BREAKING OUT

BOOK 6 OF THE SEAL TEAM HEARTBREAKERS

Teresa J. Reasor

Breaking Out

Contact Information: teresareasor@msn.com

Cover Art by Tracy Stewart
Edited by Faith Freewoman

Teresa J. Reasor
PO Box 124
Corbin, KY 40702

Publishing History: First Edition 2016

ISBN-13: 978-1-940047-08-9
ISBN-10: 1-940047-08-0
Print Edition

DEDICATION

To the MWDs (Military Working Dogs), and their trainers and handlers. Thank you for your service, and for putting your lives at risk to protect so many others.

If you're moved to support these wonderful dogs, go to facebook.com/MilitaryDogs for more information.

Also. For our military veterans who suffer from PTSD there is a program that provides service dogs for them. They rescue appropriate dogs from high-kill shelters and train them. If you're interested you can check them out at: www.k9sforwarriors.org.

TABLE OF CONTENTS

PROLOGUE

ENSIGN ZACHARY O'CONNOR, aka Doc, stood inside the shadows between the two buildings. He had to shake off this distraction and shut his thoughts off to everything but the mission.

He could not think about Patricia and the distance she was forcing between them. Not while he was standing out here with enough C-4 and blasting caps on his back to ionize himself. The trip on the chopper had already given him too much time to plan reasons for them to stay together once he got home to see her.

He and his teammates were nearing the end of their deployment, and the final few weeks were wearing on everyone. He had to forget about the things that could go wrong and think about getting this shit done. A sliver of moon shone in the star-studded sky, the weak light it cast providing shadowy cover on the east side of the structure he was scoping out.

He'd slip inside the building, do his work, then get out, and just think about making it home. That's all he needed to do. He breathed in the soupy, lukewarm air, and wanted to gag. Why was it the entire country reeked of sewage?

He scanned the hundred-foot span between him and the building. Without the Night Vision Goggles (NVGs), he'd never have noticed when his teammate Daniel Rivera, aka Bowie, slithered up to the window diagonal to his position. Despite the weight of Bowie's pack and his combat assault rifle, he moved like a gymnast when he heaved himself up through the opening and disappeared into the darkness.

Doc grunted in satisfaction. No reason to look a gift horse in the mouth. Bowie had already done the hard part. He'd breach the building through the same window.

He eyed the distance between his position and the window and waited for the rooftop patrol's attention to wander elsewhere. The sentry moved to the corner and looked north. Doc followed Bowie's path across the sun-baked sandy soil, hugging every clump of brush and shadow. Once he reached the side of the building, he paused for half a second to scan his surroundings. The blacked-out windows of the buildings surrounding them stared back.

Doc heaved himself up and through the window, caught his weight on his hands on the floor and wriggled his way in. His pack slid forward and he held it stationary with the back of his head. Not his most graceful entrance, but it had been silent.

Climbing to his feet, he wiped his gritty fingertips, the only part of his hands not covered by gloves, on the rear pockets of his BDUs. He moved to the door and eased it open.

The hall stood empty. He slipped through the door and, placing each foot with care, walked down the hall. He paused when the passageway angled to the right and darted a look around the dark corner. Nothing. Good. He slinked around the bend and paused outside the second door on the right. Every nerve came to life while he slowed his breathing and concentrated on hearing any movement from inside. Silence. He twisted the knob and the door swung open. He hustled inside and closed it.

The room glowed pale green through the NVGs. Crates lined the walls, making it feel cave-like, and the smell of machine oil and gunpowder permeated the room. At least the smell affirmed their Intel. Al-Qaida terrorists were using the building as an armory.

And the terrorists had chosen the building because it sat in the heart of an entire neighborhood of families. Probably their own. The fuckers knew Americans wouldn't drop a bomb, because they would want to preserve and protect the same families these Al-Qaida bastards were willing to sacrifice.

Goddamn them. He couldn't understand their mind-set. He'd give his life to protect his family. They'd sacrifice theirs...

He didn't have time to argue with himself about the fucked-up thinking of these terrorist cocksuckers. *Forget about this shit and get down to business.*

God, he hated working with explosives. The other guys loved blowing shit up. He couldn't feel the same way. Being the medic of the team, he'd dealt too many times with the carnage left behind after IEDs ripped guys apart. Seeing the aftermath had made him wary. The C-4 they were using to bring down the building wasn't what spooked him. The stuff could burn like a log if he set it on fire, but it wouldn't blow up until he added the blasting caps he was carrying... In fact, just one of those blasting caps could do significant damage and set off the entire cache in his pack.

He dragged in deep breaths to stifle the rush of anxiety. Sweat rolled down his sides. As soon as they returned to base, he'd email Patricia and feel better. The thought steadied him, and his hands only shook a little while he set his supplies out and paused to check the stability of the stacked crates in his way. Moving them would take too long and be too noisy.

He rested a booted foot on one of the wooden boxes and shifted his weight atop it in increments. The lid gave a little, but seemed strong enough to support him. He tucked the hated blasting caps into one of the many pockets in his BDUs and laid the bars of C-4 atop the crates. He climbed the first tier. The lid of the top box wobbled, and he eased it aside. It was packed with rifles. How many were in the room?

And what else might there be?

They were sitting on top of one huge IED with the fuse in their hands. He reached into his front pocket for his cell phone and took a quick pic of the interior of the crate, then another to document the crates in the room. Satisfaction blocked out some of his anxiety while he mashed several blocks of plastic explosive along the weight-bearing wall behind the boxes.

Working quickly, he linked the explosives, embedded the last blasting cap, and hooked it to the timer, finishing the circuit. He glanced at his dive watch. The clock had to be set at just the right second so they'd all go off at once. The steel supports of the building created too much interference for them to use a remote to set off the explosion. This would give them time to bug out and be long gone before the building collapsed.

Clicks on his com system signaled his team members, first Hawk, then Bowie, exiting the building. *Need to get a move on.*

The sound of voices outside the door sent an electric charge through his system, and he jerked his sidearm free. With the stacks of crates in the room lining the walls, there was nowhere to hide. If they opened the door, they wouldn't see the charges, but they'd damn sure see him.

Gingerly, he stepped down off the boxes, placing one foot, then the other, on the floor. Even the rustle of his clothing sounded loud. The voices receded. He snagged his pack, which still held his med kit and other supplies, and slipped it onto his shoulders, grabbed his assault rifle, and sidestepped to the window.

If all hell broke loose, he'd take his chances outside the building, away from the explosives. Every bump of the wooden frame as he raised the window sounded like a sonic boom. He slid, legs first, out the window, then lowered himself to the ground.

The crunch of the sandy grit beneath his boots grated as loud as an avalanche. He froze and waited while he scanned the area. The buildings around him seemed to lean in, waiting, watching. Nothing moved, and he sneaked from shadow to shadow, away from the building and back to his position across the street, just catty-corner to the structure's façade. It wasn't until he was under the cover of a broken masonry wall that he signaled his all clear on the com.

Derrick Armstrong, aka Strong Man's signal followed a few seconds later.

Fifteen seconds passed, then fifteen more. *Cutter. Where the hell was Cutter?* Shit!

Derrick broke radio silence. "Cutter's a no-show."

Every nerve in Doc's body went taut, prickles of concern racing over his skin, all his attention on the building. *How the fuck could Strong Man's voice be so calm?*

His commanding officer, Lieutenant Hawk Yazzie, replied over the com, quiet, controlled. "Cutter, come in, over."

Silence.

"Last location, over?" Hawk asked.

Derrick's tone remained flat. "Ground floor. I thought he was right behind me."

Greenback, Oliver Shaker, the teammate protecting their back door cut in, "Five minutes."

A slight movement diagonal from his position drew Doc's attention. He focused on the spot, and the NVG-green illumination picked out a shadow shuffling along the side of the building just behind some scrub. A guy with a Boonie hat hiked himself up over the edge of the window, his hat fell off, and his hair, light in color, shone in the odd, greenish glow. Was it Cutter? Why the fuck was he going back inside the building?

"I'm going back in for him, over," Hawk's decisive voice cut through the silence.

No. If it was Cutter climbing inside the building... Maybe... Why the fuck would he go into a building set to explode? Was it Strong Man? If it was, why hadn't he acknowledged he was entering the building?

He needed to say something to rescind Hawk's decision. He needed to break radio silence and see if it was Derrick. He needed to fucking do *something*.

Doc's heart started doing a salsa dance, and he broke out in a cold sweat. Jesus Christ. He stared at the building. The lookouts on top paced back and forth. How the hell had any of them gotten inside without alerting them? In his mind's eye, he saw the minutes ticking down on the timers, then all those boxes of weapons, stacked one atop the other.

They weren't going to make it home. Not if those boxes held anything but rifles.

Every muscle in his body froze. Even his vocal chords had locked.

The sound of machine-gun fire dragged him back to the here and now. Like a drunk he staggered to his feet, fumbled for his rifle. He had to do something.

Hawk crashed through the front door of the structure, a limp body hanging over his shoulder. The rooftop guards aimed their weapons down and bullets ricocheted off the uneven, battered street. Doc pulled the trigger and peppered the upper ridge of the building with return fire.

The explosives went off inside, cascading into the rumble of a locomotive bearing down on them. The ground heaved, throwing him back.

Seconds later, Bowie, coated in gray dust and looking like a ghost, reached in and dragged him to his feet. "Brett's hurt bad. Get a move on."

CHAPTER 1

THE DRONE OF the C-130 transport's engine vibrated beneath Ensign Zach O'Connor's feet, the sound so loud it made talking without the com system inside his helmet impossible. If he wasn't busy sucking in the pure oxygen. He'd be falling fast during the first part of the dive, and he wanted no part of the bends.

The neoprene suit under his flight suit held the heat in and protected him from the plummeting temperatures outside the aircraft while it climbed to their target altitude. He rubbed the duct tape he'd used to seal the seam between the wrists of his suit and his gloves. The wind was an icy bitch and could cause frostbite on even a thin strip of exposed skin.

Their jump had been scheduled for zero three hundred, to simulate a night insertion, but they'd gotten a late start and now fought the clock to get this practice dive behind them before sunup.

Even without the urgency of a mission, it was still a dangerous part of training, and the men were quieter than usual, most of them focused on their gear. Each of them carried seventy pounds of equipment, everything they'd need for a regular mission.

Once they exited the aircraft and fell a hundred feet or so, the trip down would be a long, slow float to the ground. With Hawk in the lead, they'd follow him down to the coordinates in the desert.

"Five minutes," the pilot's voice came over the com system.

Lieutenant Hawk Yazzie signaled for the team to take their jump positions and check their gear. Zach checked his oxygen flow, put on his goggles, and took his position behind Bowie, Ensign Dan Rivera, then "Greenback" Oliver Shaker settled in behind him, and the rest fell in. Hawk walked down the line and got a thumbs-up from each of the men before returning to his position at the head.

"Twenty-five thousand feet and holding. Thirty seconds out." One of the flight crew took a position next to Hawk and prepared to close the ramp once they had deployed. The crewman pushed the release. A loud buzzer sounded, and the cargo ramp cranked open. The wind blasted through the interior of the C-130 like a cyclone, dragging at their clothes and whipping at their gear. The dark sky was turning purplish-blue. The sun, a promise just below the horizon, cast a dusky glow.

The pilot's voice fed through his helmet. "Almost over the drop site. Five seconds."

The wait was the worst part. Five seconds seemed like an hour when you had yourself psyched to jump.

"Jump's a go."

Hawk showed no hesitation when he rushed forward and fell into midair. His chute deployed five seconds later. Bowie followed.

Zach's heart raced as fast as the air whirling around him. He didn't allow himself to think about everything that could go wrong, only the things he was trained to do. With a running jump, he dropped over the edge of the platform and into the empty sky. He waited five seconds, then pulled the ripcord. The impact of his parachute opening called a halt to the seventy pounds of momentum his gear created, drove his harness straps up into groin, giving his junk a hard squeeze, and yanked him upward. He grunted in pain and breathed an oath. Damn, he'd be feeling the aftereffects for the next couple of days. He might be singing in a higher key, too.

He looked down and saw the indistinct shape of Bowe's parachute below him. Checking his altimeter and GPS, he saw it would take some time to reach the ground, and their plan was to travel thirty miles to the landing site by manipulating the air currents.

"Sound off," Hawk's voice came over the com.

Since this was a practice run they kept their call signs brief.

"Alpha 2, on course," Bowie answered.

"Alpha 3, on course," Zach said.

"Greenback" Oliver Shaker, "Lang" Chief Petty Officer Langley Marks, "Bullet" Seaman Jeff Sizemore, "Box" Seaman Jack Logan, and "Celt" Seaman Kelsey Tyler sang out in turn. Everyone was in position and doing well.

If someone wasn't, there wasn't a whole hell of a lot they could do about it. They'd never locate him in the dark. It would be up to the team member to fall back on his training and deal with it. They had to maintain radio silence unless they were reporting information about the dive. If it were a mission, he'd be going over the things he needed to do the moment he hit the ground, and keeping an eye peeled for trouble below.

As it was, a hundred things flitted through his mind that had nothing to do with the dive. He needed to do some work on the boat. And call Kathleen, his sister, to come over for a meal some time this week, since it had been almost three weeks since they'd seen each other. And how pathetic was it that his sister was the only woman in his life at the moment?

Lately he'd been filling his off time with work on the apartment, the boat, anything to hold the emptiness of his life at bay. His teammates shared their families. His brothers, sister, and parents shared their lives with him through calls, letters and emails. His military calling was his life, but lately it just hadn't been enough.

But he'd learned through experience that he couldn't be romantically involved and do the job. Every time he was tempted, memories of the mission in Iraq when he froze rose up to warn him off. So what was the answer?

Hawk's voice came over the com. "There's a cross wind at nineteen thousand feet. You'll need to adjust your heading."

Zach caught the crosswind and pulled the handles on either side of his chute to correct his course, then checked his altimeter and GPS. He glanced down, making sure the dull gray glows of Hawk and Bowie's chutes were still aligned with his, then tilted his head back and caught a faint glimpse of Bullet, Box, and Celt's positions, while his own chute concealed Greenback and Lang's places in the stack.

Around zero five-forty the sun appeared above the desert horizon like a yellow-orange ball, and for several moments, Zach was mesmerized by the pinkish yellow streaks painted across the sky. The distant mountains, barren knolls, turned gold.

"Doesn't get much better than that," Hawk murmured. "Transport is ten miles ahead."

Twenty minutes later Hawk came across the com again. "There's a strong hot air downwind over the landing site. Be prepared for a rough landing."

From his position above, Zach watched Hawk land with his normal badass control, downwind or not. He scooped in his chute. Bowie landed two minutes behind him. Zach prepared himself for the sudden rush of the ground up to his feet, and thought he'd manage to touch down in as decent a descent as the others, until a quick rush of hot air filled his chute and jerked him back up, carrying him thirty feet farther. The chute curled over him, dragging him forward. His feet brushed the hard-packed sand, and he stumbled over a small rock, lost his footing, and plowed into a waist-high boulder hip-first. He yelped as he dropped and fell, rolling onto his back while the chute still dragged at him, his arm tangled in the lines. "Fuck me!" He tugged the oxygen mask off his face and let loose a stream of curses his Irish Catholic mother would have washed out his mouth for even thinking, much less using.

Bowie ran across the sand and brush to where he lay. "Jesus, Doc. You okay?"

"Yeah." The weight of his gear felt as heavy as the boulder he'd just plowed into. Fuck, no, he wasn't okay. He'd have the imprint of his sidearm stamped on his hip like a tattoo, his left leg was numb, and he needed to check and see if there was damage to his weapon.

Concentrate on the immediate problem. He untangled his arm from the parachute lines while Bowie grabbed his chute and started rolling it up so the wind couldn't catch it again.

Zach rocked to get to his feet, the weight of his gear making it difficult. His left side was numbed by trauma, but it was going to start aching like a son of a bitch in about five minutes. Hawk and Greenback loomed over him and bent to grip his hands. He braced his good foot, and they levered him to a standing position. He gritted his teeth to keep from groaning aloud when the first spike of pain hit him. He still had a job to do. He was the medic of the team. He needed to look out for their welfare. "Did everyone get down okay?"

"Yeah." Hawk's features were sharp with concern. "Everyone else is fine. Drop your gear, and we'll get you to the transport," Hawk ordered. The truck sat a hundred feet away. This was going to hurt. In fact, the whole rocky, bumpy trip in the back of the truck was going to hurt like a bitch.

PIPER BERTINELLI SPUN the steering wheel and pulled into the parking lot. She braked and spent a moment studying the front of the office. The new sign stood out nicely from the main road. San Diego Veterinary Clinic. The painting of two pups, one lying down, the other sitting, gave the businesslike facade a friendlier feel. They had a good location. Though wedged between a strip mall and an office supply store, they had their own access, and were separate from the businesses on either side of them. Luckily the whole back side of the lot provided a deep field of grass which they could use to exercise the dogs they boarded.

She let her foot off the brake and pulled around to the back of the building where the staff was encouraged to park, leaving the front slots open for customers. The faint sound of barking reached her as she unlocked the back door. The soundproofing they'd done in the kennel area did a good job of blocking the noise. The hoops they had to jump through to get permits for the business had been a challenge, but worth it. They were settled in and getting established.

And she was doing the one thing she'd always dreamed of, caring for animals. She'd studied so hard. Worked her ass off during school and after. And now it was paying off.

She turned on lights as she walked toward the front office, pausing to check on the ten boarded animals and make sure they had fresh water, then moving on down the hall to the kenneled animals they were treating.

The two dogs who'd gotten into a bag of year-old chocolate Halloween candy and eaten every bit wagged their tails when she paused by their kennels. After inducing vomiting, they'd given the dogs activated charcoal to absorb as much from their stomachs as possible, and put them on IVs to flush their systems. Both had shown mild symptoms of chocolate poisoning, one more than the other, but they were recovering, and would be sent home today.

She moved on to the next kennel to check on the golden retriever who'd been attacked by a pit bull. His thick coat saved him, that and the owner's quick response with a water hose, but they had to put a drain in the dog's neck to filter out the infection. He raised his head and wagged when she spoke to him, the most activity she'd seen in the past two days. The antibiotics were taking hold and doing their work.

Last but not least, she checked the mother cat someone had dropped off with her six kittens. Piper already found a foster home for the cat and her litter, and they'd be picked up at noon.

She stopped by her office to put her purse in her desk, then swept down the hall to the reception desk, but paused when she noticed the computer was on and files already pulled. She was usually the only one who came in early.

She raised the divider and walked to several very large metal bookcases with dividers to hold the office files in place, checking between each one. No one was there.

She backtracked to the counter and opened the first file. It was for a German shepherd named Otto. His owner brought him in for shots three months before.

Piper opened the appointment book on the computer and scanned the listings to see what Otto was being brought in for this time. His name wasn't listed. Nor were his owners'. She ran through the rest of the files quickly. Every dog was a large breed, ranging from the German shepherd to a Rottweiler.

Was one of her partners doing some kind of study?

Someone had pulled the files and left the computer on overnight. She'd need to remind the staff to shut things down before leaving.

Piper resisted the urge to put the files back in their proper places, in case someone was working with them. She studied the appointment book instead.

They were going to be busy. Which was a good thing. And she needed to make sure the surgical instruments were sterilized and ready to go for the two spayings scheduled for this morning.

She'd do the surgeries, go home for a few hours, and return for evening duty. She didn't mind working a split shift, and she'd certainly done it often enough at her family's restaurant. After all, she didn't have a family to go home to like two of the other three partners.

She went into the surgical bay to make double sure everything was ready and heard a sound through the open door. She glanced at her watch. Seven-thirty was too early for any of the employees to arrive. She walked to the door and paused there to listen. The squeak of a rubber shoe on the tile floor shot her heart rate into the stratosphere. Anxiety rushed her system. Someone was inside the building with her. Her limbs grew weak, she started shaking, and her breath came in shallow pants while she rubbed the chill bumps on her arms.

In a flash, she was back at the robbery. She and her father stared down the barrel of the gun aimed at them by a drug-crazed maniac. Helpless. Terrified. Her face went numb as she gasped for air. Every muscle in her body turned to stone.

She had to move, had to hide. It took twice as much energy to force her legs into action. She shuffled back away from the door and spotted plastic-covered tray of surgical instruments on the adjustable table next to the operating table. She ripped the plastic off and grabbed one of the scalpels. Her legs wobbling, she crept to the corner closest to the door. If the intruder walked by, he wouldn't be able to see her if he looked into the room, not unless he stepped inside.

She waited. One minute turned into five. The sound of a door opening, then closing, came from the direction of the kennels. The dogs barked. What if they took one of the animals the clinic was caring for?

And why didn't she have her cell phone with her? Because she rarely carried it while at work. If she got out of this alive, the phone would never leave her pocket.

She glanced at the phone on the wall across the room. Her muscles trembled while she geared up to cross the space. What if there were more than one, and they walked by just as she reached for the phone? And if they were at the reception desk, they'd see the light go on. Why were they at reception and in their records instead of breaking into the drug cabinet? But they might have already been there.

Piper covered her face with one hand. She had to do something. She wouldn't be victimized again. Listening intently for any sound coming from outside the room, she crossed the floor to the wall phone. Her muscles felt weak as jelly while she lifted the receiver from its cradle and keyed in nine-one-one.

She debated where to hide. If she got into one of the cabinets, she'd be trapped, but if she didn't, she'd be out in the open, and they might see her and attack. She got down on her knees and crawled into the cabinet beneath the sink. Her hands shook, and her clammy palms stuck to the phone.

A voice came over the line. "Nine-one-one operator."

Hearing that calm, dispassionate voice did no more to reassure her than it had the last time.

"There's someone in our office raiding our files. They're still in the building." She rattled off the address.

"Are you safe?"

She hadn't felt safe in the past seven years. Especially from the police. But there was no one else to call.

CHAPTER 2

WITHOUT A CLOUD in sight to soften it, the midmorning sky burned bright blue. It appeared as though the plane, flying diagonal to his position, might hit a flat blue wall at any moment.

Ensign Zachary O'Connor flipped open the console between the seats, extracted a pair of dark sunglasses, and shoved them on his face. He ran a hand over his scruff-covered jaw and raked his fingers through the long auburn hair curling and waving back from his forehead. He needed a haircut. He'd have to sweet-talk his sister, Kathleen, into giving him one. He didn't trust the post barbers not to scalp him.

Shit! The team's HAHO (High Altitude High Opening) dive this morning had gone off with textbook perfection, and when the sun broke over the horizon, the view had been spectacular. Everyone else's perfect, synchronized landing, just made him feel more like a clumsy-ass shit. He had more experience than most of the others, so he should have had better control. The only good part about the experience was no one else had been injured, and his skills as a medic hadn't been needed for anyone but himself.

His left side ached every time he moved, and was already turning purple. The two-hour emergency room visit for X-rays had been a real joy, too. Luckily his teammates looked out for him. After transport took them back to the base, Bowie drove him to the hospital and left his SUV in the hospital parking lot so he'd have wheels. He even offered to stick around, but there'd been no reason for him to waste his time sitting in the ER, so Bullet, Seaman Jeff Sizemore, picked up Bowie and they went back to the base.

And now he was limping home like a pussy for a few weeks, until the biggest part of the bruising passed. Doctor's orders. Fuck!

He hated being off duty. With no steady girlfriend to spend time with, and his sister working full time and tangled up with Cal, her almost-fiancé, he had no one to hang with or distract him.

Doc yawned and shook his head. He was already bored out of his skull and he hadn't even made it home yet. He'd end up sitting in his recliner watching reruns of stuff he hadn't seen in the first place, or zoning out in front of ball games he had no interest in. Maybe he could go out on his boat and fish a couple of days.

From his peripheral vision, he caught movement from the left. Instinct kicked in, and he stomped on his brakes, sending the car into a skid even before a man dressed in jeans and a T-shirt, darted out from behind two parked cars. The guy skimmed past the front of the SUV by a hair, but the dog running full-out behind the guy didn't make it. Doc gritted his teeth against the sickening thump of the impact. The animal cried out and tumbled down the street like a child's stuffed toy. He jerked the car into park and bailed out as quickly as he could manage, his bruised hip screaming with every move.

The man tossed a glance behind him. His features were distorted, flattened by something, his hair plastered to his head. He jumped a chain link fence and disappeared between two houses.

The dog lay motionless in the street. Zach rushed to it. Though its eyes were open, the canine appeared stunned. A puddle of blood formed at an alarming rate around its hips. Doc thought it was a German shepherd until he was upon it. He immediately recognized the breed. The animal was a Belgian Malinois. Doc knelt beside him and ran a hand over the animal's head. Inside the ear was a tattoo.

"Jesus Christ!" It was an MWD, a military war dog. It

wouldn't have gone after just anyone. It had to have been chasing a tango on command. Doc moved its back leg to see where the bleeding was coming from. The hip looked displaced and the upper leg bone projected through the skin above the joint. It had possibly torn an artery, because with every pump of the animal's heart blood gushed from the wound.

Other motorists pulled around his stopped vehicle, moving slowly and rubbernecking, kicking up exhaust. No one offered to stop and help.

Assholes!

The animal, starting to come around, breathed a high-pitched whine. Ignoring his own injury, Doc staggered to his feet and rushed to his vehicle, hit the lock release for the back of his SUV, and dragged out the med kit he kept packed there. Though his hip ached like a son of a bitch, he double-timed it back to the dog.

He unzipped his kit, shook out the medical gloves, and put them on. Rifling through the medical instruments sealed in paper-wrapped packages, he located the scalpel and clamp, ripping open the packages and using the scalpel to slice the tissue away from the bleeding artery and clamp it off. Using a tongue depressor as a splint, he secured the limb with gauze to immobilize it. He wrapped gauze, then tape, around the wound to hold the clamp in place and put pressure on the injury.

As it became more aware, the Malinois gave a yip, then a growl of pain and jerked its head toward his hand when he moved the limb. Doc was surprised it didn't bite him. It was probably too weak from loss of blood, shock, or in too much pain.

He lifted the dog, which had to weigh at least sixty-five pounds, as gently as possible and carried it to the back of his SUV. He positioned the animal on a blanket and covered it. Now he needed to know where the closest vet's office was. Otherwise *she*, he'd noticed it was female, was either going to bleed out, lose her leg, or both.

He jerked his gloves off, retrieved his med kit and slid back into the vehicle before tugging his cell phone free of his pants pocket to search for vet's offices. Thank God there was one within a few blocks.

SHE SHOULD HAVE gone home after the police left. She could have used an hour or so to settle her nerves. But she had two surgeries scheduled. The medicine cabinets had been raided, and some of the patient files disturbed, but nothing else was damaged. And, most important, none of the animals were harmed.

And the interview with the police detective hadn't been nearly the ordeal she'd braced herself for, but then he didn't know about her unpleasant history with one of their own.

She did learn they were not the only animal clinic to be hit. She was just the only vet to walk in on the thieves while they were still in the building. Lucky her. But the intruders were gone by the time the police arrived.

The police took some fingerprints and noted where the lock had been picked at the back of the building. Hunter Rawls, one of the partners, was doing an inventory of the drugs they'd taken, while the rest of the staff held down the fort.

Their early-morning customers had been rescheduled, including the two spayings, and now it was close to one, and they were seeing patients again.

Piper ran her glove-covered fingers over the inside of the kitten's leg. The small swollen area along the stomach wall felt spongy and soft, but didn't appear to give the animal any discomfort. Although it would if it wasn't repaired. "It's a hernia. The exterior wall of the abdomen has a small tear, and the intestines are protruding through it. It will need to be repaired; otherwise it may grow larger and possibly strangulate. If that happens, it will cut off the blood flow to the protruding intestines, and Tabby will need surgery to save her life."

The kitten climbed her lab coat and butted its head against her jaw. She disconnected her claws gently and placed her back on the examination table.

The owner who'd brought the kitten in bounced her baby girl

on her hip, more a nervous gesture than because the infant was fussing. "How much is it going to cost?"

Piper could see where this was going way before she got there. "Including anesthesia and shots, about three hundred dollars."

The woman's eyes widened. "Uh—Look, I just got the kitten to entertain my kids. I didn't think it would cost an arm and a leg to keep it. As it is, I can barely afford the food and the litter. There's no way I can pay three hundred dollars to get shots and have surgery done."

"I understand it's expensive, but you don't want a pet around your children who hasn't had its shots. Some diseases can be transferred from pet to human. Not many, but they do exist. And you don't want your children to grow attached to a pet who may die because it wasn't protected from distemper or feline leukemia."

The woman shook her head. "I can't do it. Three hundred dollars could feed my kids, or pay *their* doctor bills."

"There is a pet care plan that will pay for the surgery and you make payments by the month. We could do just the shots, then next month you can bring her back for the surgery, although you'll need to watch her carefully in the meantime. If the hernia strangulates, she'll start throwing up and be off her water and food, possibly run a fever. You'll have to bring her in as quickly as possible. Without care, she could die."

The woman reached out to touch the gray tabby. She was already tearing up. "Could you find her a home with someone who can afford to take care of her?"

If Mrs. Taylor refused and dropped her at a shelter because she already needed treatment, they'd put her down.

Piper stifled a sigh. "Are you sure you can't make payments on her treatment, Mrs. Taylor? She's a beautiful kitten, lively, healthy except for the hernia. She'll make a good pet for your family. And kittens and cats are very independent and don't require as much care as other pets. Once she gets past this rough patch, she'll be okay. Then you just have to get her annual shots."

"I can't do it. We're barely squeaking by as it is. Just paying for this office visit—" She cut off what she was about to say, her cheeks flaring with color.

"I understand, Mrs. Taylor." Piper counted to ten. "I'll keep her until I can find her a home."

"You'll take care of her?" Relief flooded the woman's face.

"Yes, I'll take care of her. We'll repair the hernia and find her a foster home until she can be adopted."

The woman's eyes were glassy with tears. She laid a hand on the kitten while she climbed Piper's lab coat again and cuddled under her chin. "I'm sorry."

Piper didn't know if she was apologizing to her or the cat. "I am, too, Mrs. Taylor. I hope the children don't take it too hard."

Mrs. Taylor nodded, gathered her purse and the diaper bag, and bolted from the room as if afraid Piper might change her mind.

Later, despite her tears, she'd be relieved to have gotten out from under the care of a pet she couldn't afford. The woman's fifty-dollar office visit fee would pay for the shots and the kitten's food, but not the cost of the surgery Piper would have to perform before the kitten could be adopted.

Why did people take on the responsibility of a pet when they knew beforehand they couldn't afford it?

And why was she such a soft touch? Dammit! They'd find a home for the kitten eventually, but until then… She had to harden her heart, grow a thicker skin. Every time she did this kind of thing, it cost their practice money. The kitten purred against her face while she petted it.

Sherry Sams, their receptionist, rushed in, her normally rosy-cheeked face white. "There's a man in the waiting room with a bleeding dog. He said he hit it with his car and it's a military war dog. Its leg is…barely hanging on." Sherry's complexion turned a little green.

"Here," Piper handed her the kitten. "Put her in one of the crates. I'll be giving her shots and performing hernia surgery on Wednesday morning. I'll do the paperwork later."

Piper rushed out into the large waiting room. The L-shaped

seating area, with its long row of wooden, cushion-covered benches, was crowded with customers. She focused first on the red-haired man holding the injured animal wrapped in a blanket and nearly stumbled over her own feet as her heart jolted with recognition, then fear. David. It couldn't be him. He was... He'd been gone for almost seven years, and shouldn't be out of jail for another year.

She caught her breath and took two long strides, intent on reaching the dog. Then the man turned his head and his eyes settled on her.

The resemblance had been a trick of the light or her imagination. She knew David was in prison. She had no reason to be afraid. But her heart was still beating high in her throat, and she was having trouble breathing. She concentrated on the man in front of her, searching for the differences between him and David. And there were plenty.

The man's wide, square-jawed face was tense with concern. She'd have known he was military even if he hadn't been dressed in desert camouflage. The way he stood, the sharp way he focused in on her, underscored the rest. His auburn hair needed a trim. It rolled over his forehead in out-of-control waves and curled around his ears. And his biceps bulged from holding the weight of the dog.

She motioned to him. "Come this way."

He fell in behind her.

She glanced over her shoulder, noticed his limp, and asked, "Are you hurt?"

"It's a previous injury. I've already been checked out."

Instead of leading him into an examining room, she took him straight back to the surgery. The dog yelped when the man laid it down on the metal table.

"I tried to stabilize the limb as best I could, and I've clamped the vessel that was torn by the break. She was bleeding out." He folded back the blanket. The limb was wrapped in gauze holding a metal clamp in place, a tongue depressor keeping the limb stationary.

Battlefield medicine at its best. He had to be a medic. Who else would have a clamp handy? "How long has it been since you hit her?"

"Fifteen minutes."

Shit! She had to get the blood supply reestablished to the limb as quickly as possible, or the dog would lose it. But she also had to see what other damage might have been done by the car. Opening a drawer, she reached for a muzzle.

Though the dog growled, she allowed her to place the device over her face and secure it.

"She'll need X-rays." And Kathy hadn't come in yet, since surgery for the day had been canceled.

"Let's do it."

"Are you assuming responsibility for her treatment?" she asked.

"Yes, I hit her. She's a WMD. You have to do something." The way he bit out his words, as though he couldn't get them out fast enough, spoke of his anxiety. "They spend upwards of twenty thousand or more to breed, raise and train these animals. They save lives. Do whatever you have to save hers."

"Okay. Will you lift her so I can remove the blanket?"

"Sure." He did so effortlessly while she slid the fabric free.

Easing the dog back down on the table, he said, "You need to scan her for a chip. If she's retired, she'll have been chipped and assigned to whoever adopted her."

"First things first, Mr.—" She handed him the bloody blanket and went to the sink to wash her hands and put on gloves.

"O'Connor. Ensign Zach O'Connor." He ran a large hand over the dog's head and ears, soothing her. With his long hair and scruff, he didn't look as military as most enlisted personnel she'd dealt with. It had been his curling tumble of red hair that triggered her moment of heart-stopping fear mixed with... Yes, she'd felt pain and panic at the thought of seeing him again. She was still paying for what he'd done to her, done to her family.

Had this man been freshly shaven and his hair cut, would she have mistaken him for David? No. His features were more masculine, the look in his eye focused and sharp. David had never looked that directly at anything. He'd been a charming con artist. A liar. A criminal. Worse.

Piper did a quick but thorough examination of the dog, looking into her eyes and ears. Her lungs sounded clear, her heartbeat fast and thready. She ran her hands over her, neck, body and legs, in search of any other injuries. She palpated her abdomen to see if the stomach or bladder had been affected.

The dog watched her every move but didn't react to anything other than her careful exam of her leg. She cut the wrappings from around the limb to get a good look at the injury. At the dog's high yip of pain and instinctive jerk, Piper pulled back.

Zach caught her in mid-lunge and restrained the action. "I've got her, Doc."

"Thanks." For a moment, she looked directly into his face. No, there was nothing there to remind her of David except the color of his hair. She had to block this out and concentrate on the Malinois.

Piper ran a soothing hand over the animal's brown and black coat. She appeared well cared for and nourished, and she had on a collar, but no tag.

"Ensign O'Connor." She swung the X-ray machine over the table. "I'm going to take X-rays of her pelvic region and her legs. You'll need to leave."

She went to the phone on the wall and asked Sherry to call Kathy, her vet tech to come in, and send in Tony, one of their assistants, to help. Kathy was with a patient and would be in ASAP.

Tony Chaffey appeared at the door. A college student of eighteen, he dressed in jeans and T-shirts with a white, hip-length lab coat over his clothes. He hadn't bothered to button the lab coat. As soon as he entered the room the dog struggled to rise and would have lunged off the table, damaged leg or not, had Ensign O'Connor not grabbed her and looped an arm around her chest. "Ease down, honey. It's all right."

The dog was having none of it. She had fixated on Tony and

was growling, her eyes, ears, and posture displaying a visceral aggression. Even muzzled, she projected seventy pounds of lethal muscular intent.

Tony froze, arms fanned out, showing he was not a threat.

"Move out. I've got this," Zach said. At the note of command in the man's voice, the kid's eyes, already wide, flashed open even bigger. He disappeared back into the hall.

"We don't usually allow owners back here."

"I'm not her owner. And if I'm authorized to volunteer at the naval medical facilities wherever I'm deployed, I can hold her so you can do the X-rays."

Piper ran through the liability issues of allowing a nonemployee to be exposed to the limited amount of radiation and conceded. The dog remained calm while he was with her, and she might do more damage to the leg if she thrashed around. And Piper didn't want to have to sedate her for the X-rays.

"Come on, Doc. Time's a'wasting." He urged the dog back onto her side.

She handed him a lead-lined apron to cover him from neck to mid-thigh. "Try and keep her on her side. We'll roll her onto her back next, then over to the other side. I need to check for broken bones and other issues."

"Got it." He put on the apron and rubber gloves as though he'd done it often.

Working quickly, Piper took several films, the ensign as skillful and efficient as any of the vet techs and assistants they employed. She pulled off her latex gloves and went to the computer to pull up the X-rays. Her heart sank as she studied the images on the screen. She rolled the machine on its stand, close to the table so she could show O'Connor the images.

He pulled off the latex gloves and moved in close beside her. Heat radiated from his body down her right side, and he briefly rested a hand against the small of her back in a gesture she was sure was unconscious. "Shit, the hip's broken, too," he murmured, regret in his tone. "I was hoping it was just dislocated."

"Yes. We can put pins in to hold it in place until it heals so she'll be able to move around with little pain, but the leg…" It was badly broken, the end splintered above the joint.

"I can see it for myself." He swallowed and shook his head. "She was running full out. I knew when I hit her it was bad. Jesus!" He rested a hand against his forehead, and his lips compressed. When he dropped his hand, his green eyes found her face. "If she's not retired already, she will be now. Do whatever you can to get her ambulatory. If you have to take the leg…" His expression went flat, controlled. "Even on three legs she'll be a good dog."

"I'll do what I can." She pointed out a small, rectangular shape on the screen. She does have a chip. We'll scan it and find out who she belongs to."

"Good."

The intercom buzzed and Sherry spoke to her. "There are two policemen in the waiting area. They've asked to speak to Ensign O'Connor."

Piper's brows jerked up.

"I called to report the guy she was chasing. He had a stocking mask over his face."

"So he was up to no good."

His features tightened with anger. "These dogs don't attack unless they've been ordered to. The son of bitch skimmed past my bumper with half a second's grace with her on his tail. She wasn't as lucky. It was the only way he would have been able to shake her."

"Give your contact information to one of the receptionists at the desk, and you'll need to sign a form giving me permission to operate. I'll be taking her into surgery immediately, and will give you a call as soon as I've finished to let you know how she's doing. And we'll scan the chip and see who her owner is."

She moved to the intercom and, with the dog's reaction to Tony in mind, asked for Jasmine and Barbara to come back to the surgery.

Ensign O'Connor offered his hand. "Thanks, Doctor…" He tilted his head and offered her a subdued smile that looked very white compared to the rust-colored beard surrounding it.

"Dr. Bertinelli."

He shook her hand. "First name?"

Piper hesitated. "Francesca, but everyone calls me Piper."

His smile widened into a grin, and with it his strong features transformed from tough to charming. She felt the potent charm of that smile hit her in the chest, the pit of her stomach, and lower. He was very masculine despite his boyish freckles and red hair. The resemblance to David was even less pronounced with the self-assured cockiness this man projected.

'The Pied Piper of animals, huh?"

Surprised he'd guessed, she nodded. "So they tell me."

Barbara came in and immediately went to the dog. She spoke soothingly to the Malinois and earned a weak tail wag. Ensign O'Connor stepped away from the animal to give her more room, but hovered, obviously reluctant to leave.

"She's going to be fine, Ensign. We'll take good care of her."

The way he focused on her once again gave her a jittery feeling in the pit of her stomach. He nodded. "Call me Zach. Piper suits you. I'll go deal with the cops while you deal with this."

Piper nodded.

He removed the apron and handed it to her. "I'll call back in a couple of hours to see how things are going."

"That will be fine."

When he limped out, he seemed to take most of the energy in the room with him.

She dragged her attention away from him to the injured animal lying on the stainless steel table while she reached for the cell phone in her pocket. Dr. Dorsey, the senior veterinarian in their practice, would want to observe this one. She called the front desk. "Sherry, page Dr. Dorsey to surgery and tell him we've had an emergency case come in. I'll be starting the surgery ASAP." She hung up.

"Jasmine, scan for the chip. I want to know who her owner is." She breathed a sigh of relief when Kathy rushed into the room. "Set her up for surgery, Kathy." She went through the dog's injuries. "I'm going to repair her hip and try to save her leg."

CHAPTER 3

ZACH EXPERIENCED A quick rush of blood to places south when he thought about how Piper Bertinelli's cheeks colored when he smiled at her. He'd breathed in the light scent of flowers as she stood next to him reading the X-ray, and her hair was tinted with just enough red to warm the brown and make her olive skin seem pale in comparison. He'd felt the punch of attraction to his toes when her eyes, a rich mahogany brown with gold around the iris, looked directly into his. If they hadn't been dealing with an emergency situation... He'd save the rest of his impressions to think about later, after he dealt with the police.

He spent a moment in the pint-sized restroom scrubbing the latex smell from his hands, his actions sharp and quick as his anger returned. What a waste. Because of some asshole, the dog would probably lose her leg.

If she were his dog, he'd be out looking for her. They really needed the info from her chip. He dried his hands with a paper towel, glad they'd elected to go old school and forgo one of those damn blow dryers that made the air muggy and still didn't dry your hands.

When he came out of the restroom, the two police officers were standing at the desk waiting. He greeted them with, "Ensign Zach O'Connor," and shook their hands. He turned to the receptionist he'd spoken to on arriving. "If you can get the paperwork started for me while I talk to these fellows, I'd appreciate it."

She smiled at him. "It will be ready for you as soon as you finish."

"Thanks." He nodded to the two police officers. "Would you like to go outside and discuss this in private?"

"Yes, sir." The taller of the two answered.

Zach led the way. Now the adrenaline had leached off, his hip ached with every step. He stood under the shaded eave of the front entrance and leaned back against the side of the building.

"I'm Officer Harrison, and this is my partner Officer Morgan," the taller of the two said.

Had he ever been that young? They looked like Cub Scouts. When did the police start recruiting from junior high? Morgan looked a shade wetter behind the ears than Harrison, but faced with their close-cropped, military haircuts and freshly-shaven faces, Zach felt scruffy and old.

"The dog has a chip. You'll be able to trace the owner through it. If you know who she belongs to, you may be able to discover where the guy I saw was running from."

"We already know, sir." Harrison's grave expression didn't bode well. "Her owner was attacked. His neighbor discovered him in his yard. He'd been beaten. He's in the hospital and stable, but hasn't regained consciousness."

Zach bit back an oath.

"May I ask why you're limping, sir?" Officer Morgan asked.

Of course, they'd have to rule him out as a suspect. "I had an accident this morning during a training exercise. I'd just been released from the ER at Balboa Med Center and was on my way home when I hit the dog."

"Did you get a good look at the man who was running from the dog?" Harrison asked.

Zach shook his head. "He was wearing a stocking over his face, and it distorted his features."

"But you saw him."

"Yeah, but it was quick. I was trying to avoid hitting him with the car." He closed his eyes to picture the man. "He skimmed past the front of my SUV with only inches to spare. He was wearing jeans, a T-shirt with some kind of design on the front, and running shoes. He was Caucasian, maybe five feet ten to six feet, slender build, dark hair and brows, I could see those through the stocking. He was built like a runner, and he scaled the chain link fence quick enough."

"Did you touch him with your vehicle?

"No, I missed him, but hit the dog instead. Was the man he attacked Navy?"

"Retired," Morgan answered.

"A SEAL?"

"Yes."

Zach clenched his teeth to keep from swearing. "What's his name? I may know him."

"Master Chief Clifton Flynn."

Zach shook his head. He didn't recognize the name, but he'd ask around.

"How's the dog?" Harrison asked.

"She lost a lot of blood, her hip's broken, and she may lose her leg. Dr. Bertinelli is doing what she can to save her."

"That's a real shame. The guy who owns her has a training course built in the back yard. It looked as though he worked with her a lot."

Zach gave a brief nod. "She's a military war dog. Probably retired."

Harrison's gaze sharpened. "How do you know that?"

"She has a tattoo inside her ear for identification. I've worked with the dogs and their handlers. The dogs love to train. They can sniff out explosives, hunt down the bad guys, and keep them occupied until we get there. After they've been through several deployments, the dogs get too stressed to return to combat, and they're retired. Their handlers adopt them sometimes. The guy who owns her may have been her partner while in the teams."

"We'll check into it. So you're accepting responsibility for her until things with her owner are clarified?"

Zach drew a deep breath. Accepting financial responsibility while she was at the vet was one thing. Taking her after she came home would be different. Maybe Kathleen, his sister, could help out. "I can try it until her owner's in the clear."

An idea occurred to him. "She may have gotten a piece of one of them. You may want to check medical facilities for anyone coming in with an animal bite."

"Too bad she didn't get the guy she was chasing," Officer Morgan said.

The three of them lapsed into silent agreement.

Harrison broke it by saying, "I'll need your contact info in case we have to talk to you again, sir, and I need to see your ID."

Zach took out his wallet, removed both his license and military ID, and passed them over.

Officer Harrison copied down his information as well as his cell phone number and Kathleen's. "Thank you, sir. We'll notify you as to the master chief's condition."

"I'd appreciate it." He watched the two get into their vehicle and pull away. A retired SEAL and his dog were attacked. Why wasn't NCIS involved?

Zach limped back into the vet's office to sign the paperwork.

At loose ends after dealing with everything, he drove home. His hip was getting more painful by the minute, and he decided the doctor's prescription for the anti-inflammatory meds wasn't for wusses after all. He swung through a pharmacy, got it filled, and bought a bottle of water on the way out. In the car, he cracked the bottle and swallowed one of the pain pills. Maybe by the time he got home the pain would have eased off. He'd put some ice on it after a shower and wait for the vet to call.

Thinking of her call triggered thoughts of Dr. Bertinelli. The name Piper suited her. There had been a moment of connection between them, despite the tension and urgent activity caused by the emergency. He'd seen the color rise in her cheeks when he smiled at her. Once things were taken care of with the dog...

What was he thinking? She wasn't a party girl. He could read that clear enough from her no-nonsense attitude on the job. And the only women he hooked up with were party girls who didn't want a commitment. Well, come to think of it, he hadn't hooked up with anyone in a long time. His dissatisfaction when he wasn't training or at work screamed *you need a woman.*

Piper's big mahogany-brown eyes just...did it for him.

And her petite, perfectly proportioned body.

And her thick, dark brown hair with just a hint of red for spice.

Shit! He needed to forget this. His last emotional entanglement had damn near cost him his career and his life. And rocked his confidence. It took him a long time to come back from it. The helpless, frozen feeling during those moments he and the team waited for Hawk to exit the terrorist's armory had proven to him he couldn't get involved and still do his job. He couldn't afford the distraction. Or the attachment.

Besides, what had all that emotion gotten him last time?

Jilted before he even made it home.

Never again! He needed to keep his distance and stay focused on his team.

He had to put Piper out of his mind.

Once at home, he took the shower he'd promised himself and dressed in sweatpants and a T-shirt. He found a bag of frozen peas left over from when his sister Kathleen stayed with him, and wrapped them in a dishtowel as an ice pack. He settled in the recliner and wedged the peas against the arm of the chair to hold it to his hip. He turned on the television for a distraction, but found himself checking the time every few minutes.

When would they call? Would it be Piper, or one of the receptionists?

What difference did it make? He just wanted to know how the dog was.

Yeah, right. Damnit!

He phoned Hawk, his commanding officer, and gave him a rundown on the man he'd almost hit and the dog he had.

"Come to find out the police were looking for the guy. It had to be more than one. They broke into the home of a retired

SEAL, beat him, and left him unconscious in his yard. Master Chief Clifton Flynn. Do you know him?

"No. But I'll ask around. You do the same. We'll spread the word that he's in the hospital. If he got a look at these guys, they might try something more. It wouldn't hurt if there's a military presence around to deter them."

"Hopefully the cops have thought of it already. I'll be taking the dog in temporarily when the vet discharges her. Just until Flynn is released from the hospital. I figure since I'll be on sick leave for a few weeks, I'll have the time."

"How's the hip?"

Zach didn't see any reason to play it down. "It's purple and hurts like a son of a bitch. I'm icing it right now." The dog's hip was much worse. He grimaced.

"Good. After a few days of ice off and on, use heat. Zoe may have some suggestions to help ease the pain. I'll ask her."

"I appreciate it."

"You're talking about taking care of a sick dog, but have you ever had a dog?" Hawk asked.

"A couple when I was growing up. This one is a retired war dog. And she seemed to respond to me. It may have just been the uniform, but we'll see." He found himself getting excited about it. It would certainly beat sitting here alone watching television.

"It might do you some good to have something in your life other than the job and fishing." Hawk was nothing if not straightforward. "There's something to say for having someone to come home to every night."

But at what cost? He'd committed himself to someone and became so obsessed with her, or actually the idea of who he thought she was, he'd choked when he was needed the most.

"Zoe keeps me grounded, steady, and helps me maintain a cool head. She's who I hold on to when things get tough."

Hawk had been on his case more than once lately about his actions sliding close to reckless during some of their training.

Zach knew where this was going. Time to nip it in the bud.

"I let someone get close once and it fucked me up. I screwed up because of it. I'm not sure I can have someone in my life and still do the job." Hawk and Zoe knew about it since he broke down in front of them and admitted everything. He'd been a wreck then. He had a long, hard road fighting his way back, and he hadn't allowed a woman truly close since.

"It's been years since then, Doc. You're different now than you were then. And the way I see it, every one of us has that one thing we do that scares the shit out of us. I've had to deal with mine, just like you've dealt with yours. You saved a man's life. You kept him going until we got him back to base and medical attention. Brett's doing fine, he's moved on. You're allowing one experience to keep you from doing the same."

Zach tugged at the long hair falling over his forehead. Why was he talking to Hawk about this now?

Because he'd met a real woman, not a SEAL bunny or a party girl. The instant attraction was strong, and he couldn't make a move on her because of this issue. How the hell could a guy who spent months at a time either deployed or training have a regular life? What kind of woman would put up with that shit?

Women like Hawk's Zoe, Brett's Tess, and Langley's Trish, that's who. They were all three strong, independent women. Even though Greenback's wife Selena had breast cancer two years ago, she was still strutting her stuff, independent, and, thank God, in remission. Despite Greenback's schedule, they seemed to make it work.

"Everyone deserves to be loved, Doc. It's human nature to crave love and physical contact. Why not enjoy getting it from someone you can actually care about instead of someone you're just scratching an itch with?"

Why not? But could he compartmentalize his life the way Hawk did? Hawk had to, otherwise when things got dangerous, he'd freak out... No, he wouldn't. He never freaked out about anything. He saved Zoe's life when Derrick Armstrong broke into his house and threatened to kill her, her brother, and Marjorie, Derrick's girlfriend. He'd held it together because he loved Zoe. Zach had never seen him as focused.

But could Zach do the same?

PIPER LISTENED TO the dog's deep, drugged respirations and the steady beat of her heart. Had she done the right thing? If it worked, it would be. It was going to take more time for her leg to heal, but she'd still have the use of it, barring the numerous complications that might follow such a complicated surgery.

Hunter Rawls, one of her partners, stuck his head in the door. "I heard you did some fantastic work today." He wandered into the room.

"I won't know until she's awake." Piper hung her stethoscope around her neck and ran a hand along the dog's side. "She's a retired war dog. The police came by a few minutes ago and told me she and her owner do volunteer work with disabled vets. They also pitch in with the police department at large events in the area. Gracie can sniff out explosives."

"How's she doing?" Hunter asked. He came to stand across the table from her. He looked as immaculate now as he did when he arrived this morning. Even his brown mid-length hair was still in place.

"So far, so good. She's still sleeping. I've repaired the torn vessel, put in pins to hold the hip together, and a plate in the leg to hold the tibia together."

"And who's paying for her treatment?"

"The man who hit her."

"Good. We can't take on any more charity cases, Piper."

She knew where this was going. "I know."

"What about the kitten you took today?"

"I'm going to create a social media page to advertise for her adoption and medical treatment. We need one for the office anyway. And I have someone to foster the mother cat and her kittens. She came by to pick them up at noon today."

His brows rose. "Good. The social media page is a good idea."

Piper focused on Gracie. Now she knew the dog's name, she thought it suited her. "Do you want to help me move her to a crate? I have everything ready for her, and I'd like to move her before she wakes."

"Sure."

She unlocked the wheels on the metal gurney and Hunter guided it through the surgery to the back room where they kept recovering animals. Side opening metal crates were mounted against the walls, larger ones down low and smaller ones above. At the moment, three crates were occupied. A Jack Russell who'd had a run-in with a neighbor's Maine Coon cat, and two sick cats.

"I'll stay late tonight, since you and the others covered some of my patients while I did the surgery."

"That would be a nice gesture."

Asshole. She detested Hunter's condescending tone. And she certainly didn't need him looking over her shoulder. She knew what her duties were, and what her priorities needed to be. She remained silent, not trusting her temper.

Gracie weighed seventy pounds. Piper lifted her hindquarters while Hunter raised her upper body, and they laid her gently in the crate. She made sure the dog's wrapped leg was positioned comfortably, and checked her respiration one more time before she closed the container and straightened.

"I hope the man who's paying for her doesn't stiff you on the bill."

"He won't."

"How do you know?"

"Because he cares about the dog. She's a military war dog, and he's military. He left his credit card number with Sherry." Which didn't mean she was going to take advantage of him and bill him for anything that wasn't absolutely necessary. Not that Hunter would condone it, but lately the man had been on all of them. Maybe he was having personal financial problems.

"How did the drug audit go? What did they take?" she asked.

"Painkillers, which wasn't surprising, but they also took some antibiotics and bandages. Makes you wonder if it isn't someone running a puppy mill or something worse. I've turned it over to our insurance company."

"Good."

"I've also called a locksmith to add a deadbolt to the back door." He laid a hand on her arm. "You were very brave this morning, sticking around and calling the police."

"I was afraid to leave the surgery. Afraid I'd run into them trying to exit the building. He was looking at some of our patient files, too, Hunter. What do you think that was about?"

"I don't know, but I'd hate to think they were using our files to case someone's home."

"I told the police which files I saw on the counter. I hope they follow up with the customers to make sure they're okay."

"Let's hope word doesn't leak that our office was compromised. It could cost us some business."

He was right, but it seemed selfish to think about it that way.

She preceded Hunter through the surgery to the office area to pick up her next patient's file, taking a moment to update Gracie's chart, and remembered she'd promised to call Ensign O'Connor. Zach. She found the number listed on the file and pulled her cell phone from her pocket. She paused when jittery nerves attacked her stomach.

He was just another customer. Who cared if he had a strong, in-charge vibe? And who cared if during those moments of standing next to each other she'd felt enveloped in his warmth? And she wasn't going to think about his smile and the kick to her heart rate and libido it gave her. Or when he'd looked directly into her eyes, how she'd felt an immediate arousal.

She didn't need to get involved with a man who carried a gun. And it didn't matter what kind of capacity he carried it in. She'd already seen what it was like to lose someone to gun violence. Besides, Zach was military and had an even greater chance of losing his life to it. She didn't want to invest her heart and have it ripped out again.

And those few things about him, his hair mostly, that reminded her of David could trigger flashbacks.

She keyed in the numbers. He answered on the first ring.

Though she felt breathless with nerves, she tried to keep her tone professional. "Hello, Ensign O'Connor. Gracie is doing well. She's still asleep, but the surgery went well."

"Good. Gracie?"

"Yes. A police officer called to check on her and told us her name."

"The police told me her owner was a retired SEAL. Any info about his condition?"

"No, I'm afraid not."

"I'll call and ask. How's Gracie's leg?"

"It pinked up as soon as I had the blood flow reestablished. I'll keep a close eye on the circulation issue for a few days. I've put in a plate to stabilize the limb, but it's going to be months until she fully heals. She may also need some physical therapy."

"And the hip?"

"I had to put in pins. As long as she doesn't develop an infection or throw a clot, I think she'll be fine."

"Fantastic." He sounded relieved.

"I have to warn you, these treatments aren't cheap."

"I didn't think they would be, Piper."

His use of her name threw her for a second. She should never have told him her name. "I didn't want you to be surprised."

"When can I come see her?"

"I'll be staying late until she wakes to be sure she's doing okay. Tomorrow midday would be good. She should have thrown off the anesthesia completely by then."

"Okay. Is orthopedics your specialty?" he asked.

"Yes. I'm usually the one who does surgery for broken bones if it's warranted. We get some specialty cases here."

"I'm glad you were there when I brought her in."

Pleasure heated her cheeks. "Thank you. I have to go. I have patients waiting."

"I'll come by tomorrow to see Gracie."

"I'll tell Sherry to expect you."

She closed out the call and focused on the next patient, but it didn't keep his masculine jaw and emerald green eyes from coming to mind off and on for the rest of the afternoon.

CHAPTER 4

KATHLEEN O'CONNOR MANIPULATED the image on the screen of her computer while she held the telephone in the bend of her neck.

"Can you give me a haircut, sis?"

Distracted by the design she was working on, she barely heard what her brother was saying.

"Hum?"

"Do you have time to give me a haircut?"

Once she had the support pieces in place, she lifted her finger from the pad. "You know they have barbers on the base."

"I prefer the way you cut my hair, as in, I still have some once you're done."

"Obviously you don't give them clear instructions."

"I don't have to give you any."

Kathleen shook her head. How could Zach expend so much energy in everything else he did and leave his hair to sprout from his head like a red bush? It was thick, coarse, and had enough natural curl to be a pain to cut, and took at least an hour to style.

"All right. Be at the house in an hour, and we'll eat dinner, then I'll cut your hair." Did she even have anything to fix? Maybe...

"Cal coming?" he asked.

"Cal's brother, Douglas, is visiting and they've gone to a ball game. They're going to grill steaks after, but I begged off to give them some brother bonding time."

"Okay."

She couldn't ask for specifics about Zach's schedule for training or deployment, but she could ask in broad terms. "Is this sudden desire for a haircut inspired by some event you want to share with me?"

"Yeah. It's called being hotter than hell in the desert during training. I'll buy you dinner after you cut it. Better yet, I'll show up with dinner."

He was up to something. His usual check-in call lasted five minutes, and typically included her talking about what she was designing at work, while his was about maybe something funny one of the guys said or did, but little about anything else. He had so little in his life other than his team and his work.

She'd pump him for info at dinner. "I'll see you in an hour at my apartment."

"I'll be there."

Kathleen worked another forty minutes, then saved her design to the server, an off-site storage e-site, and an external hard drive. Would she ever be able to relax again at work?

Since Hillary Bryant and Paul Warren—two ex-coworkers, both deceased—had played fast and loose with her architectural designs at work, then damn near killed her, she felt more than a little anxiety about continuing to work for Wiley Design. But she couldn't afford to quit her job.

She'd been moved to a different pod with three other architects, Jack Sutton, Tyler Unger, and Kenton Frasier. The work space was very similar to the one she'd occupied before, but she was on the other side of the building.

The change in location did help. The three men she worked with did their best to treat her with understanding. They were careful to knock on the side of her work area before entering it, since the short dividers between their workstations provided the only walls in the room. She'd been easily startled and noticeably tense at first. She was more at ease now, but still not back one hundred percent.

She said good night to her three pod mates and rode the elevator down to the lobby. The reception area reminded her of her last run-in with Paul Warren, and instead of crossing it, she turned toward the rear exit.

She took a deep breath as she shoved out the door. She didn't mind that it was warm and a touch muggy from the summer heat, or that the smell of the new surface they just put on the parking lot reeked of oil. She closed her car door, and the tension inside her released.

What could she do to get past this? She'd fought the PTSD caused by her kidnapping, and believed she'd made strides in overcoming it. This residual anxiety she experienced at work just would not go away. In fact, if she was honest with herself, she had never truly been happy at Wiley Design. The work was challenging and the pay good, but she couldn't shake the feeling she needed to watch her back every minute. Would it be different somewhere else?

She pressed the heels of her hands against her eyes and rested them for a minute. She had to get past this or make a change.

Maybe leaving would be for the best.

She could research some of the other design firms in the area and submit her resume. Her supervisor, Mr. Allison, had expressed surprise when she said she'd stay. She'd done good work for the company, and was sure he'd give her a recommendation so she could move on.

But she couldn't worry about this now. Zach would be waiting for her.

Twenty minutes later she parked in front of her apartment to find Zach sitting on the steps, a large takeout bag next to him. She ought to give him a copy of her key in case of an emergency, especially since she still had a copy of his.

He was dressed in jeans and a pullover knit shirt with a collar. It had been so long since she'd seen him clean-shaven, she studied his square-jawed face with interest. He looked younger without the beard, though just as masculine. His features were strong like her father's, with thick brows and a firm mouth, eager to smile.

"Hey, stranger," she greeted him. Though they'd talked on the phone, it had been nearly three weeks since she saw him last. She frowned when he eased to his feet much more slowly than usual, and her heart gave a sisterly thump.

"Hey." Zach leaned forward and brushed her cheek with a brotherly kiss. "You look good."

She braced a hand against his chest. "You look like you're in pain. What's wrong?"

"I had a small accident. I made a clumsy landing after a sky-dive, tripped, and fell on a fucking rock."

"Ouch!" She reached past him to unlock the door and motioned him in.

"That's not what I said." He bent and scooped up the bag and preceded her into the apartment. He limped noticeably as he bypassed the living room and went directly into the kitchen area.

Knowing his creative vocabulary, she could imagine. "Have you been checked out by a doctor?" She tossed her purse on the table next to the door and followed in his wake. She knew how stubborn he was about going to the hospital for anything short of bleeding to death.

"Yeah." He placed the bag on the counter. "They X-rayed my hip, and I'm bruised, but nothing's broken."

"Good. Are you on pain meds?" She opened the refrigerator.

"Yeah. The pills are taking the edge off."

Which meant the pain level was probably just below a scream for anyone else. She reached for the pitcher of iced tea on the top shelf. He wasn't drinking beer on top of his pills on her watch. She fixed them both a glass, added a wedge of lemon to soften the blow, and set the sugar bowl next to him with a long-handled iced-tea spoon.

Zach grimaced, but scooped some into his drink and stirred it.

"Come have a seat." She urged him toward the living room. "Can I get you an ice pack?"

He hesitated. "That would be good." He lowered himself carefully into one of her overstuffed chairs.

She got a package of frozen peas out of the freezer and wrapped it in a dishtowel. He smiled as he wedged it against his hip. "I found the package of peas you left in the door of the freezer at home. It came in handy about two o'clock today."

"I left them for you to *eat*, but they do come in handy for other things." She settled on the couch, toed off her shoes, and propped her feet on the coffee table. "So, what's the big rush for the haircut?"

"No rush. Needed a trim, and I haven't seen you in a few weeks."

"So you decided to kill two birds with one stone." She narrowed her eyes at him. Typical brother.

"And I did bring dinner to pay you back."

She smiled. "You did." As brothers went, he was pretty good, though she didn't get to see him often enough, even though he only lived thirty minutes away. "So how long will you be off your feet?"

"A couple of weeks, maybe three."

He'd go insane at home with nothing to do. "What will you do with your time?"

"Well, I sort of had two accidents this morning. One sent me to the hospital, and one sent the dog I hit on the way home to the vet."

Darn. He'd be upset about the dog. He had a soft spot for them. Or had when they were growing up. "You've had a rough day."

"Yeah. I feel like shit that I hit her. After you cut my hair and we eat, I thought I'd roll by and check on her on my way home."

"Will the office be open so late?"

"Yep, until nine tonight."

"I guess we'd better get started on the haircut so you're not late." She rose to get a towel and the spray bottle, scissors, clips, clippers, a mirror, and comb. By the time she returned, Zach had moved from the chair to one of the dining table chairs. Kathleen spread the towel over his shoulders and wet his hair. "What's the name of the vet you're getting cleaned up to go see?"

Zach looked over his shoulder at her and quirked a brow.

Kathleen's lips twitched in amusement. "You didn't press your shirt to go see a dog, Zach."

A wry smile flickered. "Her name is Francesca, but everyone calls her Piper."

Kathleen pinned up part of his hair. "Blonde or brunette?

"Brunette with just a hint of red."

"Blue eyes or green?"

"A kind of sherry brown. She's Italian. But I'm going by to see the dog, too."

Kathleen controlled her smile with an effort. Sherry brown? Her brother was actually waxing poetic about a woman's eyes. "I'm sure you are. You know you're allowed to have a life outside of your job, right?"

His expression closed, and she avoided saying anything else. If she pushed too hard, he might change his mind about going to the vet's office. She concentrated on layering his thick hair without gapping it.

"The dog's owner is in the hospital and won't be able to care for her until he gets out himself. So I've volunteered to take her until he's on his feet and she is too."

"You'll need to be ambulatory yourself if you intend to take her. You're not moving very well."

"I'll heal. I'm doing okay. She's not going to be moving very fast either for a while. Her leg is pretty banged up and her hip is broken." He changed the direction of the conversation. "Remember Rusty?"

"Yeah, I remember him." How could she ever forget him? He'd slept at the foot of her bed from the time she was four until she was sixteen. Her eyes stung and she blinked fast to clear her vision.

"He was a great dog. Not trained like Gracie, but smart. He'd catch a ball until my arm felt like rubber from throwing it and his tongue hung out of his head like it might fall off."

She chuckled. "I remember. What's Gracie trained to do?" She thinned the thick hair at the back of his head and trimmed it close, but left just a little length on top so it would lie nicely.

"Take down the bad guys and sniff out explosives or weapons."

"So, she's a military war dog."

"Yeah. Retired. We've got handlers who train with the dogs. I can't tell you how many times the dog has gone in first and saved us from walking into an IED. Having them in our unit gives us an edge on the job, and they provide us with a little piece of normal when everything's all fucked up. The dogs are trained, but they still like to be scratched behind the ears and loved on. Sometimes it helps a lot just to love on a dog."

Wow! He was giving her a small peek into his world. She paused in mid-clip until she had her emotions under control. "Dogs do seem to offer comfort when you need it the most. Like they have some kind of sixth sense."

"Yeah, they do."

She finished sculpting around his ears and shaved the back of his neck, then handed him a mirror so he wouldn't have to walk all the way to the bathroom to check it out.

He turned his head one way, then another. "It looks good. If you ever give up architecture, you can open up your own barbershop. Thanks, Kathleen."

"You're welcome. If you'd come by more often for a trim, it wouldn't get so out of control." She removed the towel and shook the big tufts of hair onto the floor at her feet, then brushed his shirt off here and there. Crossing the narrow kitchen space to get the broom, she glanced over her shoulder at him. "Now, what did you bring to eat?"

"I got veal Parmesan from Bertinelli's." He stood and returned the chair to its usual place at the table.

Kathleen couldn't help but smile. "Did you buy your vet something to eat?"

"Yeah. It's in a container so she can reheat it in a microwave."

"Smart man. If she's anything like me, the way to her heart will be through her stomach." He had so few people in his life. If he was trying to make a connection with someone, she'd encourage him. He was so alone, too alone when he wasn't with his team. "I won't mind if you want to go on over and take the food with you so you can share a meal with her instead of me."

"Are you trying to get rid of me?" he asked.

"No. But I'm your sister, and you'd probably enjoy other female company more."

He looked away. "I just want a date. I'm not shooting for love at first sight."

"It wouldn't be bad to have both, would it?"

The uncertainty she read in his expression gave her heart a little squeeze. Was he still hung up on Patricia? Or was it something else?

"Let's eat. Then I'll run the food by to Piper and visit the dog." He carried the takeout bag to the dining table.

It was his call, but she'd like to know why he was reluctant to go the extra step. Not just with this woman, but with *anyone*. What had happened to make him so wary of getting involved with someone on a long-term basis? Had his breakup with Patricia been so painful?

She knew all about painful breakups. Hers had been contentious, and she'd lost her best friend along with her fiancé. How could she spur him into getting out of the rut he'd fallen into? She gathered silverware, napkins and their drinks.

"How's Cal?" He asked as soon as she sat down across from him.

"He's good." Good try, but he couldn't get her off topic so easily.

"Every other man I know your age, besides Bowie, has a steady girlfriend. I haven't seen you go out even once since I've lived here, and I've been here five months. All you do is work. And when you finally find someone you'd like to go out with, you're hem-hawing around about it."

Zach leaned forward. "Would you want to go out with someone who might be called up at any moment, knowing if you got involved you'd have to put your love life on hold until they got back? If you'd even be willing to do it."

His last sentence said more than the rest. "If Cal were active duty, I'd still love him, Zach. I knew the day I met him he was special. Otherwise, I wouldn't have gone out with him when he called me two days later. And all we'd had was a two-minute conversation, and we had to practically yell at each other to be heard over the rumble of heavy construction equipment, too. So, yeah, if I didn't already have Cal, I'd take a chance on someone. But how's she supposed to know you're unique unless you show her you are?"

There was a question brewing behind his masculine features, but he didn't ask it.

Kathleen sighed inwardly. He just wasn't going to open up to her. With eight siblings, there was always some kind of drama going on to talk about. Their oldest brother's family was experiencing the latest. "Maggie's having another baby," she announced.

"Michael Junior's wife?"

"Yeah."

"Isn't she almost forty?"

"Thirty-seven."

"Isn't she a little old to have a baby?"

"For some, but they're all a blessing, aren't they?"

"Sure, but how does Trey feel about it? He's sixteen, isn't he?"

"Yeah. He's embarrassed because everyone knows his parents still have sex."

Zach's hoot of laughter triggered a grin.

"Wonder how Mike senior feels about being a dad at forty," Kathleen mused.

"There's two ways it can go. He could be in a panic, or he could be strutting around like he's done all the heavy lifting himself. How much you want to bet that's the one he's going with?"

Kathleen grinned. "Is that how you'd feel?"

"Hell, no. I'd be breathing into a paper bag."

Kathleen laughed.

"The closest I've ever been to a woman in labor was when we landed at Miramar and Zoe went into labor. Scared the hell out of me, and it's the only time I've ever seen Hawk freaked out."

His expression stilled, and Kathleen wondered what thought had suddenly arrested his attention.

She filled him in on the other family news she learned from her mother's call the night before. In a way it was a curse and a blessing to be so far away. Living in the maelstrom of Clan O'Connor had been emotionally exhausting. None of the family members thought a thing about sticking their nose in each other's business. At least this far away she didn't have to hear anyone's thoughts about whether or not she was or should be sleeping with Cal. It was nobody's business but her own.

In fact, she wished Cal was here now, because her brother's loneliness had triggered a need to be held close. Zach deserved better. He'd put his entire life on hold to serve his country. If there was anyone who deserved to be loved, it was him.

She waited until they cleared the table before she said. "Thank you for dinner and the company. I appreciate it."

"Me too."

"You have exactly two and a half hours before the vet's office closes. I bet it's quiet there this time of night, and you might even get to hang with Piper while she eats." She brushed her fingers through the short ruff across his forehead, combing it in place. "I bet she'll take one look at you and think, 'gee, he cleans up pretty good and has a killer smile. I want to see what else he has to offer.'"

His uncertainty returned, though he tried to cover it with a cocky smile. "Thanks, Sis. If she needs a reference to go out with me, I'll give her your number." He hugged her tight and kissed her cheek.

He limped up the sidewalk to the parking lot but stopped midway. "I gave them your number in case they release the dog and can't reach me."

"Oh, you did?"

"Yeah. Just in case I should need backup."

It was part of being a family to help each other out, and he'd unhesitatingly run to her rescue when Hillary held her hostage.

"Call me if you need me, and even if you don't."

He grinned again. "Thanks. It's been a while for us both, having a dog around."

Their mother still had one, but the loss of Rusty still hurt. "It might do us both good, as long as neither of us gets too attached." Why had she said that?

"I won't. I'm not home enough to have a pet. And it's too hard to find someone to take care of one when you're gone for six months or more at a time."

"You'll get to enjoy the responsibility until her owner can take care of her. The two of you can heal together."

He looked away. "Yeah. Maybe so."

Why did she get the idea he was talking about more than their hip injuries? Now she was more worried about him than she was about herself.

CHAPTER 5

CALLAHAN CROWES STARED at his brother. Shock reverberated through him like he'd been zapped with a cattle prod. "You're shitting me, aren't you?" His comfortable living room suddenly seemed claustrophobic, and the pleasant weekend he'd hoped for was fast taking a spiraling trip down the toilet.

"It's not like you've been there working in the past five years, Cal."

"I was a little busy fighting a war, Doug." He tried to keep the anger out of his voice, though it was rushing through him like a tornado through a cornfield. "Then when I fought my way back home, Dad wouldn't let me on his crew."

"Yeah, I've heard that tune before. Nobody asked you to enlist."

Wow, Doug didn't fall far from the same bitter tree. When was Doug going to be his own man instead of mirroring their father in every aspect of his life? If Dad told him to shit green tomatoes, he'd try it.

Cal attempted to choke back the bitterness. "Besides being the right thing to do, the business was close to bankruptcy when I enlisted. I had dreams of being an engineer. I thought they might go for helping me complete the training but—you get what you get. I still took as much of the burden off of Mom and Dad as I could. Or didn't they tell you I floated one of the loans he had on the business the whole time I was enlisted, and paid it off for them? I have the receipts to prove it. How much of your money have you sunk into it?"

Doug's cheeks flushed red. His coloring, more like their father's, tended to reflect his emotions in that telltale sweep. With his darker hair and eyes, he was a mirror of Jameson Crowes in looks. Cal had gotten his blond-streaked light brown hair and blue-green eyes from his mother.

"No, they didn't tell me." His grudging tone granted little concession.

"No, I don't guess Dad would."

"I'm there working building the business alongside him."

"Just as you would be if you worked for someone else. And you're drawing a pretty good salary for doing it, too. Better than you would if you worked for anyone else. You're not sweating any more for him than you would for anyone else, either. You may be the favored son, but I'm still his son, too. Even if he doesn't see it that way anymore."

Doug's expression revealed a shadow of remorse. "He still sees you as his son, Cal."

Cal narrowed his eyes and once again swept Doug with a searching look. "Then what the fuck are we talking about here?"

"Dad's been having some issues lately."

"Like what?"

"They're not sure yet. His blood pressure's been up, and he's been having what they thought were digestive issues at first. Now they've decided it's his heart."

Heat swept into Cal's face. "So you thought, just in case he dropped dead, you'd come here and see if you could convince me to sign over any inheritance I might get? Jesus Christ, Doug!" He didn't even attempt to color the disgust in his tone.

"You can't blame me for wanting to cement my position with the company."

"By trying to jerk the rug out from under me like Dad did? Jesus Christ!" Nausea rose like he'd been kicked in the nuts. His father was sick, and his brother was circling like some kind of money-grubbing vulture. He wanted to grab him by the scruff of the neck and throw him out of the apartment.

Cal jerked the cell phone from his pocket and dialed his mother's number. As soon as she answered he said. "Tell me about Dad."

His mom, always practical, did just that. "He's worked eighty-hour weeks for the last five years, and it's caught up with him. They have his blood pressure under control now, but he's on a restricted diet, and he's had to cut back on his work hours."

Cal glanced at Doug and read the guilt in his expression. This wasn't kindergarten, and he wouldn't burden his mother with his younger brother's bullshit. No matter how pissed he was at him.

"What else do they plan to do?"

"More tests. Then the doctor will know what he needs done. Medication or surgery. As long as he does what they tell him…and I'll see that he does…he'll be fine."

"From the way Doug talked, I thought he was at death's door." He shot his brother another look.

"He needs to be careful until we find out how bad things are. He wouldn't take care of himself, wouldn't eat healthily. This scare has been a wake-up call.

"Well, as long as something good comes out of it… If you need me, let me know."

"He needs you, too, Cal. I know how unfair he's been to you. He knows he was, too. He loves you. And is proud of you. He read every article they wrote about how you rescued that woman on the top of the building."

He had a damn funny way of showing it. "That woman's name is Kathleen, Mom, and she and I are dating exclusively. It's serious."

"I'm thrilled you've found someone special."

"Me too, and she is. Keep me posted on his progress, Mom."

He heard her sigh on the other end of the phone. "Sometimes it takes a bigger man to bend and make the first move."

This was not the time to step into the breach between him and his father. "Call me if you need me. He can, too."

They both knew a man like Jameson Crowes would never make the first move. He and Cal hadn't spoken in nearly two years. His father saw him as a cripple because of his prosthetic leg, and refused to allow him anywhere near any of his building sites. Cal had been given no choice but to leave and make a life for himself.

Poetic justice would have been for him to get a job on a rival firm's crew there in San Antonio. He'd made it possible for his Dad to keep his business, and the man repaid him by pushing him out. He'd been too hurt and bitter to be anywhere near his family. Instead he returned to the area he called home during his recovery from the IED which destroyed his leg, put him in the hospital for nearly three months, and required therapy of one kind or the other for another year.

He refused to allow his father's judgment to hold him back from making a living in his field, a field he'd worked in every day since returning to San Diego.

He closed out the call and turned to face Doug. Cal hadn't come close to dealing with his anger, and he'd never felt less like being in the same room with his brother. The emotional punches just kept coming every time he let his father and brother get close enough.

Luckily he had steaks to cook. He went out onto the front porch and lit the grill.

Doug wandered out onto the porch a beer in each hand. Cal took the bottle and set it on the railing. He went back into the apartment and retrieved the two steaks he'd marinated and the ears of corn he'd shucked and wrapped in aluminum foil.

Why had he gone to all this trouble? Feeding people was a symbol of fellowship and caring. That wasn't what he was feeling right now. For the first time in months, he fought the urge to rub the top of his head. Which made him even angrier.

Using tongs, he flipped the steaks on the grill, tossed the corn on with them, and shut the lid.

"I'm sorry," Doug said.

No he wasn't. There had always been a brotherly competition

between them. But since Cal had come back from Afghanistan without a leg, it had changed to something darker. Doug had wanted to be the only son, and now he was, he still wasn't satisfied.

"I'm a prick."

There was no arguing with that.

"You don't know what he's been like since you walked away and never looked back."

Cal glanced up. "That's the way he wanted it."

"No, he didn't. Now I know the whole story... He's eaten up with guilt because you lost a leg so he could keep the company."

"I didn't lose a leg for him. I lost it fighting a bunch of religious fanatics on a power trip, bent on killing anyone who didn't want to be oppressed by them. Killing anyone they could to intimidate people into accepting their beliefs. I lost it because some asshole wanted to kill me because I was defending people who couldn't defend themselves. It didn't have a damn thing to do with Dad or the business. Not everything is about you guys."

Doug laughed.

After a moment's pause, the sound actually brought a wry twist to Cal's lips. He raised the lid on the grill, flipped the steaks again, and used tongs to roll the corn.

Doug rubbed the back of his neck. "You're not going to let this go, are you?"

"I can't un-hear something. And all I'm hearing is, 'you're no longer part of the family, so fuck you, Cal.' Isn't that what you meant? The double fuck you and Dad dealt me when he refused to let me work for him. I can't be a part of the business, so I'm no longer part of the family."

Cal stood facing away from Doug for a moment, then turned back. "Well, how about, fuck you, Doug! How about you use a tiny bit of that selfish, asshole brain of yours and think how you would feel if Dad kicked you off the crew and said you couldn't work there anymore. That you're fucking useless, a cripple, a liability. Try to un-hear that."

Cal threw the tongs onto the built-in shelf on the side of the grill and stormed into the house. Fuck it. He was out of here.

He grabbed his keys and wallet from the table next to the door. "I won't be back tonight. Lock up when you leave in the morning."

"Is this how you solve your problems? By walking away?" Doug yelled.

Doug was a goddamn fool. Cal jerked open the door to his truck. "I'm walking away so I don't pound your face into mud. *Don't. Poke. The. Bear.*"

CHAPTER 6

PIPER UPDATED THE Chocolate Lab's chart, left it on the counter for Tiffany, the evening receptionist, to deal with, and retreated to her office for a breather. Her shoulders were stiff and her back ached from being on her feet for the past eight hours.

And why had she volunteered to stay late? Oh, yeah, because she felt guilty for taking up the first half of the afternoon with an emergency surgery. The other three vets would have amputated the leg, but she just couldn't do it. The animal was too healthy, and she knew MWDs thrived on being active. Besides, the Malinois had served her country in Iraq and Afghanistan. She deserved a shot at keeping the leg.

Once inside her office she kneaded the small of her back, then leaned down to touch her toes. When she got home she'd do some yoga exercises to relieve the pain. And sleep like a log.

Tony appeared at the door just as she was sliding behind her desk. "The SEAL who brought in the war dog this morning is out front. He wants to check on Gracie."

"What makes you think he's a SEAL, Tony?"

"Those guys have a different air about them. With special permission, they're allowed to let their hair grow longer. Keeps them from looking so military when they go to foreign countries."

Zach was a SEAL. It explained a lot. She knew a little about them—not much, just what she'd heard on television. Did she really want to be attracted to someone who did such a dangerous job and carried a gun? And disappeared for months at a time? *No!* The whole scenario seemed way too familiar.

Even as she followed Tony to reception, her heart was racing and her cheeks felt hot. At the open bathroom door, she paused to yank off the scrunchie she used to keep her hair out of the way, finger-combed out the tangles, and put the scrunchie on again. But she couldn't do anything about the thumbprint-like shadows under her eyes.

She was tired, and it showed, so she pasted on a smile. Maybe then he wouldn't notice her exhaustion.

Zach was lounging against the front counter, and straightened as soon as he saw her. His green gaze tracked her progress around the large reception counter.

She felt a little out of breath when she said, "Hello, Ensign O'Connor. Why don't you come back, and I'll discuss Gracie's progress with you?"

He bent to grab the handles of a bag at his feet and followed her. Noticing his limp was worse, she slowed her pace to accommodate him. "She's doing very well," she said over her shoulder. "She's already thrown off some of the aftereffects of the anesthesia." Piper crouched at one of the cages and released the levers, securing the cage door in an open position before stepping back.

Zach set the bag just outside the kennel room door and moved to the open cage.

Gracie raised her head and wagged her tail as, with some difficulty, he knelt on the floor next to her.

Piper saw the dog's eyes still looked a little glazed. "I've given her some pain medication. I felt she needed it."

Zach nodded. "I feel guilty as hell that I hit her."

"An accident is an accident. And you did everything at the scene you could do to save her life. She might have died before you got her here otherwise."

He offered Gracie his hand to sniff before reaching in and rubbing her behind the ears. He cupped the dog's bottom jaw in one hand and ran the other over her head and neck.

Piper observed her behavior with him. Despite the cushioned wrappings around Gracie's leg and body, she looked pretty good considering what she'd been through. Her tail thumped the padding, slow and steady, like a drummer keeping time, and she angled her head, directing Zach's touch where she wanted it.

Piper smiled at the behavior.

"Yeah, we're a pair aren't we? Both hobbling a bit, but we'll get through it, won't we, sweetheart?" He petted her for a few minutes, talking to her all the while. When he attempted to rise, he braced a hand on the floor and shoved up with his good leg. Piper gripped his other arm above the elbow to help him as much as she could.

"Thanks." He covered her hand and held it against his arm.

He had large hands. Strong hands. Totally different from David's. By focusing on the differences, she was obliterating that momentary stumble she experienced the first moment they met. She turned aside, afraid of what he might read in her face. "Have you heard anything from the police about her owner?" She closed the cage door.

"I called one of the cops I met with this morning. Master Chief Flynn isn't out of the woods yet. He's got a fractured skull, a broken arm, several broken ribs, and a bruised kidney. More than one person attacked him, and one had a baseball bat."

"It was a miracle he even survived." Piper shook her head. "Do they have any clue why?"

"No. Nothing was stolen from the house. He must have seen something suspicious and gone out to investigate. Luckily the neighbor heard the commotion and called the cops. He might not have made it otherwise."

"That's horrible." What kind of person could do such a thing? It might be a long time before Gracie could go home. "Come to the office and we'll talk about Gracie's progress."

She paused outside the kennel room to look down at the bag.

"That's your dinner," he said. "I promised my sister I'd buy dinner tonight if she gave me a haircut, so I got an extra meal for you. You'll have to reheat it in the microwave. There's a salad and bread in there, too. Dressing on the side. Kathleen rescued the salad and refrigerated it so it wouldn't wilt."

Touched by his thoughtfulness, she smiled. "Thank you. I don't know what to say." Was he leading up to something?

"It's just a small thank-you for jumping into the emergency. I didn't expect her to survive at first. Then I didn't expect her to keep the leg."

"We'll have to be a little cautious about that for a few days and see how she does. She's had a little water today, but I'm waiting until tomorrow morning to offer her food."

He followed her down to a small office, where she placed the bag on the desk and gestured for him to come in and sit down. She studied the familiar logo on the bag. He had no idea he'd brought her food from her family's restaurant. She wondered how long it had been since she swung by there.

She settled behind the desk and turned her attention back to Zach.

"Animals don't process pain like we do, so I'm monitoring her carefully. She'll be in for a longer recovery than a simple broken leg would require, and she'll need some physical therapy once she's on her feet."

"Like water therapy?" He asked.

"Yes. And passive-range massage to keep the circulation going and the range of motion normal."

"I can do the massage. I've done some training. For humans. Just a couple of classes, but if someone will show me the right techniques, I can do them."

"It's a good idea, but let's wait and see for now." She leaned forward on her elbows on the desk. "How are *you* doing? Your limp is worse."

"I'm sore and bruised. It'll be worse tomorrow. Then I'll start to heal."

"You should be staying off your leg. How were you injured? Unless you're not allowed to tell me."

"It's okay. We were doing a high altitude, high opening train-ing dive. We call it a HAHO. Everything went great. Took us about sixty minutes to reach the ground, and I landed just the way I was supposed to until the wind caught my chute and carried me off target, dragging me along. I tripped over one rock, crashed into another, and got a little banged up. Nothing's broken, but the bruising is coming out in Technicolor."

She grimaced in sympathy. "Oooo! It smarts to even think about it."

He grinned. "I've had a few colorful things to say about it at the time and since."

She laughed.

"I'm sorry you were hurt."

"Thanks." He leaned forward in his seat. "It would make me feel much better if you'd go out to dinner with me, or for coffee or a drink."

She hesitated. She studied his strong, square jaw. "I don't know if it would be such a good idea."

His smile folded, to be replaced by a frown. "I didn't ask if you were married or committed."

"Neither. I mean—other than to my work here. But to date one of our clients…"

"I'm not really one of your clients since I don't own Gracie. Or actually, I'm only a temporary customer until she goes home to her owner."

"You seem to have a way with her. She responded to you from the first."

"We had several big dogs while I was growing up, and I've missed having one."

"Why don't you get one?"

"I'm a SEAL. We have to go wheels up at a moment's notice. And we train a lot, which means long hours and sometimes weeks away from home. It wouldn't be fair to the dog or cat to be left alone like that. This way I can enjoy Gracie for a few weeks while she and I are laid up, and return her when it's time."

His job sounded like it didn't leave him very much time to date. Then again, she hadn't had time, either, since starting vet school. Starting a business and working didn't leave much time for anything but sleep. And even if she'd had time there'd been…the fallout from David. And Lester. No, she wasn't going to go there. "And if you get called up?"

"I don't think it will happen in the next four or so weeks, but, just in case, my sister Kathleen said she'd take her. She loves dogs, and she'll be good with her."

"If she can't take her, I'll keep her until Mr. Flynn gets out of the hospital. I have a golden retriever named Trouble. I'm sure they'll get along."

He smiled amused at the name. "Trouble, huh?"

"Yes, and he still is at times, but for the most part he's pretty well behaved nowadays."

Tiffany, the evening receptionist, came to the door. "We have a woman with a sick cat. I've put her in room four." She stepped in to lay the file on her desk.

Piper rose and picked up the folder. "Thanks, Tiffany."

Zach stood with some difficulty. The urge to help him had her pausing on the way to her office door. Once on his feet, he ran his fingertips down her forearm and cuffed her wrist in a light grip. His dark green eyes had interesting yellow flecks around the iris. But beyond the color, the hungry look she read there arrowed down into the pit of her stomach and lower. "I'll be back tomorrow to see Gracie. In the meantime, why don't you think about my dinner invitation?"

The man could barely walk and he was asking her out. But she couldn't go out with him. She'd just bring trouble to his door. Although she hadn't seen Detective Lester around since she moved back. She was keeping a low profile, and there was no reason for him to know she was back in San Diego.

If he ever discovered she was… Her throat tightened and her heart raced. If they started dating and Lester came around…Zach deserved better than to have to deal with her stalker cop. She came with far too much baggage for any man.

Why couldn't she have a normal life?

An idea suddenly occurred to her. "Did you shave and get a haircut…?" she let the question drift off.

He smiled. "Yeah. I wanted to make a better impression." He brushed the newly cut hair back from his forehead. "When I'm working a lot, those things are low on my to-do list."

She'd been impressed with his focus and skill during Gracie's X-rays. His patience and care. He looked younger clean-shaven, but she rather liked his long auburn hair and the scruff.

The close shave did leave the clean lines of his jaw and lips bare. "I imagine you make an impression wherever you go, Zach. But I'd better get to my patient."

She didn't want to. She wanted to sit with him, listen to the hint of New England in his accent, and continue to resist the temptation. It had been a long, long time since she'd been on a date. Or even been attracted to someone.

The temptation was strong.

The threat of Lester stronger.

"You rest your hip, now."

"Roger that. See you tomorrow."

CHAPTER 7

K ATHLEEN WATCHED CAL pace across her living room and back. His anger stood like a clenched fist between them. Not that he'd ever raise his hand to her. He might with a man, but never a woman.

She was always amazed by his ability to walk so flawlessly on his prosthetic, but anger made his quick movements choppy. It had been some time since she'd seen him this upset, and he hadn't as yet spilled why, but she could see it was affecting his whole body.

"If you tell me what happened, I might be able to help you work through it," she suggested.

"It's my fucking selfish asshole brother. I want to beat the fucking shit out of him."

Whoa. Cal rarely cussed in front of her. Even so, it wasn't the words that shocked her. It was the passion with which he delivered them.

"He wants me to see a lawyer and sign over control of my part of the business to him in case something happens to Dad."

Shock held Kathleen silent for beat. "You're kidding."

"No. It's what this trip was all about. Dad had a heart attack and isn't working, and right now he's supposed to do nothing but rest and avoid stress until they finish the tests."

"So Doug is marking his territory. He thought you'd move in

and try and take over."

Cal laughed for the first time since arriving. "Marking his territory?"

"It's what you guys do, isn't it?"

Cal shook his head then sat next to her on the couch. "Yeah, I guess we do."

Now he was sitting down he was more approachable. Kathleen rested a soothing hand on his thigh. "He's doing this without your Dad's knowledge, isn't he?"

"Yes. When I called Mom, he acted like someone had driven a stake up his ass and wouldn't look at me, so I don't think Dad knows. Why would he think I'd give up my job and move back to Texas to try and take over? I'm making more money than he is, and he's part of the business."

She understood why Cal was hypersensitive about issues with his family. He'd gotten a raw deal from his father after returning from Afghanistan. "There's no reason to get worked up unless your Mom or Dad call and say you need to go home and sign paperwork."

"Doug waited until tonight to tell me. He acted like it shouldn't matter to me that he wanted to cut me out."

She couldn't even imagine how much it must hurt to be treated like this by a brother. It was taking sibling rivalry to a whole new level. "You did the right thing by leaving and coming over here before things escalated to more than an argument. But it might be time to go to San Antonio for a visit and check on your dad."

Time to heal this chasm between father and son before something happened and they never got an opportunity to fix it. Cal carried enough guilt without adding any more to his burden.

"Don't allow your brother to influence the way you feel about your father. These are two completely different issues, Cal. Your father has nothing to do with how Doug behaves."

He made a sound in the back of his throat, filled with bitterness. "Doug doesn't shit without asking permission from my father. And he doesn't have a thought of his own without Dad putting it in his head first. Dad's attitude toward me has led to all of this."

She leaned into his shoulder and rested her head there. She wanted to wrap herself around him and protect him from further hurt.

He was the same way about her.

His body relaxed and he drew her in against his side. "I'm sorry. I'm being an asshole."

"As long as your assholery isn't directed at me, I'm good," she replied.

He laughed. "Is that a real word?"

"Probably not."

He was easing up about it, but it would take days for him to get over this last bout with his brother.

"If I make a trip home, will you go with me?" He breathed against her temple. "I want my mom to meet you."

Did she want to go? Would she end up being a buffer between Cal and his father? "When would you want to go?"

"We could take a long weekend next week, just an extra day or two, and fly down and back."

"I'm finishing up on a project right now, and I won't be done for another week at least. It would have to be the end of next week before I'd feel comfortable asking for a couple of days off."

"Okay."

"I'm not sure you should wait, Cal. If your brother is talking control of the company, he must think things are serious. You could go on ahead of me and I could fly in later."

Cal's cell phone rang and he reached for it. After looking at the screen he vacillated, then, with a grimace, finally tapped it and answered the call. His expression changed from controlled anger to grave concern after listening to only a couple of words.

"I'll call the airport to see if we can get a flight out and call you back."

Kathleen knew before he ever said the words, and everything in her wanted to reach out and hold him.

"Dad had another heart attack and is in the hospital. It happened right after I talked to Mom." He rubbed his hands over his close-cropped hair. "It looks like you were right. Doug and I will try to get a flight out tonight."

CHAPTER 8

THE PAIN WOKE ZACH at zero seven hundred. He rolled out of bed with a groan he'd have chewed back if anyone had been there to hear him. The bone-deep ache didn't let up. Every move twisted it higher. He needed to use heat on the injury and take some meds.

He limped into the kitchen, swallowed two of the pain pills dry, then reached into the refrigerator for a bottle of juice. He lay on the couch, and after twenty minutes the medication kicked in, and the tension the pain had triggered eased.

The silence of the apartment was a welcome relief most of the time. Much of what the team did was noisy. Target practice, weapons training, drills, blowing stuff up, even most of the transports they used were loud. The emptiness of the apartment while he was in pain bothered him. He thought about calling Kathleen, but she'd be getting ready for work.

He lay for a long while, hoping without success to go back to sleep, and finally reached for his cell phone.

Hawk answered on the first ring, and he asked, "Did you find any of Master Chief's family or friends?"

"Yeah. Team members will be going to the hospital to check on him."

"I thought I might, too. Let him know about his dog."

"You're supposed to be taking things easy and staying off that hip until it heals, Doc."

"I will. I have a pair of crutches around here somewhere. I'll drag them out and give it some rest. Sitting here at home watching television isn't exactly conducive to my mental health. I'll be batshit crazy by the time I get back to work."

Hawk laughed. "I keep telling you, you need a woman. They're a great distraction—among other things."

Doc ignored him, but he couldn't ignore the way Piper Bertinelli popped into his head. "Any news coming down the pike?" They suspected a deployment was coming. With ISIS or Daesh actively encouraging terrorist bombings all over the world, Boko Haram kidnapping women and children, and Al Qaeda still wreaking havoc, he'd never be out of a job. Even the drug cartels threatening American borders were a danger to national security.

Hawk's tone took a turn to serious. "I have a feeling we'll hear something soon. You need to do what the doc said and get back in peak condition. I don't want the team to be a man down if we have to go wheels up. We depend on your medical training too much to leave you behind."

"I'm taking care of business here, I promise." Jesus, all he could do was wait for the injury to heal on its own.

The sound of a toddler crying came through in the background. "If I hear anything, I'll let you know. Zoe's in the shower and A. J.'s just conked his head on the coffee table. Gotta go."

Zach closed the call then tossed his phone onto his coffee table and stared at the ceiling. "Damnit!" He'd done this to himself. Closed himself off to everyone but his teammates. Because of Patricia. It wasn't even her fault. He was the one who'd gotten in too deep emotionally. Or had he? He'd been just as lonely then as he was now, and needing to know someone was at home waiting for him.

His family always did, but they were across the country, busy with their own lives. And sometimes he wondered just how much it would affect them if something happened to him. Sure, his mom and dad loved him, he was their child, but the physical distance kept them from having the same emotional closeness they had with the five siblings who lived nearby.

He'd been through two more six-month deployments to the Middle East and a couple of shorter deployments to South America since Patricia. And another loomed, although he didn't know where yet.

And now he'd met someone he was interested in....

What would be the point of getting involved when he was leaving soon? It wouldn't be fair to her, or to him. And he couldn't get in so deep he'd let it screw with his head again, either.

It would be better to stick with the party girls. No-strings-attached sex and a little company.

Piper was more than likely going to turn him down anyway. She'd delayed a decision last night, and that was the first step. If he didn't pursue it again, she'd let it go. It would be best for them both.

A hollow disappointment settled in the pit of his stomach. He tried to ignore it.

The phone rang and he reached for it. The veterinary office number showed on the screen. He tapped the screen to answer the call.

"Hello, Zach." Piper's voice, a little breathy and uncertain, came over the line.

Just like that, he had a boner. He shook his head. Fate was either playing him for a fool or fulfilling a prayer.

"I thought I'd call and give you an update on Gracie's progress before starting with patients. I didn't wake you, did I?"

If he were to go by his Grandma's superstitious Irish beliefs, this would be a sign. "No, I've been up a while. How's she doing?"

"Much better now the anesthesia has worn off. She drank water and has even shifted around in her kennel. I plan to take her out and get her moving today."

"Great. I'm going by the hospital today to check on her owner. His teammates are going to be there, and if he's awake, I'll have to tell him about the accident. He'll naturally be upset, so if I can tell him about her progress, it might soften the blow."

"What time are you going?"

"I don't have a definite plan." Just whenever he could be certain his hip could stand the walk.

"I work a split shift. I do surgery early morning and see patients until noon, and then don't come back in until five, so I could go with you after lunch if it's convenient. It might help to have some backup to reassure him Gracie's going to be fine."

"Sure. I'll come in about eleven. I could help get Gracie moving. She's a big dog, and if you intend to use a sling to support her hindquarters, it will be easier for me to handle than you." He'd have to make sure his meds hadn't worn off by then.

"Have you been researching physical therapy for dogs?" she asked.

"Some." More than some. Television bored him, so surfing the net seemed more mission-productive. Fuck! Hawk was right, he needed a life outside of work. Piper's slightly breathy, nervous voice drew him back in. Why would she be nervous around him? Attraction or something else?

"She does well with the female assistants here, but not Tony. I haven't asked the two male vets we have on staff to approach her, because I don't want to cause her more distress. You seem to be the only man she isn't aggressive with right now." In professional mode, her breathless nervousness seemed to be evening out.

"It could be she's still traumatized from the attack the other night."

"Could be. Come at eleven. We'll just walk her a few minutes to see how she does."

"Okay."

"I'll see you then."

He closed out the call, but lay there mulling over things. He'd grown lazy romantically, having dated so many women who were a sure thing instead of someone who expected to be wooed and tempted to join him between the sheets. But two or three weeks wasn't enough time to do things right. It would be better if they just kept things on a professional level.

PIPER PLACED THE kitten inside the kennel. The tiny cat remained a little groggy from anesthesia, but was breathing normally and was even purring. The hernia had been small and easily repaired. Now if they could find her a forever home… She gave the sweet animal a gentle rub and closed the door.

She glanced at her watch for the fourth time in an hour. Zach O'Connor would be here any moment.

Why had she called him again? And why was she volunteering to go to the hospital with him? There was just something…so damn sexy and…lonely about him. She was drawn to him, just like she'd been drawn to… No, it was stronger, much stronger. God, this was such a mistake! She had to back away from whatever *this* was.

For her, for him.

She knelt on the floor and opened Gracie's kennel door. The dog's tail went into wag mode immediately. She was beautiful, her coat shiny and healthy, her lines perfect for her breed. From a distance, she looked like a German shepherd, but she was sleeker, her body muscular and slim. Her dark chest, legs, muzzle, and ears contrasted with the warm brown of her body.

Piper knelt to pet her, but her eyes went to the door instead of Piper. Gracie's ears went up and she cocked her head to one side. Jasmine's voice came from down the hall. "Just this way." When the sound of uneven steps reached Piper, she knew why the dog had perked up, and she had nothing to do with it. When Zach walked in, Gracie's tail went wild.

Jeans and a blue pullover shirt with a collar never looked so good on most men. The knit fabric of the shirt stretched across his broad shoulders and the sleeves banded the muscles in his arms.

"Hey, Doc. How's she doin'?" he greeted her.

Piper dragged air into her lungs. "Happier now you're here. I've never seen anything like it. She's really taken with you."

He grinned and threw his arms wide. "What can I say?"

Piper shook her head at his cocky humor, but smiled.

"I probably smell like someone familiar," he said as he moved closer. His walk, stiffer today than the day before, concerned her. He didn't attempt to kneel, but bent to pat and stroke Gracie. The dog got to her feet, her actions as tentative as his. She held her leg up and hobbled to him to lean against his leg.

"Boy, we're sure a pair, aren't we, sweetheart?" he murmured as he ran his hand over her muzzle and ears, then down her body.

Piper couldn't help but comment. "Your hip is worse today."

He looked up, and hesitated just long enough to let her know he didn't want to admit it. "Yeah. I'll go over and use a friend's hot tub later, which should ease it some."

Was the friend female? The twinge of jealousy surprised her. She shoved it aside. She had no right to feel anything. "Actually you should probably wait another twenty-four hours before applying heat."

"Thanks for letting me know. Where do you plan to walk her?" he asked.

Now she'd seen him move, she had serious reservations about him doing even this small task. "I can do this, Zach. Why don't you take a seat in my office and wait for me?"

Understanding lit his eyes and he grimaced. "The hip will just get stiffer and sorer if I don't work it, Doc."

"I think you need to rest it."

Zach cocked his head, and a grin spread slowly across his features that she felt all the way to the bottoms of her feet. "I'm okay, Piper."

"No, you're not." She bit back the rest of what she wanted to say. What he did was none of her business. "We have a run out back. It's important we keep her from getting too rambunctious for the first couple of weeks, until her hip starts to recover and the leg break starts to heal. The soft cast will slow her down some."

He nodded. "Today, when we visit the master chief, I'll ask him about commands. They usually choose words in another language that won't be spoken by mistake. If we know how to get her to heel and lie down on command, it might be helpful."

Piper placed a collar around Gracie's neck and hooked a leash to it. The dog stood at attention, as though waiting for a command. "Has the master chief regained consciousness?"

"Yes. One of his team called to let me know. But his attackers did a job on him. It may be a month or more before he's out of the hospital."

"How did you find them?"

"Hawk, my CO, called around and got in touch with the master chief's CO. The team is going to take turns visiting the hospital to make sure he's covered. If he can identify the guys who attacked him, he may be in danger."

She hadn't thought of that.

"NCIS may get involved since it was a retired SEAL who was involved."

"I thought that only happened on television."

"No. They really do get involved in cases concerning active duty members. Master chief just retired, so I think they might want to look into his, too."

It made sense to her.

She handed Zach the leash. "You lead on and I'll follow. Just go two doors down to your right and out the back kennel door. I want to see how she does with her leg." And she'd check him out, too. The way he moved troubled her.

Zach held the loop of the leash in one hand while he held the strap straight up and short, just as she would have instructed him to do. He guided Gracie down the hall. He was patient with the limping dog, allowing her to move at her own pace. Piper doubted he could move much faster himself.

Why were men so stubborn?

Once they were outside, Gracie lifted her head and sniffed the air, then seemed to heave a sigh of relief. She didn't attempt to put any weight on the leg, though the cast kept her from bending her leg and displacing anything. She and Zach had almost done one full circuit of the small run when the dog finally managed the awkward business of squatting to pee with one stiff leg.

"I think one circle is enough, Zach. She'll be slow for a few days until the trauma of the injury starts to heal." She held the door for him to go through. "Do you have steps at your apartment?"

"No. It's a ground-level four-plex on the beach. The three guys who rent the other units are military, too." He walked Gracie back through the kennel room and down the hall while Piper followed.

"Does your landlord have any issue with you bringing a dog in?"

"No, I called to ask this morning. He was good with me taking her until the master chief goes home."

"Good. I want to keep her here for three or four more days to be sure the hip and leg are doing okay. And I'll take another round of X-rays before you take her just to be certain there are no issues."

He walked Gracie slowly back to her kennel, his limp very pronounced.

"Which will also give you a few more days to recover before you take her home."

"I have crutches in the car. I'll use them for a couple of days until this eases off."

"You might need to get another X-ray, just to rule out a break. Sometimes they don't show up on the first X-ray."

He unclipped the leash and bent to rub Gracie behind the ears. He looked up. "I'm okay, Piper. If I thought I wasn't, I'd go in. We're expecting a deployment, and my team will need me."

Her heart seemed to drop into her stomach. "How soon?"

"We won't know until it comes down. It could be a week, a month, six weeks, we never know."

So this is how he lived. What if something happened to him? What if he left and she never saw him again? Her throat hurt when she swallowed. There was such a presence about him, an energy. She'd never experienced such an instant attraction to anyone before, not even David. A jittery, needy feeling swamped her.

She knelt to urge Gracie back into the kennel and closed the door. Rubbing her hands nervously on the seat of her jeans, she straightened. She turned to face him and lifted her hands to cup his face.

Zach's eyes settled on her in surprise, then darkened with heat, offering her encouragement.

As she rose on tiptoe, he bent his head and met her halfway. Their lips came together. Instead of pushing, he kept the pressure a light caress, splaying a hand against the small of her back and urging her closer. He smelled like soap and something citrus, and when he strengthened the pressure of the kiss, she looped her arms around his neck.

Her stomach did a slow, sensual roll while her body came into contact with his solid, muscular one, yet his lips remained tender, taking hers, then releasing them, then taking them again. Though he didn't use any tongue, the kiss still set off a series of combustible longings in intimate parts of her body, and turned her legs to jelly.

When he pulled back a little and looked down at her, embarrassed heat warmed her cheeks. "I don't normally kiss strangers," she said.

His smile was quick, and his eyes lit with humor. "I'm not a stranger anymore."

The tingle of arousal ramped to torment level. No, he wasn't. She took a step back and ran her hands down his shoulders to his chest, then dropped her hands to her sides. She looked at anything and everything but him.

He took pity on her and asked, "Would you like to get some lunch before we go see the master chief?"

She jumped at the suggestion. "Maybe a taco or something quick."

"Good enough. I know just the place. It's on the way to the hospital."

After that buildup, she wanted to grab his shirt and drag him to her apartment.

But it wasn't going to happen. Not now, at least. She jumped into something once, and it had been a horrible, life-altering mistake. A mistake she and her family would never stop paying for.

CHAPTER 9

ZACH'S HEART DRUMMED against his ribs and his breathing was still a little rough. It had been the hardest thing he'd ever done, keeping the kiss at a low level when he wanted to consume her. The jasmine fragrance she wore was feminine and sexy. When her slender body had rested against his, it had set off a chain reaction he was still trying to deal with. At least the adrenaline from the sexual charge eased the pain in his hip.

He fought the urge to rest his hand possessively against the small of her back while they wandered down the hall to the waiting room.

Piper stopped by the desk and placed Gracie's chart on the ledge there.

The receptionist, Sherry, laid a newspaper folded to an article in front of her. "There's something in today's paper I thought you might be interested in."

Zach glanced at the headline. *Rash of Robberies Hits Area Veterinary Offices.*

Piper scanned the article. "Have you shown this to the others?"

"Not yet, but I will." Sherry glanced up at Zach...then her attention shifted to Piper again, and something passed between them.

Piper brushed back a thick strand of hair from her cheek. Her hand trembled. "I'll be back at five. I'm going to the med center to visit with Gracie's owner." She removed her lab coat and laid it across the rail. "Would you hang this up for me?"

"Sure." Sherry flashed Zach a quick smile, took up the chart and the lab coat, and disappeared around the file shelves.

On the way to his car, Zach hit the key fob to unlock the SUV and opened the passenger door for Piper.

Once in the car, he buckled his seat belt and turned on the car. "When was your office broken into?"

Piper stared at him, her lips parted in surprise. "How did you know?"

"The way you reacted to the article. Your hands were shaking."

"We're a new office, and just building our clientele. If word gets around, it may cost us customers. I'd appreciate it if you wouldn't say anything to anyone."

"I won't."

When she continued to study him, he felt compelled to add, "Trust me, I can keep a secret, Piper."

She shifted, obviously uncomfortable. "It was yesterday morning. I always come in early when I'm due in surgery. Someone was still inside the office. I hid in the surgery and called nine-one-one. They went out the back door."

His muscles tightened at the thought of her trapped inside the building with someone who could have hurt her. "Jesus. Did you see them?"

"No. I was too busy being scared to death and praying they didn't see me. I crawled inside a cabinet and clung to the phone until the police arrived."

"I'm sorry." He laid a hand over hers, which were gripped tight in her lap. After a moment's hesitation she turned her hand to hold onto his.

Her throat worked as she swallowed. "They stole drugs, but they also stole bandages, sutures, needles, syringes and even some bottles of saline."

"Sounds like more than just a break-in. They may be running

a vet clinic of their own."

"It's what I think as well." She paused and her voice dropped to nearly a whisper. "They got into our computers, too."

That caused a ripple of unease. Gaining access to people's home addresses and credit card numbers was a big deal.

"If you like, I can look around the business and give you some pointers about how to make it more secure. In fact, I have a friend who put in security systems for several months while he was undercover. He and I could put in some cameras and tell you how to update the security on your computers as well." If Flash wasn't gearing up for a deployment, he could help him do it. If he was, Zach could figure it out himself.

He withdrew his hand and put the car into reverse.

As he pulled out of the parking lot onto the street, she asked, "Why are you volunteering for all this, Zach?"

He glanced over at her and she continued. "I, mean taking care of Gracie and visiting Master Chief Flynn. Offering to help me."

He drew a deep breath. If he was completely honest, she'd think he was pathetic. The truth was, if he didn't have something to focus on, the walls would close in on him, and he'd have too much time to think about how empty his life was.

He stopped at a red light and ran his hands restlessly around the steering wheel. "Master Chief Flynn is a SEAL, and we look out for our own. And as for offering to help you..." He shrugged. "I have skills, I might as well use them."

"What do you do on the weekends when you're not working?"

"I bought a boat from a friend, a cabin cruiser. I take it out on the weekends and fish some."

"Alone?"

"Sometimes. I have teammates who go with me most of the time, and my sister's boyfriend, Callahan, comes out with me now and then."

"No girlfriend?"

He realized there hadn't even been any party girls in months.

"No one steady for a long time." He pulled through the intersection when the light changed to green.

"Why not?"

Was she going to try to talk herself out of going out with him? He could paint a rosier picture, but then it would end up biting them both on the ass later.

But, no. "I've done four deployments in the last five years, and we train a lot when we're in the US. It doesn't leave too much time to develop close relationships." He glanced in her direction. "Women like boyfriends who are going to be around physically now and then to help keep the relationship going. When we're working we can't be *here*. There are times we don't have access to a working phone or a computer. So, communication can be—difficult." Non-existent. God, this was such a bad idea. She deserved so much better than he could give her.

The restaurant came up on the right. He hit his blinker, whipped the car into the parking lot, parked, and killed the engine. He'd had enough of this negative stuff.

They got out of the car and met along the back of it. "My oldest brother is forty and his wife, who is thirty-seven, is pregnant with their fourth child. I called my Dad to see how things are going. Mike's been having sympathetic morning sickness for days."

Piper chuckled. "You said your oldest brother. How many are there?"

"Seven brothers and one sister."

"You have me beat. I only have four brothers and one sister."

"With out-laws and in-laws and the kids, my mom and dad have to rent the recreation center at their church for Thanksgiving and Christmas dinners."

"We have our own restaurant, so we just shut the place for the day and have everyone over there."

His brows rose. "Bertinelli's? That belongs to your family?"

"Yeah. I worked there summers and weekends through high school."

"Great food."

"They cater weddings and other things. I used to help with those, too."

"Maybe I should suggest that one of my nephews or nieces should open an Irish pub to solve the family dinner issue."

"In Boston, right?" she asked while they walked around the building to the front entrance.

Zach tried not to limp so badly, but the hip was stiff as hell, and every step was starting to hurt again. "Yeah. I know I still have the accent. I've tried to shake it, but it always comes through."

"Why would you want to? It's part of your heritage."

Jesus. He had to stop thinking in terms of his job. "I can speak Gaelic. Thanks to my *maimeó*."

"That means grandmother, doesn't it?"

"Yeah. She moved to America when she was eighteen, and married my grandfather at twenty."

"And she taught you Gaelic."

"Yeah. She felt the same way about heritage playing a part in our lives. I don't have an ear for the languages, so I really struggled to learn it. Unlike one of my old teammates. Brett hung out with two girls in Ireland on leave and came back speaking it like he'd been born there. *Maimeó* was ready to adopt him."

She chuckled, the sound light and feminine. "You sound a little jealous."

Zach focused on her upturned face. "Naw, my *maimeó* and mom have enough love to go around for everyone. Plus, they've sort of embraced my team as part of the family. They have this habit of grabbing your face and looking you right in the eye, like they're seeing everything you've been up to for the last year, and then they lay a kiss on you, like they're either forgiving you for the stuff you've messed up on, or blessing you for the stuff you didn't."

Piper laughed, her cheeks flushed. "I thought only Italian mothers did that."

They stood at the counter and ordered their tacos, and Zach paid the woman while Piper carried the tray over to the table and unloaded it, and Zach didn't object because of his uneven gait. He didn't want their food or drinks to end up on the floor.

"I assume you speak fluent Italian?" He held her chair.

"Yes," She slipped into her seat. "My mom and dad were both born here, as were my grandparents, but they all grew up in bilingual households. They passed it on to us."

"My bud Bowie is Mexican-American and speaks fluent Spanish. So I'm pretty good with it."

"There are some similarities in the languages. I'm sure you'd be able to follow along when you hear it."

"Maybe. Italian seems to have a little more music to the flow. Spanish speakers tend to race through as quickly as possible, like they're trying to say as much as they can in one breath."

"You haven't been in the back of the restaurant at rush hour."

"No, I haven't. I imagine it gets a little crazy."

"Crazy is a good word for it." She raised her taco, took a bite and hummed her appreciation.

They spent a few minutes concentrating on their food.

Zach ate to give his stomach something to gnaw on so he could take more pain medication. It had been more than six hours since his first dose of the day, and his damn leg ached.

He popped the two pills in his mouth and swallowed them with his soda.

To take his mind off the pain, he concentrated on her again. Her skin had a light olive tint, and looked smooth and soft, the hint of color in her cheeks warming it. The red highlights in her hair, and even the sherry hue of her eyes, brought to mind the warmth of the Tuscan countryside he'd visited on leave one summer. "Your brothers aren't going to go Mafioso on me if I take you out on a real date, are they?"

Piper shook her head. "No. My mother might, though."

He smiled. "That's a given."

"You don't seem too concerned."

"I don't plan to do anything to piss her off."

"I hear special ops guys can be pretty sneaky."

"Only against the enemy, darlin'. Moms are a whole different deal. You do something to get on a mom's bad side, they may forgive, but they'll never forget."

"Sounds like you might have experience with that."

He was tempted to tell her about his mom breaking Kathleen's ex-fiancé's nose, but decided against it. "Cynthia Stevens' mom."

"What happened?"

"I took Cynthia to senior prom, and we went to a party afterward. By the time I got her home, she was less than sober. I didn't ply her with drink. Or anything else." He held up three fingers like a boy scout. "Mrs. Stevens sicced Father Hansberger on me and I got a lecture. And she gave me the evil eye every time she saw me from then on."

"What's Cynthia doing now?"

"She's been married three times and has five kids."

Piper covered her mouth to stifle her laughter. "She hasn't really, has she?"

He couldn't suppress a chuckle. "Naw. I think she's an accountant and been married to the same guy since college. But her mom still gives me the stink eye when she sees me."

Piper shook her head and a speculative gleam shone in her eye. "Did she have reason?"

"No. Cynthia and I were just friends. Dancing isn't my thing, since I have two left feet." He gestured to his side. "Thus the hip injury. She and I only decided to go together at the last minute. I got up to my share of mischief, but my dad was a cop. Still is. I knew if I got into trouble anywhere, it was going to follow me home."

"My mom has always been like that too, although my dad was a little more laid back about everything...everything but the restaurant." A melancholy smile crossed her face.

He didn't have to be told her father was dead. He knew the look well.

He changed the subject and smoothed things out again.

As they left the restaurant, Piper said, "I hope you'll use those crutches you have in the back of your car when we get to the hospital."

"I plan to. I need to rest my hip. It has to heal fast."

"In case you're deployed."

"Yeah. But mostly because it hurts like a—well, pretty bad."

"You know, I have four brothers, and I have heard a cuss word or two."

"Don't encourage me. I'm trying to be on my best behavior."

She smiled and looped her arm through his while they walked across the parking lot. She was beginning to relax around him and come closer on her own, even though she put out this vibe of being a little wary, despite the kiss she'd given him.

"How long do you think you can keep up your good behavior?"

He shook his head. "I wouldn't lay odds I won't slip. But though we talk like salty dogs when we're together as a team, we all try to curb our language around ladies."

"I appreciate it. Ice will help today, maybe the hot tub tomorrow."

"I'll call my CO, Hawk, later and find out when I can use his hot tub."

He handed her the keys. "I just took those meds. You'd better drive."

CHAPTER 10

MASTER CHIEF FLYNN looked like just what he was, a man in good condition for his fifty-four years who had been brutally beaten. One side of his face was bruised, his eye was black and swollen shut, and his right arm was in a cast. No wonder the poor man didn't move unless he had to.

Though he looked a little groggy, his one clear eye sharpened when Zach introduced Piper. "Is Gracie going to be okay?" he asked, anxiety in every syllable.

"I've had to put pins in her hip and a plate in her right leg, but she was up today and walked the perimeter of the run we have at the clinic. So she's doing as well as can be expected. Ensign O'Connor is going to foster her until you get out of the hospital and can take her home."

"You know what you're doing, son?" Flynn asked.

"I know how to take care of her physical needs, and I'll do massage with her. I'm a medic, so I can dispense any kind of medication she needs. But I don't know the commands she's used to hearing. Or if there's any special routine you need me to follow with her."

Flynn seemed to relax. "You on the injured list right now?"

"Yeah. I banged up my hip, and I have three weeks off until it heals. So I have time to spend with her."

"You going to deploy soon?"

"Possibly."

But the way he said it, it sounded like a sure thing.

"If I do, Dr. Bertinelli says she'll take Gracie until you get out of the hospital."

"Okay. But I'm going to be out of here before then." The stubborn determination in Flynn's expression had Piper smiling. It was very much like Zach's at times. They were surely born with it. But they'd spoken to a couple of his nurses before visiting him, explaining about his dog, and the truth was the master chief was having balance issues, and one side of his body was weak. Not paralyzed, but weak. So there was some brain trauma from the beating. He was going to have to have some physical therapy and be monitored closely, probably for a longer time than he wanted.

"She's in good hands right now, Master Chief. I really hate that I hit her. If I could have stopped, I would have."

"From what Dr. Bertinelli said, you kept her alive until you could get her to the vet's office. And you've paid for her care. She's going to be fine. I know my dog. She won't lie down and quit, any more than I will."

"Have you been together long?" Piper asked.

"I did four deployments with a dog just like her. During my last three deployments, her handler and I were teammates. When he was injured, I took care of her until he was back on his feet. She did two more deployments after, and was showing signs of PTSD. She's also got some age on her, so they decided to retire her, and I decided to go out with her. Her handler loves her as much as I do, but he knows I take good care of her, and he has other responsibilities. He comes by now and then to visit when he's home. She's always excited to see him."

Piper looked away as emotion threatened. To have gone through the things he did during deployment, and survived to come home, only to be beaten by the same people he had protected through his service... There was no justice in that. Not unless the police found the people who did it and arrested them.

"She's really taken a shine to Ensign O'Connor. When he's around, it's like there's no one else in the room." Piper moved close to lay her hand on Flynn's weak arm. "I'll do everything I can to make sure she comes back to you whole. You do the same to come back to her, okay?"

He patted her hand. "Roger that. You can call me Flynn, Dr. Bertinelli. You're taking care of my girl. No need for formality between us."

"I'm Piper."

He nodded.

Zach set aside his crutches and drew a chair up to the bed, taking a small notebook out of the back pocket of his jeans and balancing it on his knee. "Tell me anything you can think of that I might need to know while I have her. If I go wheels up, Dr. Bertinelli,... He looked up at her. "Piper will need to know, too."

Piper listened to the two men. They spoke the same language. Conducted themselves in the same manner. Even in casual conversation, there was something similar about the way they phrased things.

Was this the way Zach would be in twenty more years? Alone, with only a dog to keep him company? She hoped not.

Flynn knew his dog, and listed everything from her favorite toy to her favorite treat. "I'll have one of my guys drop her toys by the vet's office tomorrow." He went over her feeding schedule and the kind of food she ate. He had a routine she followed, and they continued the training exercises she had done in the past. Being in such good physical condition had saved her life.

"She gets along well with other animals. Even cats."

"I have a golden retriever." Piper said. "They'll be good buddies, I'm sure. He's very laid back."

"She'll want to be the alpha."

"Trouble doesn't want to be in charge of anything but the next meal," Piper commented drily.

Flynn laughed.

"He's not very bright, but he's great with kids, and he's loving."

"She likes children, too. And she's good with other animals."

"Maybe he'll learn a few things from her." She hoped so. "I'm taking her to my apartment this weekend to keep a close eye on her. If everything looks good, I'll turn her over to Ensign O'Connor on Monday."

"Think you'll be up to it by then?" Flynn asked, studying Zach.

"She's supposed to take things easy and not overdo. So am I. We'll be great together. And I've put Dr. Bertinelli's number in my phone on speed dial."

Flynn seemed satisfied. "Don't lose your heart to her. I want her back."

Zach smiled. "I already have, but Uncle Sam has my ticket, and I know this is temporary."

A quick pinch of loss hit Piper when he said it. He didn't have a life outside of the Navy, because the Navy was his life. Did she really want to get to know him, possibly get attached, and watch him fly away to places unknown? And what if he didn't come back?

Who was she kidding? She was already getting to know him.

Would he want to get closer to her if he knew about her past?

No, it would be too much, and he'd probably disappear afterwards, just like every guy she'd dated since. All two of them.

Zach rose. He wrote something on one of the small sheets of paper and tore it out of the notebook. "This is my cell and my address, so you'll know where she is and how to reach me. You can call me any time."

Piper removed a business card from her purse, jotted her cell number on the back, and laid it next to Zach's.

"Thanks," Flynn offered her his hand. Piper clasped it and gave it a pat. Zach laid a hand on the master chief's shoulder.

"I don't remember any of the guys who came after me. I was supposed to meet up with some friends and play chess at zero twelve-thirty, and I was running late. Otherwise they'd have been able to just take her, and I wouldn't have known until I got back. I went out when I heard Gracie bark. It wasn't just a bark like she'd seen a squirrel, there's a different sound to it when she's gone into attack mode. I understand why they wanted her, but I don't get why they'd try to kill me to get her."

"Do you always go out on Mondays to play chess?" Zach asked.

"Most Mondays."

"They may have been watching you to see when it was most convenient to snatch her, Master Chief. She's trained. She'd be worth a lot of money to someone who wanted a dog like her."

Or a dog trained to attack on command. She could see where he was going with this.

Flynn did as well, and said, "Keep a close eye on her for me."

"I will, Master Chief. I'll be back to visit, too."

Zach stuck the notebook in his back pocket and then gathered his crutches and swung forward with practiced ease. On their way by, they nodded to the two men sitting outside Flynn's room.

They were almost to the elevator when she thought of something. "Wait a minute, Zach, I want to check with the staff about something."

"Okay."

She backtracked to the nurses' station and leaned against the divider separating their work area from the hallway. A woman, slender and dark haired, was keying information into the computer, so Piper waited until she looked up and asked, "May I help you?"

Piper introduced herself. "I was wondering if service dogs are allowed on this floor. Master Chief Flynn has a service dog, a retired Military Work Dog, and he's pining for her. She was injured at the same time he was, and I thought perhaps a visit might ease his concerns. It would help them both to see each other."

"You have to fill out paperwork from the main office downstairs, but I'm certain they'd allow you to bring her in to see him. In fact, why don't I call and see if they can email it up here, and I'll print it out for you now." The nurse reached for the phone.

Zach wandered over and leaned against the divider beside her. A blond nurse returned to the station, clipboard in hand. She peeked up at Zach from beneath her lashes and offered him a smile. He nodded to her, but returned his attention to Piper.

The dark-haired nurse hung up the phone, did something on the computer, then stood and said, "I'll be right back with the paperwork. If you fill it out and fax it to the office with her picture and her shot record, they'll email you a conformation and a badge."

"Great! Thank you so much."

The nurse went inside an office behind the divider.

"This is an excellent idea," Zach said.

"I've thought about trying to train Trouble to be a therapy dog, but he's still in the puppy stage and too rambunctious."

"How old is he?"

Piper grinned. "Four."

Zach chuckled. "There's still time."

"I have to go back and ask Flynn what vet he normally uses so I can get the shot record."

"I'm good. Take your time." He balanced easily on the crutches and held his left foot off the ground.

"How's the hip feeling?"

"Better."

"Good. I still think you should have another X-ray. Just to be safe."

His smile was part amusement, part temptation. "You wouldn't want to do it for me?"

"You know I can't. I take care of man's best friend instead of man, because they're not nearly as stubborn and they don't talk back."

"Amen to that," the nurse sitting behind the counter murmured.

Zach tossed a glance over his shoulder at her. "I don't want to sit here for hours waiting for an X-ray."

"Are you whining?" Piper asked.

"Roger that!" he said with feeling.

She laughed. "Think about it." She patted his shoulder and walked back down the hall to Flynn's room.

By the time she got back, the blond nurse had struck up a

conversation and was smiling at him in a way he'd have to be deaf, dumb and blind to miss.

The dark-haired nurse who had helped her leaned across the counter and handed Piper the paperwork. She gave Zach a card. "Zoe said she'd see you in fifteen minutes in the emergency room, so I suggest you double-time it down there now."

"Will do. I appreciate it, Jeanine."

"You're welcome."

So when in the last three minutes had he gotten on a first-name basis with the nurse?

Zach fished into his jeans pocket and pulled the car keys free. "I'll catch a ride back to your office after I've finished getting the X-ray."

Piper smiled in relief. "I can run home, let Trouble out for a few minutes, do some laundry, and then come back to pick you up."

"You sure?"

"Yes. It's no problem." She accepted the keys from him and the paperwork she'd asked for from the nurse, murmuring her thanks.

"Thanks, ladies." Zach flashed a white grin at the two. "I appreciate your help." He shifted on the crutches. "You ready to go?"

"Yes." She walked down to the elevator while he swung on the crutches. "So how did you manage to get an appointment so quickly?"

"It seems Jeanine knows Zoe, my CO's wife, and Zoe works with several of the ortho guys. She called and got me in to see one of them. Zoe's meeting in the emergency room with an X-ray tech. Then I'll have to stick around for the ortho guy to read the X-ray and check me out, so take your time and do whatever you had planned before we went on this little side trip. I'll be a while." He grimaced.

"You don't want anything to hinder your recovery, Zach." They stepped into the surprisingly empty elevator.

"No." He narrowed his green eyes at her, and she smiled.

"I'm not happy about the way you're moving. With a soft tissue injury, you could develop a blood clot. Is your leg swollen?"

"Yeah, but I'm bruised from my waist to my knee, Piper."

She flinched. She couldn't believe he was even mobile. Her worry doubled. "Then I'm glad you're staying to get checked out again."

The elevator stopped on the next floor and picked up two people. They fell silent. After stops to pick up three more people, they arrived on the ground floor, and filtered out with the rest of the crowd.

"The car's in lot A. You can take the tram." He gave her the row. "Look for the frog sticker on the back window."

The way he watched out for her was refreshing. She was an independent woman, but it was nice now and then for a guy to act like he wanted to take care of her. "If I get lost, I'll ask for directions. Would you like me to stay with you?"

He tilted his head and smiled. "I'd enjoy the company, but you probably have things you need to do which are more important than hanging around here waiting. I'll be fine."

He wasn't fine, but he'd never admit it.

"Call when you're done."

"I will." He nodded.

She watched him make his way down a wide hall on crutches, the muscles of his arms working as he swung himself forward. He clearly knew where he was going, and that worried her some. How often had he, or one of his teammates, been here?

Her phone rang and she fished in her purse for it. It was the office.

Sherry's voice was hushed. "Piper, there were two detectives here wanting to go back over your interview about the break-in."

"Was it Detective Sherman?"

"No. One's name was Detective Schneider. I'm not certain about the other one. He was older, blond, and looked like a body builder. Schneider asked a bunch of questions about you."

A rush of terror stole her breath and shot adrenaline into her system. The hand holding the cell phone shook. "What kind of questions?"

"The nosy kind, like where you went to school, how long you've practiced, that kind of thing."

Lester already knew where she'd gone to school. He wouldn't have to ask. She forced the tension from her shoulders and dragged in a deep breath.

"Did they say they needed me to call them or anything?"

"No. He said he'd call you if they needed any other info."

"Okay. Thanks, Sherry."

She tucked the phone into the back pocket of her jeans. It couldn't be Lester. He already knew all her basic information. They were probably double-checking on something.

But her heart continued to race the entire tram trip to Zach's car.

ZACH TOOK A power nap in X-ray while he waited his turn. The pain meds made him drowsy, and without a mission of some sort to keep him sharp, he couldn't keep his eyes open.

Downtime did give him time to think about Piper, and relive the kiss they'd shared. She was worried about him, but he didn't want her pity. He wanted *her*. She was too concerned about his physical well-being to realize that his hip might be sore as hell, but the rest of him was in excellent working order, and went on high alert every time she came within touching distance.

To distract himself, he used his smartphone to access the newspaper article about the break-ins. While he read it, an idea came to him, and he called Flynn through the hospital switchboard.

"What vet office do you use?"

"Dr. Bertinelli asked me the same thing."

"She needed the information to get Gracie's shot record. There have been some break-ins at area vet offices, and I was just wondering if yours was one of them, and if there might be a connection between the burglaries and Gracie's attempted dognapping."

He gave Zach the name.

"Are they on the list?"

Zach's jaw clenched. "Yeah, they are."

"If they'd called me, I'd have kept a closer eye on my dog."

After he hung up, Zach dwelled on the ramifications. It was three-thirty by the time he saw the doctor, and the diagnosis was no broken bones, but an impressive hematoma from the collision with the rock. No blood clot. The doc sent him on his way with the same advice as the first. Avoid aspirin, stay off the leg and hip, and take the pain medication as directed until he didn't need it any longer.

He called Piper from the doctor's office and meandered through the hospital to the main entrance. During the twenty-five minutes he waited for her to pick him up, he tried to plan how he might approach her about contacting their pet owners to issue a warning.

She looked small behind the wheel of the SUV when she pulled to a stop beside him. He stowed his crutches in the back and climbed into the passenger seat gingerly.

"How did it go?" she asked.

"No breaks, just a prize-winning bruise. He even took a photo of it for his scrapbook, since you can see the imprint of my service weapon on my hip."

"Ouch. It must be really horrible."

"He did say something about using leeches to suck the blood out from under my skin so it wouldn't look so bad, but I decided to forgo that pleasure."

She tilted her head and glanced at him. "He didn't."

He grinned. "Just teasing. I thought of something while I was waiting."

"What?"

"Flynn's vet was on the list of veterinary offices broken into recently. What if they accessed your files in order to steal the dogs they want? They have a list of your clients and the kind of dogs they own. I think you should call the people whose files have been compromised and give them a heads-up. Caution them to keep a close eye on their dogs, and not to approach these guys if they catch them in the act."

Piper remained silent a moment as she turned onto the main road. "We have one partner in particular who'll be against doing it. I don't know about the rest."

"If someone were to be injured trying to save their pet, Piper, they might not be as lucky as the master chief. It isn't just the four-legged customers you have an obligation to."

"I agree, Zach, but I'm in partnership with three other people. We're a team, and I can't take action without their agreement. I'll have to discuss this with them first."

"I understand. But you need to move quickly."

"I will. I promise."

Zach studied Piper while she drove, and couldn't completely suppress his disappointment about her response to his suggestion.

But there were times he disagreed with the chain of command, and he had to follow their orders instead of what he felt was right. His team had done an extra six-month tour in Iraq and Afghanistan because they'd done the right thing and the powers that be thought otherwise.

When more than one person was involved, decisions were seldom black and white.

Silence, heavy with unspoken thoughts, lay between them the rest of the way to her office.

"Thanks for visiting Master Chief Flynn with me," he said when she pulled into the lot and parked.

"You're welcome."

"How was Trouble?"

"Waiting at the door for me with his leash in his mouth."

"I think he's getting a bad rap. He sounds like a good dog."

"Until he chews up a brand new pair of shoes or eats the corner off a twenty-five-pound bag of dog food and has it spread from one end of the house to the other."

Zach looked away to hide his amusement. "Why don't you bring him to work with you? He's probably lonely and needs company."

"You may be right, but there's no guarantee he wouldn't get bored and chew something important here."

"You know your dog." He didn't have to have a map drawn for him to see the distance she was putting between them. It was in her body language and her tone. Was it because of his comment about calling their clients? Or was it because she'd decided getting to know him wasn't worth the effort when he'd be shipping out soon. For the second time in ten minutes, disappointment lay heavy in the pit of his stomach. "I'll call tomorrow to check on Gracie. I need to stay off the leg more."

"I think so too."

He reached for his seat belt and exited the car to limp around the back of the vehicle to the driver's door.

She stood next to the SUV, her brown eyes searching his face. "Take care of yourself, Zach."

"I will. You do the same."

She turned away and regret even deeper than his disappointment took root.

He adjusted the car seat and gritted his teeth while he hauled himself up into the vehicle. He reached for the door only to find her standing in the way.

"It isn't because I don't want to do the right thing, Zach."

He drew a relieved breath. "I work for one of the largest bureaucracies in the world, Piper. I know about how things can get skewed when more than one person has a say. I'm not sitting in judgment on you."

"You don't know my situation."

"No, I don't. Are you going to give me a shot at understanding what it is, or are you going to end things here?"

He was grateful to see uncertainty flicker across her features. Her lips parted as though she meant to tell him something.

"I don't know." She ran her fingers through the long tail of hair hanging over her shoulder. "Come to dinner on Sunday and you can pick Gracie up. I'll have dealt with things by then."

The curve of her cheek and the full pout of her lips was driving him crazy. He bit his lip to keep from saying something. If she was on the fence, he needed to figure out a way to ease her off and in his direction. Pouncing on her in the parking lot didn't seem like the right way. He wasn't in pouncing condition anyway.

"If I'm going to come to dinner, I need the address."

She took out her phone and typed it in, and he heard the ding when the text arrived.

"What time?" he asked and slid back off the seat.

"Six o'clock."

He settled his feet on the ground with only a little pain. "Red or white?"

"Call me on Sunday and I'll tell you then."

"Will do. Hey! You're not going to send me away without a good-bye kiss, are you?" Not a pounce but a nudge. As wary as she was, it was a better strategy. "If you're trying to make up your mind, you might as well try things out to see if I'm worth your time."

She looked away and bit her lip but he caught a glimpse of a smile. "I've already kissed you." She brushed a hand across her forehead, as though trying to hide the quick color in her cheeks.

"Darlin', that wasn't a kiss, that was just an appetizer." His arms went around her and pulled her against him until her breasts pressed against his ribs. Everything south responded with stubborn enthusiasm, like she was naked and he could feel every inch of her skin against his. His mouth covered hers, and she tasted of sweet iced tea and smelled like jasmine. When her mouth parted, inviting him to take the kiss further, his tongue searched for hers.

CHAPTER 11

E VERY NERVE IN PIPER'S body sprang to instant, tingling life. Thanks to his lips brushing against hers, and the tempting thrust of his tongue tangling with hers, a sensual lassitude invaded her limbs. She didn't want to think beyond this moment. Couldn't think beyond it. She wanted his hands on her. Wanted her skin against his.

He increased the pressure, the kissed deepening into no-tomorrow-land, like he wanted to experience what he could before life as they knew it ended. A raging need tightened muscles down low and shot her heart rate into the stratosphere. She clung to him, her legs weak as cooked pasta.

"What the hell are you doing making out in the parking lot, Piper?"

Hunter Rawls voice shot ice crystals of reality through her and tore her out of the sensual haze she'd fallen into. She stiffened, but when she attempted to pull away, Zach's arms tightened holding her firmly against him. His cheeks were as flushed as hers as he raised his head.

Zach's eyes narrowed and his scowl flared into intimidating masculinity. He raised a brow, challenge in his glare. "I wasn't aware we had a morality police in this country. But we were kissing, not groping each other. And why did you walk all the way around the SUV to check us out?"

Hunter's cheeks reddened, and he shot Piper a look, then continued into the building.

"Is he the prick who's going to give you a hard time about calling your clients?" Zach asked.

"Yes." Hunter was a prick. And lately she'd begun to wonder more and more often of late about why she agreed to go into business with him. But the fact was, they were stuck with him, because none of them had the money to buy him out, and they needed a fourth partner. But she was getting pretty fed up with his bossy, judgmental, prickish attitude.

"Who drove the sharp stick of prissy righteous up his ass?"

"I think he was born with it."

Zach gave a bark of laughter she would have smiled about at any other time. His expression quickly became intent. "If he says anything to you about this, lay it on me."

"No." The longer she thought about Hunter's tone and the look he gave her, the angrier she got. She'd allowed someone to dictate how she lived her life seven years ago. Hunter wasn't going to get away with doing the same thing. "I won't do that. He may try to dictate how things happen here in the office, but my private life is mine."

She was distracted by the sudden spark of sunlight on Zach's beard stubble. It glinted red against his skin. She rather liked his scruff. She reached up to trace the square shape of his jaw and felt the prickle of his beard against her skin. He gripped her hand and guided her fingers to his lips to kiss them. The gesture left her breathless, and she sounded it when she said, "I need to go to work. Call me on Sunday about the wine."

"Okay."

Reluctantly she withdrew from his arms. She had to fight the urge to look back the entire way across the parking lot until she entered the building.

Sherry handed her lab coat across the counter and a file. "A woman just brought in a Chihuahua. One of her teenage sons stepped on its foot, and she's afraid it might be broken. She's in room six."

Shit! "Okay."

She hurried back to the exam rooms. When she spotted Hunter sitting behind the desk in his office, she paused in the doorway. He looked up.

She stepped into the small room and lowered her voice. "Don't you ever, *ever* talk to me that way again. What I do in my personal life is my business. Do you understand?"

His cheeks flushed. "What if a client had seen you? He's a *customer*."

"A *temporary* customer, until Gracie goes back to Master Chief Flynn. And we were in the employee parking lot all the way in the back, so the only witnesses besides you were the dogs. We are entitled to our personal lives. I imagine our customers kiss their boyfriends, girlfriends, spouses, or partners. There was nothing indecent about what we were doing. And who are you to sit in judgment on me, anyway? Don't talk to me like that again, Hunter."

She strode out of his office before she let other resentments take over and she lost control of her temper. This was not the time. Tomorrow morning would be soon enough. She had patients to take care of.

She stood in the hall outside the exam room for several seconds, waiting for her temper to settle. Out of the corner of her eye, she saw Hunter come to the door and look out. She ignored him, opened the door, and walked into the exam room.

An X-ray confirmed the tiny Chihuahua's foot was only bruised, not broken. The owner was as relieved as she, and Piper sent her on her way with a caution about big feet and tiny bones.

She took a minute to check on her recent surgery patients, and was relieved to see the kitten up, moving around, and curious about her surroundings. Piper gave her a quick exam and cuddled her for a moment before securing her back in her kennel. Next she turned her attention to Gracie, who had risen to greet her when she entered the room, and had been pawing at the front of the kennel, wanting out. A good sign. She gave the Malinois a quick exam, listened to her heart and lungs, and checked the tightness of the wrappings around her leg. She stroked and spoke to her reassuringly, then fastened the kennel door again.

The evening progressed with a steady stream of patients and Hunter keeping a low-key presence around her. Her tension didn't ease until he left at seven.

A lull came around eight, and she went into her office and activated the computer with a flip of the mouse. She looked up the addresses of the clients she remembered had been pulled, wishing she'd paid closer attention to the files lying on the counter.

Next she looked through her desk for the business card Detective Sherman, the officer in charge of the investigation, had given her. She stared at the card, her stomach muscles cramping, her tension like a spring being wound around her insides.

Not all policemen were stalkers. Not all of them became obsessed with their cases and accused innocent people of unspeakable things.

The police knew professional burglars had broken into the clinic. And she wasn't a professional burglar.

She needed to know if they'd contacted her clinic's clients, just in case. She hoped they had. Otherwise, she'd have to call them herself, and she didn't relish doing it. She dialed the detective's number.

Detective Sherman's voice sounded brusque. "What can I do for you, Dr. Bertinelli?"

"Our receptionist, Sherry, called and said someone came by earlier to go back over my statement. Was there something you needed clarified?"

"No. Who came by?"

"A Detective Schneider. He had another man with him."

After a short pause, Sherman said, "Everything seems to be in order."

That was strange. "I also want to know if you have contacted the clients whose files were compromised. I have concerns about their safety."

His tone sharpened. "What do you mean?"

"I visited a man in the hospital today who was nearly killed by two men attempting to steal his retired war dog. He tried to stop them, and was badly beaten with a bat. His vet's office was identified in the paper as one of those burglarized. They're not breaking in to steal only meds, but to possibly find particular breeds of dogs they intend to steal. All the files I saw opened on the desk were for large breeds capable of aggression, Detective."

"Look, Dr. Bertinelli, I think you and I should meet."

"We can meet whenever you like, but I need to know whether you've contacted the clients. If you haven't, I need to do so myself."

"We've talked to every person on the list, doctor. They've been warned to keep close watch over their pets. But we weren't aware of this man and his dog."

The tension went out of Piper, and she relaxed for the first time in hours. "He's retired Master Chief Clifton Flynn, and he's in the Naval hospital. They fractured his skull, cracked some ribs, and broke his arm. He's experiencing brain trauma from the attack, and having some balance issues and weakness on the right side. I have his dog. She was hit by a car while pursuing one of the men who attacked Flynn. The dog and her handler were close to the master chief in Iraq or Afghanistan, and since the dog was retiring at the same time he was, he adopted her on his way out. He was a SEAL."

"I can't believe we missed this." She heard the shuffles of paper on the other end of the phone.

"It just happened yesterday, Detective. It was actually the man who hit the dog who put it all together. He's been coming by to see how she is and invited me to go with him to the hospital to see Master Chief Flynn."

"Who is this guy?"

She bit her lip. Zach would be overjoyed about being dragged into this. "Ensign Zach O'Connor. He's an active duty SEAL. He contacted the police and gave a statement after he brought the master chief's dog in. He recognized her war dog status from the tattoo in her ear, and was upset about hitting her. I'll give you his number and you can call him, but his statement should be with the policemen who interviewed him."

"And he saw the guy she was chasing?"

"Yes, but he said he was wearing a stocking over his face."

"If you have his number I'd appreciate it."

She gave him Zach's number and, as soon as she ended the call, skimmed through her cell phone for Zach's number so she could warn him the police would likely call or visit him sometime in the next few days. A movement just outside her office caught her attention...more the shifting of a shadow than a movement.

Was someone out there listening to her conversation? Had anyone checked the back door to make sure it was secure? A deadbolt could only work if everyone remembered to use it when they visited the run out back.

Piper's heart raced, jamming her breath up into her throat. She rose and slipped around the desk and eased to the door. Tony appeared and she yelped in surprise.

"I'm sorry. I didn't mean to scare you."

Piper pressed a hand to her chest as her heart continued to drum in her throat and ears. "Was someone out in the hall?"

"Dr. Rawls came back in. He left something in his office he needed." Tony waved the chart he held. "We have a black lab who's lethargic and not drinking or eating."

Piper released a relieved breath, closed her phone, and dropped it in her pocket. "Let's take care of him."

CHAPTER 12

C AL SLOUCHED IN one of the two chairs. Hospital rooms were interchangeable, be they military hospitals or civilian. They all had the same beds, the same tables, and the same white sheets, bleached until they were rough as sandpaper.

The smell lingering in the room was also universal. It was blend of bleach, cleaning solutions, and alcohol. There was also the sour smell of sick sweat hanging in the air.

He propped his foot on the side support of the bed and tried to focus on the newspaper he was reading to pass the time. His father slept much of the time, which worried him, because Rob Crowes never slept. He was always in motion, always barking orders.

But he wasn't now. While he'd been confined to the hospital and home during his illness, he'd lost his tan. Silver threaded his hair, and he'd lost weight, which he'd needed to do, but he didn't look healthy. Wires snaked out from inside his hospital gown to a machine next to the bed, monitoring his oxygen level, pulse, and blood pressure.

For the first time, his father looked old and the emotions the simple observation unleashed were too complicated to unwind.

If his dad hadn't been such a hard-ass, there wouldn't be this wedge of anger and resentment hammered between them, a wedge that changed them into polite strangers.

Cal had been monitoring everything he said carefully to keep from antagonizing his dad, and his father in turn replied using words designed to push his buttons. Which made him resent his father even more. But he needed to find a way to set their tangled, contentious emotional history aside. If his father died, he'd be left holding the guilt and pain while his dad skipped out to the afterlife, fancy-free and with a clear conscience. Rob Crowes didn't apologize for anything. Everyone was expected to just get over it.

So why was Cal still holding on to so much hurt and resentment? He'd moved to San Diego and built his own life. He was settled in a job he enjoyed and was good at. He had a girlfriend he was crazy about, and who loved him. What difference did it make if he wasn't a part of a business he said good-bye to four years ago?

Being cut out of the business wasn't what had caused the rift. It was being thrown out of his father's life. He lost his leg and lost his father at the same time. On occasion he still had shadow pain from the leg amputation. The pain of losing his dad reared up just as often.

His father's voice cut into his thoughts. "I don't know why you're staring at the damn paper so hard. You haven't read a word in the last five minutes."

Cal jerked his attention away from his thoughts. He folded the paper and set it aside. "How are you feeling?"

"I'm okay. Where's your mother?"

"She had some scheduling issues to take care of at the office. Something about cabinets being delayed."

"So she left you here to babysit me?"

Cal breathed a sigh. Why was this man always combative? "You're a little old for a babysitter, Dad. If you don't want me here, I can go sit out in the hall until she comes back."

His father looked away. "No. You're fine where you are."

Cal straightened in his chair and rested his elbows on his knees. "Do you want some water or something?"

"Yeah, I could use a drink. I can have liquids until midnight."

Cal poured some water into a small cup from the plastic pitcher on the bedside table, stuck in a flexible straw, set it on the hospital table, pushing it over the bed. Then he raised the head of the bed so his father could sit up and reach the water.

"You seem to know how to work everything around here," his father commented.

"One hospital is the same as another. I had plenty of practice when I was in one."

His father reached for the cup and took a long drink. "You look good."

"Thanks. I'm doing good."

"Tom Hill came through for you."

"Yeah, he did. I like my job, and I'm good at it."

"And this girl you're dating?"

"She's not a girl, Dad. She's a woman. Kathleen is beautiful and talented. You'll meet her next week."

"She's flying here?"

"Yeah. I want her to meet you and mom."

"So it's serious?"

"As it gets."

His father nodded and studied him for a long moment. "I guess if you can survive surgery in a makeshift hospital in Afghanistan, I can make it in a state-of-the-art hospital here in the states."

Was his dad afraid? Hell, who wouldn't be? They were going to crack open his chest and do bypass surgery. "You're going to be fine. The surgeon doing your operation has an excellent reputation and no lawsuits on record. He knows what he's doing."

"You must have looked him up."

"Yeah, I did some research on him."

"That's the most interest you've shown in a while."

Cal cocked a brow at him and shrugged. "I call Mom every week, Dad. You could ask to speak to me any time." He drew a deep breath and bit back the words of resentment begging to be spoken. "Why did you tell her not to tell me about your heart?"

"I figured you were busy with work and stuff."

"Yeah, I have been busy, but not so busy I couldn't listen to an update about your health." Unlike his father's disinterest in his son's ability to walk again and lead a normal life. He turned away to look out the window and across the San Antonio cityscape.

Silence stretched, and Cal let it. It was better not to say anything, because if he said half of what he thought, they'd have a blowup, and his dad would have another heart attack.

"This woman you're dating…what does she do for a living?"

"She's an architect for a large commercial firm."

"She must be a smart cookie."

"Yeah, very smart and beautiful."

"Where did you meet her?"

He was tired of this slow, painful process. "On a building site. She's the woman in the newspaper articles, Dad." He turned to face his father. "We were already dating when she was kidnapped and tortured."

"I see."

There was the tone he'd been waiting for. He didn't see a thing.

"How long have you been dating?"

"Nearly nine months. Her brother and his SEAL team saved my life in Afghanistan."

His gray brows went up. "That's a wild coincidence."

"Yeah, it is. She had just moved out from Boston to start work at her job, and was living with her brother while she hunted for an apartment. She invited me to dinner, and I recognized him."

"So, her brother is a SEAL?"

"Yeah. She has two other brothers serving, one army, one marine, and her father and oldest brother are Boston policemen."

"She has a large family."

"Yeah. Eight brothers and her mom and dad, plus an army of nieces and nephews. They're Irish Catholic."

"Different from us, huh?"

"There are certainly more of them. Her mom and dad are good people."

"When did you meet them?"

"About six months ago. They came out to check on Kathleen and stayed a week."

He could see his dad's mind working, trying to figure out a way to ask what they thought about their daughter dating a man missing part of a leg. He settled for, "And you got along okay with her family?"

"Yeah, the ones I've met so far. Zach and I fish together now and then."

His dad looked away. "Sounds like you've moved on."

Like he had a choice. "I had to make a living." Cal shrugged again and held his tongue.

"We've got five crews working with only your brother and mother supervising, Cal."

He studied his dad's face. "Doug will step up to the plate."

"He's not ready."

Then what the hell had Doug been doing? "My impression was you don't want me anywhere near your business."

"Your mother is overwhelmed and I…The doc's already said I may never be able to go back to the job full time."

Cal remained silent to keep from voicing the string of curses going through his mind. Doug was a number-one fucker. "Doug's worked with you for more than six years, Dad. He should be up to running things. He'll get used to supervising and delegating. I'm only going to be here for a week or so. After your surgery, I have a job to go back to."

"You could help him find his feet while you're here, Cal."

Why hadn't his Dad helped Doug find his feet in the six years he'd been working with him? "He'll see my help as interference. I didn't come here to start a power struggle over the business. I won't be a party to that."

"Okay. I'll talk to him about it."

"No. You're not supposed to be under any kind of stress, and the minute you start talking about any of this your blood pressure starts to rise."

He frowned. "How do you know?"

Cal pointed to the machine next to the bed monitoring his

dad's vitals. "It's there on the screen." He wasn't going to be held responsible for his Dad having another attack, and the only way to avoid it was to avoid him. "I'm going downstairs to get a soft drink. Do you want anything?"

"You're running away," his dad accused.

"I'm glad to know you finally realize I can," Cal commented and wandered out of the room. He stopped by the nurses' station and spoke to the one who'd been assigned to his dad since he arrived. She was short and round, had an engaging smile, and a great mass of dark hair rolled into a casual bun at the crown of her head.

"I'm going to the cafeteria for a drink, but I'll be right back."

"We can give you a soft drink, Mr. Crowes."

"I need to stretch my legs. If you could check on my Dad, I'd appreciate it. He's a little worried about his business. I've tried to reassure him, but he has a tendency to get worked up. I left so he'd quit talking about it and get it off his mind."

"We'll keep an eye on him."

"Thanks." He took the elevator to the first floor and followed the signs to the cafeteria. He wondered if hospitals had a universal plan their cafeterias had to follow. This one looked like all the others he'd been in. He grabbed an apple from the salad line and got a bottled soft drink out of a refrigerator unit. He paid for it, and then wandered back toward the elevators, taking his time. He didn't want to return to the same argument. It was like being stuck on a treadmill covering the same ground over and over and never moving forward. He was tired of it.

His mom walked through the front entrance, so he paused near the elevators to wait for her.

Looking up, she spotted him and angled in his direction. "How's your father doing?"

"He's fine. The nurses are keeping an eye on him. I just ran down to get a drink."

It was easier for the gray to hide out in her blond hair, but it was there, around her face. Lines at the corner of her blue-green eyes, the same color as his, deepened while she studied him with a troubled expression. "He's already started on you, hasn't he?"

She'd put on makeup and hidden the dark circles under her eyes he noticed this morning.

"What was he after you about?"

"He wants me to help Doug out at the business until he gets his feet under him. I'd think Doug would already have the rhythm of the job after six years, Mom."

"Your Dad likes to keep a tight rein on things. And your brother hasn't really put in the kind of time he needs to catch on to the way we do things."

Cal raised a brow. According to Doug, he was in charge, and their Dad was just there to supervise. "I don't want to get into a tug-of-war with Doug over the business, Mom." And he had a life back in San Diego he wanted to return to. He'd been gone forty-eight hours, and he missed Kathleen every minute. He should never have encouraged her to fly out. She'd land dead center in a family feud if his mom and dad continued to push him toward helping with the business.

"Doug's bragged a bit, hasn't he?"

Cal remained silent. He wasn't going to tell his mom what her youngest son had been up to.

"We are a bit overwhelmed, Cal. It would be a help to me if you'd go by the sites and check on the crews' progress. You know how the workers slack off if they think the boss isn't watching."

Yeah, he knew. They needed deadlines; otherwise, they'd drag their feet and draw their check. Not all of them, but enough to screw up a construction schedule. "After Dad's surgery, I'll make the rounds with Doug. If I do it alone, he'll get the idea I'm trying to take over."

"All right."

"I'll need to see the plans for the projects and the materials ordered. What kind of problem did you have with today's order?"

"Just a delay in receiving some kitchen cabinets. The bathroom cabinets were in the same order. We have the flooring done in both bathrooms and the kitchen. They were going to deliver the granite counter tops tomorrow, so I've had to put them off for a couple of days until we get the cabinets in. The guys went ahead and worked on laying the hardwood flooring in the bedrooms and hallway on the second floor today. The cabinets will be here tomorrow."

"I'll look at things tonight so I'll be up to speed."

"If Doug has anything to say about it, just tell him I asked you to check on some things for me."

Great! This was going to go over like a cherry bomb in a manure pile. Shit would fly.

They hopped on the elevator and rode upstairs to the cardiology wing. "He's never going to relax while I'm here, Mom. Every time I'm in the room his blood pressure goes up."

"He's got a guilty conscience."

He didn't want guilt to feed his dad's illness. He just wanted him to acknowledge he'd been wrong.

She drew a deep breath, impatience radiating off of her. "You're both idiots."

Cal bit his lip to keep from smiling.

"I'm over this thing between the two of you, Cal. One of you has to apologize so we can move on."

"I didn't do anything to apologize for, Mom. He didn't want me, and I left. What else was I supposed to do? My leg isn't going to grow back. I wasn't going to stick around and be treated like a cripple the rest of my life."

"No. I didn't expect you to." Her shoulders fell and she looped her arm through his. "Your dad thought you'd leave for a few months then come back. He never thought you'd stay away."

"He should have given me a chance. But he wasn't willing to do it, so I found someone who would."

"He was going to, Cal, but you never came back."

That revelation came four years too late to change anything. "His finger wasn't broken. He could have called me."

"He's a stubborn man. And so are you. And Doug has always been stuck between you."

"Between us?" From his standpoint Doug had been front and center for the last six years. It was on him if he hadn't taken advantage of the situation.

"Both of you are driven and determined. Doug wants to be just like you, but lacks the initiative. He'd rather put in his eight hours and go home for a cold beer. He'd rather watch television than spend half the night tracking down a faucet lost in shipping."

"I'm with him about the faucet. Just go out and buy one and send the lost one back when it comes in."

"Customers want what they want, Cal. We're in the business of making their dreams come true. If they want a certain kind of faucet, we get it for them."

"I'd be on the phone telling them it was lost and I was going to find a comparable one."

She shook her head, and though she didn't roll her eyes, he could tell she wanted to. "Which also takes time."

It sounded like his mom was just as run-down as his dad, and if she got sick, too...

Cal pulled her to a stop down the hall from his dad's room. "Until Dad is on his feet, I think you need to hire someone who can help with the day-to-day aggravations. Dad's going to be a full time job." He drew a deep breath. "While I'm here, I'll make sure the crews stay on task and get the job done, but I have responsibilities back in San Diego. A job, friends, and—most important—Kathleen. I can't just tear up roots and move back here. And even if I could...I'm not at all sure I want to."

"I understand, but we need you, Cal. The last month since your father's been sick it's been plain to him and to me."

Shit! "I'll think about it, and I'll talk to Doug. Or maybe we can do it together."

"Okay. Once your father's surgery is behind us."

He'd carried his resentment and pain over this situation for so long, it was hard to lay it down, hard to know what to do with himself when it wasn't there in the background, goading him. Now he was needed, he wasn't sure he wanted to turn his entire life upside down again to move back to Texas.

And what about Kathleen? No way was he leaving her behind. If she couldn't come with him, he wasn't going anywhere.

CHAPTER 13

KATHLEEN PARKED IN front of her apartment, but was slow to get out of the car. She sat for a moment, willing her muscles to relax and her nerves to unwind. She'd worked her ass off the entire week to put the finishing touches on the design for the client, only to have them come back and want some additions. It always happened, but it couldn't have come at a worse time.

Through every moment of the hard work and meetings, she'd wanted to drop everything and hop a plane to be with Cal, but she just couldn't. Not until the changes were finished. She'd go in tomorrow and complete them, and then first thing Tuesday morning ask the clients to come in and okay the changes. That way she'd be on the plane to San Antonio on Tuesday afternoon, just as she and Cal had planned.

She missed him. Since finding each other, they hadn't been apart more than a day, and now it had been three days…and it felt like a year.

What had happened to her? She had been eager to make new friends and build a life here in San Diego. Since the kidnapping, she'd done was hide out at her apartment and hang with Cal. She had grown too dependent on him. Too clingy. But she felt safe while she was with him. And when she wasn't…the words vulnerable and shaky came to mind.

When she stepped outside her apartment or car, she was hyperaware of everything around her. And though she thought she was controlling her anxiety, since Cal's absence, she'd been anxious and having trouble breathing just walking from her car into the building at work. Or from her apartment to the car.

She had to get over this.

With that thought in mind, she shoved open the car door and climbed out. She hit the button to lock the vehicle and forced herself to walk slowly up the sidewalk. Her hand shook a little when she put the key in the lock.

She hadn't had anything to eat since lunch. It was just low blood sugar, she told herself, though deep down she knew it was much more.

She shoved open the door, rushed inside, and set the dead-bolt. Immediately her tension released, leaving her trembling.

She tossed her purse on the table close to the door and moved into the living room, where she sat on the couch, rested her hands on her knees, and waited for her heart to stop racing.

Why was she suddenly going through this again? What had triggered it?

She needed to go back to the psychologist she'd seen for three months after the attack.

And how the hell was she supposed to fly to San Antonio when she couldn't walk from her car to her apartment without being scared shitless?

ZACH SETTLED BACK in the hot tub on Hawk's sun porch. The sun slipped in through the privacy blinds in strips that shone on the painted wooden floor.

Hawk turned up the jets for him, and the heated water bubbled around his legs. "Zoe says fifteen minutes."

"Okay." Zach leaned his head back and stretched his arms out over the edge of the tub.

Hawk sat down on the couch. "So how are the master chief and his dog?"

"They're both recovering, and already trying to work their way back. Master chief will need some therapy to regain the strength on his right side, and Gracie will need some massage and therapy to walk normally again. In the MC's words, he'll never give up, and neither will his dog."

Hawk walked over to the small refrigerator in the corner. He removed a beer and held one up for Zach. "It's a real shame both of them are having to go through this."

Though he could practically taste the brew, Zach shook his head. "Better not. I'm still on the pain meds the doc gave me. And, yeah, it is a shame. That fucker led her right in front of my car. I damn near hit him, too."

Hawk palmed a bottled soft drink and handed it to him. Zach unscrewed the lid and took a healthy gulp. The drink buzzed his tongue and tasted sweet, instead of the bitterness he craved. Maybe it was good he had to deny himself something now and then. It built character.

His thoughts swung to Piper. He wondered if it would build character if he denied himself her.

They were barreling down a path that might be wrong for them both.

He heard himself saying. "I met a woman."

Hawk turned to look at him. "Who is she?" He sat down in the glider across from Zach.

"Her name is Francesca, but everyone calls her Piper. She's a vet. And her family owns Bertinelli's Restaurant."

"And?" Hawk urged.

"She's smart and beautiful. Not a party girl or a SEAL groupie."

Hawk raised his brows, encouraging him to continue.

"We haven't been out yet. Well, we stopped for lunch on the way to visit Master Chief Flynn. I'm not sure that counts. But I'm going to dinner at her house on Sunday." His thoughts kept hanging up on the kiss they shared in the parking lot before her asshole partner interrupted. And the one before. The way she looked at him, touched him.

Hawk's voice interrupted his musings. "I'm glad to hear it. You need other friends besides the team, and other interests besides bandaging wounds or blowing things up."

"And fishing," Zach added.

Hawk shot him a look. "And fishing."

Zach drew in a deep breath and tasted the chlorination in the mist around the tub. "We're about to deploy. It isn't the greatest time to start dating someone."

Hawk leaned forward to rest his elbows on his knees and let the beer bottle dangle between his legs. "In our line of work, we have to grab our opportunities with both hands. Life isn't about acting when it's convenient. It's about living as fully as we can, and making every moment count."

Zach dwelled on that a moment. "How do you leave them, Hawk? How do you walk into the fire and leave them behind without going crazy?

"Who the hell says I don't sometimes?"

He'd never seen Hawk reveal even a hint of being out of control. He had a reputation for being one of the most professional operators in the teams. The best of the best.

Hawk raked his fingers through his hair, roughing up the stick-straight dark strands. His gray gaze looked pale against the dark tan of his face. "When we're gone, there are times I feel like…if I have to go one more day without seeing Zoe, or hearing her voice, I might rip something or someone to pieces. That's when I get on SKYPE. I have to see her face while I'm talking to her. I have to see A. J."

"She talks me down off the ledge. She offers me encouragement and tells me how much she loves me. She gives me a little touches of home to cling to, and tells me every detail of what's going on with her and A. J., makes me a part of their lives. Even if he's asleep when I call, she gets him out of bed before I say good-bye so I can see him." A wry smile tweaked his lips. "Sometimes she even succeeds in not waking him up. I don't know how I'd do what we do without them, Doc."

Hawk looked up. "You can't keep the people you love at a

distance and do the job. You have to make them as much a part of it as possible. I can't share what we do or where we are, but I can share pictures and small events, funny stories, to bring them closer. I can tell them how much I love them every opportunity I get."

Zach swallowed against the knot in his throat. Man, that was tough. Would it have worked with Patricia?

He'd had plenty of time to think about the mistakes he made in their relationship, and dissect the feelings he had for her. He'd found it difficult to sort them out, much less express them to her.

Hawk was waiting for a response, so he said, "Talking about my feelings is like walking around naked in public for me, Hawk."

"You have to trust someone, sometime, Doc. We have too many things we can't talk about. It's a mistake not to share the things we can."

Zoe tapped at the door. "Sorry to interrupt." She nodded to Hawk. "A. J. wants you to rub his back until he goes to sleep."

Hawk set aside his beer and stood. "I'll be right back. You have five more minutes in the tub before you need to get out."

"I'll keep an eye on him," Zoe offered. She limped into the sun porch and sat down on the glider Hawk just vacated. "He'll only be a few minutes. He has the magic touch with A. J." She flashed him a smile that said *with me, too*.

Zach wondered how she dealt with a child alone when they were gone. A child who was missing his Pa, as A. J. called Hawk.

"How's the hip feeling?" Zoe asked, cutting into his thoughts.

"Better, I think."

"Good. Hawk can give you a key and the alarm code. We're not here during the day, so you could slip in and do ten or fifteen minutes in the mornings, and then another ten or so at night."

"I wouldn't want to intrude, Zoe."

"You're family, Doc. It isn't an intrusion."

"I appreciate you saying that." He touched a spot in the center of his chest with a fist and gave a thumbs up gesture.

"All I ask is that you make sure the kitchen door is locked when you leave. A. J.'s determined to get into the tub every time it's uncovered, and he's as sneaky as you guys. He gets into stuff faster than I can catch him."

Zach chuckled. "He's three and already training to be a SEAL."

"Let's hope he learns the self-discipline to go along with it. Otherwise, God help us. He shot through the terrible twos without any of the usual tantrums, and has hit the thunderous threes with a vengeance to make up for it."

The timer went off, and Zach braced a hand on the side of the tub to help him stand. When he climbed out and reached for the towel, he could tell he was moving a little easier.

He returned to the subject of A. J. "He's probably sensing things from you and Hawk about the deployment."

"Probably."

"I know it isn't easy for you, Zoe."

"No." She avoided looking at him, and instead removed the clip holding her long, hazelnut-colored hair in a tail, finger-combed it, gathering the loose, flyaway strands around her face, then twisted it and secured it with the clip at the back of her head again. An oval face and large blue eyes put her firmly in the category of beautiful.

A drunk driver hit her while she was out riding her bicycle years before and damaged her legs, one worse than the other, leaving her with skin graft scars and a permanent limp that required a brace on one leg. She was without the brace at the moment, leaving the scars visible below her cropped pants.

"This will be the third deployment since we met. The second one since A. J.'s birth. It never gets any easier having him away."

He wanted to ask if it was worth it, but couldn't bring himself to.

"I love him, and I knew what I was taking on when I married him. I'd rather have him half the year than not at all."

And if something happened to Hawk?

He had never allowed himself to think about the people and family he left behind. He'd blocked that off, too, so he could avoid feeling guilty about putting them in such a position. But they still loved him, encouraged him, and supported him, despite the fact it left them open to heartache if something happened to him.

"I have a good support network with the other wives while he's away. We help each other out a lot."

"You gals seem as close as we are."

"We are." She changed the subject. "Let me look at your leg."

Surprised by the request, Zach eyed her.

Zoe chuckled. "I'm not saying drop your drawers, I'm saying move the towel so I can see if your leg is as swollen now as it was when you first arrived."

Zach removed the towel and pulled up on the legs of his trunks. "I don't think it is."

"No, it doesn't look it."

"Are you flashing my wife, Doc?" Hawk asked from the door.

"She'd be oohing and aahing if I was."

Zoe shook her head. "You guys are all the same. Cocky as hell." She clapped a hand over her mouth, her eyes round with shock, then her cheeks reddened.

Hawk and Doc roared with laughter.

"I didn't mean it like that." She pointed a finger at Doc. "Don't you dare tell anyone I said that. Oh, my God, I'm leaving." She started past Hawk and he grabbed her and pressed a quick kiss to her cheek and whispered something in her ear, making her color deepen. She pressed into him for a moment and hid her face against his chest, easy to do since her face was level with it. She looked fragile up against Hawk's large, muscular frame.

When she peeked out again, she avoided looking at Zach altogether. "I promised Doc you would give him a key so he can come in during the day to use the tub. If he uses it every day, it might speed up the healing."

"Okay."

Zach took pity on her embarrassment. "My lips are sealed, Zoe."

"Mine aren't," Hawk grinned.

"They better be." Her tone was somewhere between a threat and a plea.

He chuckled again. "We'll negotiate my silence later."

Her color rose again, but she was fighting a smile. "I'm out of here. I think I need to put a cool cloth on my face."

Hawk was still grinning when she limped through the kitchen and down the hall. "I am going to get so much mileage out of this."

Zach chuckled. "You don't have to give me a key. I can go out to the base and use the whirlpool in the weight room."

"That's a forty-minute drive there and back, plus the hour it takes for the water to heat for a fifteen-minute soak. We're ten minutes closer, even with traffic. And I can leave the tub heated so you can simply slide in. It's up to you."

He didn't want to be a problem. But he was trying to heal quickly so he'd be up for deployment. "Give me the key."

Hawk nodded. "You'll need the alarm code, too."

On the way home, Zach mulled over the relationship Hawk had built with Zoe. LT didn't try to hide his feelings for her from anyone.

She was partially disabled, had mobility issues, and a child to care for, and she still hung in there with him.

He kissed Piper today and showed her how he felt. So he'd started off in the right direction. Four days without seeing her didn't seem like such a good idea. But she had acted like she wanted him to keep his distance until Sunday and give her some time.

Damnit.

An idea relieved some of his frustration. She hadn't said he couldn't call.

CHAPTER 14

PIPER PULLED INTO the restaurant parking lot and got out of her car. What good was it if your family ran a restaurant and you couldn't go now and then to beg a meal? It was Friday night, and she'd just gotten off work. What did that say about her life?

That it was going to the dogs. Literally.

She thought about Zach for a moment. He'd kept his distance, exactly the way she asked him to do, and he visited Gracie after she left for lunch, so she missed seeing him for the last three days. Every day she found her heart leaping every time Sherry or one of the other receptionists buzzed her. He called every morning, though, and spoke to her. But he kept the conversation easy, with no demands, leaving her unsatisfied.

What did she expect? It was what she asked for.

Her neck tight with exhaustion and wariness, she slung her purse over her shoulder and exited the car. The sign, backlit with the family name in a curved font, acted like a beacon to customers. She paused outside and braced herself before entering. A man exited and held the door for her, so she couldn't very well turn and run away. This was her family's place of business.

Every time she walked inside, it was like running a gauntlet. She couldn't shut off the memories, and she felt the accusations bombarding her, though they were never spoken. At least not in public.

She murmured thanks to the man holding the door and entered the foyer.

She avoided looking at the front reservation desk, where the hostess stood. The memory of blood splatter across the back wall still colored the sheetrock behind it, even though it had long since been cleaned and painted.

Madeline Salmons walked around the desk and moved to embrace her. She'd been a fixture at Bertinelli's for ten years, and was more family than employee. She was dressed in a bright red polka dot blouse and red skirt. "Piper, it's good to see you."

"Thanks, Maddy. It's good to see you, too." A wave of homesickness and genuine affection hit her. She missed them, but she couldn't come back. Her brothers wouldn't want it. Plus, her vet clinic demanded her time and, besides...she couldn't face this place like her mother did.

Thank God her mother hadn't been here when it happened. It owed her to walk through the door without running straight into the memories still haunting her seven years later. What would she have done otherwise? The restaurant had been their lives for the past twenty years.

Maddy tucked a loose strand of blond hair behind her ear. "How's the vet clinic doing?"

Was that a little gray mixed in with the blond around Maddy's temples? And there were smile lines bracketing her mouth. "Very well. We're busy, and getting more customers every day."

"Good. I knew you'd do well. You can't be your mother and father's daughter without having the Bertinelli genius for business gene in there somewhere."

Piper smiled like she was expected to. "One of my partners was telling me the other day to quit taking on charity cases. I think it's a lot easier to turn down people for reservations than to refuse to take in abandoned newborn kittens. If I didn't have the others to rope me in, I'd probably have every kennel filled with needy animals. You wouldn't be in the market for a kitten, would you?"

"No. I still have the last one you palmed off—I mean, talked me into taking." Maddy laughed. "I'm only teasing. We love her.

But you're not called Piper for nothin'.'"

"So everyone keeps reminding me."

"Are you here to visit or to eat?"

How long had it been since she was here? Six weeks at least. "Both. I thought I'd just pop into the kitchen and say hello, then order something to take home. It's been a long day."

"Go on through. If your mother knew you came in, she'd already be out here, dragging you back. You know the way."

"Thanks, Maddy." Large slate tiles led the way into the dining area. The dinner rush had passed, but there were still at least twenty occupied tables. The lights were lowered, and candles glowed against the spotless white linen tablecloths. The smell of marinara sauce and garlic burst from the kitchen as one of the large blue kitchen doors flew open and a waitress entered the dining room with a tray full of plates heaped with pasta and other goodies.

Piper pushed one door back and peeked inside the kitchen. The rush hour havoc had passed, but it looked like they were still busy. She wandered in and spied her mother at the back, slicing a small loaf of Italian bread. She lifted the whole thing and placed it into a napkin-lined basket, poured olive oil onto a plate, and sprinkled herbs into it.

Piper dodged one of the waitresses and wove around the busy cooks. Someone in the washroom dropped a pot and it rang like a church bell. Irena, their pastry chef turned with a bag of icing in her hand. A smile lit her face and she grabbed Piper and gave her a hug. "It's good to see you! It has been too long, Piper."

"I know." Piper returned the woman's embrace. "I work nights now, and haven't been off early enough to stop in."

"It has been weeks since we've seen you here at the restaurant, Francesca." Her mother was bearing down on her like a locomotive. She grabbed her out of Irena's arms and gave her a hard hug. "And if you don't start eating more, you are going to live up to your nickname, *piccola*, and not in a good way." Her mother cupped her face and looked into her eyes, the way she always did when they had not seen each other in a week or more. "You look tired, *tesora*."

"I am a little. It's been a full day. I just stopped in to get some food and say hello."

Her mother slung an arm around her waist and walked her toward the back of the kitchen, out of the way of speeding chefs and wait staff. "What would you like? I'll have them prepare it for you while we visit."

"Cheese ravioli and some bread would be good. Ice water to drink. If I drink a glass of wine, I'll go to sleep."

"Okay. I'll be right back."

Piper leaned against the door facing the office, but didn't go in. There was always family stopping by, and more than one person inside the office, which was about the size of a pool table, left little room for chairs. The only furniture besides the desk and desk chair was a small settee positioned along the back wall.

Her mom returned with a goblet of red wine and a glass of ice water. She handed Piper the glass and lowered herself into the office chair behind the desk, giving Piper no choice but to come into the room and sit down.

Her mother sipped her wine, then said, "Benito said he will have your ravioli done in just a few minutes, and will bring it to you himself so he can say hello."

"Was he out there? I didn't see him." Piper wedged herself into the corner of the settee and sipped the water.

"He was in the refrigerator unit doing inventory. Our freezer went out and had to be replaced, and we had to throw out many of the supplies. He's ordering more tonight so they'll be delivered tomorrow afternoon."

"Will the insurance cover the loss?" she asked.

"Some. But not all. But business is good. We're run off our feet most nights. I changed the menu a little, and some of the new items on it have proven to be very popular. And Irena has been trying her hand at some very light pastries filled with fruit. She's doing sfogliatelle filled with ricotta and citron right now. And they're beautiful to look at as well as delicious."

"They sound wonderful."

"You can try one before you leave, if you like."

"Maybe I will." Every time she came by here, she felt guilty for leaving the business and abandoning her family to the chaos following her father's death. But walking through the door nearly brought her to her knees.

A small voice inside her whispered that they had abandoned her first. She tried to ignore it.

"How is Teresa?"

Her mother's expression brightened. "The doctor says the treatments are working."

Piper breathed a sigh. The tight knot of worry she carried around with her every time she thought about her sister eased a little. If something happened to her only sister... Her mom wouldn't do well. None of them would. And her children...

"I'm relieved to hear it. I called her a couple of weeks ago, but you never know if it's too much or not enough. I offered to take the kids, but she said they were fine." In fact, her offer was summarily dismissed. Her sister didn't want Piper anywhere near her children.

"They are doing better than the adults. Tom keeps them busy, so she has time to recover each week from the treatments. The day after is really rough, but by Friday she's found her feet again."

"I'm amazed by her and Tom."

"They're a unit. They look out for each other like husbands and wives are supposed to do."

Piper nodded. Like her father had always looked out for her mother. Until a drug-crazed bastard shot and killed him. And it was her fault. "How are you doing, Mom?"

"I'm okay. Busy most days. Just like you."

Piper sought something to say.

Her mom found something quickly enough. "When are you going to find a Tom to look out for you?"

She ought to have known that was coming. "I look out for myself, Mom."

"I know all about that, and it sucks. It's easier to deal with things if you have a partner."

Pain stabbed her. Her parents had been like two parts of a whole. Her mistakes had ended their love story long before its time.

"I have a partner," she said. "He's always thrilled to see me, greets me with a kiss, loves me unconditionally, and never argues."

A sour look crossed her mother's face. "And he's dumb as a post."

Piper forced a smile. "But he's sweet when he's not drooling on my shoes."

"Or chewing them." Her mother crossed her arms.

"He has good taste. He always goes for the most expensive ones." Not that she had any of those. Running shoes and slip-ons were the extent of her wardrobe these days. She couldn't remember the last time she'd bought any kind of dress.

"Francesca, please tell me you don't intend to be one of those women who fill their lives with animals instead of people."

"I have people in my life, Mom. I have you, and my partners, and people at work."

"You know what I mean. It's been seven years, *tesora*. When are you going to trust again?"

Never, probably. "I trust some people."

"Do you go out with any of them?"

Piper rarely allowed men close. She had tried once or twice, but the men hadn't had the patience to wait until she was ready to open herself to them.

But she'd allowed Zach close. Let him kiss her. He'd slipped right in under her defenses. She even kissed him first. She still couldn't believe she'd done something so rash. She worried now every time she thought about it.

"I met a man, and we're having dinner on Sunday. I had lunch with him Tuesday."

Her mother's gaze brightened. "That's good. Who is he?"

She was saved from saying more by Ben bringing her food. He carried the plate, a basket of bread, and a saucer of olive oil with herbs on a tray on one hand.

Piper rose to take the plate from him and was surprised when he set the tray down on the desk and stepped forward to give her a hug. She felt awkward and was slow to put her arms around him.

Was this some kind of trick?

"We missed you at Sunday brunch," he complained.

"We had a busy week, and I was so tired I slept right through brunch." She had still been stinging from Teresa's rejection. It made it harder for her to sit across the table from them, knowing they only tolerated her being there for her mother's sake.

"What about this Sunday?"

"I've invited someone to come over for dinner."

He shrugged one shouldered. "So bring him with you to brunch instead. It isn't as though we won't have enough food."

Piper shook her head. Anyone she dated would be vetted to within an inch of his life. She couldn't put Zach through that. "You guys might scare him away."

Ben laughed. "If he's scared by us, he doesn't deserve to date you."

"Actually he has more brothers than you do. Seven brothers and one sister."

Her mother's brows rose and a gleam lit her eyes. "A nice Catholic boy?"

"We haven't discussed religion, but he has mentioned a priest... I can't remember what his name was, but his family's Irish, he's from Boston, and with that many siblings..." Piper shrugged. "Don't get any ideas, Mom. He's in the military, and he could be deployed at any time."

She caught the look that shot between her mother and brother.

She felt trapped in the office with them both eyeing her, questioning her judgment about who she wanted to go out with. "I think it might be more convenient for me to eat in the dining room, Mom. Why don't you join me?"

"Okay."

They rose. Ben scooped up the tray and led the way through the kitchen and out into the dining room. He set the plate of ravioli, the saucer of oil and herbs and the breadbasket on the table with a practiced flare. He pulled out a chair for her and waited for her to sit.

After she sat down, Ben leaned over her shoulder to place her silverware next to her plate. "I will learn everything you say from Mom later."

Pain pinched her, and she controlled her reaction with an effort. "You've always been nosy. But you already know everything..." Her voice trailed off. Though he had his head turned and was looking out the window, she recognized Zach's red curls and broad shoulders. The crutches propped against the wall behind the table made her identification a sure bet. "Excuse me."

She rose and wove around three tables to where he sat, an empty plate smeared with red sauce in front of him. So he'd been here for a while. "Zach?"

He turned his head and looked up at her. "Piper." He struggled to his feet before she could tell him to stay seated. He scanned the restaurant and his own table. "I swear I'm not stalking you."

"I know you're not. Your plate is empty, and I've only been here about fifteen minutes."

He motioned to the table. "Would you like to join me?"

"My mother's at our table waiting." He scanned the restaurant and homed in on her mother standing with Ben.

"Bring her on over. I'll order desert and some decaf while you eat."

Lord, it was going to be a trial by fire for Zach if she introduced him to her mother and brother. Piper beckoned to the two of them. Ben put her food and her water glass back on the tray and brought it over. He studied Zach through narrowed eyes all the way across the restaurant.

"It is Mr. O'Connor, isn't it?" her mother spoke as they reached the table.

"Yes, it is."

"I've rung up your tickets several times."

"Yes, you have. Please call me Zach."

"You may call me Carlotta."

He limped around the table to hold their chairs, but Ben placed a hand on his shoulder. "You look like you need to take it easy. I'll seat them."

Piper couldn't tell if Ben was being kind or territorial.

"This is my brother Ben, Zach."

"Nice to meet you." Zach extended his hand and the two men shook. Ben did the sizing up thing that seemed to be universal between males, but Zach focused on her mom instead.

"I'll reheat your food, Piper. It's bound to be cold by now," Ben said and scooped up the plate and took it back to the kitchen.

Zach lowered himself into his chair after Piper and her mother took a seat.

"Piper said you were in the military."

"Yes, the Navy."

"How long have you been in?"

"Eight years."

"You were hurt during training?"

"Yes, during a skydive. I'm better than I was four days ago." He glanced at Piper and gave her a brief smile.

Ben returned with her food and she reached for her silverware.

She cringed with every question her mother asked, but Zach seemed to take it in stride. After he told her about his family, she started in on his education. Turned out he had a degree in criminal justice which he earned after enlisting in the Navy.

"Mom, I think you need to give up the restaurant and go to work for the CIA. You've grilled the poor man for nearly ten minutes."

Zach bit his lip and she could tell he was fighting a smile.

"Have I been grilling you, Zach?" Her mother asked.

"If I had a daughter, I'd be interested in the kind of man she was seeing. We've only had lunch together, so we haven't officially gone out yet. If it puts your mind at ease, though, I have had an FBI background check, and Uncle Sam signs my paychecks."

Her mother smiled, but her eyes rested on Piper.

Zach laid his hand over her mother's in a gesture of reassurance.

She seemed startled, then patted his hand and rose. "What would you like for desert?"

"What would you suggest? Or better yet, surprise me."

"You'll want decaf coffee this late. Cream and sugar?"

"Black will be fine."

"I'll see to it myself." She marched away to the kitchen.

Piper spoke softly. "Thank you for being so patient with her."

"You're her baby girl. I don't blame her for being protective. I'm the same way with my sister Kathleen."

"It's my fault she's so protective. I got involved with the wrong guy my junior year in college."

He studied her for a moment. "We all make mistakes, Piper. Especially when we're young."

But it didn't always cost a parent's life. She swallowed the bite of ravioli she was chewing and reached for her water when it threatened to choke her. She fixed her attention on her glass for a long moment. "Tell me you're the right kind of guy."

CHAPTER 15

ZACH WAS SILENT a moment while he studied her. There was uncertainty in her voice, as though she really needed to be reassured. It must have been a really *big* asshole in her past.

"I'm the right kind of guy," he said. "I can't promise I'll be here for long, but while I am, I'll be up-front with you, and I'll treat you with respect." Did that make him the right kind of guy?

Piper nodded, but spoke with feeling. "It really sucks that you won't be around, Zach."

"Yeah. It does."

Her mother returned with several deserts on one plate. "I thought you two could share. Just flag down Carol when you're ready for some coffee, Francesca."

"Thank you, Mom."

Thankfully her mother wandered back to the kitchen. Zach had been grilled by police after his sister's abduction, and by commanders who thought he might be involved in a fellow teammate's injury. They couldn't come close to Piper's mother's technique, sweet mama bear ready to rip you to shreds if you hurt her baby.

Piper studied his face, her brown eyes shadowed in the dusky overhead light. Her skin looked satiny smooth, and the reddish highlights in her hair glinted. "Are you sure you still want to go out?"

"Yeah, I'm sure."

Jesus, he wanted her.

She took a bite of ravioli, chewed and swallowed. She made eating look like an art form. He shifted in his seat, his cock so hard he had to fight the urge to reposition himself.

She looked up at him from under her lashes. "You're not in any shape to look at me that way."

Zach grinned, damn thrilled that she'd finally started to flirt a little. "I'd soldier through."

Piper laughed. "I wouldn't want you to risk any permanent damage."

Zach chuckled. "I'm tougher than that, but I'd rather be in top shape just in case."

Piper bit her lip and shook her head, but a smile tugged at the corners of her delectable mouth.

He'd succeeded in lightening her mood, and she hadn't turned him down. Yet.

She reached for a slice of bread, broke off a small piece, dipped it in the olive oil on the saucer, and popped it in her mouth. There was such grace and sensuality to the way she ate, Zach paused with a bite of ricotta pie halfway to his mouth. God, just watching her set him on fire. He set his fork aside and reached for his coffee.

"How do you keep from being rolled out of here?"

Her laughter was sexy as hell.

"I've been eating Italian food my whole life, so I like to try other things. Mexican, Thai, Indian. I'm not fixing Italian on Sunday."

"Once you've lived off of MREs—short for meals, ready to eat—for a month, you'd eat the north end of a southbound elephant…if they weren't an endangered species. Gives me the shudders just to think about the chicken fajitas." He grimaced at the memory. "Thank you, Jesus, and the Bertinelli pastry chef who made this pie." He finally forked in the pie and held the sweet in his mouth, letting it dissolve.

Piper chuckled again. "What's your favorite besides Italian?"

Zach swallowed the bite. "Grilled steak and loaded baked potatoes."

"Typical guy food. I notice you didn't even mention salad."

He shrugged and set his fork down to take up the coffee cup, which had miraculously been reheated while he wasn't looking. Hell, the waitress walked by and left a fresh cup, and he hadn't even noticed. He'd been too busy looking at her. "What can I say? I'm a guy."

"I think I can arrange steaks for Sunday."

"You don't have to. I'll eat anything."

"What kind of beer do you like?"

"You don't look like a beer girl. I can bring my own if I'm off the meds by then. I used to think beer was beer until the guys and I found some on sale at a liquor store and bought up cases of it. We called it turtle piss because it was so bad it took us forever to drink it all. I used it to make chili and steamed clams just to get rid of it."

Piper shook her head and laughed. "I have been known to drink a beer now and then, but you're right, I prefer wine. But then I've been raised on it. You bring your beer, and I already have a good bottle of red to go with the steaks."

He folded his arms and leaned forward. "What about tomorrow? I've kept my distance, Piper. Isn't three days enough since we're planning dinner for Sunday night?"

Her heart was beating hard in her throat. He could see it and wondered if it was fear or excitement.

She moistened her lips. "What about tomorrow?" Her voice sounded breathy, and a rush of desire raced straight to his groin.

He cleared his throat and swallowed. "You could bring Trouble over, and we could enjoy the sun, sand, and water. My apartment's on the beach. We might even be able to swim some if the wind isn't up. We can grill some yellowtail. I have some in the freezer. You can just relax, no pressure."

She took a sip of her water. "I have to work until noon. Then I'm off the rest of the day."

"Throw a swim suit or wet suit in a bag and come over." He

whipped out his phone and texted his address, just as she had done for him three days earlier. Her phone chirped, signaling the text had gone through.

"Okay. I'll come over around one. Are you sure you want me to bring Trouble?"

He'd never had to work so hard in his life for a date. He wanted to run around the room and high five everyone. But even though he was improving, he couldn't walk to the next table without pain, let alone put the move on this lady with any grace. Damn it.

"Sure. He can hang out and play in the water. Retrievers like water, don't they?"

"Oh yeah, he likes water. He'll drink out of your toilet and wipe his mouth on your clean pants, too."

Zach laughed. "You're talking to a SEAL, Piper. A little water is nothing. We'll keep the lid down. I have an outdoor hose we can spray him off with, and plenty of beach towels. In fact, why don't I go to the office and collect Gracie? The master chief had a friend drop her kennel, toys, and food off at my house."

A waitress came by to clear the table and spoke for a moment to Piper.

When the woman left, Piper went back to their conversation. "Come by at noon, and you and Tony can load Gracie into your SUV. Bring her kennel. She'll need to be stable inside it while you transport her so she won't have to fight against the movement of the car."

He was still smiling when they stood to leave. Piper excused herself to say good-bye to everyone in the kitchen and Zach waited for her.

She had the leftover deserts with her in a Styrofoam container when she returned. "I thought we could finish these off tomorrow."

"Sounds good."

He paid for his meal and offered to pay for the desserts.

"That was Mrs. B's treat," the receptionist said with a smile.

"Thanks."

"You and Piper have a nice dinner on Sunday."

He looked up, surprised. "I'm sure we will."

"If I'd been smart I'd have texted you at your table and warned you to pretend you didn't know me," Piper said as they left the building.

The air brushed against them like chilled fingers, damp, cool, promising rain. The fragrance of greenery from the landscaping around the entrance surrounded them. The sound of the passing traffic was only a soft whooshing sound.

"I'm glad you didn't. I wouldn't have had the opportunity to wear you down about coming over tomorrow."

"You only met two members of my family, and they were watching you like a hawk, and had everyone in the restaurant doing the same."

The guy she'd hooked up with must have been a really bad asshole, and now he was paying for it in a small way. "I can take it, Piper. Once they get to know me and see I'm harmless, they'll calm down."

"I have to tell you, even on crutches, you don't look harmless, Zach."

He didn't know whether to smirk with satisfaction or be worried.

She fidgeted for a moment, then took a deep breath. "It isn't your fault, Zach. It's mine. My dad was killed in a robbery here while he was trying to protect me." Her throat worked as she swallowed.

Her shoulders didn't look wide enough to carry such a burden. "I'm sorry, Piper." How did she bear coming into the restaurant? He wanted to ask her what happened, but decided she'd tell him when she was ready. He reached out to grip her hand and held it for a moment.

"It's getting late." She walked with him to his SUV and while he put the crutches in the back seat, she placed the container of desserts on the front passenger seat.

Zach limped around the front of the vehicle and met her halfway. "I'll see you at noon." He slipped an arm around her and brought her in close to hold her, because it seemed to be what she needed. After a moment of hesitation, she relaxed against him and tucked her head under his chin. He ran a hand up and down her back, and with each caress she leaned in a little closer. He was aware of every inch of her body resting against his and tried to control his response, but, damn, it was hard. When she started to draw away, he released her and didn't try to push for anything more. It wasn't the time or the place.

"Thanks, Zach." She rested a hand on his chest for a moment. "See you tomorrow."

She took two steps away then paused. "Did the police contact you about Master Chief Flynn?"

"Yeah. A detective named Sherman. I gave him the name of the two officers who questioned me so he could pull the interview. He said he'd get back to me."

"He had already talked to the clients whose files were compromised, so I didn't have to convince the partners to call them."

"Good."

"I'd appreciate it if you wouldn't mention the burglary in front of my family...I mean—when you meet the rest of them."

If she didn't tell them and they found out, all hell would break loose, for sure. But it was her family, not his. And, hey, she was talking like he would meet the rest of them. "Okay."

"Thanks."

He watched the subtle sway of her hips as she walked to her car, a Chevy Equinox. He waited for her to get in before limping around and getting into his own, where he watched until she pulled out of the parking lot.

He wondered what kind of situation she'd fallen into in college, and why she kept her family at a distance. She'd been embarrassed when her mother questioned him, but there had been pain and resentment mixed into her expression as well when she asked her mother to stop.

Something bad had gone down, either before or after the robbery, and it had scarred Piper and her family. He'd just have to wait and see if she would share it with him. Or, he could look it up on the Internet so he'd have an idea what went down. Maybe he could figure things out for himself.

CHAPTER 16

AHEADACHE POUNDED BEHIND CALLAHAN'S eyes. He stayed at the hospital all night, just outside the intensive care unit, so his mother could go home and rest.

Since noon he'd been following up on things she asked him to check.

He stood in the center of the barren living area of this particular construction project, then looked at the plans stretched out on a long sheet of three-quarter inch plywood laid atop two sawhorses, studying the structural changes. The crew had begun the renovation, and with the walls down, he could visualize the space.

He'd already driven by one site and looked over the work. They were on schedule at this one only because he picked up a hammer and lit a buzz saw under the crew.

And where the hell was Doug? He'd gone to all three of the other sites, and Doug hadn't been at any of them. He even called his cell twice and gotten only a voice message.

He reached for his cell phone again. When his brother finally picked up, he tried to temper his tone of voice. "Where are you?"

"I've been making material deliveries all day. Where are you?"

"I went by the sites and looked for you. Mom asked me to check out how things were going.

"And?" Doug sounded a little testy.

"And nothing. I did what she asked me to do. I checked out

the sites."

"Where are you?" Doug asked his voice icy.

"I'm at the Sutton house."

"I'm on my way."

He hung up so quickly, Cal gathered he was beyond angry. So be it. He was tired of his little brother. He'd kept his mouth shut and stayed out of things until he was invited.

Cal shut his phone and stuck it in his pocket. He continued to study the plans for a minute.

He wondered what Kathleen would think if they were building their house. He jerked the phone out and flipped it open. He hit Kathleen's number. Her voice came over the line.

"Hey, sweetheart. How's it going?"

"Everything's fine. It's really quiet around here without you. How's your father?"

"He's still in intensive care, but he's doing well. They had him sitting up today and walking. He still has a drainage tube and all that, but his color's better, and he seems to be feeling better. No shortness of breath, and no pain other than the incisions."

"Fantastic."

"How are the plans going?"

"The clients wanted some changes, so I'll be working all weekend. I've set up a meeting on Tuesday morning first thing to turn the finished plans over to them. My partners at work will be looking them over on Monday to make sure I haven't left anything out."

"So you still plan to fly in on Tuesday evening?"

"Yes. Zach will drop me at the airport so I don't have to leave my car in parking. He said he'd pick us up when we fly back here."

"Good. That's a big help."

"How are things with your brother?"

"I'll know in a few minutes. He's on his way over here to the building site I'm on. We have a crew who's renovating a house, and I'm helping Mom keep things going like they should."

"I thought that was Doug's job."

"It is." He didn't want to get into Doug's exaggerations/lies with Kathleen until they were face-to-face.

When the silence stretched, he heard Kathleen draw a deep breath. "I think I understand. We'll talk about it when I get there." She switched topics. "I'm feeling a little separation anxiety. I keep looking up, expecting you to walk through the door."

"Wish I could, Kathleen. I'm walking a minefield with Dad every time I go in to see him, because he wants to argue with me, and he's not supposed to have any excitement. And Mom wants me to look over Doug's shoulder until Dad is on his feet enough for her to do it. And we'll talk about Doug when you get here. Anyway, I saw a beautiful house plan today. In fact, I'm looking at it right now, and I thought about you. Have you got a dream house in mind to own one day?"

"Well, yeah. Most women do. No matter how much we fight it, we women have a nesting instinct, and home and hearth fall into that category. For the house I have in mind, though, I'd have to win the lottery." She laughed.

"If you're going to dream, you might as well dream big. What about a starter home?"

"Realistically, I suppose I'll have to work my way up to the Hollywood mansion." She gave an exaggerated sigh, and he could almost see her doing it and smiled.

"I want to show you this house when you get out here. Have you ever thought about drawing residential plans?"

"Yeah. I have a few plans I drew up for people during summers when I was doing my co-op. I'll show them to you."

"Excellent."

"Have you been bitten by the residential bug, Cal?"

"No. But this is going to be a beautiful house, and I'd like one like it one day." He wanted to say "I'd like one with you," but he wanted to say it in person. Lights flared in the windows, accompanied by the sound of a vehicle pulling up outside. "Doug's here, sweetheart. And he and I have a lot to talk about. Can I call you back later?"

"Yes, sure."

"Love you."

He hung up after her quick "love you" and turned back to the empty room. Doug shoved open the door and stepped in. Glimpsing his sulky expression, Cal mentally shook his head and counted to ten.

Doug stalked toward him and led with, "I thought you said you didn't want to take over, Cal."

"Believe me, I don't. But you lied about your place in the company. You made it seem like you were dad's go-to guy and you could run the show."

"I pick up the slack in every way I can. It isn't my fault Dad left things in a mess and we're having to scramble to keep up."

"You can't work nine to five and run this company. It's impossible. So if you want it, you're going to have to start putting in some hours after everyone else has left for the day. Coordinating orders. Making sure the crews are staying on task and on schedule, and doing the paperwork to make sure the men get paid. Mom does the orders and the paychecks. Think she's going to have time to do it with Dad underfoot while he recovers? And that doesn't even cover meeting with clients and landing the jobs to begin with."

"I can't be on five sites at the same time."

"Yeah. The crew at the Gibson place had fallen behind, but they aren't anymore."

"And how did you manage that?" Doug's tone grew ominously quiet.

"I picked up a hammer and saw and worked with them for a couple of hours. I recommend you put someone else in charge of pickups and deliveries and stay with the crews, Doug. Pickups are grunt work. Anyone can do it. They need you working with them so they aren't tempted to slack off."

"Says the guy who walked away."

"Says the guy who was kicked to the curb. You want to be in charge? Get with the program and prove to Dad you can run the show. Put someone else in charge of the grunt work, get in the trenches, and keep the crews moving. This is going to fall on you when I go back to San Diego." And if Doug couldn't handle things, the whole show would crash and burn. His father's company would go down the tubes.

He didn't have time to pussyfoot around this shit. "This is your livelihood, not mine. But it would be a real shame to see it fail after the hard work the three of you have put into it. I don't think any of you can afford to lose the income."

"We've got five jobs going and only two trucks to pick up supplies."

He was still focused on the minutia when the larger picture was more important. "Every guy you have on the job has a truck. Pay them a twenty-five or thirty dollar stipend plus gas if they'll use their truck to pick up a delivery. Or have the companies deliver. It'll cost more, but it will free you up to keep things going. A large order will be a flat rate."

"All right. I get what you're saying."

"Find someone who can take care of some of the weekly responsibilities, like taking care of the orders and deliveries, and maybe the paychecks."

Doug's features tensed. "I thought that's why you were here."

"I promised Mom I'd help out until you get your feet under you. That's it. I have a girlfriend I'm missing more every day, and responsibilities at home." Cal looked away. "Besides, it isn't good for me to be around Dad. His idea of communication is ripping everyone around him a new asshole every chance he gets. I've held my tongue for two days, but it isn't going to last."

Doug crammed his hands into his jeans pockets and wandered around the site, checking the work. "It looks good," he said, his tone grudging. He rubbed his eyes with the heels of his hands. "I might know someone who can take care of the paperwork. I can put a couple of the guys in charge of deliveries and get a system going. You can take a couple of the sites each day, and I'll do the other two, and we'll share the fifth one between us.

"Good. Get on the phone and get whoever it is to come in to talk about the job first thing in the morning. Paychecks are due next Friday. You and Mom can interview—is it a woman?" At Doug's nod, he continued. "Mom knows more about what the job entails, since she does it. It would be good for her to sit in on the interview, since she'll be working with the new person afterward, if she thinks she can handle things."

"You don't realize it, but the reason you and Dad go at each other all the damn time is you're just alike. I may look more like him, but you act just like him. Throwing your weight around, demanding things."

He wasn't like his father. He didn't try to browbeat people into doing things, he just told them what needed to be done and expected it to be taken care of. If he could teach Doug that one basic approach, he'd be able to walk away from this.

"If you'd spent more time learning the ropes instead of just putting in your time, I wouldn't even be involved in any of this, Doug."

Doug's features took on a bitter cast. "What do you know about it? *You* try wrestling away any small piece of control from Dad. Every time I tried to take the initiative, he shot me down. He doesn't even know the concept of constructive criticism, just plain hard criticism. He never looks for the good, just the other stuff that needs to be taken care of."

The underlying pain in his brother's voice struck a chord with Cal. "Bosses aren't usually very good about handing out compliments. They figure you get paid, so what are you whining about? I *know* Dad's like that. In the military, I didn't get pats on the back, but I did get promotions.

"There's no such thing as a promotion when the man in charge is your father and the boss. The men think I'm only on the job because I'm his son."

"Then it's up to you to show them you know the job as well as they do, or better. Like today, I had to take up a hammer and show them I knew what needed to be done and how to make it happen. Once they saw I was as competent as they are, and knew how to get it done, they got with the program. You can't give an order and jump in the truck and take off. You have to provide a presence. Let them know you're in charge."

He'd been upset about being shut out, but he didn't envy his brother's life with his father. He paused a moment to really give the core issue some consideration. If he could assume control of the company, would he want it? In fact, it wasn't control he wanted, just the recognition that his leg didn't create a barrier to it. The realization eased the bitterness he'd carried for such a long time.

He took charge on the job all the time back in San Diego. He was treated with respect because he did the job, and did it well. His brother needed this more than he ever had. Doug had lived in his father's shadow long enough to have earned it.

His Dad had done a fine job of tearing Doug down. Now he'd have to build him up so he could take charge. Otherwise Cal would be stuck here indefinitely.

CHAPTER 17

MIRACULOUSLY, DR. DOWLING was able take her on the spur of the moment. And now she was here in her office, Kathleen wanted to be anywhere else in the world.

Kathleen stared at an original watercolor on the wall and tried to make out the name of the artist from where she sat.

"Have you changed jobs, or had any other change in your situation since we talked before?"

"No, I haven't changed jobs, but I'd like to. Every time I walk across the lobby, I remember the confrontation with Paul Warren. I've started going out the back entrance to avoid going through the lobby at the end of the day.

"Staying at Wylie's probably wasn't the best decision after everything that happened there. But I'm afraid if I quit, I'll have to acknowledge I'm a quitter, and I just can't allow myself to do it."

Dr. Dowling leaned forward in her chair and rested her elbows on the desk. "If you were a quitter, Kathleen, you'd have turned tail and run home to Boston nine months ago."

She almost had. A psychotic woman who'd killed her lover held Kathleen hostage for twenty hours, tortured her with a Taser, and attempted to kill her by shoving her off the top of a building under construction. It was mind-bendingly crazy to even think it could happen, let alone happen to her.

"You chose to stick it out and try to move on. That was a

brave decision, Kathleen."

"I couldn't leave Zach and Callahan. I'd just gotten to spend some time with Zach. He came home to Boston maybe one time a year. Now I see him at least two or three times a month."

She turned her head to look directly at Dr. Dowling. "Why is this coming back on me now? I was doing great, or at least I thought I was."

"Has there been any other changes recently?"

As much as she wanted to ignore the possible repercussions of Cal and Zach's leaving… "Cal has gone to San Antonio to be with his family. His father had open-heart surgery this week, and they needed him there. And my brother Zach may be deployed soon."

"I see."

"I can intellectualize the connection between my boyfriend leaving and my broken engagement. And my brother is leaving soon to go to God knows where, and I can see how the anxiety about the two of them leaving could trigger things. But Cal is only going to be gone a few weeks, and Zach is always gone for trainings and deployments."

Dr. Dowling remained silent.

"Okay, I was having issues at work before Zach got his orders or Cal had to leave for San Antonio."

"Tell me about work."

"I have three men in my pod. They're very supportive and careful around me. In fact, everyone is careful around me. It drives me crazy, while at the same time I'm grateful for it."

"But?"

"I can't get past what happened there. They moved me to a different pod, in a different part of the building, but it looks the same. And I feel like I'm constantly watching my back. I'm OCD about saving my work. And it's difficult for me to share anything but work with the guys in my pod. If I did, they might think I was coming on to them. So I'm isolated. I keep wondering if it would be different somewhere else."

"Maybe you should look around and see what's out there."

"I want to, but I still have the feeling that if I leave, Hillary and Paul Warren will have won. If I quit, it will be a failure."

"It isn't a failure to be happy in what you do, Kathleen. If being in the building is painful for you, why would you force yourself to go back inside every day?"

"Because I'm not a quitter. No one in my family is."

"It isn't quitting to move on to a better work situation or better pay."

It wasn't, was it? She bit her lip. When she looked up, Dr. Dowling's patient silence embraced her, nonjudgmental, supportive. Her eyes stung with tears.

"I'm carrying everything that happened out the door with me every day when I leave work."

"Yes, you are."

Twenty minutes later Kathleen stared at the prescription in her hand. She hated having to take any kind of medication. It just seemed defeatist to have to take a pill to deal with something she should have been over months before. She switched her attention back to Dr. Dowling.

The psychologist was an expert in anxiety and PTSD, and she trusted her. But her habitual need to maintain control kicked in. "Are you sure there isn't any other way?"

"The medication will help alleviate some of the anxiety, Kathleen. It won't dope you up or make you dull, just take the edge off. But you have to take it every day and maintain a level in your system for it to work.

She didn't want to be on meds. But even Cal had admitted he'd taken them at the beginning of his treatment.

"Okay." She rose to leave. "Thank you for seeing me on such short notice, Dr. Dowling."

"You're welcome. I'll have Becky make your next appointment for two weeks from today. We'll give the meds time to work, and you will be back from San Antonio by then. I want to see how you're feeling by then."

"Okay."

Once she left the office, she felt both relieved and anxious again. She was going to have to talk to Cal about it. She'd hidden it from him, thinking it would go away if she just kept muscling through. He'd understand, since he'd gone through the same thing. But to admit it to him was to admit she wasn't over the trauma of the kidnapping. And she truly wanted to be.

PIPER PUSHED A finger against the bridge of her sunglasses to slide them back up her nose. After thirty minutes, she'd moved her lounge into the shade of the large umbrella Zach put up, knowing the California sun could be sneaky. With the breeze coming in off the ocean, it was tempting to stay in the direct sun longer than was healthy.

As soon as her sun-kissed skin cooled from the shade, she slipped a cover-up on over her modest one-piece bathing suit. For the tenth time in an hour, she looked toward the sliding glass door to check on Gracie. She was lying on her side, stretched out in a patch of sun, relaxing.

Zach threw a ball into the surf, the muscles in his arm and shoulder coordinating with poetic beauty. His white tank top hugged his torso and outlined every delicious inch of his well-toned chest and stomach. She'd never been around anyone in such perfect physical condition, and he awed her. His black knit shorts came to mid-thigh and cupped his buttocks, and a bruise peeked out from the hem down his left thigh. She flinched every time she saw it. Had the injury happened to anyone less fit, he'd probably have broken his hip.

Trouble charged through the surf after the ball, grabbed the bright yellow sphere, and paddled furiously toward shore. Reaching Zach, he gave his large, long-haired body a shake that sent a spray of sand and salt water flying. Zach threw up a hand to protect his face, and she smiled and shook her head. The patience he showed with both the dogs was awesome.

With the ball still in his jaws, Trouble came pounding up the beach at a running lope, scattering sand and water in all directions, his thick blond hair clumped and swinging under his belly. Piper braced herself, certain he'd launch himself at her. At the last minute, a high-pitched whistle pierced the air, and Trouble circled her lounge and ran back the way he came.

He danced around Zach in gleeful leaps. Zach pointed down, and, in a commanding tone of voice, said a word in what sounded like French. She was shocked when Trouble plopped his butt onto the sand and sat, ball in mouth gazing up at Zach with adoring intensity. Zach wiggled the ball free and handed him a treat from his pocket, which lasted all of half a second.

The two of them continued up the beach. Zach's gait was a little easier, and his movements less stiff, but he was still in pain. He was being too active. She'd have to take the bull by the horns and make darn sure he got some rest.

She smiled when he eased himself down on a lounge next to hers. "Thank for saving me. I thought he was going to pounce and it would take me days to get rid of all the salt and sand."

"I thought so too. If science could bottle the energy he has, we'd have a never-ending supply."

"He's like a hyperactive two-year-old. And I was amazed when you got him to sit."

Trouble gulped water from the bucket Zach had filled for him, then went over and immediately wiped his chin on his new best friend's leg.

Piper stifled a laugh and Zach arched a brow at her. "At least it's not from the toilet." He smiled and dragged the towel hanging over the back of the lounge free, dried his leg, then dried Trouble's face and chest.

"How did you get him to sit?" she asked.

"Sheer coincidence. I think he was so surprised I spoke to him in that tone of voice, he just sat down."

She chuckled. Trouble jumped up on the end of her lounge and lay next to her. Piper squeezed against the arm of the lounge and let him have the lower half of the chair and one side, while he plastered his wet body against her leg and hip. She rested a hand on his big head and rubbed his ear. He sighed in ecstasy. "I'm surprised I don't go around reeking of dog all the time. He wants to lie as close to me as he can get. I wake up every morning with his head on the pillow next to mine."

"There are a several ways I can respond to that, but they'd all sound self-serving, so I won't."

Piper smiled and felt the rise of heat in her cheeks. She couldn't say she hadn't wondered what it would be like to wake up with Zach in her bed instead of her dog. The touch of his body against hers set off every hormone, and brought every cell to quivering attention. It had been a very long time since she experienced such a reaction. In fact, she'd never experienced it. Not like this.

If he was as good at other things as he was kissing... Her breathing hitched and she glanced up into his face to see him studying her. He grinned when a fresh wave of heat flared in her face.

She needed to warn him about what he was getting into if they pursued this. She'd thought of little else. Last night when he just held her and offered her comfort rather than pushing for more... She'd been racked with guilt for not being more forthcoming. But the truth was, she was afraid once she said the words he'd walk away.

She felt safe with him. He was the first man in the past seven years who made her feel protected. The first man she felt safe enough with to give of herself. She'd been alone for so long.

To distract him and herself she asked, "Would you like something to drink?"

"A bottle of water would be good. I've got it on ice in the cooler."

She wiggled free of Trouble's weight and got up from the lounge. He immediately stretched out and took over the whole thing. She went to the cooler set in the shade of the lounges and got out two bottles of water.

"Looks like you've lost your seat. I'll get another lounge out for you."

He started to rise, but she placed a hand on his shoulder,

handed him the water, and sat down next to him on his lounge. "I'd rather sit with you, if I don't smell too much like a wet dog."

Zach braced a hand on the chair's metal frame, leaned close and pressed a kiss to the side of her neck and breathed in. She shivered and caught her breath.

"You smell delicious," he said. "Good enough to eat."

A quick vision of his head between her thighs popped into her head. Piper bit back a groan while a tantalizing sensation blossomed within the intimate heart of her, and her throat dried. She raised a hand to touch his cheek and felt the scruff of his beard against her palm. Her heart thundered against her ribs. When he drew her earlobe into his mouth, her toes curled into the sand.

"Zach…" She turned to look at him. He slid his arm around her waist and the other beneath her legs and lifted her to sit between his thighs.

"Lean back against me."

"Your hip—You have to be careful."

"I'm good, Piper."

She'd never been so aware of a man's body. When he slipped an arm around her waist and his hand came to rest on her stomach, she bit her bottom lip and suppressed a hum of frustration. She was hyperaware of the intimacy of his body fitting against hers. And how easy it would be for him to slip his hand lower between her legs. Her heart raced, and her breathing grew ragged.

"Your heart's beating crazy fast."

"I know." If she told him how long it had been since she'd been held or kissed, he'd think it was strange. She'd never craved a man's touch like this before. She told herself it was because it had been so long since she experienced any kind of physical closeness. Every time he held her, it rammed home how long she'd denied herself those things. "It just feels good to be close."

Zach slipped the other arm around her as well. "Yeah. It does." He rested his cheek against her temple. "I'm not going to rush you into anything."

God, she wished he would. Then she'd have someone to

blame when she screwed up again.

No, she didn't mean it. Zach didn't deserve to be blamed for what she had done years before. What another man had done. "I'm not your normal type, am I?"

"What type are you?"

"The neurotic, worrywart, am-I-doing-the-right-thing type."

"What's to worry about, Piper? We're sitting here enjoying the sun and surf. Nothing has to be decided in this moment."

"What if you're gone in two weeks?"

"It's not going to happen. I have to be able to walk much better than I can now before they'll ship me out."

She relaxed a little at his reassurance. "That's why I kissed you, you know. I thought… What if he leaves and I never find out what it's like to kiss him?" She leaned her head back against his shoulder and wished she could see his expression instead of just the strong, angular cut of his jaw.

"And how was it?"

She bit her lip to keep from smiling. "You know how it was. You were there."

"Yeah." She could see the smile curving his mouth. "I haven't recovered yet." His hand moved to cup her hip and give it a squeeze.

She fell silent, afraid to push the conversation further while also wanting his hands all over her.

The ocean, stormy and gray, looked at odds with the sky, clear and cloudless. The breeze caressed her skin, a tinge of seaweed in its salty scent. "It's very peaceful here next to the water. How long have you lived here?"

"Four years. The man who owns the building is a retired SEAL, and the four of us who live here are active duty. I keep him supplied with fish, and let him use my boat on the weekends I'm not using it. One of the other guys mows the grass and trims the bushes. He knows no one's going to screw up his property as long as we're here, so he cut us a good deal."

"And when you're gone?"

"My landlord gets to use my boat whenever he wants."

"That's trusting."

"He trusts us with his building, I trust him with my boat. Last deployment I came home to find he'd rebuilt the carburetor. When I offered to pay him he said no, he'd taken it in fish, and it was well worth the money. It's a small community, Piper. We work together, sometimes play together, and always look out for each other."

"Like a big family."

"Yeah. But it's the same as a family in other ways, too. You can build a relationship with some of the guys, and not with others. You may be able to work with another operator really well, but not get along with him in other situations."

She didn't want to go into the situation with her family. "We have some personality issues at work. But as a vet, Ryan is pretty good." She deflected the situation away from her work. "I've been reading a little about what you do. Do you really deploy for six months at a time?"

"Yeah, sometimes longer, rarely less. And sometimes we spend weeks training out in the desert, or days training out there somewhere." He nodded toward the water. "Or twenty-five thousand feet above, like on Monday. But then we'll have spells where we're working nine to five just like anyone else."

"And you can't talk about what you do."

"Not where we've been, or what we do while we're deployed, or even some of the training we do."

Piper wiggled around to look up at him. She couldn't imagine how anyone lived under such restrictions. "Doesn't it get lonely?"

"Yeah, it does." His green gaze shot past her out to the water. "You may want to try to keep your emotional distance and keep things light between us. Six months can be a long time."

She experienced a dropping sensation in the pit of her stomach again. "Is that what you do, keep things light?"

"I've tried it the other way. A woman I was really serious about dumped me while I was deployed. She couldn't take the separations. And she couldn't wait to tell me when I got home, because she was already pregnant with some other guy's baby and needed to move on."

A knot lodged in her throat. "How could she have done such a thing?"

He focused on her, shaking his head. "I can give you quality instead of quantity, Piper. When I'm here with you, I'll be here all the way. When I'm deployed, I have to be there, with no distractions. Otherwise I might put someone's life in danger. My team's, or mine."

Hearing his dispassionate tone, the hard edge to it, made her ache for him. She'd seen the warmth of his smile, the amusement gleaming in his eyes when he told her funny stories, the generosity he was capable of. He'd saved Gracie's life and was using his downtime to care for her. He'd offered to install better security hardware at the office. That hard edge didn't fit in with the rest, but she understood how it had to be because of what he did for a living.

She rested back against him and felt the steady rise and fall of his chest. He was so alive. Had such energy, even injured. He made her feel alive again.

She cupped her hand over his, resting against the curve of her abdomen. She wanted to guide his hand lower and feel his touch between her thighs. The ache of need had her drawing a slow breath. She tried to concentrate on the movement of the water and think of anything else besides the need, but her legs trembled and she gritted her teeth so they wouldn't chatter.

"Are you cold?" Zach's voice, low and husky, sounded like a growl against her ear.

"No." She was on fire and he hadn't even touched her. Just the idea was almost enough to send her over the edge.

She turned to look up at him. The intensity of his bright green gaze pierced hers, his throat working when he swallowed, then cupped her cheek and lowered his mouth to hers. The corded muscles of his neck lay against her palm, and the rich feel and taste of his lips and tongue tangled with hers.

Piper's bones turned to liquid, an exquisite lassitude taking possession of her muscles. His erection pressed against her hip.

They were both breathing hard when he broke the kiss.

She smiled at his flushed cheeks and brushed her fingertips against his beard stubble.

His hand skimmed up her arm to her hand and he turned his lips against her palm.

"It's been a long time since I've felt this way," she said.

"Me too."

She doubted it had been three years for him. The pathetic dates she'd been on. The two men she'd really tried with had been in too big a rush to get to the finish line to realize she needed their patience as much as anything else. The one she'd tried the hardest with dumped her after a month. She had too many hang-ups. She was too much work in bed.

She truly believed it could be different with Zach. She wanted it to be different.

Zach wasn't a drug-hyped twenty-two-year-old. He had control. He made her feel safe.

She leaned back against him. "What were you doing seven years ago?"

"I'd finished two years of college before I came out here. After a six-month break, I started taking classes while I worked chartering fishing trips. It would have been a hell of a lot easier if I'd finished school back home, but when you're a kid, you make all sorts of rash decisions, and I had the travel bug. Two years later, I'd almost finished my degree when I enlisted and they sent me to Michigan for basic training.

"Then I applied for the SEALs. You have to take tests to qualify, and I did okay with them, so they sent me back to Michigan again for more training."

"And you've been training ever since?"

"Yeah. We do a lot of training. We get to use new tech stuff and weapons. Every time they come up with something new, we try it out."

"Do you still have the travel bug?"

"Yeah. I didn't tell you before, but I have been to Italy. My mom and dad went a couple of years ago, and I met them in

Rome for a week."

"I've never been. How was it?"

"Busy, noisy, and fantastic. The history of the place is unbelievable. We did the Colosseum, St. Peter's Basilica, the Sistine Chapel, and several other things. We rented a car and drove around some of the countryside, ate fantastic food, freshly made ice cream for dessert. Handmade rolls with butter and coffee *con leche* every morning for breakfast."

"And pizza?"

"Yes, which isn't as cluttered with toppings as it is here, but it was just as good. But it was supposed to be a second honeymoon for my parents, and I was a fifth wheel, so I took off for home and left them in Florence for the second week of their trip. It was starting to get embarrassing, watching my dad put moves on my mom."

Piper laughed. "They wouldn't have eight children if there wasn't some passion in their relationship."

His arms tightened around her. "Don't put that image in my head, *please*."

She laughed again. "My parents were the same way. Sometimes they'd slow dance on the back patio, like they could hear music, though none was playing. He would nuzzle her neck and mama would practically purr." The bittersweet images had her eyes stinging, and she blinked to hold the tears at bay. "That's the kind of relationship I want to have someday."

"I'd say it's what we all want someday."

"Yes." She glanced at the sliding glass door. "I think Gracie needs to go out."

CHAPTER 18

Z ACH DROPPED HIS LEG over the side of the lounge and gave Piper a hand up. The only thing keeping him from getting up and urging her inside the apartment and straight to bed was his injury. She was going to take one look at his hip and the mood would die.

But she wanted him as much as he wanted her. She'd been trembling with it. There was no mistaking the way she kissed him, looked at him. He tracked the subtle shift of her hips beneath her beach cover-up while she strode into the apartment…and got hard all over again.

"Shit!"

Trouble's head popped up, and he scanned the sand for Piper. "She'll be back in a minute, pal." Filled with a restlessness brought on by the sexual charge he and Piper generated, Zach shoved to his feet. Trouble leapt off the lounge.

The dog ran ahead, following Piper's tracks, and they met her coming out of the apartment with Gracie. "Let's go for a drive," he suggested. "We'll pick up some ice cream for desert."

"Okay. I'll change once Gracie finishes."

Zach slipped a knit shirt on over his T-shirt and shoved his feet into the deck shoes.

Piper came in and removed the leash from Gracie's harness and slipped into the guest room to change.

When she came out of the bedroom in jeans and a T-shirt, he held up his keys. "Dogs or no dogs?" he asked.

"I'll put Trouble in Gracie's kennel to make sure he doesn't get into something while we're gone."

Gracie didn't seem to mind that Trouble was taking up housing in her crate, but she began to whine about being left behind, and when she tilted her head back with a mournful howl, Zach frowned. At Trouble's answering yodel, Piper laughed.

"She's used to going everywhere with the master chief," Zach mused. "And she's been locked up for days."

"If we leave them and they howl the whole time, your neighbors will complain," Piper warned.

A grin broke up Zach's serious expression. "I guess the dogs are going."

"I have a harness in my car we can put on Gracie to secure her in the seat so she'll be stable."

Ten minutes later, when they pulled out, each dog sat on their side of the car, secured by a harness and seat belt, the windows cracked so the outside air circulated around them. Both had their noses stuck out the window and their tongues lolling out.

After backing around Piper's vehicle, Zach whipped out his phone and took a picture of the two. "My team has to see these two." He keyed the group into the device and sent the picture.

When he swung the phone in Piper's direction and took her picture, she threw up a hand too late. "I'm not camera-worthy, Zach."

Her windblown hair and sun-flushed cheeks just added to her beauty. A fresh spike of desire raced south. "Yeah, you are, Piper." He pulled out onto the street.

She remained silent for a moment. "I wouldn't mind if you took your shirt off when we get back so I can take your picture."

He grinned at her. "We can play show and tell if you like."

She smiled, and the way she avoided looking at him triggered an answering smile.

She surprised him by saying, "Being a SEAL and all, I'd have thought you'd be more into hide and seek."

He chuckled. "You're already getting to know me."

He'd suggested they keep things light between them. But damn if she hadn't done a great job today of blowing that idea all to hell.

They came to a stop at the light, and he glanced up to find her studying him. When they reached for each other at the same time and shared a kiss, he knew he was in trouble.

They wandered down the I-5 for a time, just taking in the scenery and letting the dogs enjoy the fresh air. They got into a discussion about rock 'n' roll or blues. They were split on that issue.

"Action-adventure, comedy, drama, or chick flick?" he asked.

"Action-adventure," Piper said immediately and turned toward him. "Why do guys call them chick flicks?"

"To remind us there will probably be tears shed during the course of the movie, and we'll have to brace ourselves for when they happen." He turned the blinker on and swung off the interstate.

Piper raised a brow. "What makes men think women can't deal with their emotions?"

"It doesn't have a thing to do with women's emotions, honey. It's all about ours. You can't have your date look over to see you bawling like a baby."

Piper chuckled. "Have you ever cried in a movie?"

"Yeah. *Dumbo.* You know, the part where the mom's locked up and she's rocking him in her trunk and singing to him."

Piper studied him, not sure whether he was serious or not. "How old were you?"

"I watch it with my brother Jason's kids every time I go home for a visit. I guess it's been six months. Gets me every time."

Piper laughed.

He loved it when she laughed. There was something so self-contained, controlled about her, but when her laughter cut loose, those constraints disappeared.

She ran her fingertips down his arm. "I promise not to tell anyone if you tear up during a movie."

The caress had every nerve firing with vivid fantasies about what it would be like for her to cup him in her hand. Jesus, he hoped he got some firsthand experience—pardon the pun—real soon.

"Thanks, my team would never let me live it down."

"I NEED TO run into the supermarket for some olive oil and the ice cream," Zach said on the way back to his apartment. "If you think the dogs will be okay alone, you can come in with me. Otherwise, I'll just be a few minutes."

"Why don't you let me go in instead and rest your hip?" she suggested.

"If you don't mind."

"I can handle it."

He pulled into the parking lot of the store and parked.

Piper collected her purse and released her seat belt. "I'll be back in just a few minutes."

He dug for his wallet. "Let me give you some money first."

She shook her head. "I'll get it," she said, sliding down out of the seat and closing the door.

She walked past the customer service desk just inside on the left, and stopped to read the aisle signs until she found the one for oils and spices. She perused the brands, picked one she usually bought herself, and swiveled to go to the end of the aisle and figure out where to find the ice cream.

A man stood at the end of the aisle reading the labels on a box. He was partially turned away, so she was unable to see his face, but the short neck and wide shoulders seemed familiar. She hesitated. Was he a client? He started to turn his head and she glimpsed more of his profile.

Her heart stuttered and her breathing hitched. The bottle of olive oil almost slipped from her grasp, and she fumbled but caught it against her stomach. Panicked, she darted around the end of the aisle and rushed past two coolers holding freshly cut meats.

Two aisles down she sidestepped around an end shelf filled with detergent and into the cleaning supply aisle, where she bent to look over the tops of the bottles of dishwashing liquid to see if he had followed her.

Detective Samuel Lester rounded the shelving. His light brown hair, sprinkled with gray at the temples, seemed to have receded some, but she could see no other change in him. He still had the same determined set to his shoulders. The same harsh line to his mouth. His gaze traveled down the length of the store, as though he was searching for someone. Oh, God! Had he seen her?

Piper jerked back out of sight and rushed to the other end of the aisle, rounding the end of the shelving so she could peek down the next aisle. The moment she saw his pale blue shirt, she bobbed back out of sight and waited for him to pass. She still had to get the ice cream.

She walked down to the opposite end of the aisle and looked toward the end of the store. The freezers holding frozen foods were the next two aisles. Creeping past the end displays, she peeked down the aisle. No Detective Lester. What if he was doubling back and slipped up behind her? The signs above the clear glass doors designated frozen pies and deserts, then ice creams. She walked quickly to the ice cream display, jerked open the door and grabbed a container of Neapolitan, then peeked around the unit at the end of the aisle to scan the checkout lanes, racing for the shortest line. A man, taller and a great deal broader than she was, pushed his buggy up behind her.

Every moment she waited for the woman in front of her to punch in her pin number seemed to take an hour. Finally, the clerk handed the customer her receipt and turned her attention to Piper's bottle of oil and the container of ice cream. Piper jerked a twenty-dollar bill out her purse just as she caught a flash of blue from the next checkout lane, she pretended to drop her purse and squatted to retrieve it.

Hidden behind the cart and the man behind her, Piper watched Lester stride by, scanning the front of the store. She bobbed up when the clerk extended her the change and the bag with the items in it.

When she exited the store, it took every bit of her self-control not to break into a run. Her lungs felt oxygen-starved, as though she'd held her breath the whole time she was inside the building. She gulped in air and gripped the plastic bag, her hands shaking.

She paused two cars down and checked her appearance in the dusty back window of a van, and dragging her composure around her. Her legs felt spongy and weak as she maintained a more sedate pace to the passenger side of Zach's SUV and slid into the vehicle.

"That was quick," he commented.

"I lucked out and hit the checkout at just the right moment."

"Good."

She tossed her purse into the floor at her feet, set the bag between her feet, and concentrated on buckling her seat belt, though her hands continued to shake like they were palsied.

Zach's cell phone rang and he pushed a button on the steering wheel to answer the call. It was his mother asking about his hip.

Grateful for the distraction, Piper concentrated on calming herself. But she couldn't control her compulsive need to glance into the side view mirror to see if they were being followed, and turning in her seat to look behind them under the guise of checking the dogs.

It had to be a random encounter. Lester would have no reason to follow her now. But he had noticed her, and had been interested enough to search for her in the store.

What would he have said? She didn't care. Nor did she ever want to know.

But what mattered was he now knew she was back in San Diego. Her stomach ached with tension, and she pressed a hand against it.

As soon as they were back at the apartment, Zach poured her a glass of wine. Piper settled at the picnic table outside on the patio and watched him cook. Between the delicious qualities of the wine and Zach's company, she calmed.

The fish was grilled perfectly. The roasted potatoes rolled in oil and spices were done to a turn, as was the asparagus. It pleased her that Zach could cook. But she he couldn't do the meal justice with anxiety twisting her stomach into knots.

She wondered at herself for thinking in terms of a relationship when they had only been in each other's company three times.

She cautioned herself to keep it light. Zach didn't want anything permanent. He wanted a fling before he returned to battle.

She wanted normalcy for them both. She could have it for a few brief days, if she could manage to set aside the panic.

Zach was funny, considerate, and attentive. And every time he kissed her she felt it to the bottoms of her feet. Her breasts tingled from just the thought of him cupping them. She couldn't think of anyone she'd ever enjoyed being with more.

And she wanted him. More than any man she'd ever dated.

The dogs were sprawled out on the living room rug, snoozing, and she and Zach wandered back out to clean up the few dishes they'd left on the table. Trouble decided he needed to join them, leaving Gracie snoozing alone in the living room, exactly what she should be doing until she regained her strength.

Piper paused to appreciate the sunset. Red-orange streaks reflected from the underside of the dark, purplish clouds out over the water, like a rare storm might blow in. They could always use the rain.

Zach's arms slipped around her waist from behind. "One of the perks of living this close to the water. There are always spectacular sunsets."

Piper leaned her head back against his shoulder. "I've thoroughly enjoyed being here with you today. It's been a perfect day."

"You don't have to go. We can make it a perfect night as well, Piper."

Her heart drummed against her throat, stealing her breath while excitement and nerves battled inside her. It had been so long since she'd felt a human touch. Or been held or kissed. Zach was so good at both. "We've only known each other five days, Zach."

"Six," he corrected her. "We're good together, Piper. We're going to be good in other ways, too. I know you want me. And you have to know I want you, too."

Oh, the temptation. But if they slept together and he found out about everything later... "It can't be that easy. You don't know enough about me yet."

"Tell me something personal you haven't shared with me yet, and I'll tell you something in return."

It was time to lay every bit of the ugliness out there.

The avid look of desire, of interest, on his face had tears stinging her eyes. She looked away. If she told him, it would kill any hope she might have of sharing more with him. It had ruined every relationship she'd ever tried to cultivate. Once people knew everything, they pulled away. They didn't want to get involved.

She didn't want to see the shutter close between them as it always did. He was special. She'd known it from the first moment they met. She wanted so desperately to hold on to the possibility of him, them, if only for a little while. Was it so selfish to want just a few days with him?

"I've only been with two men. It's been three years since...the last time..." She bit her bottom lip and shook her head. "It's difficult for me to..." She broke off, tried a different approach. "I feel safe with you, and I don't know if you understand how special that is, how seductive it is."

SHOCK HELD ZACH silent for a beat then two. *Three years.*

Six months, eight months during deployments, sure, but *three years?*

He had to get it out of his head, otherwise the hard-on pushing against his zipper was going to rob his brain of blood and oxygen, and he was going to keel over from lack of both. Possible reasons why this smart, beautiful woman might not have had sex in *three years* darted through his thoughts.

He urged her to turn so he could hold her close. She nestled in and pressed her breasts into his ribs until he felt them all the way to his toes. There was no way she was missing his response to her announcement, since she fit against him so perfectly, her head tucked just under his chin.

He smoothed a thick lock of her hair that floated up and brushed his cheek while the ocean breeze pushed against them like an invisible hand, urging them closer.

He remembered how she'd spoken about David Henderlight, her ex. The past wasn't the past when traumatic events etched every detail into your psyche. He knew it from personal experience. Kathleen pretended to be fine, but he saw the signs, just like, he was certain, Cal did.

Piper revisited her father's death every time she spoke to a family member, and every time she went to the restaurant where he died. Whatever David Henderlight did to make her break things off was tangled up in what happened to her father. And it couldn't be anything good if she clung so desperately to the need to feel safe before allowing anyone to lay hands on her.

He had to say something. "It's been nearly five months for me. Whenever we're out of the country, it can be anywhere between six and eight months. I always practice safe sex and use condoms faithfully. And we're tested for all sorts of stuff every few months, including drugs."

He backed off to give them both some time to think about it. "How 'bout a movie?" he asked. He accepted the soggy ball Trouble brought him and tossed it up. Trouble caught it on the way down.

"What kind of movie?" she asked.

"You can pick one. I have several services I subscribe to." Trouble dropped the ball at his feet again.

"Beautiful women, hot guys, and lots of action?"

"Yeah. Trouble, my man, lead the way." He tossed the ball through the open sliding door into the kitchen, and the dog raced after it.

Three years. Jesus, he was going to have to stop thinking about it...and how badly he wanted to be the one to end her long, dry spell.

CHAPTER 19

IF ONLY HE hadn't mentioned sex. She'd known it would come up sometime. There was too much chemistry between them for it not to.

Why did she even want to try it again? Because the closer she got to him, the safer she felt.

And when she was close to him, she experienced a high she'd never known before.

A temporary intimacy based on physical chemistry. Not the emotion she needed. Even Zach admitted it. He needed to keep it light, and she'd never be able to manage that. She already had feelings for him...because it was impossible not to.

She couldn't make love with a man she'd only known six days. No matter how hot he was. How good a guy he was. And no matter how much she wanted him.

There was too much he didn't know about her. If she gave herself to him and he broke it off, it would crush her. But if she didn't make love with him and he left...

If—no, when—Lester popped up in her life again... Tonight might be the only night they had. Oh, God, that sounded so selfish.

But if they didn't, she'd always wonder if this perfect day could have ended as perfectly as they both wanted it to.

When they reached the living room, she looped her fingers

through his, and tugged him down the hall, pausing outside the guest room where she left her bathing suit and bag.

Zach's Adam's apple worked as he swallowed. "Are you sure, Piper?"

Her heart pounded so hard it was difficult to draw a full breath. Nerves stole the strength from her voice, leaving it airy and weak. "Yes, I'm sure."

He studied her for a long moment, then stepped close to cup her face in his hands and kiss her gently, slowly, thoroughly, stealing the strength from her legs. He caught her hand and drew her into the bedroom.

Before she could lose her nerve, she reached for his shirt buttons. Her heart beat at her throat and wrists, and her hands trembled. She pulled his garment free of his black shorts and parted it—and of course he was beautiful. From his dark red hair and his green eyes with the yellow flecks around the iris, to his expressive mouth, to the muscular width of his shoulders, and more. She ran her hands over his shoulders and slipped the garment off. Standing on tiptoe, she encircled his neck with her arms and pressed a line of kisses along his jaw.

This might be the only time they had together. She wouldn't allow her fears to stand in the way. She wanted, needed to be close to him.

He turned his head and his mouth claimed hers. His big hands felt so good as they caressed every curve of her body, bringing her in close so she felt his arousal.

Their fingers collided when they both reached for the buttons of her blouse. Hers were faster. She wiggled her shoulders and allowed it to fall. With a sense of increasing urgency, she shed her jeans while Zach undressed.

From behind her, he slipped the strap of her bra off her shoulder and pressed an open-mouthed kiss to the spot.

The small caress brought with it a sense of being cherished, making it easier when he unhooked the bra and guided it down her arms. His hands were hot as he cupped her breasts, kneading and caressing them until the nipples peaked into tight buds.

She leaned back against him and felt the taut heat of his erection against the small of her back. When anxiety started to rise, she quashed it, concentrating on the gentle caress of his hands moving over her skin. He wasn't going to rush her, hurt her.

While his tongue traced the curve of her ear, her whole body shook with sweet anticipation. It was going to be different this time. She knew it, because Zach was different. He was generous and patient and made her want to give herself to him.

She turned to cup the back of his neck and guide his mouth back to hers. When he urged her down on the bed, she went eagerly, and got the first full view of his body when he eased in beside her.

The seventy-pound packs he carried, and the training he'd told her about, had hewn his body into muscular perfection.

A perfection marred by the ugly purplish-black bruise encompassing most of his right hip and the upper part of his thigh.

"You're supposed to be concentrating on something besides my injury," Zach said while he tucked a strand of hair behind her ear.

"I am but... Are you sure you're okay?" The injury looked too painful for him to be taking part in any kind of activity, even this.

"Ninety-eight percent of me is good to go. But you may have to be on top."

It wasn't ninety-eight percent...more like ninety. She brushed back the hair at his temple with her fingertips and ran a questing hand over the broad width of his chest to his shoulder. She rose up on an elbow to press a kiss against the strong pulse that beat in his throat. He smelled of the ocean and him. Salty, sexy.

He caressed her breasts and bent his head to taste each one. Seeing his manly mouth latched around her nipple, feeling it, sent a frisson of sensation arrowing downward. She reveled in the hotness of his mouth, the brush of his beard against her skin.

A feeling of tenderness swept through her, and she caressed the back of his neck.

Zach's chest rose as he dragged in a breath and cupped her buttocks to bring her in close against him. His erection pressed against her stomach. But she still avoided looking at that part of him. If she looked at it, she'd freeze up.

She ran her hand down his broad back, bringing him in closer, and they rocked together. He seemed to respond as powerfully as she did to him. Every brush of his hand, every touch of his lips seemed to reach inside her and drag free feelings she'd suppressed for too long.

When he eased a hand into her panties, her breathing hitched. His touch was light, careful, caressing her, leaving her aching for more.

He guided her panties down her legs, then reached in the bedside table for a box of condoms and broke the seal. His cheeks were flushed, his green eyes alight. "Want to put this on for me?"

It was just another part of him. This was Zach. He wasn't holding her down. He wasn't pushing himself inside her. He was letting her have control. She forced herself to look at that part of him. She paused to cup him in her hand, feeling the warmth of him, the blood pulsing through his erection. The intimacy of the act, and his willing vulnerability, hit her and eased her nervousness.

She'd never put a condom on a man before. Feeling a little uncertain, she tore the wrapper open and somewhat awkwardly rolled the condom down over him.

"Take me inside you, Piper," he said, his voice husky.

It was always at the moment of penetration when she lost the promise of the act. She wanted it to be different this time. Nerves stole her breath again as she rose and straddled him, concentrating on Zach's expression while she lowered herself over him slowly. There was no sensation of weight forcing her down, no panic, no flashback, only a sensation of pleasure as he filled her. Her delight and relief brought a quick smile in its wake. She leaned forward, braced her hands on the mattress on either side of his head and lowered her mouth to his.

"Is your hip okay?" she asked.

Zach grinned. "It isn't my hip that needs attention, right now." He cupped her hips in his large hands and guided her into a slow, easy rhythm he could move with beneath her.

With each downward stroke, Piper watched Zach's face, hoping to please him. When he started to massage her breasts and then worked his way down to more intimate spots, she forgot about everything but his touch. He homed in on the most sensitive, intimate areas of her body, and she began to rock faster, chasing a pleasure she'd only ever experienced for fleeting moments during foreplay.

He swelled inside her, and her need exploded to a fever pitch. Every inch of her body tautened while she sought to capture what lay just out of reach. With the first throb of Zach's release, a surge of pleasure rushed through her, and she lost the rhythm of her movements. She bit her lip to hold back a cry of pleasure.

When her vision cleared, she realized she was gripping Zach's hands and he was sporting a satisfied grin.

"I don't think I've ever seen anything more beautiful than you coming, Piper."

She didn't know whether to laugh or cry. Both were possible in that moment. She leaned down to rest her breasts atop his chest and kissed him. Would he think her pathetic if she told him it was her very first time? "You made it happen."

When Zach blew on his fingernails and buffed them against his chest, she laughed.

His masculine features took on a look of tenderness as he smoothed back a strand of hair from her cheek and tucked it behind her ear. "You did the work. Next time we'll go a little slower and make it even better."

After seven years she had been able to set aside the fear, the trauma. She wanted there to be a next time. Wanted there to be many next times.

Reluctantly, she eased away from Zach, the parting of their bodies leaving behind a feeling of emptiness, of loss.

It was then, the specter of Lester rose again in her mind.

The way he'd looked through the store, searching...Pursuing...

She needed to tell Zach.

But not yet.

CHAPTER 20

ZACH WATCHED THE slow, even, rise and fall of Piper's chest. The drab brown T-shirt she slept in, one of his, well-worn and faded from a thousand washings, had never looked so good on him. It clung to the rounded shape of her breasts and flowed over her hip, outlining every feminine curve of her body.

With a stifled moan, he rolled onto his back and covered his eyes with a forearm. If he was content to lie here and watch her sleep, he was in trouble. He was letting her get too close. But he had only himself to blame. She was beautiful and inexperienced, and he hadn't been able to resist reaching for her. They made love twice the first night, then twice more the next day. And now this morning he wanted to do it all over again.

He sensed there were things she wanted to tell him, but held back. Even after they'd shared the intimacy of making love and sleeping together that first night, she hadn't asked him questions about his family or his job, and seemed content to let him volunteer what he would. The perfect girlfriend for a SEAL.

They were enjoying each other without strings. And he'd told her it was all he could give her.

So why the hell was he feeling like something was missing?

Because there was.

Piper wasn't the kind of woman you fucked and let walk away. But she was living in the moment just like he was. Why? And why had it been three years since she'd allowed a man close? He wanted to know, but he'd tied his own hands. By saying he didn't want a relationship, he'd succeeded in limiting what questions he could ask.

Certainly she'd experienced some kind of sexual trauma. But he couldn't throw out the question, "Have you been raped?" while he was having sex with her. The idea that she might have been banded his throat with a rage so ferocious it threatened to strangle him. He fell back and breathed in and out for several moments until the feeling eased.

The alarm clock beeped, and Piper rolled away from it with a murmured moan. She flipped the bedclothes back and staggered into the bathroom while he hit the button to turn it off.

She came back to snuggle under the covers and wiggled back against him to be held. "I don't want to go back to the real world."

God, he felt the same way. "We both have to sometime, sweetheart." He nuzzled her neck. "We're both lucky to love what we do," he reminded her.

"Yes, we are. But being here was like Shangri-La. No worries, no stress, a hunky male to fulfill my every fantasy…."

Zach chuckled. "Surely we haven't fulfilled them all yet." He caught a glimpse of a smile over her shoulder.

"No, not all. I've just discovered my capacity for them."

"Sounds promising." He brushed his lips against her shoulder.

She wiggled around to look up at him. "Being here with you has been wonderful."

It sounded like she might be leading up to letting him down easy. The idea dealt him a considerable punch. "You're not dumping me after a weekend?"

"No!" She smiled, then said, "No," her tone a little less adamant. She cupped his cheek with a palm. "I want to spend as much time with you as I can before you go back to active duty, if it's what you want, too."

Relief quick and sharp released the tension of his muscles. He kissed her and pulled her into him.

Piper groaned. "I can't. I don't have time." She patted his

chest. "I have to go to work."

"Give me fifteen minutes...."

She glanced at the clock again. While her head was turned and she was distracted, he nipped her earlobe and took the opportunity to rake his teeth gently along her neck.

Piper cupped the back of his head. "Fifteen minutes." Her voice had that soft, breathy tone that jumpstarted his libido, not that he needed any encouragement.

What was building between them had the same stomach-plunging thrill of rappelling down from a hovering helicopter.

She turned her lips to his, and he lost himself in the kiss.

In only a weekend they had learned how to touch each other, give to each other. There was nothing missing when they made love. Piper's hands, her mouth drove him crazy, even as he was feasting on her with his own.

He could spend hours stroking the soft underside of her breast, breathing in her scent, buried in the heated warmth between her thighs.

When he could wait no longer, he covered himself with a condom and levered himself over her. Piper caught her breath and braced a hand against his chest, her expression anxious.

It was the first time he'd attempted to be on top. He froze.

Her hand dropped to his side. "Your hip, Zach."

At her look of concern, he breathed a sigh of relief. "It'll be okay. I'm going to be very slow." He grabbed a pillow, folded it in half, and elevated her hips, then guided himself into her and felt her body grip him. Each time their bodies came together she lit up as though it was the first time. It gave him such a sexual charge.

He stayed on his knees, seated deep inside her and, bracing one hand on the bed, rocked, slowly giving his hip time to adjust to the movement. Piper raised her knees, deepening the contact, and he murmured his approval. God, how could they be so physically in sync and deny themselves more?

As Piper's body gripped his, the need overwhelmed him, and he forgot about his hip, forgot about everything but the hunger for release. He braced both hands on the bed and leaned over her to change the rocking movement to hard, deep thrusts.

Piper murmured his name, her tone a plea, driving him on. Her hands moved over his chest, his back, as though she sought a mooring to hold onto while her hips rose to meet his every thrust. She cried out, her grimace of pleasure ripping away his control and tipping him over the brink.

His arms felt like rubber and his hip ached when he lowered himself atop her and rested his head in the bend of her neck.

Her arms came around him, and she held him while his heart thundered in his ears. When he started to withdraw, her arms tightened. "Not yet. I just want to feel you inside me, hold you close for a moment more."

He turned his head to find tears streaming down her temples.

"There are some things I need to tell you. Things about my past you need to know. There isn't enough time now, but later…"

Even though he'd expected it, seeing her in tears ramped up the concern he'd stifled all weekend to mid-grade anxiety. He made soothing noises while he wiped her tears away with the sheet. "Come here for lunch and we'll talk."

She nodded. But she continued to cling to him, hold him.

He waited until her arms slid away and kissed her softly. As their bodies separated, a fresh rush of tears coursed down her cheeks. When she sat up he drew her close. "It's going to be okay, Piper."

Her silence at his reassurance twisted his uneasiness higher.

Though she regained her composure, he was reluctant to release her, even when she said, "I have to go."

He went into the bathroom and dealt with the condom. By the time he joined her in the bedroom, Piper had slipped her jeans on and was hooking her bra.

She slipped on her T-shirt with a quick, practiced move. "I'll catch a quick shower at home."

He hated to see her leave upset, without things settled between them. He stepped into his boxer briefs and jerked on the khaki shorts he'd worn the day before.

Two excited dogs danced around them while they left the

bedroom and went into the living room. Trouble in particular looped his body around Piper's legs, his tail going wild and threatening to clear the coasters off the coffee table. Gracie, though more sedate in her greeting to first Zach, then Piper, did a three-legged rumba that almost matched Trouble's.

After giving both dogs a quick rubbing, Piper began to gather Trouble's things.

Zach said, "It'll save you time if you leave him here with me and Gracie today. He entertains us both, and I'll take good care of him."

After a moment's hesitation, Piper nodded. "Okay, thank you. I'll be back at noon." She grabbed her purse from the table next to the door and fished out a long clip. His breath hitched when he eyed the womanly profile of her body as she lifted her arms to bundle her hair into a tail and fastened it at the back of her head.

Any other woman would be fussing with her makeup and hair. With her warm Italian coloring, dark hair, and eyes, Piper looked beautiful without any.

Zach trailed her to the door, the dogs close behind.

Piper stood on tiptoes to brush his lips with a kiss. She hit the button on her key fob to unlock her car as she walked to it, then paused to look up and down the street.

It was an action he had seen her do while they walked on the beach, ran to the store for munchies, or sat out on the back patio. Zach stepped out on the stoop and closed the door behind him to keep the dogs in. "Who are you looking for, Piper?"

She paused by the open car door for a long moment, her gaze dark with worry. "Trouble."

She wasn't talking about her dog. A dropping sensation swooped through Zach's stomach and condensed into a knot.

"I'll tell you everything at lunch."

The feeling lingered even while she backed out of the drive and pulled away.

He drew in a deep breath and released it on an oath. "Shit!"

CHAPTER 21

CAL BRAKED, SLOWING the truck to a stop at the light and let the silence stretch between him and his dad. Silence was good. Silence didn't cause issues or get his dad's blood pressure up or threaten him with another heart attack. His dad didn't need the stress, and he didn't either. He needed to concentrate on driving and getting his dad home safe without any kind of conflict. He glanced in the rearview mirror. His mom was a car length behind them.

"So, your gal will be here tomorrow?"

"Yeah." God, he missed Kathleen. "Unless you don't think you want the company."

"It will be fine. It sounds like she'll fit in fine with the rest of us. Maybe we can hire her to do some architectural designs for us."

"She said she's done some residential stuff in the past."

"Can she swing a hammer?"

Cal smiled. "No. She can put up pictures, blinds, curtain rods, that kind of thing, and put in a new light switch or plug, but none of the heavy repair work." But Kathleen's mom had a mean right hook. He had the urge to tell the story to his dad, but it was hers to share, and talking about her ex didn't feel right.

"We can teach her."

Those few words had him glancing at his father.

"She'd probably like the demolition better than the repair work."

His dad chuckled. "She would?"

"I can see her with a sledge hammer, knocking down walls and tearing out cabinets. She wouldn't mind the dirty work."

"Sounds like your mother."

"Maybe a little. She has mom's patience."

"Good thing for a woman to have in this family." There was a pause. "Your mom has already asked which bedroom she should put her in, yours or the guest room."

"The guest room will be fine. We don't live together in California." Not yet, anyway. And he wouldn't want to disturb his mom's southern ideas of morality and respect. "She isn't a hookup, Dad. I love her."

"Why don't you just go ahead and pop the question?"

"I've been waiting for the right moment."

"Then I had the heart attack."

Cal shrugged. "It wasn't like you planned it, Dad. My feelings for her aren't going to change, whether I ask her this week or next."

"And you're pretty confident about her feelings, too?"

"I know she loves me." But if he had to move to San Antonio and help take care of things… Just when she'd gotten closer to Zach and been able to spend more time with him. Would she want to move to Texas?

He wanted to put it off until he was certain about his dad. And Douglas. But the ring had been burning a hole in his pocket for the past two weeks, just waiting to be slipped on her finger.

Since she'd just gotten more settled at work and seemed to be doing better, how would she feel about taking him on permanently? It had been fifteen months since she split from her cheating, lying, asshole ex-boyfriend.

Was that long enough for her to know if she wanted something permanent with someone else? With him, the man who loved her?

"Could we drive by one of the sites? I want to see how they're doing."

Cal jerked his head in his dad's direction. "You're in your pajamas, Dad. You've got a seven-inch incision down the center of your chest, and wires holding your breastbone together. You're not going to a construction site."

"I didn't say I wanted to get out of the car and walk around, I said I wanted you to drive by so I can see how things are going."

Cal debated. "If things aren't going according to your schedule, I don't want to hear you yelling about it. You *cannot* get upset or stressed out. You have sutures holding grafts in place to bypass the blocked vessels. You're not blowing one of those on my watch."

"I won't yell or make a fuss. But Jesus, Cal, your mom hasn't let me out of her sight in over a month. I haven't been on the job for almost six weeks. I'll go crazy trapped in the house watching television or walking on the damn treadmill for the rest of my days."

He knew what his dad meant. He almost felt sorry for him. Almost. But his mom had made sacrifices too. "I think it would be a good idea for you to retire. You and mom could travel. You could go up north to Canada. Mom's been talking about Niagara Falls forever. Every time she planned the trip, you always made excuses. It's time for her to have something in her life besides a husband who works himself into a heart attack."

His father pressed a hand to his forehead. "Shoot me now."

Cal laughed and pulled over to the curb. His mother swung in behind them and got out of the car. She marched up the sidewalk with the determined steps of a woman on a mission.

Cal rolled down the window.

"What the hell do you think you're doing, Jameson?" She had the steely-eyed look of someone whose patience was stretched beyond endurance.

"Nothing, Mom. Dad wanted to see the progress on the site, and it was on the way home, so I'm letting him take a look."

"Jameson, you are not getting out of that truck."

"No, I'm not. For Christ's sake, I'm just looking." He released his seat belt and slid forward to look through the side window at the two-story split level. "It looks…the new windows are in and the pavers have been put down and the guttering is up. How 'bout the inside?"

"There's some finishing touches to be done in two of the bedrooms, but the bathrooms and kitchen are done, and the painting is finished."

"Floors, too?" he asked.

"Yeah, floors too. When the kitchen cabinets came in late, Mom put the crew on laying the floors upstairs in the bedrooms and halls. The only things we have left to do are lay some baseboard, put covers on the light switches and plug-ins, and hang a couple of light fixtures. The job will be finished tomorrow."

"Shit. You've done the whole damn house in a week."

"No." Cal shot his mom a look. "We did the downstairs and some cosmetic stuff on the outside of the house in a week. Mom had the rest finished before I got here."

His mother stepped up to the window, blocking his view of the house. "The rest of the projects are on schedule. The boys have been taking care of everything. And Doug found someone to take over placing the orders and keeping the books until you're better."

His dad subsided back against the wide seat, a frown wrinkling his brow. "Good. That's good." He didn't look happy, though. He looked tired and suddenly shrunken.

Cal more than anyone understood what he was going through. His dad might never be able to go back to what he loved doing most. He was wondering what the fuck he was going to do with the rest of his life.

Cal remembered grappling with every one of those thoughts and feelings.

"You need to put your seat belt back on, Dad, so we can get home."

His father reached for the seat belt and slowly pulled it over his chest and lap. Cal helped him guide the mechanism in the slot. "I can do this, dammit. I'm not an invalid."

Cal held his tongue and started the vehicle. His mom turned aside to walk back to her car.

His father remained silent the rest of the way to the house, looking out the side window while he pretended an interest in the passing scenery.

When they pulled into the driveway of the family's sprawling ranch-style house, Cal rushed to get out of the car in case his dad needed help getting out. His mother stood by, her arms full with the bag of stuff they'd loaded up from the hospital, deep furrows etched on each side of her mouth. She looked exhausted.

His father threw out a hand. "Stop hovering, Sondra. Go on in. If I fall on my face out here, Cal can haul me back up."

"They wouldn't have sent him home if they thought he wasn't ready, Mom. Go on. I'll get the rest of the stuff out of the car in a bit."

She nodded. "Don't give him a chance to make a break for it. He'll get on the damn riding mower or something, just to prove how indestructible he is."

Cal grinned. "He won't get away from me. I can outrun him."

She shot him a tired smile and went into the house.

Cal turned his attention to his father.

His dad stared after her. "I bet you're pleased I'm getting some payback after everything I said and did while you were getting back on your feet."

Surprise held him silent a moment. "No, Dad. I wouldn't wish anything like this on anyone. It's a fucking bitch to be in pain and have everyone remind you daily how helpless you are."

"Yeah it is." Jameson's mouth flattened.

"Kathleen's brother's a SEAL. They have a saying, 'the only easy day was yesterday.' That's the way it's going to feel for awhile, but you'll get through it, just like I did."

His dad remained silent.

"You've been up quite a while. Want to go in?"

He nodded. "Yeah."

Cal adjusted his strides to match his dad's, just in case he should need some support. Since his father was being so amiable, he decided to push it a little further. "Stacy walked away because she couldn't handle things. You're lucky Mom's made of sterner stuff. I hope you know it."

Jameson shot him a look.

"Just because you've been married for thirty-five years doesn't give you the right to take things out on her, or be an asshole because you have to take things easy for a while. And you'll be tempted to do it since she's handy."

Jameson's look turned into a scowl.

"I happen to know that because I was a fucker to the nurses at the hospital, and I ended up having to swallow my pride and apologize to them later."

"You were?"

"Yeah. A real bastard." Cal reached for the doorknob and swung the front door open. "If you think marriage is going to save you from having to apologize, you're wrong. Because women may forgive a lot, but they don't forget anything, and it will end up biting you in the ass."

His dad laughed. "What's made you the expert on women?"

"Is there really such a thing as an expert on women?" Cal shook his head. "I just know two truths. You don't lie to them, and you don't treat them like shit, because eventually either one will boomerang back to you and kick you in the nuts."

He cut off the suggestions and asked, "Where are you going to lie down? Bedroom or your cave?"

"My den. Lying all day in the fucking bed just makes me feel like—shit."

Cal was careful not to grab his arm, but he could tell his dad's energy was flagging. They turned right and walked through the large, open floor plan living room. The cathedral ceiling made the room seem spacious, though it was actually not much larger than other homes of the same design. They moved on down a wide hall to another living space. His father's den.

Jameson sank into his recliner with a sigh. Cal pushed the lever to raise his feet.

His mom appeared. "Would you two like something to eat or

drink?"

Before Cal could say anything, his dad broke in, impatiently. "Go lie down, Sondra. We're fine." The tone he used with her grated against Cal's nerves and he bit back a retort.

Driven into protective mode, Cal crossed to his mother and laid an arm around her shoulders. "I'll get the rest of the stuff out of the car. You go ahead and lie down, and I'll hang out with him for a while. If he needs anything, I'll get it."

She rested her head against his chest for a moment and gave him pat. "I think I will."

The slump of her shoulders when she walked out of the room shot Cal's feelings of anger to a full-blown rage. How long had this shit been going on? Probably long before his dad got sick.

"If you keep talking to Mom in a short, pissy tone, she'll eventually get ticked off enough to knock you upside the head, or walk away and leave you to deal with this shit all on your lonesome."

"Your mom's not going anywhere."

Cal raised a brow. "Keep using that tone with her, and we'll find out. But the real question is...if you love her, why do you talk to her like a condescending prick?"

His dad's expression turned resentful. "It's none of your damn business, Cal."

"Yeah, it is, Dad. Because she's my mom, and she's done everything she can to help you through this and keep the business going. Doug has too. What have you done lately to show them your appreciation?"

With that, he walked away before Jameson had could come back with anything or get too angry.

He took his time getting the rest of the bags out of the car. His mom had spent some time writing cards, thanking the staff for everything they'd done.

He'd delivered the cut flower arrangements to the nursing stations in the pediatric wings, and given the rest to one of the volunteers to pass on to patients who had no family visiting during their stay at the hospital. They'd sent a fruit basket to the ICU, surgery, and emergency.

His mom brought two live arrangements home, and he put the delicate begonia in a moss pot in the living room on an end table, and the other, a mixed planter, in the dining room on a side table so it would get the morning sun.

He left the bags of toiletries and hospital paraphernalia in the mudroom off the kitchen, put in a load of laundry, and opened the refrigerator to see what was available for dinner. Neighbors had brought in a ton of food in the last two days. Casseroles and takeout items. So there was no need to cook. He'd put one of the casseroles in the oven in an hour or so.

He stepped into the den to find his dad asleep in his recliner, his breathing even, his color much better than when he first arrived. With nothing else to do, Cal wandered through the French doors to the back patio and took a seat on one of the Adirondack lounges under the canvas awning stretching twenty feet across the back of the house. Sunlight glistened off the pool, and he narrowed his eyes against the glare.

He hadn't forgotten the mid-ninety days, but he longed for the mid-seventies he worked in at home. Sweat beaded his skin in moments, but he preferred the outdoor air to the oppression of the house.

He'd been gone long enough to have gained some distance from his family. Everyone was making excuses for his father's behavior, but his illness wasn't what had triggered this. The truth was he wasn't any different now than he'd been the whole time Cal was growing up.

What his father was doing to his brother and mother was abusive. And he didn't like it one bit. He needed to figure out how he could talk to his mom about it. But what good would it do? She'd lived with the man for nearly thirty years and stood by while he verbally abused all of them.

He slipped his phone out of his pocket. Was it fair to Kathleen to bring her into the middle of this? Or would her presence trigger some restraint in his dad?

God, he missed her. He needed her here, but would his dad embarrass him by acting like the asshole he was? Fuck!

He tapped Kathleen's number and waited for her to pick up.

"Hey, handsome," she answered, and he smiled. His mood lightened.

"I can't wait for you to get out here. I want us to take an afternoon and do the river walk and eat somewhere nice. Maybe go to the tower of the Americas so you can check out the city.

"It's okay if you have things to do to help your mom and dad instead. You don't have to entertain me."

"Tomorrow we'll be putting the finishing touches on one of the three projects I've worked on, so I'll be able to take a day off." He paused. "I helped Mom bring Dad home from the hospital today."

"How is he?"

"Ornery as ever, but his color's good, and he walked into the house under his own steam."

"Wonderful!"

He had to talk to her about this. "He's copping an attitude with Mom I don't like. I'm trying to guilt him into giving her a break."

"From what you've told me, he's always been strong, independent, and hates to be helpless. Does any of that sound familiar?"

Cal smiled weakly. "Yeah-yeah." And his anger issues sounded familiar, too. "I was hoping to keep Dad from making the same mistakes I made."

"It's early days. He's just been through two really bad scares, plus major surgery. Give him some time."

"I will. But I don't know how Mom has put up with him for the past thirty-five years. I may not have a tongue left by the time I leave here. I spend half my time biting it to keep from giving him hell for being a jerk."

"I'm rather pleased with the things you do with your tongue. You need to think about that when you start gnawing on it."

Which made a nice dent in the knot in his stomach. "Maybe I'll have more luck getting my mind off things by thinking of some of the sounds you make when I'm—"

"Don't say it. I'm not going to be able to concentrate on work."

Cal laughed. He knew her cheeks were red right now. "You need to get it done so you can get on that plane tomorrow. I really want to see you."

"I'm working hard, and I've missed you. It's too quiet around here without you."

"Quiet, huh?"

"And lonely. I'm almost done. I just have a couple of small changes to make, then my part of the plans will be done. The whole team was excited about the design, too."

"Good. I'm not surprised. I'll let you go so you can finish. I love you. See you tomorrow."

"I love you, too. I'm looking forward to it."

"I wanted to warn you." About everything. "Mom's putting you in the guest room, but I'm sleeping in my room."

"It's okay. Remember how we had to pretend we weren't sleeping together for my parents?"

"Yeah, I do. I don't think we fooled them a bit."

"No. But the fantasy put them at ease while they were here. So I won't mind doing the same for your parents."

"Thanks, Kathleen." God, he was so lucky to have her.

"See you tomorrow."

He should have told her to cancel her flight. That he'd be home in a few days. In fact, he already could hardly wait to leave.

CHAPTER 22

K ATHLEEN FOCUSED ON the computer screen, though she didn't attempt to move the mouse in her hand. Cal's tension had seeped through more in how he said things than what he said. He had told her more than once how overbearing his father was, and his brother seemed to be following in the man's footsteps.

But they were still his family. She loved him, so she'd try to love them, too.

She just hoped they liked her. His mother in particular, because when Cal talked about her his expression and body language changed. He was more relaxed and open.

After having spoken with Dr. Dowling about her job, and giving it some thought, she'd made up her mind to move on. But she wanted to talk to Cal about it first. It wasn't really surprising she wanted to talk to him about it. She loved him, was in love with him. And she valued his opinion.

A tap sounded on the wall dividing their pod. "Kathleen?"

"Yes." She swiveled her chair and looked over her shoulder. Tyler Unger was the epitome of a nerd, with the light overhead reflecting off his wire-rim glasses when he moved his head. He was in his late forties, and always looked like he'd just shoved his fingers through his thick mop of brown hair, leaving it disheveled. He wore a uniform of blue jeans and a T-shirt, but he kept a white short-sleeved dress shirt at work to throw on for meetings.

Kathleen liked his laid-back style, the way he made it easy for her to work with him.

"The client has moved the meeting up to today at five instead of tomorrow morning. Is it going to be an issue for you?"

"No. I'm finishing up right now."

"Excellent!"

"I'd like you to look over the file, just to be certain I haven't missed anything."

"Sure, just buzz me when you're done."

"Will do."

She turned her attention back to the project and used the mouse to manipulate a small section of the schematic. In just a few minutes she had finished and rolled back to study the screen. The sense of accomplishment when she finished a project gave her a high she never tired of.

She reached for the phone and buzzed Tyler. He answered immediately, and she stood and stretched to relieve the tension in her back and shoulders.

She turned to find Tyler standing at the edge of her pod watching her. She folded her arms against her, an instant rush of anxiety seizing her lungs.

She forced a smile. "I think we need loops hung from the ceiling in here to stretch out the kinks after sitting hunched over the computer all day."

"I'll mention it to human resources," he commented. He moved to her desk chair. "Why don't you go get something to drink while I look this over?"

"I think I will." She wandered out and went into the break room. After heating some water in the microwave and adding a tea bag, she returned and leaned against the dividing wall while Tyler went over the schematic with his eagle eye. When he rolled back from the desk and smiled she sighed.

"It looks great, Kathleen. You've done good work."

She smiled in relief. "Thanks."

"Pull up a chair. I'd like to talk to you about something."

She rolled the extra office chair out from under the counter and sat down.

"How are you doing here with us?"

"I'm good."

"If you don't feel comfortable, I can see about a transfer to another pod."

A dropping sensation struck her stomach. Quick tears blurred her eyes and she looked away. "Have I done something wrong?"

"God, no. No, not at all. I wasn't suggesting the other guys or I want you to leave, either. I'm trying to be sensitive to your needs, Kathleen. You're still a little anxious sometimes. Like when I first came in here."

"I wasn't anxious...I was stretching, and I didn't want you to think I was trying to draw attention to myself."

"I didn't think you were putting on a show for me, Kathleen. I know you're in a relationship with a guy, and that it's pretty serious."

"Yes, it is." She finally looked up.

"I know we've avoided talking about what happened in your other pod. Maybe it wasn't such a good idea. It's left an elephant in the room, and we've been walking around it for months."

Kathleen moistened her lips.

"How would you feel about the four of us having a meeting right now, just talking about what happened and what we can do to help you get past it?"

Just when she was ready to throw in the towel... But was she ready to tell other people about what happened?

How would they feel about her after she told them?

How much worse could it get since she was already thinking about quitting?

"Okay."

He reached for her phone and punched in Jack's and Kenton's phone numbers.

"Bring your chairs, guys and roll on over to Kathleen's work station for a few minutes."

Tyler got up to close the door.

Jack Sutton, the oldest member of their group, rolled his chair over. He was tall and lanky, his shoulders slightly hunched. He reminded Kathleen of Jimmy Stewart, except his brows and hair were graying. He was quiet and rarely said anything, even in meetings, but Kathleen had found his laid-back attitude was deceiving. Jack never missed anything. He was apt to pop out with information the rest of them had overlooked.

Kenton Frazier was five-nine and slightly built, with dark hair and blue eyes. When he wheeled around the corner of her station, Kathleen thought he might be the prettiest man she'd ever seen. She envied his long eyelashes and naturally rosy cheeks. "Is there a problem with the design?" he asked in his slightly fussy tone. He was openly gay, and didn't mind letting other people know. He was the least threatening member in the group, though none of them had ever shown the least inclination to provoke an issue with her or each other.

Tyler answered him, "No. Kathleen's finished her part of the design in record time, so you two probably need to step up your game."

Kenton wiggled his eyebrows. "You trying to show us up, girlfriend?"

Kathleen smiled at him. "I don't think it's possible, Kenton. You guys are too good for that. I'm going out of town for a few days, and didn't want to hang you up by being late with my part of the design."

"That's real considerate of you, Kathleen."

"What do you need, Tyler?" Jack asked. He stretched out his legs and crossed them at the ankles.

"I thought we could take a few minutes to talk. We've skirted around the issue of what happened to Kathleen when she first started working here. I've asked her to tell us what happened straight out. Maybe it will help us understand. And help her feel more like one of us."

Jack moved to lean forward in his seat. "For what it's worth, I always thought Paul Warren was an asshole." He looked around the circle they had created with their chairs. "We had some dealings with him." He grimaced. "He wasn't shy about taking credit for the work, even if he didn't do it."

That he was the first one to speak when he usually hung back was telling. How long had he wanted to tell her?

"I can see that. He was a little overly friendly my first day on the job, and made me uncomfortable. He had a reputation for dating the recent hires."

"Not something the company condones, Kathleen," Ryan said.

She nodded. "My brother urged me to file a complaint, but I had just been hired, and it didn't seem the way to go after just signing a contract a few days before. I thought if I continued to turn him down, things would level out.

"The first day, while we were on one of the sites, a man went over the side on the twentieth floor, but was caught in time. The man I'm dating now, Cal, is the crewmember who saved the man's life.

"Warren had an issue with him. At the time he said it was because he's an amputee, and therefore a danger to the rest of the crew, but there was another issue that didn't come to light until later."

"How did your boyfriend lose his leg?"

"Cal was driving the Humvee he and three other men were riding in when they hit an IED and the vehicle was destroyed. Cal almost died. His leg was blown off below the knee, his jaw was broken, some of his teeth gone, and he had two cracked vertebrae in his neck. It took him a year to recover."

"And Warren's nephew was one of the other men."

"Yes." She went into Warren's reasons for being vengeful toward Cal, and about his false forgiveness for what had happened, and his relationship with Hillary Bryant.

"She was a brilliant architect. Truly brilliant. And very ill. She shocked me with a Taser until the battery went dead. Locked me in the trunk of her car in a parking structure for hours. I was dehydrated and weak by the time I got out. Every part of my body felt pulverized, and my sugar level was so low I couldn't think clearly.

"I don't know what Warren said to her that caused her to kill him, but she wasn't in her right mind when she did it. She believed he was still alive until the very end."

"Jesus," Jack murmured. "You're being more forgiving than I would be, Kathleen."

"I felt sorry for her. She loved him. I really believe she did. And he manipulated her like he did me, and used her as a weapon."

Kenton's beautiful face was creased in a rare frown. "How many other women do you think he might have victimized with her help?" Kenton asked.

Kathleen shook her head. "I don't know. I think they kept things quiet so there wouldn't be any suits filed against the company."

"You didn't file?" Kenton asked.

"No." A lawyer had contacted her about it, but it felt wrong to hold Willey Construction and Design accountable for something they had no control over. And she couldn't face legal action after everything she'd been through. "It wasn't the company's fault that Warren was an asshole, or that Hillary was mentally unstable."

Jack laughed, then leaned forward to cover his face. For several moments his shoulders shook with silent laughter. "I'm sorry. I didn't laugh because it was funny it was just... You said that the same way I would have said it."

"I have eight brothers. I suppose they've rubbed off on me a little."

"Eight brothers!" Kenton said hopefully. "Any of them gay?"

Kathleen raised her brows. "I'm sorry, Kenton, but no."

He feigned a look of exaggerated disappointment, then winked at her.

She smiled. He was trying so hard to put her at ease. She hadn't given these three nearly enough credit. She reached over and patted his hand. He gave hers a squeeze.

"If I've seemed distant, it's because I started out friendly with Warren, and he pushed the barriers. He had this passive-aggressive thing he did which kept me off balance and made me anxious. I kept second-guessing myself. Had I been too friendly? Had I said something to lead him to believe I was interested in him?

"I know I put up walls or look for behaviors when they're not there. But after this happened, I questioned everything I'd done from the first day on, thinking it was somehow my fault."

"Nothing you did could have been responsible for what happened, Kathleen," Jack said. "You were harassed by one and attacked by the other."

He leaned forward in his chair and put his elbows on his knees. "You can be friendly and joke around with me, and I promise not to think you're coming on to me. Besides, the guy you're dating could kick all three of our asses with one arm tied behind his back. All three of us at once. We're nerds, not warriors."

Kathleen laughed. "Cal wouldn't have to kick your ass, Jack. My brother is in the Navy, and he's taught me a few things since this happened. I could probably take you out all by myself."

Tyler laughed. "I guess we're forewarned, then. Is there any particular thing that makes you anxious we should be aware of?"

She thought about the anxiety of walking to her car. They'd think her a total wuss. After all, she did have those moves Zach had taught her. "I've recently continued my sessions with a PTSD specialist. I'm going to be fine. It's just going to take some time." She didn't want to mention the medication, either. "You guys have been great, really. If I've been too weird around you, I'm sorry."

"Not weird, Kathleen. Just cautious," Kenton said.

She tried not to tear up, but her eyes stung. "I'll try to get beyond it, okay?"

When the Jack and Kenton got to their feet, Kathleen rose to give each one a hug and thank them before they wandered back to their desks.

"Thanks for doing this, Tyler. It was the right thing to do, and I feel better because of the discussion."

"I'm glad. You're a damn fine architect, Kathleen. I don't want to lose you from my team. It would be Wiley's loss, and ours."

"Thanks for saying so."

He started to mosey back to his part of the pod, but stopped and turned back to face her. "It took a great deal of courage for you to walk back through the doors of this building and return to work after such an experience. Not many people would have been up for it."

"The Irish are a pigheaded, stubborn people. My family in particular. I don't want to quit. Something just won't let me."

"I'm glad to hear it. Take it easy for a little while. The meeting won't be until five. You have plenty of time to prepare for it."

She nodded. What had happened to the bold woman who'd traveled across the country to live in a new city and launch a new career?

She'd gone into hiding. She depended on Cal and Zach to give her support, but Cal was gone, and Zach had his own life to live, and would soon be overseas somewhere fighting the good fight.

He and Cal had been through worse things and functioned. She could do this.

PIPER INVESTED EVERY OUNCE of her attention on the dog on the operating table. Her veterinary training had taught her to focus on the problem before her and block out everything else. And she'd been able to do it thus far, despite the constant feelings of dread plaguing her.

The dog's name came to her after a momentary lapse. "You're going to be just fine, Rowdy," she spoke out loud, even though the animal was unconscious. She'd seen the Scottish terrier for his annual shots just recently, and he'd been Mr. Personality Plus, with a great deal of energy and a sweet disposition.

Piper used the clamp to grip the needle and carefully guided the sutures through the inside of the Scottish terrier's eyelid and sealed the eye shut. A sense of regret struck her, but there was nothing she could do. The injury to the eyeball was catastrophic, and she couldn't save it.

After performing surgery for two years, there was little that made her queasy, but this procedure had given her more than a few moments of queasiness. She left a small opening at the inner corner of the eye to allow it to drain, and ran her fingertips carefully over the field to make sure the fluid could escape. Pinkish red fluid seeped from the opening, and she blotted it away with a square of sterile gauze.

"Poor fellow," Kathy, her assistant murmured. "I remember him being in for a recent visit. He was a real sweetie. I hope he'll adjust to this okay."

"Animals seem to adapt more easily to situations like this than humans. It will take some time, but he's young and healthy. He should do fine." Dropping the used instruments into a basin, she reached for her stethoscope and listened to the terrier's heartbeat and respiration.

"The owner was freaked out. I mean to walk out and see a stick poking out of your dog's eye." Sandy shuddered.

"Hits you right in the pit of the stomach to imagine it. His owner was lucky to find him right away. He could have done more damage trying to get it out." She clipped the end of the last suture and dropped the curved needle and scissors she'd been using in a basin to be washed and sterilized later. She tugged down her mask and rotated her shoulders.

Fifteen minutes later Rowdy was already breathing on his own and she removed the tube. "I'll go call the owner and let her know how he's doing, and I'll need you to monitor him closely for the next couple of hours, just in case."

Kathy nodded. "Will do."

Piper removed her mask and gloves and placed them in a bio-hazard container. The gown went into the laundry bin.

"You're very good at what you do, Dr. Bertinelli. And you do it with compassion. I've worked with several vets in the past who were only in it for the money. I can tell you're not."

"Thanks, Kathy. And no, I'm not in it for the money." She smiled. "Not entirely. I have to have a little to pay my rent and eat.

But the reason I became a vet was because I love animals. They're the only creatures on the earth who aren't self-centered, and who are capable of unconditional love. God put them here under our dominion to care for and respect. So many people don't understand or believe that, otherwise we wouldn't have so many abused and neglected pets come in to be treated or rescued from cruel, thoughtless owners."

She looked away. "I used to volunteer at some of the shelters. I hated to see them put healthy animals down because they couldn't find them a home, or they didn't have room for them, or because they didn't have the veterinary services or the money for medications to treat the sick ones.

"I dream about being able to open a free clinic the shelters could turn to for medical services, so none of the animals would have to be put down. But it would require constant funding, and the shelters would need more, too. And the likelihood of that is, I won't say impossible, but it would be close."

"I understand."

She knew the woman truly did understand, because she'd worked with her in the surgery since they first opened. She was an excellent vet tech, an expert anesthesiologist, and conscientious and caring with the animals they treated. "Call me if you need me."

"I will."

Piper peeled the paper booties off her feet, dropped them in the waste bin, and left the surgery. She checked on the other surgical patients, then spent some time in her office updating the charts of the three dogs she'd operated on this morning. After calling each owner and notified them of their progress, she double-checked the notations for medications for each animal, including antibiotics and anti-inflammatory pain medications for the Scottish terrier, and went back into the recovery area to hang each chart on the board there.

She checked the terrier again and found him groggy, but already waking. The swelling around his eye socket was noticeable but not extreme. It was a miracle the stick hadn't penetrated farther. She gave him a gentle rub and closed the kennel door.

She hung her stethoscope around her neck and walked down the hall to the front desk.

Sherry looked up from printing out a receipt for a client. "I have a note for you, Dr. Bertinelli." She extended the receipt and a bag of medication to the customer and waited for the man to leave. She picked up an envelope from beside her computer and extended it to Piper. Sherry lowered her voice. "It was mixed in with the mail delivered today, but doesn't have a stamp or return address."

Piper reluctantly reached for the envelope. "Thanks, Sherry. It's probably just a note from a client." She turned aside to tear open the envelope and pulled out a piece of paper. In bold, black words it read, *Have you told your boyfriend about your past?* The message drove the breath from her lungs and turned her stomach inside out.

She crumpled the note and envelope into a ball and darted into the bathroom off the reception area. Tears blurred her vision while sickness burned its way up her throat.

He knew she was back. He knew where she was. And he was coming after her again. She realized she was murmuring *oh God, oh God, oh God* and forced herself to stop. The crumpled note she still gripped made her feel sick every time she looked at it. But she couldn't throw it away. It was proof he was planning to harass her again.

She slipped out of the bathroom and stumbled down the hall to her office, closed herself in and locked the door. Every muscle in her body jerked she sank to the floor behind her desk and curled into the corner. She had to think. She had to plan what she could do.

As soon as the trauma eased, the need to see Zach, to hear his voice, took over. Every moment she'd spent with him the last two days played through her mind. They hadn't been out of each other's sight from Saturday afternoon till this morning. They cooked together, walked the beach, showered together, bathed and cared for the dogs, and made love. The way he made love to her that morning played through her mind.

She gripped the corner of her desk, dragged herself to her feet, and fell into her desk chair. She checked the time. She only had thirty minutes until she could leave. She called the front desk.

"Sherry, I need you to page Dr. Dorsey and ask him to cover for me for the next half hour. I'm not feeling very well."

"I saw you dodge into the restroom up here. Are you okay? Do you need a ride home? Tony's here and can drive you."

"No, I'll be okay. I just need to go home and lie down."

"I'll buzz Dr. Dorsey right now."

Two minutes later, Sherry buzzed her back on her phone. "He says he'll check in on your surgical patients and for you to go on home."

"Thank you. I'll let you know about my evening shift in plenty of time."

"Okay, Dr. Bertinelli. Feel better."

Piper thanked her, opened her desk drawer, and got her purse. She crammed the note into her bag and got her keys.

She scanned the parking lot from the corner of the building. Was he here watching for her? The cars in the lot all looked empty. She hurried to her car and got in.

She had to tell Zach.

Her hands felt slick with sweat on the steering wheel as she wove through noon traffic toward his apartment, but she had calmed somewhat by the time she pulled into his driveway.

She caught the sound of Zach's laughter, and instead of going to the front door she walked around to the back patio. The smell of grilled meat drifted to her on the ocean breeze. Using a long pair of tongs Zach flipped chicken breasts cooking on the grill. Gracie had a squeak toy in her mouth, Trouble's favorite. She rolled on her back while squeezing the toy, making it chatter like a chipmunk.

Zach looked up from the grill and smiled. "Hey, you're a little early." He shut the top of the grill and limped toward her. Seeing her expression, he slowed. "What is it?"

She withdrew the crumpled envelope and paper from her bag

and handed it to him. "This was left with Sherry, our receptionist, today. I saw him on Saturday at the grocery store, but...I was praying he hadn't seen me. Praying he'd leave me alone."

He smoothed the paper and read the words. His dark auburn brows locked in a V.

The dogs leaped to their feet, and Trouble let out a deep base bark.

Two men appeared from the driveway, both dressed in suits.

Piper caught her breath when recognition struck like a hammer blow.

No! The one-word denial caught in her throat even as fear wreaked havoc with every nerve and cell. She had hoped never to see him again in this lifetime. He sauntered across the yard to the concrete patio with the same confident swagger she remembered. Every muscle in her body locked and there was a metallic taste in her mouth. She realized she'd bitten the inside of her cheek.

CHAPTER 23

ZACH LOOKED OVER his shoulder. He didn't recognize either man. Seeing the telltale bulge of a sidearm at the first man's waist Zach, took a protective step between Piper and the two strangers.

"Ensign O'Connor?" the first man asked.

"Yes."

"I'm Detective Marcus Sherman." He flashed his badge. "And this is Detective Sam Lester. We've been calling. We wanted to go over the report you filed with the patrol officers the other day."

"I left my cell phone in the house." Zach glanced in Piper's direction, and then did a double-take. He'd once seen the face of a guy who'd stepped on an IED seconds before it had gone off. The man's expression of abject fear and shock had stuck in his mind for months. Every time he closed his eyes it had come back to him. The similarity to expression on Piper's face set off a flood of adrenaline, and every protective instinct raged to life in him.

"Hello, Dr. Bertinelli," Detective Sherman said with a nod.

She nodded, but her eyes were riveted on the man standing next to him.

Zach slipped an arm around Piper's waist and drew her against his body. She was stiff and her eyes focused, unblinking and dark. "Excuse us for a moment." He guided her away from the men and turned to block her view of the Detective Lester.

"What is it, Piper?"

It was a moment before she could speak. "He's the man who left the note." Her voice wobbled. "The robbery at the restaurant... The man who killed my father was someone the man I was dating owed money to. He was there to shoot me because he thought I had the money. Detective Lester accused me of being responsible, hounded me for months....". She shook her head. "He nearly destroyed me...my family." Her eyes pleaded with him as she met his gaze. "I had to file a harassment suit to get him to leave me alone."

He'd been curious enough to go online and look up the shooting, but none of this was in the newspaper account. Shock ricocheted through him and brought his protective instincts to bear. He'd never seen anyone so pale who was still standing. He wanted to comfort her, take her into the apartment and urge her to lie down, but the detectives were waiting and watching. "I think the dogs need to go in. Can you take them in for me? I'll get rid of these guys, and then we'll talk."

It took a moment for her to respond. She nodded. She gripped Trouble's collar, urged him into the apartment. "Come, Gracie."

Zach paused a moment to gain control of the emotions crashing through him. This was what she was going to tell him. But there was more, he was certain of it. He had only known Piper a few days, but her self-description earlier in the week—"neurotic, worrywart, am I doing the right thing" said it all. She could no more bring harm to her family or anyone else than she would him. They were the words of a woman profoundly fearful of doing the wrong thing.

And this detective had something to do with her constant vigilance, and possibly her half-fearful, self-contained attitude.

He turned back to the two detectives to find Gracie standing at attention, her gaze focused on the two men, her nose working. She had taken up a defensive position between the officers and him.

"Se désister, Gracie." He gave the order for her to stand

down. "Don't move, guys. She knows you're armed." He opened the sliding glass door, led her in, and closed the door. The Malinois stood at attention on three legs, her eyes bright and her attention still directed at the two detectives.

He turned back to the two men.

"Isn't it dangerous for you to have a dog like that?" Lester, the heavier of the two, mopped his round face and tucked the handkerchief into his pocket. He stood five nine or ten, but appeared shorter because of his short neck and barrel chest. The sleeves of his jacket strained against the muscles beneath, and there was an aggressive cast to his expression.

Detective Sherman was taller and leaner, but in as good shape as Lester, though he appeared to be at least a decade older. His hair was iron gray, though his brows were dark. He projected calm and reason, where Lester had a pugnacious quality. They'd probably be the perfect duo to do the good cop, bad cop thing.

"Not if you're not armed or packing explosives. She's trained to attack on command. She was on alert and waiting for my word." Zach glanced at the grill. "Take a seat." He nodded toward the table. "Just give me a moment to take up the chicken I have on the grill."

He tucked the note Piper had handed him under the plate of meat, then covered the plate with a strip of paper towels and turned off the grill.

"What can I do for you, Detectives?"

Sherman spoke first. "I want to follow up on your earlier statement and see if you remember anything else."

"I pretty much covered everything that happened from the time I left the hospital emergency room to when I arrived at the vet's office with Gracie. Gracie's blood would have still been on the street where everything took place. I told the officers where to look."

"Do you have experience, caring for a dog like that?" Lester asked.

"I have experience with dogs and with military working dogs, since we work with both the handlers and the dogs during missions. And Master Chief Flynn, her owner, has confidence I can handle her until he gets out of the hospital. She very well trained."

"Did Dr. Bertinelli do her surgery?" Lester asked.

"Yes, she did. Any other vet would have probably amputated the leg, but she went the extra mile, and thus far Gracie's doing well. We're both keeping a close eye on her."

"How long have you and she been dating?" he asked.

Detective Sherman frowned and shot a look in his partner's direction.

Zach braced his elbows on the top of the table. "My personal life has no bearing on Master Chief Flynn's case or the robberies, Detective."

Sherman cut in hastily. "Will you go over everything that happened one more time for us?"

Zach started with the trip to the emergency room, what time he left the hospital, and how he'd come to miss the man running but hit Gracie. He described her injury, his battlefield care of her injury, and the rush to the vet.

"Were you aware at the time that the vet's office had been broken into the same morning?" Sherman asked.

"No. And Piper didn't say anything about it until the next day, when we went to visit Master Chief Flynn."

Lester scowled. "How was it you put the attack and the burglaries together, Ensign?"

"Piper mentioned the guys who'd broken in stole meds, but also took other supplies and accessed their computer files. I saw an article in the paper about local veterinary offices being burglarized and asked the master chief what vet normally cared for Gracie. It was one of those mentioned in the article. It didn't take any major leaps in logic to figure out that the master chief's attack might be connected to the vet robberies. They could have accessed his address at his vet's office, learned he had a military-trained Malinois, and decided they could get big bucks by selling her. They're looking for large breeds. Maybe building a dog-fighting ring, running puppy mills, selling them to laboratories, or all three."

Detective Sherman broke in. "That's speculation, Ensign O'Connor. We'd appreciate it if you wouldn't spread it around."

He raised a brow. Who the hell would he tell? "I won't." He returned his interest to Lester again and waited for the next question.

"So you and Dr. Bertinelli have talked at length about this?"

"Some. I wouldn't say at length."

"Whose idea was it to call her customers?"

"We talked about it in the car on the way back from visiting the master chief." He thought of her defensiveness about not calling right away. She'd been anxious and worried about what he thought. Not the behavior of a criminal. "Piper was concerned about their clients and their animals. She called you when she had time between patients that evening."

Lester glanced at his partner. Detective Sherman nodded, but lines had begun to bracket his mouth, and he was eyeing Lester.

Anyone with two eyes could see Lester had a hard-on for Piper. He could see it. Surely the man's partner did as well.

Lester got to his feet and reached for his jacket. "We need to interview her again instead of receiving this information second hand."

Zach stood and shifted position, hemming the detective in between the lounges. "She won't speak with you, Detective Lester."

Lester's deep-set eyes gleamed. "Does she have something to hide?"

"No. But we both know you have. Have you told your partner how you know Piper, and why you're so interested in her?" He glanced at Sherman.

Sherman clearly had no clue what was going on, but tried to hide it behind the deadpan calm.

Zach turned to Sherman. "Did he ask to work this case with you?"

Sherman's expression remained neutral. "We have quite a few detectives working on it."

"Good. The more guys you have on this, the quicker you'll find the assholes responsible." Zach folded his arms and met Detective Lester's threatening look. "In the meantime, I'll be covering Piper's six. I'm off because of an injury and have nothing else to do."

Whatever she might have done, she wasn't a criminal mastermind. If Lester had looked that closely at her before and been unable to arrest her, she wasn't guilty. And she'd never hurt an animal. She was too caring of the ones in her charge.

Lester stepped into his space, in an attempt to intimidate. Zach raised a brow and stood his ground. He'd had bigger, badder men in his face than this asshole. And those were the good guys, who trained him to remain cool under pressure. What he sensed about Lester was he wasn't a badass, but a bully. Lester had decided Piper was the one who got away, and he was using this opportunity to get in a few more hits at her. Zach would be damned if he'd let the man anywhere near her.

"I'm going to give you some free advice, Ensign. Don't get tangled up with her. Men who do end up either dead or in jail."

Jesus, this guy was a real piece of work. "My father's a police officer, Detective. He's been with the Boston PD for twenty-five years. He says the worst thing a cop can do is get tunnel vision about a case. It causes you to make mistakes and overlook things. If you're looking at Piper for this, you might want to have your eyes checked."

He shifted his gaze to Sherman. "If I think of anything helpful, I'll give you a call, Detective Sherman. I'm certain Piper will be willing to speak to you alone. You're welcome to come in and talk to her now, but without Detective Lester."

Sherman's features were stiff. "I'll call and go by her office tomorrow."

Zach gave Sherman a nod, gathered the chicken with the note and limped to the door. He slid open the back door and Gracie sat up, ears forward, eyes bright. He set the food on the stove, gathered the note, and stood at the door until Lester and Sherman strode around the apartment to the street.

Gracie wagged her tail and he bent to give her a rub. She hobbled after him from the kitchen to the living room. Piper sat in the floor, her back propped against the couch. Trouble lay next to her, but reared to his feet and nearly bowled him over with enthusiasm, though he hadn't seen him for days instead of a few minutes. His tail waved like a blond palm frond.

"Gracie insisted on staying by the door until you came in," Piper said. She'd been crying, and her lashes were clumped with tears.

Gracie eyed Trouble with aloof superiority, but deigned to touch noses with him. He went into a wiggly I'm-so-happy-to-have-a-new-friend production until she yapped at him. He immediately settled down and trailed along behind her as she went to Piper and head-butted her gently for attention.

Zach watched how naturally Piper gathered her close. Gracie folded herself to lie down next to her on one side, while Trouble took the other.

He'd read somewhere that dogs could sense human emotion. Or was it the change in the pheromones? Whatever it was, the Malinois laid her head on Piper's leg and looked up at him as if to say, *What are you going to do about this?*

He sought something neutral to begin with. "She's doing okay, isn't she?"

"Very well. The problem will be keeping her calm when she starts to feel better. She'll believe she can do everything she used to do well before her leg and hip are ready for it."

A wry smile twisted his lips. "I can identify with that."

He sank into one of the leather chairs across from her, and although it felt too far away, she appeared to have all the comfort she had room for right now.

"How did it go?" she asked, while she seemed to concentrate hard on every stroke she made over Gracie's head.

"Lester wanted to question you again."

She glanced toward the kitchen, her features tense with dread.

"I told him you wouldn't talk to him. Sherman didn't know about the history between you, I'm certain of it. He said he'd call and come by your office tomorrow."

"Lester will be back." She leaned her neck back against the couch cushion and closed her eyes, baring the fragile slope of her throat and the delicate thrust of her collarbones.

"Tell me what happened."

She lifted her head as though it was too heavy to lift. "I was in my junior year in college, and had just turned nineteen. I met David at a party." She ran a hand over her wet lashes. "He was funny and charming, and everyone seemed to gravitate toward him. I thought it was because of his personality. It was because he was dealing drugs, but I didn't find out until nearly three weeks later. By then, I realized he was using and I broke it off.

"I was afraid he might get arrested or overdose, so I went to his parents and told them what was going on. They got him into a four-week rehab. The minute he got out, he came back around. But my family had found out about the drug issues, and they were hounding me to stay away from him at the same time he was pressuring me to get back together.

"I moved out of the house and into an apartment with three other girls. It was a planned move. I'd already signed the lease before he went into rehab, and I couldn't leave the other girls holding the bag on the rent, so I went ahead and moved in."

She cupped a hand to her forehead. "It was a big mistake. The girls I lived with didn't realize how charming and how determined David could be when he wanted his way, so he was able to sweet-talk his way into the apartment on several occasions.

"His mom and dad started pressuring me. They kept saying what a good influence I was on him. I was the reason he agreed to rehab to begin with.

"I realized later that what they wanted was a watchdog. I'd gone to them before when he was out of control, and they wanted me to keep an eye on him since they couldn't."

Absently, she brushed her hand over Trouble's large head and massaged his ear. "It wasn't the first or even second time he'd been in trouble for selling drugs or using them. He just hadn't been caught, or when he had, they'd gotten him off with a slap on the wrist."

She tucked back the strand of rich brown hair that had fallen against her cheek. "He swore to me he'd cleaned up, and he was over the drugs. So I agreed to see him again. Things went okay for a couple of weeks, until he—"

She wrapped her arms around Trouble and held him close. "He did something, and I knew he was using again. I broke it off for good. I told my roommates not to let him back in the apartment. I blocked his number from my phone, changed my email address. I threatened him with a restraining order."

A hollow feeling struck Zach's stomach when she looked up.

"I couldn't permit him to affect my future. I was afraid if I was with him when he was arrested with drugs it might affect my ability to get into vet school. You can't hold a vet or doctor's license with a drug arrest on your record."

"A week later David was stopped with heroin and cocaine in his trunk. A lot of both. They arrested him."

"He accused me of turning him in. He'd been by my mom's house earlier that day, begging me to take him back. I told him if he didn't leave I'd call the police, and the police received an anonymous tip a couple of hours later accusing David of transporting and selling drugs. His parents accused me of calling them and of taking advantage of him. After they begged me to take him back, they accused me of taking money from him, drug money."

Her voice took on a note of outrage. "I was working two part-time jobs, and going to school on the scholarship I worked my butt off to get. I didn't have any money, and he certainly never gave me any.

"David made bail, but was under house arrest. But he still had access to a phone. He contacted his supplier, Duardo Acosta, and told him he'd given me the money he owed him.

"I was showing out the last customer and about to lock the door when Acosta shoved into the restaurant. He knocked me down, waved a gun at me, and threatened to shoot me if I didn't give him the money."

She drew her knees up and wrapped her arms around them. "I

didn't know who he was. My father walked in. He tried to talk him down, to give him the money out of the register and he—he shot him." She caught her breath and it sounded close to a sob. "He'd have shot me too, but he didn't have his money yet. One of the wait staff heard what was going down and dialed nine-one-one, and the sirens were getting close. He ran out of the restaurant."

Her restless movements were driving him crazy. Her body language was screaming pain and fear. His instinct was to go to her, lift her into his lap and comfort her.

"Detective Lester interviewed me for the first time the night my father was killed. Duardo Acosta insisted I had the twenty-five thousand dollars. David had told him I did. Then Lester interviewed David and his parents. Everyone else involved in the drug case. And that's when he decided I was guilty. That I was involved in the drug business somehow, and I had the money.

"I'd go to class and come out, and he'd be there waiting on me. He hauled me into the station six times before my mother got a lawyer, and we filed harassment charges and threatened to sue. He told my family it was my fault my father was killed. He harassed the other members of my family, encouraging them to turn me in. He wanted them to get me to confess that I'd sold drugs or at least still had the money for David. My sister, Teresa, quit speaking to me. My brother Lorenzo asked me point blank if I had the money. He was disrupting their lives and making it as hard for them as it was for me, and he completely destroyed their trust in me."

Tears streamed down her face. "He made the loss of my father seem a byproduct instead of the most important, painful thing that had ever happened in our lives. Wasn't the fact that Acosta and David were murderers more important than anything else?"

Zach rose and got some tissue from the bathroom.

She closed her eyes and he read the struggle to regain her composure.

"My last year and a half of college, I pulled away from my family so he'd have no reason to harass them anymore. I avoided going to the restaurant or going home on the weekends, but he was still hounding me every chance he got. I'd think he was finally done, and he'd just pop up at a restaurant where I was eating or at the grocery store."

"I just kept putting one foot in front of the other and working toward finishing my degree. It was all I had left." She paused for a shaky breath. "I didn't have anything else to hold on to. I would study myself into a coma rather than give myself time to think…to remember…" She pressed the heels of her hands against her eyes and remained silent for a long moment. "Lester did everything he could to make my life hell."

Her despair and grief deepened the hollow feeling in the pit of his stomach.

She dropped her hands. "I applied for financial aid and grants. Then, right after I graduated, I got another job to go with the two I already had and waited for vet school to start in the fall. Two weeks before school started, I moved up to U C Davis and roomed with three other women to save money. For a while I thought I'd finally been able to leave it behind.

"I stayed on campus for the most part. I went home with one of my roommates for Thanksgiving. I hadn't been home in months, and my mom begged me to come for Christmas. He—he was parked across the street on Christmas Day, watching the house."

At the weariness in her expression, Zach shifted, his muscles tight with emotion, but he didn't want to distract her. He needed to hear it all, see it all in her face.

"I took pictures of him with my phone, and I went outside and took pictures of his license plate while he drove away. I filed a complaint, but it was ignored. He said he had business in the neighborhood, and they believed him.

"In January, he came up to Davis and interviewed some of my professors. He told them I was involved in a drug case. He tried to get me kicked out of school. I contacted a lawyer, an expert in civil liberties. She took depositions from every person he'd interviewed. She filed a harassment suit, and I reported him for violating my civil liberties. We filed a restraining order against him in the county I lived in. My lawyer presented them to the district attorney's office there, and he contacted the district attorney here.

"Internal affairs went through both my father's case and David's. They interviewed my roommates, my family, and everyone else involved, including David and his parents, and went through my bank account, my computer, and all the social media accounts I had closed months before. Every dime I'd spent at school. They traced everything."

"Their finding was there was no evidence to support that I had any illegal money, or that I had ever sold drugs. I had a clean record."

"They looked through all the paperwork Lester filed, all the interviews he'd done, and filed a disciplinary action against him, suspended him for four months, and ordered him to stay away from me. It was only then that some members of my family started to think I might be innocent."

She remained silent for a moment, her features blank with loss. "By then it was too late."

"David accepted a plea deal with the understanding he would have to testify against Acosta. It was two years before Acosta went to trial for killing my father. He got life because he already had two arrests for drug distribution, and they were able to connect the killing to the drug distribution.

"During the trial—I might as well have been put on trial, too, and of course the money came up again. Lester made sure it did during his testimony. And he tried every way he could to point the finger at me while he was on the stand. He could have messed up the conviction of Acosta, but he wouldn't have cared as long as he got to me."

Her large brown eyes looked smudged with exhaustion now the adrenaline was wearing off. "If I'd had the money, no matter where it came from, I'd have given it to Acosta. I'd have given him anything to save my father. No one thought to ask me about that." She drew her knees up again and rested her arms atop them.

She raised her head to look up at him. "If Lester can figure out a way to turn this on me, he will. This will give him a toehold to start all over again. I'm over a hundred thousand dollars in debt between my school loans and my part of the business, and I can't afford for him to start stalking me again, and taking me in for questioning over and over. He'll damage our business if he can."

"Take it easy," Zach soothed, and waited, giving her time to regroup. "Have you tried to figure out what David might have done with the money?'

"Of course." She threw out a hand in frustration. "He said he put it in the back of my car in a small black backpack. But the police searched my car, my mom's car, every car at my parents' house that day, and it wasn't there. They searched my apartment, my mom's house, David's house. It was never found. The longer it was missing, the guiltier I looked to him.

"For a while I was obsessed with finding it to prove my innocence. I racked my brain, trying to figure out who he might have left it with, or where he could have hidden it. But then I realized if I found it and tried to turn it in, Detective Lester would say I had it all along, and I'd be right back where I started. He'd arrest me no matter what I did. So I let it go. I didn't want to take the chance."

Zach could certainly understand. When you have a vicious dog on your tail, you didn't go around poking him with a stick. Or maybe you do, to get him to move in the direction you wanted him to. He'd have to give that some thought.

Zach rose from the leather chair. If he'd left the money with someone, they'd have spent it by now. Twenty-five thousand dollars would be a huge temptation to have lying around. Whoever had it could have nickeled and dimed it until they spent every bit of it without drawing attention.

Even Piper could have done that. But she wouldn't have played dumb with a gun in her face. She'd have given up the money to save her father.

Chances are it would never be found. Unless this guy David's parents had it.

He extended his hand.

She allowed him to pull her to her feet. "I need to leave, Zach. I need to get far away from you, so he doesn't drag you into this."

If she walked away now, he'd never see her again. He knew it as surely as he knew the color of her eyes. Eyes he'd looked into while he thrust inside her. They'd shared their bodies, but they'd shared a lot of other things, too. They made a connection, and he wasn't ready to break it. Not yet.

"If you walk away, Piper, it will give Lester exactly what he wants. You'll be isolating yourself from your friends and family like you did before. It will make it easier for him to stalk you without witnesses."

"I don't want to cause you any trouble. Any time you're with me, you'll be a target. You can't afford to get drawn into this. He'll figure out a way to bring you in for questioning, cause trouble for you. Damage your career."

She was giving him every opportunity to step away from her, from the situation.

His stomach knotted in a visceral reaction to the hunted look on her face, in her eyes. He recognized the obsessive worry about doing the wrong thing, saw her wariness when they first met for what it was. He'd seen that the same look in his sister's eyes, sometimes still did when she was having a bad day.

"Detective Sherman didn't know about Lester's history with you. I'd bank on it."

"I've been down this road before. Even if he's curious enough to look into it, he won't do anything to stop Lester."

"Invite him to come here instead of your office at lunchtime. I'll stay with you while you talk to him. Ask him to help you find the money so you can move on with your life."

Her dark eyes searched his face. "How can you believe me when my family doesn't?"

CHAPTER 24

WHY WAS HE so sure she'd had nothing to do with drugs or the money? And how could he give trust when her own family wouldn't believe in her?

A tentative hope rushed up to collide with her doubt.

He cocked his head to one side and studied her. "If you had the money, you'd have taken off to places unknown and spent it. Family or no family, you wouldn't have moved back to the city you came from, and started a business where Lester could continue to get at you.

"Because in the seven years since your father's death, if you had the money, you'd have found a way to turn it in to get Lester off your back. You could have shipped it to the police station with a note, or left it on Lester's front porch. He never would have been able to connect you to it. It would have been a way to get back to your family.

"You drive a ten-year-old car, probably the same car you were driving when you first started college. You're also carrying a large debt, and the temptation to use the money would be damn strong, but you haven't."

All good arguments, but he still didn't get it.

She sat down and ran a hand over her face again. "Zach, you don't know what it's like having Lester after you. He has the power and you have none. If you complain to anyone, they act like they've heard it a million times before, because they have. And they look at you like you're just another criminal complaining about the system."

"I hear what you're saying. But Lester has a history with you. A history his own people know about. And now Detective Sherman knows about it too. It's not going to be as easy for him to convince people you still have the money. Or convince them to okay it for him to search your house or car. And he's welcome to search mine. There's nothing here for him to find. Every one of my weapons is registered, locked up in a gun safe, or on post. Other than them, I don't have a stash of anything to find."

It hit her stomach first, the relief of it. He really did believe her. Then it hit a little higher, dead center in her chest. Her eyes blurred as the tears rose up.

Even though she was attempting to rebuild her relationship with her mother and siblings, they still wanted proof of her innocence…and she had none.

She didn't have to prove anything to Zach. He believed her.

The weight she'd carried lifted a tiny bit, and she could breathe fully, deeply, for the first time since returning to San Diego nine months before.

She pushed herself to her feet, drew a deep breath and attempted to control her shaking. She felt exposed physically, emotionally. If she denied having anything to do with the money one more time, would it make her seem guilty?

"It's okay, Piper."

"I need to go, Zach. I need to…" If he changed his mind, it would crush her. She didn't want to buy into his trust then have it vanish overnight. "You need to think about this. We both do."

"We can think about it together."

He reached for her arm, and she sidestepped, avoiding his touch.

"We won't think." She didn't want to think. She wanted to believe. She wanted this, him, too much.

"You're offering this too easily. You need time to realize what you'll be facing." She bent to grab her purse. "He'll make you hate me. He'll hound you until you're sick of it, and you'll have to walk away."

Zach's features had settled into stubborn, intense lines. "I don't scare so easily, Piper. I've faced worse things than Lester."

Her heart ached for him. The tears rose up again and threatened to spill. She didn't want that kind of existence for him. "He'll wear you down. I don't want you to hate me like... You don't want this." She cut the words off before she said too much. "Trouble, come." She slapped her thigh to call him to her.

The golden retriever dragged his feet, head and tail down, until he stood next to her. She'd never realized a dog could look woeful. He'd fallen for Zach, with his tireless throwing arm and his patient affection.

Just as she had.

"You don't have to go, Piper."

Her resolve weakened to crumbling.

She grasped at control and raised her head to look at him. "You only know part of it. There's more. There's my family. You don't need the drama. You have enough in your life."

She should have never agreed to go out with him, never slept with him. Regret was already eating her alive. She'd never meet anyone else like him. She grabbed the leash from the table next to the door and, juggling her purse, slipped the choke chain over Trouble's head.

Zach stepped between her and the door, his features taut with determination. "Then show me the rest. I at least deserve to know the whole picture."

She couldn't tell him everything. She'd buried it as deep as she could so she could try to forget. "You saw how my family was at the restaurant. Circling us, checking on our conversation, my mother asking a thousand questions to make sure I hadn't hooked up with another drug dealer."

He grasped her wrist and ran a thumb back and forth along the curve of it. "I'll be okay, Piper. You don't have to worry about me," he said, his masculine expression tense and resolute.

He truly was pigheaded.

He obviously didn't understand what he was taking on. They'd take verbal potshots at him like they did her. Her composure cracked and her breath hitched. "I'm sorry, Zach." She'd wanted this, wanted him. "I'm sorry."

She jerked the front door open. The sea breeze hit her, bringing with it those perfect moments they'd spent on the beach, the two wonderful days they'd spent together, eating, talking, watching movies, in bed. It had been two perfect days. The sunlight stung her eyes. She opened the back door of her car and got Trouble harnessed in.

Zach's silent presence made it harder for her.

Her throat ached with unshed tears as she got in the car and backed out of his driveway.

ZACH PACED THROUGH his frustration until his hip ached and he had to stop. Gracie lay on her bed in the corner, her head on her paws and her gaze focused expectantly on him while she followed his movements.

He went back over everything Piper told him. He sat down at his computer and surfed the net for any further information about Piper's father's murder and the man who shot him. He read through the articles systematically, and the coverage of the trial was detailed. Luca Bertinelli ran a popular business, and had been beloved by many people in the community.

Acosta was a businessman, too. He ran drugs and weapons, had numerous arrests, and had shot Bertinelli while trying to kill his daughter. He shot at Piper, too, and missed, something she hadn't told him.

He did a search for Detective Lester, but the only things he found, besides a comment about his testimony during the trial, were a couple of quotes he'd given about another case. He fished his cell phone out of his pocket and keyed down until he reached Brett Weaver's number. They hadn't talked since his wedding the summer before, but they kept up with each other through sporadic emails. He pushed the button and waited for Brett's phone to connect.

"Hey Doc, what's happenin'?"

"I'm on injured leave and thought I'd check in on you. Are you on CONUS?"

"No. And I can't swear as to the strength of this signal, so if it cuts out…"

"Understood. Scuttlebutt is three to four weeks for us. I'm hoping to be in better shape before it goes down."

"Will you be joining us?" Brett was back in Afghanistan for the third time.

"Possibly. I'd prefer a dry heat to the humidity down south." They were so used to talking in code around their family it was second nature. Even with terrorists threatening them at every turn, he preferred Afghanistan to South America with its bug-infested humidity and snakes of both the animal kingdom and the human drug cartel nature.

"I want to ask a favor. I need some information on someone, and I thought Tess might be able to help me out. She has contacts in the police department I don't have access to."

"What kind of someone?"

"A cop."

Brett remained silent for a moment.

"I'm dating someone, Cutter, and he's already been called in by internal affairs and reprimanded for stalking her. I want to know who I'm dealing with."

"My instinct is to protect my wife. I'm not there to watch her six."

Shit, what had he been thinking? Zach understood that. "It's okay, Cutter. I'll tug on a few lines of my own and see what I can find out."

"What's his name? I'll pass it along when I speak to her and see if she knows something without having to ask around."

"No. If you do, she'll feel compelled to look into him. I'd cut my own throat before I'd put Tess in harm's way. Is there any message you want me to pass on if I see her? We'll probably have a get together before we go wheels up."

"If you see my mom, tell her I'm ready to walk her down the aisle any time. She just has to say the word. And tell the rest of the ladies they are missed."

"Will do."

"Tell Tess I'm be ready to work on the project we've been discussing as soon as I get home. And that I miss her."

"She's not going to smack me for saying that, is she?"

Brett laughed. "No. We're talking about buying a house."

In a surge of relief Zach breathed a sigh. "Roger that. Watch your six, man."

"Will do."

Time to go to plan B. He scrolled for Flash's number and punched it. He had better luck this time. He arranged for Flash to come by the vet's office to see what kind of alarm system they would need. Flash also offered to poke around and see what other information about Lester he could get off the 'net. Once off the phone, Zach continued to stew.

He'd been burned by Patricia, and, as concerned as he was about Piper's situation, he had to think of the emotional toll if he got involved, or how it might affect his career. He couldn't just go at this with a knee-jerk reaction. But to leave her hanging and vulnerable went against everything he believed in.

Gracie went to the door to signal she needed to go out. He rose, clipped her halter on, and hooked her leash to it. They slowly circled the yard while he used a trenching tool to clean up after her. Once inside. She followed him to the couch to be loved. And for a few minutes his mind was on the injured dog. After he fed her and gave her the meds Piper prescribed, Gracie eased up beside him on the couch, and he cuddled her close.

He'd bet the master chief didn't allow her on the furniture. "You know master chief is going to rip me a new one if you get spoiled to this."

She turned on her back for a belly rub. He hadn't the heart to put her off the couch.

He and Piper could have had a nice lunch, maybe watched a

movie with some cuddle time, and maybe a little something more. Instead…he was here, loving on a dog.

Damn that fucker Lester.

He cut his thoughts off when the idea he might not see her again began to form. She was so determined to protect everyone but herself. Because of that cocksucker. He was not going to leave her alone with this problem. It was not happening. Then why hadn't he gone to the expert first?

He picked up the phone from the end table next to him and dialed a number. "Dad, I have a problem."

NO MATTER WHAT she did or how hard she tried not to think about Zach, she couldn't ease the ache of loss clawing her ribcage like a live thing trapped inside. She'd cried until her eyes were raw and her head ached.

She mustn't fall apart like this. She had to keep pushing forward. But when did it end? When would she be able to live a peaceful life?

As she went through the routine chores of doing the laundry and taking care of Trouble, Piper dwelled on those last fraught moments at Zach's house. He believed her. His trust meant everything to her. But it promised him nothing but trouble.

He was a SEAL. After first meeting him, she'd read about their training. Over the weekend, they'd talked about how his command held them to a higher standard. A single DUI or arrest for anything could affect their career. They had to conduct themselves with as much impeccability and dedication off the battlefield as they did on, or lose the privilege of being a SEAL. Even if he didn't do anything wrong, Lester could make it appear he had and mess things up for him. He'd tried it numerous times with her.

She had refused to risk her future for David. She couldn't let Zach risk his for her.

Exhaustion weighted her body, and she went into her bedroom and stretched out across the faded quilt she used for a spread. The pillow didn't smell like Zach. It smelled like her. The bed seemed so empty without him there to mold his body against hers and hold her.

Trouble padded into the room and jumped up on the bed, pawing at the faded blanket, making a nest at her feet. She patted the bed next to her and he immediately wiggled up to lie beside her. She stroked his face and smoothed the heavy layer of fur around his neck and down his chest. He made a sound like a sigh and closed his eyes.

What would she do without Trouble? He had been her one constant in the past three years. She had cried into his fur more times than she could count, and had always gotten comfort from his closeness. He loved her unconditionally, was always happy to see her, whether she had been away five minutes or five hours.

She needed more, though. She needed Zach.

In just a few days, he had filled the emptiness of her life with laughter and the many other things that made him so special. And now everything felt different because he had opened her up to a need she denied herself, denied even existed. The need to be touched, to be held, to feel affection and have it returned. To trust.

He had given her a gift. Shown her she could be with a man without fear, and without the flashbacks.

But the only thing she could bring to him in return was trouble.

She loved him. It nestled inside her, giving her comfort despite the ache, but nothing could stem the tears. If she truly loved him, she must do what was best for him.

But how many sacrifices did she have to make in the name of love? She had abandoned her family to keep them from being hounded. She'd taken on the responsibility of dealing with Detective Lester alone.

And what had she gotten for her sacrifice? For every moment of fear she experienced when Acosta pointed his gun at her head, Lester had multiplied it by ten. He had trivialized her father's death, and the anguish she and her family suffered, by putting the price tag of a paltry twenty-five thousand dollars on it. And he had turned her family against her.

She was already reverting to old habits, acting as if she had no choice. She was clinging to the one thing she had to make up for everything she was losing.

She was allowing Detective Samuel Lester to dictate who she could or couldn't have in her life.

She deserved a normal life, with friends, family, and someone special.

It had to stop. He had to be stopped.

But how?

How?

The night passed slowly. Piper dozed off and on, but woke frequently, her heart drumming anxiously and her hands reaching for someone who wasn't there.

At six-thirty she stumbled into the bathroom, a headache pounding at her temples. She shook out two Tylenol and downed them with a little water. Standing in the shower for ten minutes seemed to help. She dressed, fixed her hair, twisting it back with a clip, and put on her shoes.

When she called Trouble's name, he slinked into the living room from the kitchen, head down and tail tucked between his legs. He hated going into the kennel. She hated putting him in it. It was to protect him from getting into things. She felt guilty and he was miserable. Something had to change.

She grabbed his leash and clipped it to his collar, unlocking the door and stepping out on the stoop.

Her heart leapt when she saw the black SUV parked behind her car. Zach leaned back against the front quarter panel, a to-go cup of coffee in his hand. Gracie sat at his feet. He straightened and waited for Piper and Trouble to reach him.

Tears welled up and she ducked her head until she beat them back.

"I got you one," he said motioning to another cup of coffee on the hood. He bent to love on Trouble, and even Gracie greeted the dog with a nose touch and a wagging tail, then came to Piper.

Piper cupped the dog's face in her hands and kissed the top of her head.

Aware of the dark bags under her eyes, Piper focused on the coffee cup Zach offered her.

"I called some people last night. Flash is up for installing a security system with cameras at the clinic, if your partners agree to it. And Detective Sherman has agreed to interview you at my apartment at lunchtime today."

A knot lodged in her throat. She set aside the coffee. "If he comes after you, I want you to step away, Zach."

"I can't do that, Piper. It isn't how I'm made."

"I know." Her composure deserted her and buried her face against his chest. His arms surrounded her, and he held her tight. The sensation of a part of her clicking back into place eased her tears.

When he kissed her, he tasted like coffee and Zach. She looked into his face and saw evidence of a sleepless night etched into his features. He didn't offer her the useless platitude about how everything would be all right, but held her close again.

I love you. The words reverberated through her psyche, her heart. But she couldn't say them. He wasn't ready to hear them. He might never be.

But he was here in this moment.

And for now, they were together.

CHAPTER 25

KATHLEEN PLACED THE freshly laundered underwear in her suitcase and studied the outfits she'd selected. She'd chosen her clothing with care, because she wanted to look her best for Cal.

She stood back and studied each color-coordinated outfit, and was stunned to realize everything was neutral, colorless, and conservative. Nothing would draw attention to her figure or her coloring.

When had she become a stodgy, matronly schoolteacher? Even when she was at her most overweight she hadn't tried to hide or fade into the woodwork. She'd been her usual, boisterous, tomboyish self.

She ran her fingers through her hair and tugged at the thick strands.

What was happening to her?

She had gone into hiding.

She was losing herself.

She went back to her closet. The clothes hangers screeched against the bar while she dragged each blouse, dress and skirt forward and studied it, this time choosing things with color. If she took unexpected things, she'd be forced to wear them because she'd have nothing else.

How long had it been since she'd worn her red blouse? The

blouse she'd worn for her first date with Cal. She'd wear it for the trip, and maybe Cal would remember. He was good about noticing details, and he loved her in skirts and thongs. She'd wear the short black skirt and sandals and show off her legs.

Remind him of what he had left behind in San Diego.

He'd been gone a week, and it seemed like a month. Her apartment was too damn quiet. And his, when she went by to check on it, already had a stuffy, abandoned feel.

And she had to face what was truly bothering her, beyond the PTSD crap. What if he decided he needed to stay and run the business until his father was well enough to take it over?

They weren't engaged. They weren't married. They weren't living together.

She loved him. He loved her.

She had no doubts about their feelings for each other.

But relationships were difficult enough without trying to make them work long distance.

It was the main reason Zach didn't get involved. He dated. But he didn't get serious. Not since Patricia.

But there were men in his team who made it work. Couples who loved each other enough to remain devoted, no matter the distance between them or the number of days they were apart.

But Cal wasn't in the Marines any longer. He had the freedom to ask her to go with him.

But would he? Did she have to wait for him to ask before she could tell him she would be willing to relocate to wherever he wanted to live?

Please, God, if he makes that decision, let him ask me.

No, no. She was getting ahead of herself. It had only been a week. He had enough on his plate without worrying about a clingy girlfriend. She had to show him she was fine without him, even though every day seemed to go on forever.

How could she have ever thought she was in love with Lee? What she felt for him was tepid in comparison.

She took most of the clothing she'd packed out of the case, folded the other items, and put them in. She added a couple of pairs of comfortable flats and closed the bag.

She pressed the skirt and blouse, then spent some time in the bathroom fiddling with her makeup, taming her hair into a French twist. When she pulled out the tube of red lipstick Cal loved, she felt more herself. When she was dressed she felt the flutter of anticipation instead of the anxiety she lived with when getting dressed for work.

She was leaving what had happened here in San Diego behind, and was going to concentrate on being with Cal and getting to know his family. She had ten days to spend with them. Ten days they could get to know her.

She checked the clock every fifteen minutes, eager for Zach to arrive. When she heard the doorbell ring she smiled in relief.

Zach grinned when he saw her. "Wow. You're going to knock Cal's socks off, Sis."

Even though the compliment came from her brother, it still pleased her. "I hope so."

"You ready to go?"

"Yes."

When she reached for her suitcase he gripped the handle first. "I'll get it, Kathleen."

As he limped up the incline to the car she asked, "How's the hip?"

"Better."

"And how did your date go with the vet?" she continued. She hadn't seen or heard from Zach since he came by to get his hair trimmed. He looked tired, as though he hadn't slept well the night before.

"It was one of the best dates I've ever had."

"Really?"

"Yeah." He settled her suitcase in the back of the SUV.

Then he didn't expand on his answer, which was frustrating, but totally Zach. She looked at him closely while he got in the car.

"What did you do on your date?" she persisted.

He pulled out of the apartment parking lot. "Nothing spectacular. I couldn't do much because of the hip. We just hung out on the beach, took a drive, cooked some good food together, took care of the dogs. She has a golden retriever named Trouble."

Kathleen understood how spending time with the right person could be more powerful than partying or other frenetic pursuits.

"That's great. Was he trouble?"

"Actually, no. He was a little exuberant at times, and would catch balls for twenty-four hours straight if anyone would throw it for him. But he wasn't any trouble at all."

His gaze shifted from the road ahead then back to her. "Are you nervous about meeting Callahan's family?"

His change of topic triggered a wry smile. It was okay for her to ask about his life, but when the tables were turned...

"Yeah, I'm a little nervous."

"They're going to love you, Kathleen. You don't have anything to worry about."

"Thanks. But you're a little biased."

"Don't you ladies say you have a signature color you wear to make you feel ready for things? Yours is definitely red."

Zach was subtle as an elephant standing on her foot.

She laid a hand on his arm. "You don't have to worry about me. I'm back on medications and seeing Dr. Dowling again, and I'm already feeling better."

His shoulders relaxed. "Good." He shot her a smile that didn't quite cover his relief. He gripped her hand and raised it to his lips. "You're tough as an old boot, Thorn. I know you'll be just fine."

"Yes, I am. And I will." She heard herself telling him about the guys at work and the impromptu meeting. "It's already made a difference. I'm beginning to relax a little more in our pod."

"They sound like good guys," Zach said.

"They're better than I ever gave them credit for."

"A few of us are out there. It's just damn hard to stand out when surround by the turds. They seem to get more press."

Kathleen laughed, then turned serious. "These guys have gone out of their way from the very beginning to put me at ease. I don't know why I couldn't see it before."

"Sometimes traumatic experiences color our world in a way that blocks everything else out. It just takes some time to get past it. You're on your way now."

"Yeah, I am." She felt the possibilities hanging there, right in front of her. She just had to reach for them.

They passed the time talking about family until they reached the terminal.

"Are you sure you don't need me to come in with you?" Zach asked, eyeing the computer bag and purse thrown over her shoulder.

Kathleen studied the busy terminal. She felt safer in crowds than she did alone. "You don't have to. I'll be fine."

Zach hopped out then swore under his breath. When he met her at the back of the car, he grumbled. "This damn hip is inconvenient as hell."

"You're moving way more easily than you were this time last week."

"Fuckin' A." He lifted her bag down and pulled the handle up for her. "If you need anything at all, call me."

"I will." She moved to embrace him and he gave her a squeeze and brushed her cheek with a kiss. "I'll check in with texts, but I'll call you to remind you of my flight information in ten days."

She'd started to step away when he said, "This doctor you go to, what kind of reputation does she have?"

"She has an excellent reputation. She's an expert in PTSD."

"What's her name?"

"Dr. Louise Dowling."

He nodded. "Thanks."

She paused to give him a long look.

"I'm not asking for me. If I was, I'd come right out and tell you."

"Would you?"

His heavy brows drew together, but he green gaze remained steady. "Yeah, I would, Kathleen. I'm asking for a friend."

"Okay." She reached up and touched his cheek. "I'll see you

Sunday." She wished he would just once take her into his confidence. He'd been trained to maintain his own counsel because of his job, but it didn't mean he had to carry it into his personal life, too. Not with her.

"I'll be here to pick you up. Let me know what time."

"I will." She tugged her suitcase forward and plodded into the airport terminal.

She checked her bag, went through airport security, and on past restaurants, souvenir shops, and bookstores, until she found her gate. She settled into an empty seat and tucked her purse in her chair beside her and placed her computer case between her feet.

In about six hours, she'd see Callahan. She needed to concentrate on that and forget her hurt over her brother's reticence. Men weren't good about sharing their feelings, or their thoughts. With eight brothers, she knew very well how they could be.

Her phone rang. She dug through her purse until she found it and tapped the face to answer the call.

"I didn't mean to shut you down, Kathleen. I just can't discuss this without the other person's agreement. I'm just guessing at things as it is."

The hurt dissolved. "It's okay, Zach. I understand. I wouldn't want you to betray anyone's privacy." This was obviously weighing on him. It had to be the woman he was seeing.

"Thanks, Thorn."

"I'll see you in a few days, but if you need to talk, I'm here."

"Be careful."

"I will. Love you."

"You, too."

When he disconnected, she went online to look up information on Piper. Nothing came up under Piper Bertinelli. Piper was a nickname. What had he said her given name was? It came to her after some thought, and she typed in Francesca Bertinelli. Stories came up about the holdup in the restaurant and the trial. After reading a couple of articles, Kathleen's stomach cramped in sympathy.

How would she have handled having to relive her attack over and over in the paper? What if she'd had to endure a trial? What if Zach or Cal had been killed while tried to protect her? It had been a real possibility when Hillary was waving her gun around. She had no doubt he and Cal would have put themselves between her and a bullet. They still would.

The articles made her worry for her brother. He had a thing about protecting women. If this woman had issues... She needed to meet her. As soon as she returned from San Antonio, she'd insist on it.

CHAPTER 26

PIPER GRIPPED HER denim-clad knees to keep her hands still while Detective Sherman took a seat across from her in one of the two leather chairs. Zach sat next to her, in silent support, but she could feel the pressure and heat from his thigh resting against hers.

"How long have you been a vet, Dr. Bertinelli?"

"Licensed in general veterinary medicine for two years. I took more classes while working for Dr. Dorsey in San Francisco for a year. When he moved down here, I came with him and bought into the practice. You met him the day of the break-in. He specializes in orthopedic surgery, so I'm in the process of doing my internship in that specialty, and will take state boards in another year."

"Your professors at Davis say you're a whiz kid."

She wasn't surprised he'd looked into her. "I'm not a kid anymore. I'll soon be twenty-six. But I studied hard in school."

"And did a lot of extra work to earn scholarships."

"Yes. I got grants and scholarships, but I still have about twenty thousand in student loans I'm trying to pay off."

"And your part of the vet practice?"

"Yes, but those payments come directly out of the business profits before we draw a salary."

He nodded. "You're usually the one to arrive in early?"

"Yes. Dr. Dorsey typically comes in an hour later if we have a number of surgeries, but on normal days I do two shifts each Monday, Wednesday, and Friday and he does the Tuesday, Thursday schedule. We consult on Friday."

"So he observes you during surgeries?"

"Yes."

"Did he come in and observe you on Monday when you did Gracie's surgery?" he asked.

"Yes, he did. I paged him right after Zach left."

"And you'd just walked in on the burglar a few hours earlier and still did surgery."

"I was pretty terrified while I hid in the cabinet and talked to the dispatcher. I kept imagining them finding me. But five hours had passed before Zach brought Gracie in. Long enough for me to calm down. Your team had just left. They were there until noon."

Having heard her name, Gracie rose with difficulty and came to lay her head in Piper's lap. She rubbed the dog's ears and massaged her neck, soothing herself as much as it did the dog.

"So there was about six hours between the break-in and the attempted dognapping."

"Possibly."

Zach spoke for the first time. "The master chief told us he usually left at noon to play chess, but he was running late. They may have thought he was already gone. He has a garage, and his car was inside."

"It's possible they'd been watching his house to learn his routine," Piper speculated. "There might be separate teams. One who does the burglaries and one who takes care of getting the animals they want."

"We're following up on those things, Dr. Bertinelli. You said they. Do you believe there was more than one person in the building?"

She hesitated and thought back on the sound alerting her to another presence in the building. "At the time I kept thinking there was more than one, because I was terrified and so hyperaware of every sound. After thinking about it for a while, I don't think I heard more than one person's steps in the hall."

"How did you know it wasn't someone who works with you?"

"Everyone at the office knows my schedule. If any of them wanted to break in, they'd know when to come and go to avoid running into me."

"You entered through the back door?"

"Yes. We usually park in the side parking lot, to leave room out front for our clients. We come in through the dog run gate and through the back door. I always pause to check on the dogs in the boarding kennels to make sure they have water. They bark when anyone comes through."

"So the perpetrator heard you coming?"

"He'd have had to when I opened the door into the hallway. We've tried to soundproof the room as much as possible, but there's no way to stifle the sound when you open the door."

"It's a shame you didn't see him."

Piper had thought the same thing for a while. Now she was just grateful she hadn't. Otherwise the guy could have attacked her to keep her from identifying him. "He waited until I was in the surgery to slip out from wherever he was—or they were—hiding. I was lucky they weren't interested in hurting me." Chill bumps rose on her arms and she rubbed them.

Sherman's gaze followed the motion. His expression never changed when he said. "Tell me about David Henderlight and Duardo Acosta."

Though she had expected it, Piper's heart still sank and her stomach twisted. "I never knew Acosta. Had never met or spoken to him until he came into our restaurant, waving a gun at me and demanding I give him his twenty-five thousand dollars. I didn't know what he was talking about. I kept telling him I didn't have the money, but he wouldn't listen. He grabbed my hair and dragged me halfway across the counter. He put the gun against my temple. My father tried to give him the money in the register and he—he shot him."

Every time she said it, she saw it happening over and over

again. Her stomach tumbled, and she folded her arms against her, feeling cold. "I went for his eyes, tried to claw him, and he swung the gun at my face and tried to hit me with it. I jerked away. He shot at me while I dodged behind the counter to get to my father. He walked around the counter and aimed his gun at me, and I thought, *I'm going to die*. But the sirens were getting closer, just up the street and he didn't have his money yet. He said, 'This isn't over, bitch,' and ran out."

She struggled to maintain her composure. "I tried to put pressure on my father's wound. There was blood everywhere, and he was having trouble breathing." She cleared her throat.

"I thought Acosta was just some crazy, deranged man until his connection to David was made clear to me by Detective Lester the next morning. I was at the hospital, my clothes still covered in blood, and I'd just been told my father was dead when Lester took me to the station and questioned me for the first time." She should have known something was wrong when he insisted she come in when she was at her weakest. And certainly when the policewoman had come in and made her strip and took her clothes and tested her hands for gunshot residue.

"He kept asking about the backpack, but I'd never seen any backpack, had no idea what he was talking about. I wasn't driving my car, I'd been driving my mother's for the last two weeks, because I was trying to avoid David. If he put a backpack in the back of my usual car, someone stole it. Otherwise my mom would have found it and turned the money in.

"But I don't believe there ever was a backpack. I believe David spent the money on drugs and partying, and threw me as a bone to Acosta as revenge for breaking things off with him."

What better way to keep a rape victim from testifying against him, than to pay her off with drug money?

There. She'd acknowledged what happened. It didn't help the pain to go away, it only solidified what had happened to her.

What else could the money have been for?

She repeated the same information she shared with Zach the day before, and the police over and over again years before. She told him about Detective Lester's determination to prosecute her, his harassment, his attempts to end her education. The internal affairs investigation.

"Why didn't you demand a settlement?" Sherman asked. "I mean other than court costs and your lawyer's fee?"

So he had already looked into the internal affairs investigation. "It wasn't about money, Detective. It was about Lester's unrelenting harassment. I just wanted it to end. For me, for my family. We'd been through enough. I can work and make my own money. I've never expected to be given anything for free. I just wanted the right to live my life. He was just as determined to make sure I couldn't.

"Two years later, when he testified at Acosta's trial, he made it plain it wasn't over, that it would never be over. He pointed the finger at me as an accessory. Painted me as part of the whole drug thing, even though every part of my life had been investigated over and over, and no evidence of any kind was ever uncovered. There was never any connection, because all I did was date the wrong man. It was a five-week mistake that cost me dearly. My father.... It's still costing me to this day." She closed her eyes against the rush of emotion.

Finally she cleared her throat and continued. "During the original investigation, I offered to take a lie detector test. They refused to give me one. They tested my blood and took hair samples to see if I'd taken drugs. I hadn't. Lester ignored everything."

"My family has never recovered from my father's death or the things Lester did." They'd never forgiven her for it, either. She was a reminder of what they'd lost and what they went through afterward. "He harassed them every bit as much as he did me."

"Then why did you come back to San Diego?" he asked.

"My mother begged me to. And when Dr. Dorsey asked me if I wanted to buy into the business, I told myself the chance that Lester would find out I was back were slim. I prayed he'd moved on. So I said yes. I just wanted to be close to my mom."

Her throat hurt, her head pounded, and she felt slightly sick.

She fought it back and reached for her purse. She withdrew the envelope and note.

"Sherry, one our receptionists, said a Detective Schneider and another policeman came by asking questions about me on Friday. Her description of the second policeman matched Lester. On Saturday, Zach and I stopped by a grocery store, and I ran in to get something.

"Lester was there. I don't know if he was already there, or followed me inside, but when I saw him, I slipped through the aisles so I wouldn't have to speak to him. I spotted him actively looking for me, so I pretended to drop my purse so he wouldn't see me when he came by the checkout line. Then yesterday Sherry found this note in the mail, but it hadn't been mailed, just slipped into the stack delivered yesterday. After I got out of surgery yesterday, I came here to see Zach, and Lester showed up with you."

Nausea overwhelmed her and she rose. "I have to have a minute…Please excuse me." She rushed down the hall to the bathroom.

ZACH FORCED HIMSELF to stay seated when every instinct insisted he go check on Piper. Instead he turned his attention on Detective Sherman. The longer Piper had spoken, and the paler she'd become, the more ferocious his anger grew.

"I know there are issues with you opening a closed case. Piper's father's death and Costa's arrest are cut and dried. Henderlight's arrest is old news, too. But are you going to look into any of this, or are you just going to allow Lester to jack her around again?"

Sherman's gaze went flat and dispassionate. "I'm going to look into everything, Ensign."

"Lester knows the steps to take to isolate his target. He used them all before. He harassed the people around her until they got out of his way and left Piper to cope alone. Destroyed their trust so they'd stay away. Then he had free rein. Seven years ago, he made it so difficult for Piper's family, she shut herself out of their lives rather than allow him to harass them any longer. I may be shipping out in three or four weeks, and she'll be alone. At his mercy again. That note proves he means to pursue this again."

When Sherman remained silent, Zach continued. "This is not what being a police officer is about. It's about finding facts and evidence to prove guilt. Piper's been investigated. Several times, and in several different ways. She doesn't know anything about the money. I'd bet my SEAL pin on it. You need to go back to David Henderlight and find out who does know, so she can put this behind her."

Sherman's brows, much darker than his hair, clenched in a frown, his first show of emotion during the entire interview. "You don't need to tell me what my job is, Ensign." He paused. "How do I know you weren't the one to write the note to stir the pot on Lester?"

"You don't. But I'll be glad to give you a handwriting sample. I knew about Piper's father's death, but I didn't know anything about the harassment until yesterday, after you left when Piper told me the whole story. They don't put internal affairs investigations in the paper."

Sherman reached for the note, but didn't ask for a handwriting sample. "I need to take this with me."

Zach nodded. "I scanned and copied it after Piper showed it to me yesterday."

Sherman reached inside his jacket for a notebook and wrote out a receipt.

They continued to stare at each other while they waited for Piper to return.

"Was Lester ever partnered with Detective Schneider?"

"I don't know, but I'll find out."

At least he'd gotten that much.

Piper returned, composed but pale.

Detective Sherman rose. "I need to take the note, Dr. Bertinelli." He extended the receipt he'd written.

She nodded and accepted it.

"What store was it you stopped at on Saturday?"

"Vons, close to the Silver Strand."

"I'll be in touch to update you and your partners on the break-in."

Her voice sounded hoarse. "Thank you, Detective."

Detective Sherman saw himself out.

Piper sat on the couch and raked her hair back from her face. "Thank you for being here with me. You'd think this would get easier, but it doesn't."

"It was a traumatic time for you, and having to relive it over and over again may help in some ways, but current events have brought the pain and the stress back to the surface."

She stared at her hands as she clenched and unclenched them. "Do you ever have flashbacks?"

"Yeah. I've had them. And I have memories that leap out and grab me now and then. And dreams. Some of things I've seen and had to do are hard to put away. Which is why we go through psych evals periodically to make sure we're steady."

He gripped her hands. "We have some time. What kind of sailor are you?"

She brushed a long strand of hair behind her ear. "I've only been on a boat twice, but I didn't get sick."

"Good. You'll be fine, but we'll take some Dramamine with us just in case." He drew her to her feet.

Gracie raised her head from her paws, her ears going up. The hopeful look on her face made him feel guilty as hell. He'd been taking her with him everywhere he went, but on board a boat would be a little risky. He bent to give her a quick rub. "Sorry, baby. Not this time. But we'll only be gone a couple of hours."

As they came out of the apartment and walked to his SUV, a red Hyundai zipped by, and he followed its progress down the street. Three cars down the street, a man sat in an older Chevy Tahoe too far away for him to clearly see his features.

Zach blocked Piper's view as he opened the SUV door. She'd had enough for one day.

After he got her settled in the car, he took out his phone and pretended to be checking a text while he took a picture of the car. He'd told Sherman Lester wouldn't give up. He hoped he wasn't right.

CHAPTER 27

THE WIND STUNG PIPER'S cheeks and had a briny smell to it. Chilled, she tugged together the desert camouflage shirt Zach loaned her and buttoned it. It hung down over her hands, almost to her knees. Piper braced her hip against the aluminum support for the awning overhead and enjoyed the view from the fly bridge atop the cabin cruiser, where she could see past the bow. The water was a little choppy, but she found the bouncing motion of the bow stimulating.

Zach motioned for her to come closer and offered her a hand. He drew her in front of him and placed her hands on the wheel, speaking directly into her ear so she could hear him. "You're the captain. Just stay parallel to the shoreline."

How was she supposed to do that? They were far enough out to be out of the ebb and flow of the surf, but still within sight of land. The distance seemed impossible to judge.

He rested his hands on her shoulders and she relaxed. Though his touch wasn't sexual, and there were layers of cloth between her skin and his hands, she still felt safe, a powerful experience, since she hadn't felt truly secure with a man in years. But she did with Zach. Safe led into a giddy tug of desire that heated her blood and had an ache of need blossoming inside her. Not just for sex, but other things, too.

The mistakes of the past didn't seem so horribly insurmountable with him standing at her back.

Piper caught her breath when a black and white shape leapt out of the water in front of the bow of the boat, then another, racing ahead of them breaching in the spray of the bow and the waves. She was surprised by their size until others of every size and length suddenly appeared around them, breaking the water with sleek power. Beneath the surface she could see their powerful tails working.

"What should we do?"

"Just keep going. There's probably a school of fish they've been following, and they've decided to race us."

"What if we hit one?"

"We won't unless we make a sudden turn."

"Oh, my God, they're beautiful." Her heart raced. And every time one got close to the boat, she caught her breath.

Finally the dolphins cut away, disappearing beneath the surface as quickly as they had appeared.

"That—" She drew a breath. "Wow. That was amazing."

Zach's smile mirrored her own "Yeah, it was. In all the years I've been fishing in this area, it's only happened to me one other time. Do you want me to take over now?"

She nodded and realized she was shaking. She'd been afraid of hitting one of the dolphins if she turned the wheel. But she was excited, too.

Zach guided the cabin cruiser around in a large U and headed out to sea.

Piper nestled in close to him. "Thanks for bringing me out here."

Zach's arm tightened around her.

Her breathing came easier. The feeling of oppression from the emotional pain eased. She breathed in the sea air, releasing the last of her tension.

She'd never met anyone so willing to put himself in harm's way for someone else. But it was what he did for a living. It wouldn't be right for Zach to try and shield her and be rewarded by having his life disrupted. She couldn't permit herself to depend on him. She had to deal with this herself. But not yet. Lester couldn't reach her out here. She was safe for these few moments.

Zach slowed the cabin cruiser and the boat rose and fell as it was caught in the wash of its own wake. His arm tightened around her, holding her steady. "I'm going to drop anchor. You okay with hanging out here for a little while?"

Piper nodded.

He released her and descended the ladder to the deck below.

ZACH TRIED TO judge Piper's mood while he unfolded two deck chairs and waited for her to take a seat.

"After I get back from deployments, I spend a lot of time out on the water. As soon as you cut ties to land, it's like you've cut ties to things weighing on you, and you're able to leave them behind. And when you get way out here," He nodded out to the horizon. "Where you can't see land anymore, the quiet sets in, and you're able to think without a dozen voices yammering in your head. So when I have to make important decisions, I want to be out here."

"I can understand that."

"Sky diving is the same way. You're cocooned in your gear, and you're surrounded by nothing but open space and your chute above you as you float down."

"So you won't be afraid to jump again?"

He didn't want her to fixate on how dangerous some of his training was, or his job. He stubbornly brushed aside the reasons he felt that way. "No. My hip was a freak accident. You have a greater risk of getting killed in a car accident than skydiving."

She looked out to sea. Sunlight glinted off the warm, chestnut highlights in her hair and kissed her light olive skin. The wind had whipped color back in her cheeks. He could spend the rest of the day just looking at her, even though her eyes were shadowed by what must have been as sleepless a night as he had.

Her sherry-tinted eyes swung to him. "That's the feeling I get from working with animals. At UC Davis we worked with horses. Some of them had been abused, others had behavior issues, some were really ill. But there were times when I could look into their eyes and make a connection. There they were, these fourteen hundred-pound animals, trusting me to do what was right for them. And there was a kind of peace working with them. Solving their health issues. Earning their trust."

The stress seemed to drain from her just talking about it. They fell into an easy silence that lasted a few minutes.

"You need to walk away from me, Zach."

The calm resolve he read in her expression punched him harder than the combined emotional fallout of the last two days.

He scooted his chair to face her and caught her hands. "We don't know for certain Lester will come after you again." He couldn't bring himself tell her about the car across the street from his house, or that he was certain it had followed them to the marina. If he did, the moment they docked, she'd run as far from him as she could.

One perfect weekend together wasn't enough. They deserved more. "We don't know Sherman will refuse to look into the things you told him today."

"They always stick together. It's their code." She withdrew her hands and tucked a strand of hair behind her ear. "It's like being caught in a spider's web, and you're the fly. It doesn't matter that you're innocent. He can twist the law to point a finger at you, whether you've done anything or not. You can't risk your career, Zach."

His career was important. He'd worked hard to become a SEAL. But what he was made it impossible for him to retreat. A SEAL never gave up. "We need to take things one day at a time. Okay?"

He read the struggle in her face. "Is this why you were reluctant to go out with me?"

"Yes. It's part of the reason I've held everyone at a distance for a long time."

"How long will you let this convince you to put your life on hold? I'm not talking about your career; I'm talking about your life."

She seemed reluctant to answer, but murmured grudgingly, "I haven't felt like I had a choice. Part of being in a relationship with someone is being able to share the truth about yourself. Once I shared my truths, no one wanted to stick around."

"I want to stick around and help you resolve this, Piper."

"Why?" She searched his face.

"Because I think we've both wasted enough time dwelling on the past. Don't you?"

"We both know it's not so simple, Zach."

His dad had said the same thing. Given him warning after warning. Telling him to stay clear of all of it, of her.

"So what do you plan to do? Run? Sell your part of your practice and leave San Diego?"

"If I have to." Her expression had gone blank when she looked up. "I'll have to distance myself from my family again, until I know what's going to happen. I wish I didn't have to say this, but it's easier. I don't have to worry about how they're being treated."

He wasn't surprised.

"Are you going to tell your partners?"

"Dr. Dorsey already knows the whole story. He was one of the professors Lester interviewed. If Lester pursues me again, I won't have a choice but to tell the others."

She was in an impossible situation, but was making decisions with an eerie calm he didn't trust.

She tucked her hair behind her ears. "I'll ask my mom again about the day David came to the house, but I don't think she'll remember anything I don't. David was high. I remember arguing with him and telling him to leave or I was going to call the cops. Lorenzo fought with him and threw him out of the house. Then Armando showed up, and they almost came to blows. Benito and Lorenzo had to hold Armando back. I think the story about the money was a lie to pay me back for threatening him."

"The temper tantrum of a spoiled rich kid."

"Yes, and it cost my father his life."

"That's on Henderlight and Acosta, Piper. Not you. You've carried enough guilt, enough responsibility for what happened. Your family should be a source of support."

"I can't risk Lester harassing them. Teresa and Tom have enough to worry about with Teresa's cancer treatments and the kids. Alana, my brother Armando's wife, is due to have their second child any time now. My mom's been through enough."

But hadn't she been through enough, too? He thought it through for a moment. "We'll have to wait for Lester to make the first move." He couldn't count Lester's watching his house as the first volley…if it had been Lester.

Anxiety tightened her expression and he motioned to the water. "We're out here in the fresh air and sunshine, completely alone, with no one to bother us, so let's enjoy the silence and solitude and forget about things for a while."

A brief smile flitted across her features. "You were supposed to think things through."

"I did."

"You've only known me for a few days. What if I'm conning you?"

"You just poured everything out to a police detective who's probably going to dissect every part of your life again. I don't think you're conning me or him."

Her brown gaze locked onto his.

He cupped her face and brushed a kiss over her lips. "I believe you, Piper." Though he kept the pressure light, he hardened as soon as he touched and tasted her lips. When he broke the kiss, Piper leaned forward to press her mouth to his to continue it.

"I didn't bring you aboard to do the lonely sailor seduction dance, Piper."

A half smile crossed her face. "I didn't come aboard to do the lonely vet seduction dance, either. I need you to hold me, touch me. I need to be close."

An iron man couldn't resist an invitation like that. He tilted Piper's face up to him. Took his time when he kissed her, building the simple brush of her lips to something more. He molded her slender frame against him with hands hungry for the feel of her.

Their tongues tangled until he drew hers into his mouth and sucked.

Piper's groan sent an answering rush of need straight to his groin.

Piper's voice was soft. "Can we go below?"

The narrow bunk across from the dining area folded out to make a twin-size mattress. He reached into the overhead for clean sheets and some pillows. "We'd be more comfortable at my apartment, Piper."

She shook her head. "You love your boat. It's a special place to you, and you're sharing it with me because you know I need it."

She was right. He and Bowie'd brought women on board before, but he never made love with one here. It hadn't felt right, because it was his private space. He wasn't going to think about why this time it did feel right.

PIPER KICKED HER SHOES off and slipped free of her blouse and jeans, but left her bra and panties on.

"You can get undressed and dressed faster than anybody else I know," Zach said, his gaze trailing down her body with open appreciation, from her face to her bare feet. "Not that I'm complaining." He toed off his deck shoes.

She sauntered up to him. "Do you need a hand taking off your clothes?"

A slow grin spread across his face. "Yeah, I could use a hand."

She paused to rest her palms against the powerful width of his T-shirt-covered chest and looked up at him. "I didn't know what it meant to truly want a man until I met you."

Zach's smile died. Her stomach tumbled at his expression of single-minded focus. A blossoming heat took root deep inside her.

He caught her waist in his hands and brushed his lips against her temple, her cheek. His voice was husky when he murmured against her ear, "You're killing me here, Piper."

He felt so solid, so strong. She slipped her hands up under his T-shirt and over the sparse patch of rust-colored hair on his chest. She dragged the shirt up, and he raised his arms to help her. She tossed it on the table. Then she leaned into him, aligning her body with his. She wanted to revel in the feel of his skin against hers, the way his body fit against hers.

Zach unhooked her bra, guided it down her arms and tossed it atop his shirt. He trailed his hands down her back and cupped her buttocks to pull her in close.

"I can feel how much you want me." The anxiety that had plagued her at such a response in the past never raised its head. She sighed with a sense of relief and release. He had given her more than he knew. So much more. She loved him for his generosity, his humor, his giving nature, his trust. How could she not love him? He deserved so much more than she could ever give him.

When he left to go to places like Afghanistan or God knew where, he'd be taking part of her with him. Because he mattered to her, more and more each day.

She unfastened the top of his shorts and unzipped his fly with an exaggerated slowness. When she slipped his shorts and boxer briefs down over his hips, he bent his head and took her lips. He cupped her breasts and ran his thumbs with a feather-light touch over her nipples until they peaked.

She trailed a hand down over the muscular tautness of his belly, then lower. Her fingers closed around his erection and stroked him.

He hummed against her mouth and broke the kiss to nip her shoulder then hooked his fingers in the elastic of her panties and peeled them down until they dropped to her feet.

He guided her to the mattress and they lay down together.

She pressed an open-mouthed kiss to his chest, right over his heart, then slid lower to his stomach. She gripped the base of his distended cock and looked up at him to find him watching her, his cheeks ruddy with desire. She ran her tongue over the head of his penis, then took him into her mouth.

ZACH'S HEART LABORED like an engine stuck in full throttle while Piper's mouth closed around him. Pleasure raced through him and he groaned aloud.

Her enthusiasm, while she licked and sucked more than made up for her inexperience. He pulled away when the need for release became too intense. "I want to be inside you when I come, Piper."

He rolled above her and positioned himself between her legs. Her arms went around him to pull him down. She rose to meet him as he thrust inside her. It was then he realized he'd forgotten the condom. The intimate sensation of her gripping him like a glove, taking him in, nearly drove him over the edge. He groaned as he beat back his need and withdrew from her. He grappled to reach his shorts, jerked his billfold free and hooked a finger in to remove the condom he'd tucked there only days ago, right after meeting Piper.

He covered himself and came back to her. Her sherry brown eyes, dark with desire, settled on his face, her hands following the curve of his spine. He eased back into her. "I got a little crazy there for a minute," he murmured and nuzzled her neck.

"I feel the same way. You feel so good inside me."

"Darlin', you don't need to remind me of that right now. Not if you want me to be any use to you at all."

"I think you've more than proven how useful you can be in bed and out, Zach." She looped an arm around his neck to pull him down for a kiss.

Need rode him hard, and there was no finesse in the way he plunged into her again and again.

Piper's breathing sounded as ragged as his, her breath hot against his neck. Her fingers found his nipples, and she ran her fingertip over them. His control went to hell, and his release crashed over him like a runaway locomotive.

He was still breathing heavily when he lifted his head to look down at her.

A smile crooked up the corners of her mouth while she smoothed his hair.

Zach rolled onto his side to lie beside her.

She curled into him and laid her head upon the pillow close to his. The scent of her shampoo and the jasmine body wash she used wafted from her heated skin. "I've discovered something."

"What is it?"

"I really like making love with you."

Zach laughed. "I'm really glad you like making love with me. I guess it's kind of obvious I feel the same way."

"I thought you might." She ran the backs of her fingers back and forth along his jaw. "You're right about me putting my life on hold. I've let the past become a prison, and I'm not going to do it anymore. I'm breaking out."

"I'm glad to hear it."

"I'm not going to let Lester put me back in the box again. What do you think I should do to keep it from happening?"

"I have some ideas, but it will require some help from friends and maybe your family."

"I won't be able to depend on them, Zach. I made excuses for them earlier, but the truth is…they blame me for what happened to my father. They won't get involved."

Jesus what was *wrong* with these people? "We'll think of something, Piper." Without her family's help, it would be just the two of them.

"I think you're more like your *maimeó* than you realize. You told me she had enough love to go around for everyone in the family and your SEAL team, too. I think you have to guard against going down that path." She stroked his cheek. "I guarded against it, too. But the way you are with me. The way you talk about your sister, your grandmother, so caring, so tender. I needed you. So now it's too late for me. You've taught me how to be generous, too. I haven't been able to be generous for a long time, because I've been afraid of to let anyone get close. I didn't want to have to watch them walk away after I shared everything."

"Don't, Piper." Zach placed a finger over her lips.

He was through with listening to her absolve everyone else of their actions. "You can't take the blame for everything. I saw how you cared for Gracie, and read the empathy in your face when you saw Master Chief Flynn's injuries. That's the person you are. If they couldn't see that person and want to get closer, it's on them, not on you. If your family can't see that person, it's their loss, not yours."

She remained silent for a long moment. "Are you going to call me when you deploy, Zach?"

She was asking if he was going to walk away, too. He didn't want to. But he'd learned the hard way to ask someone to wait for him wasn't a realistic expectation. She was just coming into her own. Just learning she could enjoy sex.

The idea of her being with someone else almost made him ill. If he found out about it through an email while he was in the thick of things... "It would be better for us both if I didn't. You wouldn't be waiting for a call that might never come. I wouldn't be thinking about hearing your voice, seeing your face, wanting to be here with you instead of there."

"I'll be wishing those things whether you call or not. Won't you be, too?"

If he said no, he'd be just another asshole, walking away. If he said no he'd be lying. The pain lanced deep, he breathed his way through it. He rolled onto his back, uncertain of his composure. "Yeah, I'll be wishing I was here with you, Piper."

Silence stretched between them, making the two or three inches of space between their bodies seem as wide as the Grand Canyon. When he couldn't stand it anymore, he rolled on his side to face her again and draw her close.

With her head tucked under his chin, her body pressed close to his, her thigh wedged between his, the distance shrank again.

"I think you need to break out, too, Zach," Piper murmured softly, her breath hot against his chest.

"Yeah, honey. You're probably right."

CHAPTER 28

Zach guided the boat back to the marina. The distant row of vessels grew larger and larger. Small clusters of people were packing up for the day. Many of the boats' sail-barren masts looked forlorn, even from afar.

The pressure of Zach's arm around her waist was protective, but she wondered if now there wasn't just a little possessiveness to it as well. Piper stepped away to give him room to maneuver while he wove the vessel through the opening into the marina area.

Zach eased the boat back into its berth as though he'd done it a million times before. She climbed down the ladder, hoping she could be helpful.

A security guard stood on the dock, a little overweight, but young, with sandy blond hair. "Toss the rope and I'll tie it off for you, miss."

Piper rolled the nylon rope into a loop and threw it to him. He tied it down with the ease of long practice.

Zach climbed down the ladder and swung around onto the narrow ledge along the port side of the boat, and reaching the bow, tossed the bow line to the man. As soon as the boat was secure, two policemen and a dog wandered down the dock toward them. "What's going on, Charlie?"

"Someone phoned in a tip saying you have drugs aboard. I told them they were crazy, but they want to board you. You can tell them they have to get a warrant."

"No need. We don't have anything but Dramamine on board. Tell them to come ahead."

Hearing their conversation, Piper's legs threatened to fold and she leaned against the starboard side of the boat, and she gasped for breath like she'd been gut-punched. After all he'd done for her, she'd brought trouble to Zach's door.

"I'D PREFER TO have Charlie accompany you while you search," Zach said his gaze on the K-9 officer. He wouldn't put it past Lester to make more trouble by trying to plant something.

The officer shrugged. "The dog will be doing the searching. But he's welcome to watch."

Zach nodded to Charlie.

"Are there any weapons on board, sir?" the K-9 officer asked.

"A couple of spear guns mounted high on the bulkhead above the table in the galley."

As Charlie and the dog's handler disappeared downstairs, Zach turned his attention to the other policeman.

"Have either of you been drinking, sir?" he asked.

The question set off Zach's temper and his face flared hot. "No. We haven't. There isn't any alcohol on board. You can check for that, too if you'd like."

He glanced at Piper. Since the police had come on board, she had tucked herself in against the starboard railing and turned her back to them. He limped to stand next to her at the railing. "It's going to be fine, Piper."

Ten minutes later Charlie, the K-9 officer, and his dog appeared from below.

The two officers conversed for a moment, then approached the two of them.

"Your boat was clean, sir."

Zach raised a brow. "I'm an active-duty SEAL. I don't do drugs. We're tested for drugs on a regular basis. Who sent you out here?"

"Dispatch sent us out here on an anonymous tip."

"Did you do a background check on Ms. Bertinelli and me before you came out?"

"Yes, sir."

"And?"

"You're clean."

"And Ms. Bertinelli?"

"The report said she was a known associate of two drug dealers, both in prison. One for murder and one for possession with intent to sale."

"Associate?" Piper's outburst had them turning toward her. "Duardo Acosta walked into our restaurant and murdered my father in cold blood. He tried to shoot me and missed. I'd never seen him before in my life. I was *never* his associate. My father, family, and I were his *victims*. The other man I dated for five weeks and dumped, specifically because I found out he was dealing and taking drugs. His name is David Henderlight. I wasn't his associate. I was stupid for believing his lies, but I was never his associate. When you get back to your cruiser, I suggest you look up the files."

Zach laid a hand on Piper's arm to sooth her.

"How do I find out who called the request into dispatch?" he asked.

"You can write a formal request for the information from the dispatch supervisor, but unless it's linked to a criminal file, it's doubtful they will release it. Since your boat was clean and no arrests were made, it's not an open investigation."

"I'd like the dispatch number."

The policeman wrote the number down on a slip of paper and tore it off his notepad. "I'd also like your names and badge numbers added to it."

The two police officers exchanged a glance. The one with the pad wrote them both down and extended it to him.

Zach drew a breath to rein in his temper. The two officers climbed off boat and the dog led the way while they returned to their car. Zach gripped Piper's arm. "I have to go up on the dock and talk to Charlie for a moment."

Charlie stood by the stern waiting for him.

"I'm real sorry this happened, Zach," Charlie said. "I told them it was bogus. That you're a SEAL and straighter than straight. They said they still had to check it out."

"It's okay." He lowered his voice to keep Piper from hearing their conversation. "I'd appreciate it if you'd keep a close eye out for anyone hanging around my boat. Someone's trying to cause me some trouble."

"I'll do it. And I'll pass the word to Jordan and Hank as well."

"Thanks."

"Are any of your security cameras pointed toward the road leading in to the parking area?"

"No, they're all directed back here at the boats."

"Okay. What about the parking lot?" Maybe Lester had pulled in and waited for them to return.

"Yeah. We have them on the parking lot."

Zach pulled out his phone and showed him the picture he'd taken. "Can you look through the digital footage from the past couple of hours and see if a car this make and model came in and parked. The man in it is muscular, medium height, with a short neck. Really bulked in his upper body. About forty-five."

Zach paused briefly, the nodded. "If you find any footage of him or the car, make a copy of it. I'm going to turn him in for harassment."

"I can do that."

Piper turned as he re-boarded the cabin cruiser. "You okay?" he asked.

"Yes, I'm okay." She leaned back against the railing.

"I just need to check everything below."

She nodded.

He quickly scanned the galley, cabin and bathroom. Nothing was disturbed. He locked the door leading below decks and pocketed the key.

Piper remained silent while they walked along the dock and crossed the gravel parking area to his SUV. Once inside the car, she leaned back against the passenger door to face him. "He won't stop. This was just the first volley, so you'll know how he can get to you."

"I know."

"You can't get involved in this, Zach."

"You just talked to Detective Sherman. Let's report this to him and see where it goes."

"It won't go anywhere, because he won't turn on a fellow cop. Trust me, he won't."

"I have some contacts in the PD, Piper. I'll give them a call and talk to them about what happened to you and what's happening now. Maybe they'll be able to help. You're not alone now." And he wasn't either. He'd talk to his team and see what they thought.

She ran her fingers through her windblown hair. "You're too good for your own good, Zach."

"No, I'm just pissed off this guy is able to use San Diego PD resources to stalk people and get away with it. If his commanding officers knew, they might have a different perspective on things. They may not give a shit that he's abusing his power, but they will if they know he's calling in bogus crimes and taking up valuable resources."

She shook her head. "I believe you might just be more stubborn than he is."

Zach grinned, making light of the situation, though it was anything but. "Pigheaded, darlin'. That's what my mom and sister call it."

"He was parked down the street from my house when we left, Piper."

A red flush stained her cheeks. "Don't hold things back from me Zach. I can't protect myself if I don't see him coming."

He grimaced. "It won't happen again."

"How can I end this?" she asked.

"I have some ideas."

He turned the key in the ignition and started the car. "We've talked about show and tell and hide and seek. How do you feel about tag?"

CHAPTER 29

CAL PACED IMPATIENTLY just outside the baggage claim area while he waited for Kathleen to appear. It seemed like a month since they'd been together. The days passed quickly, since he was working to complete another project for the company, but at night it dragged.

He'd been out with Doug the night before for a beer, and ended up leaving his brother talking up one of the girls who'd bought them a drink. Even sitting at the table with someone else had felt like a betrayal of Kathleen, so he got up and left the moment he finished his beer. Jesus, he had it bad.

He caught a glimpse of dark hair and something red and scanned the crowd. There she was, towing a suitcase behind her, and hitching her purse and her computer bag over her shoulder. As soon as she saw him, she smiled, totally unaware when a guy she passed did a double take and turned to watch her walk away. She was beautiful, and super-sexy, and didn't even know it.

She still saw herself as the chunky, overweight college freshman she'd told him about. She wasn't. She was a freakin' bombshell.

He knew he was grinning like a fool by the time she made it past the security barrier. He couldn't wait to get his hands on her, to hold her.

"Hi." She sounded as breathless as he felt.

"I'm so freakin' glad you're here!" He tried not to grab too roughly, but he had to kiss her. Despite the baggage, he dragged her close and sealed his lips over hers with a week's worth of hunger. God, he'd missed her. Her arms went around him, holding him as tightly as he was holding her. She tasted like Kathleen and sweet iced tea.

When he lifted his head, her cheeks were flushed and she nestled into him. "I missed you, too."

"You have no idea, honey," he said with feeling. He bent to grip the handle of her suitcase and took the computer bag from her shoulder and slipped it over his own. "Whoever said you can't go home again knew what they were talking about. Though they probably ought to have said 'you shouldn't go home again.'"

"I understand. Even the thought of moving back in with my parents gives me the willies. How's your father doing?"

"Physically he's doing good."

He didn't want to bring up his father's behavior right off the bat, but he didn't want Kathleen to be caught unaware. He changed the subject. "How have you been? Everything okay?"

"Yes. Everything is fine. I have some things to tell you about the guys at work, but we'll talk about them later."

"Okay. Tomorrow I'll show you some of the work we've been doing, because I think you'll be interested."

"And the house you mentioned?"

"Yeah, I've been waiting to show it to you. You'll probably have some ideas of your own to improve the design, but I thought it turned out pretty nice."

"You sound excited about the work you've been doing."

"It's different from business construction. It's not on such a huge scale. Doing ironwork is just the skeleton of the building. Doing tile work in a bathroom makes you feel a little more creative. I'd forgotten how much easier it is than what I do, too."

"I'm glad you've enjoyed it. You could always switch to residential when you go back to San Diego."

He shook his head. "I make better money at business construction."

She hugged his arm against her. The soft brush of her breast against his arm had him wondering if they might find somewhere private on the way home to make up for the week they'd been apart.

"Sometimes it's not about making more money, it's about doing what you love. If you enjoy residential construction more, you could move in that direction. I wouldn't mind having the opportunity to draw residential designs. They're much less stressful than the industrial plans."

"It's about paying the bills and saving some money so we can follow a dream." He brushed her temple with a kiss and led her through the terminal to the walkway outside. The heat had abated somewhat, but exhaust from the many cars, vans, and shuttles lingered in the air, faint but persistent. "There's a shuttle we'll catch to the place where I've parked," he explained, then asked, "How's the design coming?"

"I finished my part ahead of schedule, and the guys are working on theirs while I'm gone. We had a meeting with the client yesterday, and it went very well. But I had to bring my laptop just in case changes are requested."

She was a talented architect, and he'd worked on enough designs to know special when he saw it. "You amaze me. You'll have to show my dad some of your designs. He'll be interested in them."

"If he feels up to it."

It didn't have a damn thing to do with how he felt. It was all about whether he could control his attitude and his mouth.

A shuttle pulled up and Cal nodded to it. "This is us." He handed off Kathleen's suitcase to the driver, and they boarded the small bus.

Once at the car, Cal put the suitcase and computer case in the trunk and broached the subject he'd held back. It wouldn't be fair to let her walk into the situation with his father without warning. "Dad's going through some of the same stuff I did after I lost my leg. Depression and anger."

Kathleen looked up from fastening her seat belt. "He's angry about being laid up?"

"To put it mildly. The only good thing is I'm not at the house most of the day to set him off. And I think he's been doing this since long before the surgery."

"There was a kind of balance while I lived here. Doug was the peacemaker, and I drew Dad's fire and kept him from riding Mom and Doug too much. Because I wasn't here to act as a buffer, he's turned on the two of them. It's become such a habit he rarely has anything pleasant to say to either of them."

"What about you? Does he take issue with you?"

"No. He doesn't say much to me." He'd given some thought to why he wasn't. "I think it's because he knows I can walk and will away."

He scanned Kathleen's features. "You're a peacekeeper, too, Kathleen. When I'm at my worst, you talk me down and keep me from being too big an irritable asshole. Until now, I didn't realize what a burden that can be."

"It isn't a burden, Cal. Everyone needs a sympathetic ear now and then. Even I do. It's part of being a couple. Besides, you've never been verbally abusive to me."

"I might have been, if I hadn't joined the military, gotten the discipline I needed." Or hadn't walked away when he did. "But Dad isn't verbalizing what's bothering him. He's just being an asshole to everyone. I can't protect you from it when I'm not there. And I won't be around some of the time. Don't let him browbeat you."

She had been rock-steady before the situation with Hillary. But now she'd faced death and discovered her own vulnerability, there were chinks in her armor. Some days they were wider than others. Right now they seemed to have closed a little, and she seemed more relaxed than before he left.

Her expression was earnest when she said, "I won't let him push me around."

"Good."

Cal took the direct route to the house. He'd take Kathleen sightseeing one day before she left, but right now he wanted to see her settled and let her meet his mom.

She'd been cooking when he left, nervous, excited, and eager to meet Kathleen. His dad had been sour and taciturn.

Cal was tired of walking on eggshells around his father, and more and more he was coming to understand and sympathize with the nurses' actions when he behaved the same way.

He turned into the gated community his family moved into while he was in high school. The houses in the neighborhood ran anywhere between two hundred and fifty to four hundred and fifty thousand. His father built quite a few of them, and now flipped houses in similar neighborhoods when the renovation and building projects allowed.

"I like how they have a combination of brick and stone, one on top, one on the bottom."

"You may see brick, stone, and stucco combined as well. And Spanish architecture similar to what we have in California."

"I've always loved the openness of the Spanish design. Covered walkways with the arches and open courtyards in the center of buildings. You won't find anything like that in Boston."

"But you have the MIT building and other progressive architecture."

"But a lot of the residential architecture is just the same as it is everywhere else. In some neighborhoods in the city there are block after block of attached homes sandwiched together. It makes me feel claustrophobic to drive down there."

"So your parents and siblings live in detached houses?"

"Yeah. Mom and Dad have owned theirs forever. Michael and Jeanine bought theirs ten years ago." She turned from watching the houses go by. "Taylor and Thomas live in a very unusual loft apartment they rent together. The kitchen and living area are one big open room, but the bedrooms are sectioned off with walls, and each has its own bathroom."

"Makes for a less awkward situation when they have company."

Kathleen laughed. "I'm sure. They're twins, and they even roomed together in college. You'd think they'd want a break from each another."

"They say twins have a bond tighter than other siblings. Maybe it's true." Cal pulled into the driveway of the ranch-style house. "There's a pool around back, and the privacy fence encloses the whole back yard. I hope you brought a swim suit."

"I did, but I couldn't transport the sunscreen. Airport regulations."

"My mom has some."

He exited the car and went around to get her suitcase and computer from the trunk.

The front door opened before they reached it and his mother stepped out onto the concrete porch. "I couldn't wait a minute longer," she commented. "I'm so glad you could come, Kathleen."

Cal watched the two most important women in his life size each other up.

"You're so gorgeous," Sondra said.

Kathleen smiled, and color blossomed in her cheeks. "Thank you. Callahan has your beautiful eyes. He's told me so much about you. I'm very, very glad to finally meet you."

They reached for each other and exchanged a heartfelt hug. He drew a relieved breath while he opened the door for them to go in ahead of him.

He stowed Kathleen's things in the guest room and wandered back to the kitchen, where he could hear voices. Kathleen was helping his mother put dishes on the dining room table after his mother filled them.

"Your father and Doug are in his cave. Would you get them?" Sondra asked.

He wandered back through to call them to the table. His father had actually taken a shower and changed into flannel sleep pants and a San Antonio Spurs T-shirt. He looked weak but alert.

Doug was stretched back in one of the recliners.

"Mom and Kathleen are putting dinner on the table," he announced to them both. "If you don't feel like sitting at the table, Dad, I can set you up a tray in here."

"Afraid I'll embarrass you in front of your girl?" his dad

asked.

"Kathleen won't hold anything you say against me, Dad. You might want to worry about embarrassing yourself."

Doug dipped his head to try and hide his grin.

Jameson shot Doug a look. "What are you smirking about?" He lowered the foot of his recliner and wiggled forward to get his feet under him.

Cal stepped forward to grasp his arm. When his Dad didn't complain, he eyed him closely.

KATHLEEN STUDIED JAMESON CROWES' features. Though he and Doug shared a stronger resemblance, with their dark hair and eyes, Kathleen recognized similarities in the shape of Cal's jaw and the strength of his build. Though Jameson's hair was gray, and he had the pallid look of someone who had been ill recently, Cal's father was a handsome man.

While they ate the dinner of baked chicken and stuffing, mashed potatoes, green beans, and rolls, they talked about the attractions available to see in the San Antonio area. Sea World, the Aquarium, tours available of the city, the tower of the Americas, the park, the Alamo, the river walk, and the malls.

"I came just to visit, not to sightsee, and I'll be going back ten days from now, on Sunday. I had to take my vacation days or lose them. I'll be content to hang out by the pool."

Jameson spoke for the first time. "You'll have to be careful with your fair Irish skin. Sondra has sunscreen around here somewhere."

After what she'd heard about him, Kathleen felt a little wary, but smiled. "I'll need it. I brought a hat as well."

"Some time while you're here, I'd like to see the project you're working on," he said. "Cal's been bragging about how talented you are, and I'd like to see some proof."

Kathleen laughed. "Okay. I have a few things on my computer. A couple of residential projects and few more industrial."

"Good."

"Kathleen draws as well, Dad," Cal broke in.

She bent her head to hide the flush of embarrassed heat. "A little. Mostly just the projects I'm involved in."

"Don't be shy about tooting your own horn around here, Kathleen. The boys come in bragging all the time," Sondra said with a laugh.

"All my brothers are the same way but Zach. He's so close-mouthed you're lucky to get anything out of him."

"He's in the Navy, isn't he?" Doug asked.

"Yes. I have a brother in the Marine Corps, one in the Army, and my oldest brother and father are police officers. The twins are both I.T. guys. They work for a firm that builds secure websites and systems for corporations. The other two, one's a lawyer, and the other is an aircraft mechanic."

"Does your mother work?"

"She babysits for two of my sisters-in-law, taking care of four of the children, ages one year to six. She's all about family."

"What did she think about her baby girl leaving the nest?" Sondra asked.

"She wasn't thrilled about me to being so far away, but they visited and saw that I'm thriving away from home and doing well in my job. And of course they met Callahan and really liked him." She placed a hand over Cal's.

"The most you can hope for is for your children to be self-reliant and happy," Sondra commented.

"That's similar to what my mom said. But she was crying the whole time she said it while she kissed me good-bye. Most of the boys have scattered like dandelion seeds. Being the only girl, I think she hoped I'd be at home for life."

"It's hard to let go, even when you know it's the best thing to do. Especially when your child's had some hard knocks along the way." Sondra said. Her gaze rested on Callahan for a moment.

"Everyone has hard knocks in life, Sondra. And we all have to deal with them the best way we can," Jameson said. "It's called living." He tossed his napkin on the table and pushed himself to his feet by gripping the edge of the table.

Doug and Cal both rose. He waved them back down. "I can make it back to my recliner on my own. Finish your dinner. I'm going to have a nap. We'll look at those plans together in the morning, Kathleen."

"Sure." His hard-edged, no-nonsense tone gave her a glimpse of what Cal meant. Even sick he projected a strong will, and his brusque delivery left no room for argument.

"I'll check on him," Doug said after a moment, and left the room.

"I have chess pie for desert," Sondra said with a strained smile.

"I'm full as a tick, Mom. Why don't you go rest and let Kathleen and me deal with the dishes? We can have some dessert later, after the rest of our food has settled."

"Kathleen's a guest, Cal." Stress had tightened the skin around Sondra's eyes and mouth.

"I didn't come to be an added responsibility, Mrs. Crowes. I came to be of help." And because she hadn't wanted to be apart from Cal a day longer than she had to be. "Since Doug and Cal are busy during the day, I thought I might help you around the house, run errands, grocery shop, whatever you need done. I know you'll need to do some work for the company while I'm here, and I can stay with Mr. Crowes so you won't have to leave him alone. I did the same for my mother when my grandmother was ill."

A battle waged behind Sondra's pleasant features. "I wasn't expecting…"

"Cal will be busy, and Jameson will require someone to be here. I knew that before I came. I don't expect to be entertained."

Sondra's shoulders dropped. "I appreciate it. Thanks so much for offering. Please call me Sondra."

Kathleen smiled. "Deal."

Doug wandered back in. "He's already nodding off. You need me to do anything before I take off, Mom?"

"No. You want to take some pie home with you?"

"I'll swing by at lunchtime tomorrow to check on Dad and get a piece then." He brushed Sondra's cheek with his lips. "Thanks for dinner. Good to see you again, Kathleen."

"Thanks. You, too." She hadn't yet decided how she felt about Doug, knowing what he had tried to do to Cal the week before. Had it truly only been a little over week? A cramp of hurt and outrage settled in the pit of her stomach every time she thought about it. Following through with the urge to slap him upside the head and demand, "What the fuck were you thinking?" might have helped resolve the issue for her. But she couldn't do it with his mom standing there. And she doubted he or Cal had told Sondra about the confrontation.

Cal shot Kathleen a smile, then drew his mother out of her chair "I'll bring a glass of wine to your room. I noticed a book on the table in the family room. I can get it for you, if you'd like to read."

Kathleen stacked the dishes and carried them into the kitchen. She'd already begun to load the dishwasher when Cal swept in a few minutes later with the platter holding the remnants of the baked chicken and the bowl of potatoes. He caught her around the waist and snuggled in close against her from behind. "Have I told you lately how fantastic you are?" He nuzzled her neck.

"I haven't heard words to that effect in at least a week."

"After we've dealt with the dishes, maybe we can slip into your room and I can show you how fantastic you are."

Kathleen's heart rate kicked into hyperdrive, and a tingling heat settled in deep to taunt her. "Sounds like a wonderful, idea and completely contrary to what your mother had in mind when she suggested separate rooms."

"What my mother doesn't know won't hurt her. She's stretched out in her room—on the other end of the house—with a glass of wine and her book, and Dad's asleep in his chair in his den."

"You'd better finish clearing the table if we're going to have a few minutes alone."

"I'm on it." He slipped back into the dining room so quickly she stifled a chuckle.

They had the pots and pans washed and the dishwasher loaded and set into action in record time.

"Let me show you your room," Callahan said snagging her hand and tugging her out the kitchen door, through the living room, and down the hall. "This is my room, in case you want to visit in the wee hours of the morning." Kathleen took in the brown, black, and cream comforter covering the queen-size bed with its decidedly masculine look, and the open-weave brown curtains hung on either side of the sliding glass doors leading out to the pool. Throw rugs lay scattered on the dark hardwood floors.

"The next room down on this side was Doug's. And this is your room." He drew her across the hall. The guest room was decorated in shades of aqua and had a relaxing coolness to the décor. A white over-stuffed comforter with matching pillows covered the queen-size bed. Rugs braided in a chevron design of different shades of blue from aqua to navy stretched next to the side of the bed and in front of the dresser, with a braided wall hanging made of different colors of jute hung behind the bed.

Nightstands flanked each side of the headboard, and cylindrical glass table lamps glowed on each one. The overhead ceiling light matched.

Her suitcase sat on a bench-like ottoman at the foot of the bed with her laptop case. Through an open doorway to the left gray tile gleamed on the floor and walls of a bathroom.

"It's a beautiful room. I know I'll be comfortable."

He nudged the door closed, drew her in and kissed her with slow, lingering thoroughness. Kathleen leaned into him with a sigh of homecoming and wrapped her arms around him.

When he raised his head she read tenderness and desire in his expression. He pulled the pins free holding her hair into the twist and tucked them into his shirt pocket. He ran his fingers through her hair. "Lie with me."

He flipped the comforter down. Kathleen slipped her shoes off and wiggled back onto the bed. Cal tugged his tennis shoes off and joined her.

He drew her close, and his sigh said more than any action he could have taken or word he could have spoken.

"When I asked you to come, I hadn't thought past you just being here with me for a few days. I don't think I considered what it would be like with my dad sick and mom worn down from it."

"My grandmother has diabetes. She had to go through heart surgery to repair a valve, and my mom cared for her the whole time. So I came knowing how it would be. It's going to take him more than a year to recover, and then the damage to his heart might still slow him down."

"I figured as much." He drew a deep breath. "We have five crews working on five projects right now. I just started a new one today. Doug can't handle all of them alone, but he's coming along. And Dad can still supervise some once he's up to it."

Kathleen ran her palm back and forth over his T-shirt-covered chest. "I know you're torn in two different directions right now. The life you have back in San Diego, and the responsibility to family here. This is what you expected to have five years ago, Cal. You've proven you can do it."

"All I ever wanted was for my Dad to acknowledge that I could still do the job. Now he's seen that I can, but it's been forced down his throat. God, he's such a hard-headed son of a bitch. And the way he talks to Mom…."

"Doug keeps his head down and avoids rocking the boat. Your Dad's afraid to take you on right now, because he knows you can walk away again. And he's smart enough to know he needs you more than you need him. Your mom is the only one he knows will take it and stay."

"I wish she wouldn't. Maybe if he sat here alone, hurting and abandoned, for a few days, he'd wake up to what he has and appreciate it."

He'd stepped away from his family and experienced the same thing. Alone, hurting from the loss of his leg, and feeling abandoned by his family, he'd started a new life and come through it stronger.

"Are you saying that because you want your father to experience just a little of what you went through, or because you're worried about your mom?"

Cal cast a narrow-eyed glance down at her and remained silent for a moment. "Maybe a little bit of both, but mostly it's for my mom's sake. If I ever talk to you the way he does her, smack me upside the head."

Kathleen laughed. "Trust me, I will." She snuggled closer. "You're so like your father. The way you gesture with your hands. The tone of your voice. The shape of your jaw." She ran the backs of her fingers along his cheek and chin. "And you can be just as hardheaded."

He shot her a look and she smiled.

"You know you can. But you're a better man, because you have an empathy for other people he may lack...which you learned because of everything you've been through."

"I've also had some distance from my family, and from him. It's made me recognize how dictatorial he's always been, and how we're responsible for creating the monster by going along with what he wanted without ever bucking him."

"He's not calling the shots now, though. Maybe the experience will encourage him to change."

"Maybe." There was doubt in his expression.

"We had a meeting at work before I left. It was a kind of intervention on my behalf."

His brows rose.

"I've been having some adjustment issues at the office. Being over-careful with what I say and how I act. Tyler asked me to sit down and explain to them about...what had happened...so we could clear the air and bond a little. So I did."

Cal's concern was palpable. "How did it go?"

"It went well. I felt better afterward, and now they're a little more relaxed around me. They're trying very hard to make me more a part of the team. Show me I don't have to always be on guard with everything I say and do."

"I'm glad." His brushed her forehead with his lips and drew her against his body. "You were born to do what you do, Kathleen. I don't want anything to hold you back from making your mark in your field."

"I've gone back on my meds, Cal. And I've started seeing Dr. Dowling again."

"Whatever it takes, Kathleen. Making a conscious choice to take control is a huge step."

She narrowed her eyes and studied him. "You knew, didn't you? Why didn't you say something to me?"

"I learned, when I was going through it myself, that the more you push someone to do something, the more resistant they become, especially if it has to do with doctors and medication. You're so take-charge where your work is concerned, I knew it would only take a little while for you to realize you needed to take charge of other things, too. But just because I didn't say anything doesn't mean I wasn't keeping a close eye on you for the past couple of months."

Her feelings of anxiety had been worse for exactly that length of time. Just about the time Zach started mentioning another deployment. Cal had started spending nearly every night at her apartment about the same time, too. He'd been calling her during her lunch break every day. Why hadn't she noticed? Because she'd been tied up in her head with the struggle. "I won't resent you if you mention things like that to me. I'll know you're saying it out of love."

"I knew you'd turned a corner when I saw you dressed in red at the airport. You were strutting your stuff, and guys were turning around to follow your progress while you wove through the crowd. And I thought what a lucky guy I am. Want me to show you?"

She slid her arms around his neck and drew him down to her. "Always."

His hand slid up her leg from knee to thigh, dragging up her skirt. His hand felt hot against her bare bottom as he palmed, then kneaded it. His pupils expanded, darkening his pale blue-green eyes. "I love it when you wear a thong. It makes it so much easier for me to touch you. He slid a hand around to caress her through the thin scrap of fabric.

Her body quickened to his touch, and she cupped him through his pants.

Cal brushed his lips along her cheek to her ear. "You're already wet for me."

"You're already hard for me," she replied, and unbuttoned the top of his jeans and unzipped his fly one-handed. She reached in to free him.

"We'll do a more thorough job of this later, but I need to be inside you right now, Kathleen."

"I need you to be inside me." She wiggled free of the thong while he pulled his jeans down. When he moved between her legs, she was ready for him. He thrust inside her, and they both sighed in pleasure and relief. She cupped his buttocks and rolled her hips.

"Jesus, Kathleen. You feel so good."

She was too breathless to say anything when he started moving inside her. With each thrust he hit the spot inside that drove her pleasure higher. She ran her hands up under his shirt to caress his back, the muscles working beneath her hands. He felt strong, solid, and everything she wanted, needed.

She tightened around him, and his thrusts became intent, his expression focused, his features hardening as his orgasm approached.

His movements became sharper, deeper, and shoved her over the edge into an intense, sweeping pleasure, leaving her fingers and toes tingling. She bit her lip to keep from crying out. He thrust twice more, and she felt the answering pulse of his release.

As he rested between her thighs and braced himself up on his elbows, she looked up into his face and knew she'd do anything to stay with him, wherever he might be. She felt whole when she was with him.

She pressed a kiss to his throat against the heavy pulse beating just there. "I love you, Callahan."

"Thank, God. I was worried you might be keeping me around just for sex."

His slow grin triggered her laughter.

He withdrew from her gently and paused to give her a sweet kiss before climbing off the bed. "Let's go for a swim, then we'll chow down on the best chess pie in Texas."

"Is it really that good?"

"Yeah. It's Mom's specialty desert, and she's spent years perfecting it."

"I'll need to work off dinner before I eat it, then. So a swim sounds like the perfect solution."

He tucked everything in, buttoned, and then zipped his pants. He offered her a hand up. She tugged her skirt down, then reached for the thong lying in the center of the bed. Callahan jerked it up and out of reach, then shoved it into his jeans pocket.

Having his mother put them in separate rooms was a clue that Sondra cared about appearances. The discovery of her thong in Callahan's room would breach the 'don't force me to acknowledge you're having sex' rule.

Kathleen eyed him. "You aren't serious."

"You can come collect it later, unless you want my mom to find it." He brushed his lips against hers and sauntered out of the room.

CHAPTER 30

PIPER PACED THE short, narrow span behind her desk, and tried to take deep breaths to settle the nervous nausea threatening to overwhelm her. She could have just waited and asked her mother. It was a simple question.

But anything to do with the trial upset her. The entire family avoided even mentioning it in front of her. She'd been through enough.

She couldn't ask her brothers or sister. They shut her down every time she brought it up.

The trip to city hall to find out the name of David Henderlight's lawyer during his trial had panned out. To avoid speaking to the man, she'd tried to get a transcript of her father's trial, but it would be months before she would get it, and it would cost a lot of money.

Her phone calls to the lawyer remained unreturned until her fifth and final try in the last three days. And now she had to answer the freaking phone.

It wasn't like she was talking directly to David. This was just the man who represented him after he was busted with a trunk full of drugs.

"I can't talk to you about David Henderlight's case, Dr. Bertinelli. Even though I no longer represent him, I'm still bound by attorney-client privilege."

The impatience in the man's voice did nothing to ease her discomfort. "I don't want you to discuss the case, Mr. Brittain. I just need to know about something he told the police during questioning. He said he gave me twenty-five thousand dollars in a backpack in the back of my car, but he never specified what kind of car he put it in. I was driving my mother's car at the time, and she was driving mine. I just need to know which car he put it in."

"Dr. Bertinelli, I'm not at liberty to share information about my past client."

"The transcript of my father's trial is thousands of pages long, Mr. Brittain. I was only there at the trial part of the time. And I wasn't there to witness David's testimony. They wouldn't allow me in the courtroom during that time. It will take me three months to get a copy. I just need to know what car he put the money in."

"He said it was in a small black backpack, and he put it in the back of your car, an Equinox. The back was open, and it was sitting in the driveway. He put the backpack in the car and shut the rear door. He was adamant about having given you the money."

"The police searched my car, Mr. Brittain. I hadn't driven it during the two weeks before my father was killed because I was trying to avoid David. I was driving my mother's Altima during that time, so he wouldn't know when I was at my apartment."

"I don't know about any of that. All I know is David testified that he put the backpack with the money in it into the back of your car, the car you usually drove."

Piper felt like she was going around and around in circles. "I never found the money. I never had it. I've told everyone who will listen. I've been investigated time after time about it."

"So why are you asking about it now?"

"The detective who investigated my father's death harassed me about the money, stalked me. I had to file a civil rights suit against him to get him to leave me alone. And now he's back at it again. I'm trying to find out what happened to the money to so I can get him off my back for good."

"What's this guy's name?"

"Detective Samuel Lester."

"You won the civil liberties suit?"

"Yes. And he was investigated by internal affairs and suspended for four months without pay."

"If he's stepped on your civil rights, Dr. Bertinelli, chances are he's done it before. Maybe you should call a few more lawyers and spread the word. Turn up the heat on him."

"I don't exactly run in the same circles he does, Mr. Brittain. I wouldn't even know the names of the people he's investigated, let alone their lawyers. And even if I did, I'm not sure I could approach them."

"You also can take the high road and suffer the consequences of his harassment. That's up to you."

He was probably a very good defense attorney. His mind certainly worked well in that vein.

"Are you sure David was telling the truth about putting the money in my car? Couldn't he have spent it on drugs or partying and just told Acosta he gave it to me to pawn off the trouble it would cause? We'd just broken up."

"There's always the possibility he lied, but he never changed his story with me or with the prosecutor. And he was under a great deal of pressure to tell the truth. Otherwise, the plea deal we arranged would have fallen though, and he'd spend more time in prison."

She rested her head in her hand and massaged her temples. She had a choice. She could believe David as Detective Lester had, or she could go on burying her head in the sand. "What reason did he give for giving me the money?"

"He said you agreed to hold it for him, and he was going to give you a cut. That you must have decided to keep it and refused to give it to Acosta."

So he had placed the blame for her father's death on her as well.

"He was protected at home. Acosta couldn't get to him. Why do you think he called him to tell him I had the money?"

"I can't speak to my client's thoughts, Dr. Bertinelli. But this is just an observation I made at the time. David is very good at deflecting blame for things. He put the money in your vehicle to make sure you reaped the consequences of having it."

After a brief pause, the attorney added, "One more thing, Dr. Bertinelli. If you didn't get the money, someone who had access to the car did. You need to think about who it might have been, and start asking questions. Because they left you holding the bag, literally, and unleashed a shitstorm of trouble for you."

She'd thought about that many times over the years. The most likely suspects were people who were supposed to love her. Why would anyone take the money and leave her at Lester's mercy? When they took it, they also signed her father's death warrant. And the blame for it had lain at her feet ever since.

And because she dated David, the catalyst who caused everything that followed, she accepted the burden. Her own feelings of guilt had demanded it. But not any longer. She couldn't live like this anymore. She brushed at the scraps of hair hanging on either side of her face.

Brittain's voice cut through her thoughts. "Are you still there?"

"Yes."

"It just so happens I may know a few lawyers who might possibly have had run-ins with Detective Lester. I'll ask around."

"You're not my lawyer, you don't have to do it."

"No, I don't. But we all have a part to play in the system. We all have a framework we have to operate within. Apparently Lester doesn't believe those boundaries apply to him. Otherwise IA wouldn't have come down on him, and you wouldn't have won the suit. If he's done it to you, he's done it to other people. Possibly some of my own clients. Some of them possibly as innocent as you are."

"How do you know I'm innocent, Mr. Brittain?"

"I saw your testimony in court, Dr. Bertinelli."

She'd seen his picture online when she researched him, but didn't remember seeing him in court. But she'd been under siege during her testimony and hanging on by her fingernails.

"The defense hammered at you for nearly an hour and a half. You were upset, crying, in pain, but your story about the money never changed. The prosecution couldn't rattle you, because you were telling the truth. Look to the people who had access to the car. The answer will be there."

Which was what she was afraid of. "Thank you for your help."

"Hey, if you ever need a defense attorney, you have my number."

She hoped and prayed the day would never come. She hung up the phone and took out her cell to call Zach, paused, and keyed in Jake Brittain's number and saved it, just in case.

She'd needed to know if what she was about to do to her family was the right course of action. At least now she was certain it was.

CHAPTER 31

THERE WERE ALWAYS LEADERS in a clan. Since Piper's father was dead, Zach tried to figure out who had stepped into his shoes.

The Bertinellis were used to serving strangers at the restaurant, but clearly having one invade their family Sunday luncheon was different. Not knowing why they had been called together might possibly have something to do with it.

They were outwardly polite, but wary. Were they waiting for him to whip out a bag of cocaine, or what?

Piper tried to warn him, but he hadn't been prepared for the open enmity they demonstrated toward her. They truly blamed her for everything that had happened.

"How long have you lived in San Diego?" Teresa, Piper's sister, asked.

Her face was thinner, and her eyes a darker shade of brown than Piper's, but the bone structure of her cheekbones and the shape of her eyes were similar, and marked their shared heritage. Her bare head was covered by a scarf, and she had no eyebrows or lashes, the result of recently undergoing chemo. For a moment Zach flashed back to some of the renaissance paintings he'd seen in Italy.

"I've lived here almost eight years. I came out and worked for two years chartering fishing trips while I took some college classes and trained to try for the SEALs. I enlisted, and right after boot camp I was transferred back out here, but sent back as soon as I applied for SEAL training." Which seemed like a million years in the past.

"So you're a SEAL?" Lorenzo said.

"Yeah." He toyed with the salad with grilled shrimp on his plate. Whatever else Piper's family did, they knew how to cook. He stabbed one of the hors 'd oeuvres of thinly slice prosciutto wrapped around bites of mozzarella and served with pesto and cherry tomatoes. Olives were the least fancy thing on the table, and even they complimented the cheese and bruschetta wedges.

"Seems like you're going a completely opposite direction, aren't you, Piper?" Lorenzo commented.

"How would you know, Lorenzo? You never visited me in San Francisco to learn anything about my life there."

Zach suppressed a smile at the dig. She'd remained silent in response to several already aimed at her. It seemed the lot of them were only waiting for an opportunity to draw blood.

His muscles remained taut, waiting to see if someone at the table would succeed. He'd have to control his reaction. Otherwise he'd be tempted to punch whoever did it and draw the real thing.

"How's the vet business treating you Piper?" Tom, Teresa's husband, asked, guiding the conversation in a different direction.

In the group of olive-skinned, dark-haired Italians, Zach thought the guy's pale blond hair and fair skin probably stood out as much as his own freckles and red hair.

Piper's smile revealed nervous relief. "We're slowly building a clientele. We're getting busier by the day."

"That's good. I'm glad to hear it."

"I'm trying to start a fostering program for animals who are brought to us for adoption."

"I thought that's what the shelters are for," Teresa said.

"In the poorer areas of town, a lot of them are kill shelters, and I'd rather see the animals go to foster homes until we can place them, instead of being stuck in cages waiting to be euphemized. Some of the shelters don't have access to a full-time vet, or the funds to pay for medications, and if the animals contract any kind of problem, they're put down. I repaired a hernia on a sweet little kitten a few days ago. Had she gone to the shelter, they'd have put her to sleep for a condition that took ten minutes to repair."

"Did you find someone to foster her?" Tom asked.

"Yes, and the foster family thinks they've found her a home."

"That's good."

"You're so passionate about saving *their lives*, Piper." Teresa's tone held a bite that was unmistakable. "To bad you don't have the same drive when it comes to humans."

A beat of silence was followed by, "Teresa!" Tom's voice blended with her mother's.

The stricken look on Piper's face had Zach's heart thundering. He slipped an arm along the back of her chair and his gaze swept the table. The rest of the men at the table concentrated on their food and remained silent.

Tom jumped up from his seat and threw his napkin down, his cheeks bright red and his anger unmistakable. He left the table and a door slammed somewhere at the back of the house. Teresa followed him.

"Her illness has been stressful, Piper," her mother said.

"Don't make excuses for her, mama," Piper's voice was soft, but betrayed a note of weariness. Carlotta subsided.

Alana, Armando's very pregnant wife, rose from her seat, removed the tray to the highchair at the end of the table, and hiked little Armando onto her hip. "I'm going to check on the other children." Her cheeks were flushed and she was fighting tears. "I'm sorry, Piper."

"It isn't your fault, Alana."

Zach tensed to rise, but Piper placed a hand on his thigh.

"Just a few more minutes," she murmured.

He had never felt more helpless in his life, so he did the only thing he could at the moment. He gripped the hand that rested on his leg.

Armando, Piper's oldest brother, started a conversation about the Dodgers vs. the Padres, as though nothing had happened. It was telling when they ignored their youngest sister's pain.

Tom and Teresa returned to the table. Both seemed to be pushing their food around on their plate rather than eating it.

The brothers batted team statistics back and forth until their mother rose to clear the table.

As they got to their feet, Piper gripped Zach's arm "I'll be ready to go in just a few minutes. I just want a minute alone with my mother."

She had yet to look at him. "Okay," Zach automatically began to clear the table.

"You don't have to do that, Ensign O'Connor," Carlotta said.

"I don't mind, Mrs. Bertinelli. I've done my share of KP at home and on post." He sure as hell didn't want to spend time with anyone in Piper's family right now, since he wanted very badly to punch one or all of them.

PIPER LED THE WAY up the stairs. Piper looked for the spindle the nine-year-old Lorenzo broke when he slid down the stairs on a cardboard box. A new banister had replaced the old, and the spindle was gone. The scratches and notches from the boys' baseball cleats were now covered by an oatmeal-colored carpet, which had been installed while she was away at vet school.

The carpet extended along the hall, and she paused before the door to the room she'd shared with her older sister. She opened it and stepped inside. The oatmeal carpet had been laid here, too, and the room painted a pale moss green. The double bed she'd slept in alone once Teresa left for college was still there. The flowered comforter flowed over the mattress like a watercolor painting, the shams and bed skirt adding an accent of solid color darker than the walls. Everything had been changed, and there were no remnants of her life left in the room.

It seemed appropriate that things should end here.

She drifted to the window and looked out at Alana playing

ball with Little Armando. His hair curled around his head like Dante's, but his features were Armando's in miniature. His short two-year-old legs toddled across the freshly mown grass while he chased after the plastic ball that rolled between his feet. He hadn't even been a thought when she left for school up north, and she'd only gotten news of his birth ten days after the fact. She'd never held her nephew. Never babysat him. She hadn't had the nerve to try and visit Armando and Alana for fear of being turned away. Not after Teresa refused to allow her to visit her children.

Her family was lost to her. She had to face it and accept it.

Her mother's voice interrupted her reverie. "What is it, Piper?"

She felt tired as she turned from the scene below.

"I want to ask you some questions about that last day David came to see me here."

"It was a long time ago, Piper."

"I know, but I can't stop playing it over and over in my head. I keep wondering why he came. I'd broken it off. He knew it was over. That I didn't want to ever see him again."

"What is it?"

"Who answered the door?"

"I was in the kitchen with Teresa making ravioli, and Lorenzo called out that he would get it. By the time I got to the door, Lorenzo was at the top of the stairs calling for you, and Benito was trying to force David back outside. Then Armando showed up, and he and David were about to come to blows, but Benito and Lorenzo held him back. David got in his car and left."

"Did David have anything with him when he arrived, a gym bag or anything?"

"There wasn't anything in the foyer. I'd have noticed it, because I'd been after the boys to put their shoes on the bench down there after I tripped over them when I came in with the groceries. Lorenzo kicked them out of the way and went out and got the rest of the groceries. Someone picked them up and put them in the basket on the bench."

Her mother took a step farther into the room and sat down

on the bed. "Why are you asking?"

"It was the last time I saw David, Momma. The only time he could have given me money. But you were there when he came. He didn't give me anything. You saw it. Armando, Lorenzo, Benito, and Teresa saw it. He wouldn't have given me anything, because he knew I was finished with him."

"I know he didn't give you anything."

Piper eased down on the bed beside her. "I would have given Acosta anything he wanted, Momma."

"I know, *tessoro*." Tears rolled down her mother's face. "I know you would have."

"I can't come back here anymore, Momma. I can't sit at the table and be punished for something I couldn't prevent. I won't be the target of everyone's unjustified rage anymore." Shouldn't she feel grief or at least anger? All she felt was a numbing weariness.

Carlotta's arms came around Piper and she held her tight. "I thought once you came home we could be a family again."

Piper clung to her, trying to offer her mother what comfort she could. Her mother's pain brought the tears she had yet to shed. "They don't want me, Momma. And I won't ask forgiveness for something I didn't do."

"I want you, Piper. You're my baby. I love you."

For a time it had been enough. It had given her hope to cling to. But not anymore. Not now Lester knew she was back.

LORENZO VACATED HIS SEAT and sat on the couch next to his brother to make room for Zach. It had taken a few minutes for Zach to tell him and his brother, Benito, apart. They looked enough alike to be twins, with the same warm brown hair as Piper and her mother, and similar sherry brown eyes.

"How did you and Piper meet?" Lorenzo asked.

"I hit a dog and took it in. She had to do surgery to save it. When I went back in to check on the dog, I asked her out."

"How long have you been seeing each other?"

"Just a short time." After everything that had gone down since they'd met, it seemed longer than two weeks. He waited to see if her brothers were going to warn him off like Detective Lester.

Lorenzo's gazed probed Zach's. "You must be pretty important to her if she invited you here."

"I asked her to bring me along because I wanted to meet her family."

"I bet you're regretting it, too," Dante said. His eyes narrowed and his mouth clamped into a thin line.

"Shut up, Dante," Armando said from between gritted teeth.

"Fuck you, Mando."

"Her last boyfriend had red hair, too." Benito said, a frown crimping his brows.

"You mean David?"

"She told you about David?" Lorenzo's tone sharpened with surprise.

"Yeah." But not that he had red hair. Uneasiness tightened the muscles at the back of his neck.

"You don't look like David. And you're nothing like him," Dante said, his tone flat. His dark hair had a curl to it and his eyes were hazel. He shot a look around the room at each of his brothers. "Don't let them try to make trouble between you."

The man's words relaxed Zach's momentary uneasiness. Maybe, just maybe, he was a source of support for Piper.

"David was a snake oil salesman," Dante continued. "He poured on the charm to sell himself to people. He became whatever each person needed so they'd like him. For a time he even had Mom fooled, just as he fooled Piper."

"How do you know I'm nothing like him?"

"Because you don't give a shit whether we like you or not."

Zach gave him a level look. "No, I don't." He didn't like them very much, and didn't care if they knew it.

He leaned forward in his seat. "Piper told me about everything. Your dad, Acosta, the money and Detective Lester."

"Most guys would have run for the hills after hearing about the kind of trouble she attracts," Armando commented.

Zach raised a brow. "I'm used to running toward trouble, not away."

Armando eyed him, his jaw working. "She brought that fucker into our parents' house. Because of her, our father's dead."

"Because of that fucker, your father's dead. Only a cold-blooded bitch would have sacrificed her father for money. Piper isn't cold-blooded. If anything, she's been traumatized more than any of you. After all, she deliberately drew Detective Lester's heat away from you by staying away, didn't she?"

The uneasiness he read in their faces gave him some satisfaction. "She couldn't give up the money, because she didn't know where it was. I knew it the moment she told me what happened."

Complete silence like an indrawn breath reigned for several moments, until Tom broke it with, "I helped her and the other vets set up their partnership and write the proposal for their business. I don't believe there ever was any money. And Piper certainly never had it if there was."

Benito shifted to look at him. "You never told us you did any of that."

"And have to put up with being abused like she has? It's time this ended. I had access to all four of their financial records. There's nothing there. If she'd had money, she'd have used it. And I've never blamed her for Armando's death. The two men responsible for it are behind bars."

Tom shoved free of his seat. "For God's sake, they were drug dealers. I never understood why Lester believed them over Piper. I've never understood why you guys believed them over her, either. You've treated her like shit for years, and she's taken it. I'm not going to sit by and watch it any longer. I won't be back. If you can hate her and treat her like this, who's next?" He stalked across the room and out the front door.

Zach mentally listed Piper's possible supporters, Dante, Tom, Alana…and possibly her mother. He eyed her three other brothers. "There's something else to consider. When a woman's being systematically harassed and abused, she'll either shut down or do anything to escape her abuser. If she had the money, she would certainly have given it up to get Lester off her back. And she never would have returned to San Diego, where he could start harassing her again."

Armando's head whipped in his direction. "Is he harassing her again?"

Finally, someone showed some concern. But Zach couldn't tell if it was for Piper or if Armando was worried about the inconvenience for himself.

"He and another detective came by my apartment on a different case. The owner of the dog I hit was beaten and left for dead in his yard. The minute Lester saw Piper, his eyes lit up like he'd gotten just what he wanted for Christmas. Chances are he'll come back at her now he knows she's in his jurisdiction again. He'll keep at it until he drives Piper out of San Diego for good. You're going to lose your sister if you don't do something."

He'd had enough of their company, couldn't sit still any longer, but before he walked out of the room he added, "Just a heads-up in case any of you want to *man up* and give her some support." Who knew? One of them might shock the shit out of him and actually do it.

He wandered down the hall toward the kitchen and noticed for the first time in days his hip wasn't aching like a son of a bitch. He wasn't discounting the adrenaline his anger had pumped into his system to have numbed it, so he took his time. But he needed a cool down period.

When he wandered back toward the living room, he heard steps on the stairs. Piper's eyes were red, as though she'd been crying, but she was composed now.

Her jaw was set when she marched into the living room. "Lester's back and he's harassing me again. And he's going after Zach because he's standing by me. We all know none of you will be in that category, don't we?"

She moved to stand over her four brothers. "I'm done. Done with all of you. Done with your blaming me for everything. Done with you punishing me for everything in your lives that you don't like. And I'm especially done with bearing the brunt of the blame for not being able to stop the bullet that killed our father. If I could have, I'd have gladly stepped in front of that gun, but I couldn't."

When the three started to argue. "Shut. Up!" Piper said with such passion their protests died. "I will have my say, and then I'll be gone out of your lives for good. You've treated me with less respect than you would your worst enemy. Used me like an emotional punching bag for years, and I've turned the other cheek for the last time."

"If I had the money Acosta was looking for, I'd have given it to him without a single argument. But I didn't have it. And that means whoever took the money out of my car will have to bear the heat, because I'm finished doing it for you.

"I didn't see any money. Never had it, never spent it. I was still driving mom's car, and she was driving mine that last week. I left right after David did that day *in her car*. You three were here when I left," she pointed at her brothers Lorenzo, Benito, and Armando. "And Teresa. If anyone took the money, it was one of you." Her gaze swept their faces. "That means the next time Lester talks to me, I'm throwing you four under the bus to take the heat."

Benito shoved to his feet, exclaiming, "You can't do that!".

The other two sitting next to him jumped to their feet to add their arguments.

Piper turned the full brunt of her intensity on Benito while color rose to her cheeks, and for a moment Zach thought she might take a swing at him. Part of him hoped she would. "Watch me."

Her features were still set and her eyes dark with anger when she glanced at Zach. "Let's go."

"I'm ready." He placed a hand against the small of her back and let her lead the way. He reached for the doorknob.

"Piper." Dante stood behind them in the entrance to the living room and took two long strides to reach her. "If you need anything at all, call me." When he hugged her, she froze for several seconds, then slowly returned the embrace. He drew back, and for a moment brother and sister looked into each other's faces. "I'm so proud of you. I mean it."

He cast a glance in Zach's direction, gave him a nod, and moved on past them to go out the door.

Piper gaze shifted to him, dark and intent. "You said something to my brothers before I did, didn't you?"

He gestured toward the door for her to walk through it. "I'm not a big baseball fan, so I changed the subject to something I was more interested in. He and your brother-in-law were the only two who spoke up for you."

"Thanks for telling me."

"My pleasure."

Once they were in the car, he started the engine, but didn't put it into gear. "How do you feel?"

Piper drew a deep breath. "Free. I'll always feel guilty that I couldn't save him." She closed her eyes and swallowed several times while she struggled to suppress her tears. "But I don't have to carry the weight of their hatred any longer."

"Good." Zach put the car in gear and pulled away from the house.

CHAPTER 32

THOUGH IT WAS early morning, the physical labor of climbing the ladder and wielding a drill had sweat running down the back of Zack's neck. He knew he was being pigheaded, but he was the one who'd asked for Flash and Bowie's help. He needed to be the one to do the lion's share of the work.

"Are you doing this to get laid?" Bowie asked. He accepted the cordless drill, changed the bit and handed it back. "'Cause if you are, there are easier ways."

Zach eyed him as he wrapped his fingers around the handle of the tool. "No, I'm not doing it to get laid. I'm doing it because Piper and her partners are on a tight budget, and they can't afford a professional service that will charge them an arm and a leg. This way they'll be able to monitor their business from their phones and keep an eye on things. At the first hint of trouble, the signal will go out to the police department, which will be the only thing they'll have to pay for."

"Seems like a hell of a lot of trouble to get laid."

"Bowie…" He loved the man like a brother, but sometimes the iron wall he'd built to keep women at arm's length for anything but sex really made him wonder. How he could be charming and get any woman he wanted when he felt that way was a mystery.

"Piper isn't a hookup, Bowie. I like her, man. We're dating.

We've been dating for two weeks." At least he had dates that involved more than bedroom action.

He guided the electric wiring through the center of the plate and turned his attention to screwing it in place.

"I've never known it to take two weeks for you to get—"

"Watch yourself, Bowie. Piper isn't a party girl. Don't talk about her like she is."

Bowie threw up his hands in surrender. "I'm just saying you need to be careful, Doc. You don't want to get too involved just before we deploy."

Zach concentrated on securing the camera to the eave of the building. He'd been thinking of what Hawk said on the subject. "When would be a good time to get involved?"

Bowie's silence stretched while Zach secured the unit onto the base. He turned to look down at him. "I've been visiting Master Chief Flynn every day while Piper's at work." The man had started hitting the wall of depression once he realized the extent of his injuries, and he needed all the encouragement he could get to move forward. "If we both keep going the way we are, bro, we're going to end up like him. No family, only a dog. And a legacy no one can share because it's all classified. Don't you want more than that?"

Bowie frowned, his dark brown brows knitting over a nose straight as a blade. His lips compressed. "Love is a trap you pay for the rest of your life, Doc. Be careful you don't end up being caged by it."

Whoa. The bitterness in his tone clung to each word like tar. Bowie never allowed any of the ladies he took out to see it. He was a ladies' man, giving pleasure and attention for the few hours he was with them, then moving on. He never dated any woman longer than a month.

Zach climbed down from his perch. The hip was so much better he only felt a twinge or two when he descended the ladder. But it still looked like hell.

Once on terra firma, he turned to face Bowie. "Don't you think it depends on the woman you fall in love with? Surely there are one or two good ones."

"Yeah, like Patricia?" Bowie threw the name down like a gauntlet.

Zach was surprised how little reaction he felt. "I'm over that, man. We were both responsible for what happened. I held back from her, and she cheated on me. But we weren't married, and we weren't engaged. I hadn't proclaimed undying love to her any more than she had me. Sure, it messed me up for a while." Longer than a while. "But I'm moving on from it."

Bowie's expression smoothed out, but there was a distant look in his eyes. "I'm glad for you, man. But it wouldn't be good to get involved when we're three weeks away, possibly less."

"And I repeat... When would be a good time, Bowie? We've put our lives on hold for our country. I know my family loves me, but how much of a loss would it be to them if I died during a mission? I moved away from home after high school, and it's been ten years. Ten years of more phone calls than face-to-face meetings. You say the words, but without some daily physical contact to keep the bond strong..." He stopped. "I need more, Bowie. I need something more than a quick fix. I need to look into another person's eyes and know I matter to them."

"And you think you're going to get that from Piper?"

"I don't know. Right now we have this powerful physical buzz, but we haven't completely dropped the walls yet to see if we can establish a deeper connection." Because of this bullshit with Lester. "But I'm willing to find out if we can have it."

Bowie's features had hardened. He gripped the aluminum ladder and lifted it. "Let's get to the next camera. Flash will be out here on our asses if we don't get a move on."

Zach suppressed a sigh. On this one subject, Bowie's mind was set in stone. Whatever had gone down to make him feel this way had been *bad. Really* bad. He'd never spoken about it, not even with Zach. Maybe if he could, it might lance the boil.

But there were women Bowie respected and had a real affection for. He loved Kathleen like a brother. And he had a special affection for Zoe, Hawk's wife. He often called Selena Shaker, teammate Oliver Shaker's wife, 'little mama' with a special affection, and Langley Marks' wife Trish. They were all women who had proven themselves to be steadfast wives.

Zach spotted Piper as she strode around the side of the building. Dressed in jeans, a button-up blouse, and a lab coat, she looked professional and beautiful. "I thought you both might need some water." She extended one bottle to Zach and one to Bowie. Then offered each a hand towel.

"Thanks." Zach unscrewed the lid and took a deep drink. He wiped his face and the back of his neck with the towel. "We have three more cameras to install. How's Flash doing in there?"

"He's shown the girls pictures of his wife and daughter, put extra password protection on the main computers, connected the cameras you have installed so far up to the laptop we bought, and loved on every animal in the place. He has more energy than anyone I know. He's talking about taking one of the pups someone dropped off yesterday home to Joy."

"He'd better call Sam and ask if it's okay, otherwise she'll tie a knot in his—" Zach caught himself. "Uh, tail."

Piper grinned. "I can't give him a pup yet. I'll have to check them out first, and give them shots. If he wants one after that, I'll be glad for him to take one. Two would be better. They do better if they have someone to play with." Her smile widened. "It's the very least I can do to repay him for all the work he's doing."

Zach chuckled. "I'll do my best to encourage him to take two. At least with Joy and Samantha, you can be sure they'll receive good care."

Piper's phone pinged with a text and she glanced at it. "I'm being paged." She sighed. "Is there anything you need before I go back in?"

"No. We're good. We'll have this done in another thirty minutes or so."

"I really appreciate everything the three of you are doing." Her eyes shifted to Bowie, then back to him. "I know it's mostly for me, but my partners appreciate it, too."

"You're here at night more than the others, Piper. I'll feel better if you have some safety measures in place."

Her slow smile, and the way she brushed a hand down his arm, had blood rushing south. "I'd better go." She took a few steps away. "Think I should mention to Flash that the pups probably need to be wormed?"

Zach laughed. "That might be a deal breaker. I'd keep it to yourself. We'll be finished in time for us to meet up at my place."

"Okay."

Bowie kept his eyes on Piper until she disappeared around the corner of the building, and Zach fought the urge to step between them and get in his face for even looking at her.

"She's beautiful," Bowie commented.

Zach bit back a growl.

"And she's going to lead you straight down the garden path into trouble," Bowie continued, his eyes narrowed when they flicked to him. "You'd better think about that promotion coming down the pike."

"She isn't the trouble, Bowie. Lester's the issue." He'd shared everything with Bowie. "I've got the video of him at the marina watching us leave the dock through binoculars, and leaving just before the cops pulled in to search the boat."

"She's more trouble than Lester ever thought of being. She's already got her hooks into you. And you're going to be miserable when you have to go wheels up."

It wasn't so. He was keeping everything light. He was more concerned about the game Lester was playing. That was all.

No, actually it wasn't all. He wanted Piper so badly his heart rate rocketed and his palms got sweaty every time she was within touching distance. He walked around semi-hard just thinking about her. Since they'd made love frequently during their two-plus weeks together, he'd have thought those feelings would taper off. But they weren't. Days of making love with Piper, of sharing meals, cuddling on the couch, walking the dogs, sharing, cooking. Worrying about her when she wasn't with him.

And when she laughed. It would be her laugh that stuck with him when they went wheels up.

He handed Bowie the drill and folded up the ladder to move on to the next camera position on the eave at the far corner of the building. Bowie hefted it in deference to Zach's hip. As he walked, Zach texted Flash to flip back on the breaker controlling the electricity to the two cameras they'd just installed, and flip off the breaker that controlled the two at this end of the building.

Bowie set up the ladder and held it steady while Zach climbed up. He waited for Flash's text, pulled the wiring through the hole the electrician cut in the eave the day before, and reached for another mounting plate from his carpenter's belt. He stood one-legged on the ladder while he worked, resting his hip as much as possible.

Bowie spoke from below him. "We always had a mutt around while we were growing up. Every summer when we left to visit my Dad in Mexico, we had to leave the dog behind. By the time we got back home, it was gone. Mom wasn't good about taking care of things. But we always lived in hope that the dog would be there, waiting for us, when we pulled up."

The wistful note in Bowie's voice had Zach glancing down. "Did she give them away?"

"No, just forgot to feed them long enough for them to wander off to someone else's house to beg for food, or for them to be picked up and hauled off to the pound."

Jesus. He was already getting attached to Gracie, and it was going to be hard as hell handing her back over to Master Chief Flynn. He couldn't imagine how hard it had been for Bowie to lose a pet every summer.

He'd wondered why Bowie had woman issues. He didn't have to be slapped upside the head to get a clue now. His mom sounded like a piece of work. "I'm sorry, bud."

Bowie shrugged one wide shoulder and handed up the drill.

"Why didn't you take them with you when you went to Mexico?"

"They have to be quarantined going in and coming back."

"Damn."

"You're taking care of my girl?" Bowie asked, changing the

subject.

"Yeah. She's running good. McMichael's rebuilt the carburetor, and the motor sounds like it's purring. Any time you want to take her out, just let me know. I have the key at home." He hadn't felt comfortable leaving the keys on board since Lester had fucked with him.

"Maybe we can all go out one last time before we go wheels up," Bowie suggested.

Zach glanced down at him. "Sounds good. We need to think of a name for the boat, Bowie. It's about time she had one, don't you think?"

After a minute hesitation he said, "Yeah."

"I'm going to paint her name on the hull before our next fishing trip."

"Do you even know how to paint something like that?" Bowie's dark brown eyes narrowed.

"Would I do anything to disfigure our girl after you entrusted her to me?"

"No."

No hesitation there. That was trust.

He didn't take Bowie's trust lightly. He never had. He was gaining a new understanding of what Piper had experienced. How a lack of trust could make you doubt yourself. Doubt other people.

"Our friend is back," Bowie said, drawing his attention back to the fenced-in dog run.

"That's Tony. He works here, Bowie. He's walking the dogs."

"He sure has an interest in where the cameras are positioned. He's checked them out every time he's come out. And the vet, Ryan something, has been out three times."

"They're probably both just interested in our progress." Zach handed Bowie the drill and climbed down off the ladder. "Ryan is a tightass. Even if he's getting the labor free, he'll be out here checking everything we do. He's worried we're not going to get the cameras up before clients start to arrive."

"After these last two, we'll have mounted twelve cameras in

three hours. What the fuck has he got to complain about?"

Zach shook his head. "I kissed Piper out in the parking lot, and you'd have thought we were ripping each other's clothes off in front the of pet owners."

"Maybe he has a thing for her."

"Maybe." He'd already thought about the possibility. Piper didn't seem to like the guy much, though; otherwise he'd be concerned about it.

Keep it light, he reminded himself. He'd be going wheels up again in three weeks or so. He had no right to get possessive. Damnit.

They finished the last two cameras, texted Flash, and loaded the ladder into Bowie's truck.

A tone sounded when they opened the door, part of the alarm system Flash had installed. He'd done the doors, but not the windows. The motion sensors he placed in the hallways would catch anyone inside when the alarm was on.

Flash cuddled a gray tabby kitten against his chest with one hand while he typed something into the computer with the other.

He glanced up from the screen when they came to lean on the counter. "Good job, guys. All twelve cameras are working great."

"Who's your friend?" Bowie asked, reaching for the kitten.

"Piper's calling her Clementine, but Joy can change it if she doesn't like the name. I've decided on a kitten instead of a pup, because it won't be as much work for Sam. Joy will be crazy about it."

"I hope you called Sam before you said yes," Zach said.

Flash glanced up. "I'm not insane, Doc."

"That's debatable." Bowie cut in. "I've seen you do more than a few crazy things," The kitten climbed his T-shirt to perch on his shoulder.

Sherry the receptionist and, Jasmine, one of the vet's assistants, watched avidly while he cupped a protective hand around the kitten's body. But it wasn't the kitten they were interested in. Zach had seen the response before. All the man had to do was walk into a room.

Bowie could turn on the charm and get any woman he wanted. He might distrust them, but it didn't stop him from wooing them.

Zach left Flash and Bowie bickering good-naturedly and moved around the counter to check on Gracie.

"How's my girl behaving?" he asked Sherry, the receptionist.

"She's incredibly well-behaved. The kitten decided to explore and climbed all over her. She just sniffed her and laid back down."

"Gracie knows she's not a threat. Don't you, gal?"

Her tail thumped in return and she sat up. Physically she was feeling better, and had started to try to push a little. He had to hold her back when they were out in the yard. He didn't want to stress the pins in her hip or encourage her to overuse the leg. She'd begun to rest the foot on the ground for balance. Six weeks was a long time to not be able to run or do other physical things when you were used to training every day. Malinois were known for their high energy levels. And now she'd started to bounce back from the initial trauma, she wanted to push herself. It was going to be tough controlling her.

He probably wouldn't be around to see her recovered, walking normally, and back in training shape. He ran a hand over his hair.

"She still doesn't like Tony." Jasmine commented while she keyed something into her computer.

Zach wondered about that. Maybe arriving at the vet's office, traumatized and injured, and seeing someone similar in looks to the man she'd been chasing had cemented Tony in her mind as someone to dislike. Young, dark-haired, wearing jeans and a T-shirt. Easily described a million men Tony's age and older. Except for the stocking mask.

Still, he planned to ask Piper what time Tony arrived for work the morning of Gracie's accident.

He checked his watch. "Guys—" he broke into Bowie's and Flash's conversation. "It's nearly zero-nine-thirty. We need to finish up and bug out."

Flash looked up from the computer screen. "You guys can go ahead. I just have a few small things to tweak. And I have to sign adoption papers and settle up for the kitten's shots and stuff."

Zach used his phone to text Piper, who was in surgery, that he was leaving and he'd see her at noon. He needed to clean up the apartment. It was starting to look like the dog lived there instead of him.

He'd often wondered how parents lived amidst the clutter children seemed to generate. It had only taken him a couple of weeks to understand how easy it was for things to get out of hand.

He hooked Gracie's harness to her leash and she perked up immediately.

He said his good-byes and left with Bowie in tow, scanning the parking lot and the surrounding area for Lester. They stopped by his vehicle. Wary that Gracie might attempt to jump into the car herself, Zach gave her the command to sit. Her hip and leg weren't ready for a jump yet.

He opened the door and bent to lift her into the car. She settled onto the back seat and waited for him to feed the seat belt through her harness. Then she swiped his cheek with her tongue while he fondled one of her ears.

"Do you honestly believe putting in security cameras is going to do anything to dissuade Lester?" Bowie asked.

"They will when I check the video footage each night and catch him following Piper or driving by. And even if they don't, Piper was trapped inside a cabinet in the surgery while the asshole or assholes who broke in were still in the building. At least the alarm system and the cameras will be a deterrent."

Bowie's dark brows crimped in a frown. "Lester may just turn his sights on you because you're trying to protect her. He can cause you trouble, Doc. Why do you want to get involved in this?"

He hadn't told Bowie about the cops searching his boat for drugs and guns. He hadn't wanted to hear him go ballistic. And if he were honest with himself, he didn't want to hear his comments about Piper bringing trouble his way.

"Piper's lived the last seven years looking over her shoulder. He's using his power as a policeman to stalk her. If we were in any other country besides the USA, wouldn't we be protecting her?"

"Man, women can look you right in the eye, lie, and make you believe everything they say. They have skills."

"Isn't that the pot calling the kettle black, Bowie?" He'd seen Bowie spin yarns a thousand different ways, with just enough truth to make everyone believe he spoke the gospel.

Bowie grimaced. "All right, I'll give you that one."

"She was going to walk away from me to protect me from Lester. She urged me to keep my distance. She's told the same story twice, with no inconsistencies, since I've known her. Once to me, and once to a police detective. Does that sound like a guilty person?"

Bowie shook his head. "But you need to be careful, Doc. You need to watch your back."

"I am, my man. I promise."

PIPER LOOKED FLUSHED and beautiful when she arrived at his apartment. "Flash has been able to get us some information on Lester. I thought it might be a good idea if you share everything with him. He's dealt with a situation similar to yours in the past, so I thought he might have some ideas."

Piper bit her lip as she took a place on the couch and Zach sat down next to her.

Flash leaned forward to place his water on a coaster. "Look, nothing you tell me will go any further than the three of us. It might help you to know Sam's ex stalked her for over a year. He still considered her his property, even after the divorce was finalized."

"I'm sorry she had to go through that. I understand how she felt."

"In a way, what you're going through is more difficult, because Lester has more resources to call on to harass you. Samantha's ex tried to screw with my business and intimidate me, but he didn't have an entire police force at his disposal to mess with me."

Flash's easy manner put her at ease in turn, and she started to open up to him. While Zach listened to her go over the whole story again, he noticed, though her hands shook, and she paused now and then to fight off emotion, the telling of it seemed to be easier.

She got up to get a drink from the kitchen and returned with two bottles of water, offering him one.

Flash gave her a moment to recover before picking up the folder of paperwork he'd brought with him and handing it to her. He rolled the bottle of water he was nursing between his palms. "Lester has a reputation for being an overzealous cop. He's arrested a lot of bad guys and cleared a lot of cases, but his methods aren't exactly police department-approved. He'll hound and stalk whoever he's targeted as the guilty party until they do something he can pounce on."

Piper sat down beside Zach and he reached for her hand. "And if they don't do anything?" she asked.

"There's never been any proof he's planted evidence, but he's had some arrests that were nothing short of miraculous. And once he has his target behind bars, he makes a case."

Piper's fingers tightened around his. "Who told you this?"

Flash exchanged a glance with him. "I'm sorry, I can't tell you. Let's just say I have people out there who owe me big favors, and I called one in. People who, in my opinion, should be crawling up this guy's ass, aren't doing it for some reason."

Zach was aware he could be following in Flash's footsteps if he wasn't careful.

Flash had put his SEAL career and his freedom on the line to capture a major drug dealer, take down a cartel, and expose a dirty FBI agent. He deserved more than a favor now and then.

Instead, his career had stalled because of that nine-month absence. But he'd gained a beautiful wife and daughter out of the experience.

SEALs didn't risk their lives for accolades or promotions. But all their teammates knew what had gone down, and were a little bitter about the injustice of it.

Gracie moseyed up to Flash to be petted, and he immediately started rubbing her ears.

"I hope the favor you called in wasn't something that will cause you any trouble," Piper said, a worried frown creasing her brows.

"No. It won't cause me any trouble." He leaned forward to rest his elbows on his knees. "My wife's ex-husband tried to kill her more than once."

Shock blanked her expression. "How awful."

"She's great now. But my point is… These guys don't give up, and they don't think like regular people. Lester stalked you under the guise of a police investigation, and he took a hit professionally because of it, and upped the stakes for him. He has something to prove now. Which makes him doubly dangerous. But it might make him reckless as well, and that may work in your favor."

"You need to be hyperaware of everything around you. Keep someone with you as much as possible, so you'll have a witness to whatever happens. Check your house and car for any kind of tampering every day. Record every phone conversation if he calls, and if he shows up, record that as well.

"With the resources he has at his disposal, he can jack with you without even being there to witness it. Don't do anything to make it easy for him to cause you trouble. Which includes no drinking in public, not even beer, no drinking even one beer and driving, no speeding, nothing. Check your head and taillights every day." He patted Gracie's side. His attention shifted to Zach. "Keep your firearms locked up or on post."

"Already done. And all my guns are registered."

Flash turned his blue eyes on Piper, and she shook her head. "I don't own a firearm. I'm afraid of them."

"Sam was, too, after everything she's been through. I've been taking her out to one of the local ranges and letting her target shoot. I want her to be able to protect herself when I'm gone. And I'm teaching Joy gun safety. It's cost me some money, but I've gotten trigger guards for every weapon in the house. Though I keep everything locked up, my fear is she'll get curious and gain access to one at someone else's house. So, I'm doing everything I can to make sure it doesn't happen."

"Seeing the damage they can do firsthand…I'm not sure I'd ever be able to pick one up," Piper said.

Zach jumped into their conversation. "They're safe enough if you know what you're doing, Piper."

Flash finished his water and stood to leave.

Piper rose with them. "Thanks for everything, Flash. You've gone above and beyond on my behalf."

"I almost lost Sam because of a crazy asshole. This is a crazy asshole with a badge. Be careful."

Piper looked him in the eye and nodded, firmly. "We will be."

Once outside in the driveway, Flash paused next to his car. "I got you the information you asked for about the ex-boyfriend, but I didn't want to give it to you with Piper in the room. It even includes some psychological evaluations that are damn scary."

While he spoke, he opened the door to the car, got out several sheets from the front passenger seat, and extended the packet of papers to him. "It might not be a bad idea to get one of those dash cams for your cars in case you're stopped. And an alarm. A GPS on her car wouldn't be bad, either, so you can track it if something happens."

Jesus! "I've already been thinking along those lines, but none of it comes cheap. Gracie's vet bills have pretty much wiped me out for now."

"Understood. Piper wouldn't charge me for the kitten's shots. And she gave me flea stuff and such for when the kitten gets older." He looked away. "She's a strong lady."

"Yeah. She hasn't had much choice but to be strong."

"When you can, buy the equipment, and I'll help you install it. If you need any more info, let me know." They bumped fists.

"Once we've gotten past this, and it's safe, I'd like to introduce the ladies. I think Sam and Piper would hit it off," Zach said as Flash got into his car.

"Sounds good." He shut the door and gripped the steering wheel, but didn't move to turn the car on.

"I've also promised Bowie we'd have a fishing trip on the boat before we go wheels up. I'll call you to come out with us."

"I'll be ready. I haven't heard anything, have you?"

He shook his head. "No. I'm working the hip, trying to get it back in shape, but it's still sore as hell. I still can't run on it."

"Don't push it too much." He looked up, his expression serious. "This guy's going to come after you so he can get to her, Doc. You need someone to watch your back. He'll jam you up."

"He hasn't done anything since he sent those bozos out to search the boat."

"He will. These guys don't give up. They're as focused as working dogs like Gracie searching out drugs. You don't want your career destroyed by this asshole."

Hearing his own concerns coming out of Flash's mouth gave his insides a twist. "I can't walk away and leave her to face this alone, Flash."

"I couldn't leave Sam, either. I was already in love with her by then. But I figured my career was gone already, and I'd be in prison for twenty years for being AWOL. I was living each day as it came. You still have everything to lose. Be extra careful."

Jesus. He hadn't really allowed himself to think about what Flash had faced. "I will."

He watched Flash back out of the drive, giving himself a moment to settle down before returning to the apartment. He scanned the street, but saw nothing suspicious. He folded the paperwork from Flash and tucked it in his back pocket. He'd have to put it away until later.

Why couldn't he walk away?

Because being with her was more than he'd expected. They saw each other at lunch and dinner. Always had something to say to each other. In bed, Piper was awakening to her needs and wanted to fulfill his. It was a strong sexual high to know he was the first to give her pleasure. That he might be replacing bad memories with good.

But beyond all that, she'd sneaked in under the barrier he'd erected after Patricia's betrayal. He cared about her, and she cared about him. He knew it, felt it.

She was naturally nurturing. The wall she threw up with people when she first met them hadn't come naturally until after David Henderlight and Lester entered her life. He'd bet his Budweiser on it.

When he entered the apartment, Piper looked up from the floor where she sat cuddling Gracie. "Everything okay?"

"Yeah." He offered her his hand and pulled her to her feet. He homed in on her lips and kissed her, cradled her in his arms, and absorbed the feel of her.

When the kiss ended, she continued to lean into him. "If you need to walk away, Zach. I'll understand."

He shook his head. "Not happenin'. In fact, I want you to move in with me until this is over."

CHAPTER 33

NERVES FLUTTERED IN the pit of Kathleen's stomach when she left Jameson in his recliner, studying the files on her computer. While he was busy, she rubbed salt, garlic, and pepper into a roast, cut up vegetables to go with it, put it in a baking bag, and popped it in the oven.

She checked the time and set the timer for two hours. Sondra was still training the woman they'd hired to do orders, and had been called into the office to take care of a materials issue. Since this was the first time she'd been left alone with the difficult patient, tension had knotted her shoulders.

Kathleen eyed Jameson's color when she wandered back into the family room. For the first week he'd slept quite a bit, but he seemed to have found his balance today, and felt able to sit up long enough to visit with her.

He closed the computer when she came into the room. "Cal knows more about the industrial plans than I do since he does steel work. They look very impressive."

"Thanks. I'm just one part of a team. Once the guys have their part of the design completed, we'll combine them and print them out for the owners."

"Did you do the house plans for clients?" he asked.

"One was for my brother and his wife. One was for a client who contacted me after seeing my brother's house. Two of the others were for a company who sells house plans. I get a commission for them each time they're sold."

"And the other?"

"It's my never-ending dream project. I keep revamping the plans every time I get a new idea."

"Show me which one it is." He handed her the computer.

Kathleen opened it to her dream house and scooted her chair next to his. "It has four bedrooms and four baths."

"So you don't plan to have nine kids like your parents."

"No. Two would be plenty. But I think a guest room and a sofa bed in the downstairs den would be a must for when family comes to visit. Thus the full bath downstairs."

"With property values so high in California, you'll both have to go into debt to your eyebrows to build it."

Kathleen's cheeks heated. He was talking as though she and Cal were already talking marriage, houses, and children. "I couldn't afford to build it in Massachusetts, either. Which is why I call it my dream plan. I couldn't do a basement in California anyway. They're not permitted because of the earthquakes."

"Property values aren't as high here. We could probably build it for about three hundred thousand, maybe three twenty-five, basement and all, including the land to put it on. One of the crews we have in place now could have it under a roof in about three weeks. Has Cal seen it?"

"No."

"Why not?" His dark brown eyes scanned her face. "He took you to see the house he liked, didn't he?"

"Yes. It was beautiful."

"Can't hold a candle to the one you've designed here." He tapped the computer screen with his index finger.

"I meant to show it to him, but it slipped my mind." And she hadn't wanted him to think she was pushing for something he wasn't ready to offer on his own.

Jameson laughed. "If you don't think he's ready, Kathleen, you're blind as a bat. I don't understand why the two of you are dancing around this, like you're walking barefoot over tacks."

Kathleen studied him. Because they both had issues, and they wanted to be at their best for each other. PTSD was a bitch. "Don't you think this might be between me and Cal, Mr. Crowes?"

"Jameson," he corrected her.

"Jameson," she repeated.

He smirked. "You're telling me to mind my own business."

"Well, yeah." She bit back the duh.

He laughed, the sound deep and masculine like Callahan's. "You know you could get a job at any architectural firm here. You're probably one of the best I've seen, and I've been in the business a while."

"I'm glad you think so. But there has to be a need before you can apply for a job."

"Have you looked around?"

"No." If she did and Callahan didn't ask her to stay with him, she'd be devastated.

"I've worked for quite a few firms. I could put in a good word when you do."

When? "If I decide to relocate, I think I can probably come up with a few references from people I've actually worked for."

He gave a quick bark of laughter. He closed the laptop and handed it to her. "Sondra always wanted a girl, but there were complications after we had Doug, and they told her she shouldn't have any more children. She hemorrhaged, and we almost lost her."

"I'm sorry."

"Seems like you've bonded with her."

"She's easy to like." Sondra had gone out of her way to make her feel welcome and part of the family. And she hadn't even said anything when she caught Cal sneaking out of her room at six in the morning.

"Unlike me?"

She wanted to love him because he was Cal's father. But he was a difficult man. Abrasive, opinionated, and impatient. "I don't know yet. This is the first conversation we've had that's lasted longer than two words."

"I suppose it is." His smile was more a grimace. "Damn ticker."

"You'll get through this, but it will take time. You're young, and they have better technology to diagnose and treat heart problems, plus there are medications to keep your cholesterol and heart enzymes in good shape."

"Young, huh?" He raised a dark brow and looked dubious.

"Well my grandmother is in her seventies and diabetic, and she's back to fighting form now. She had open heart surgery two years ago."

"Two years?"

"You'll have to make use of the pool out there, walk, maybe do more exercise, eat healthier."

He scowled.

"Cal fought his way back. You can do it, too."

"How satisfying is it for you to say that? Cal's bound to have told you what kind of asshole I am."

"It isn't satisfying at all." She shook her head. Even after all the pain he had caused Cal, she couldn't feel that way toward him. "And I know Cal doesn't feel that way either. He never wanted to see you in pain. But I would like to know why you didn't want him to work with you."

He remained silent for a long moment. "He... The idea of him walking atop a roof or even climbing a ladder scared the shit out of me. Now he's doing it, and I'm not there to watch out for him."

"He does a job ten times more dangerous in San Diego. And does it well."

"He'd be safer closer to the ground. It can still be dangerous now and then, but never as much. If he'll come back to Texas."

"You should be saying this to your son, not me." Kathleen rose. She held the laptop against her. "Talk to Cal. Tell him how you feel."

"I could tell you to do the same."

"He knows I love him."

"Then what the hell's the holdup?"

Kathleen laughed, then grew serious. "We've both been through some difficult things. I thought I'd be able to shake it off and go back to my life, but it hasn't been as easy as I hoped. I want to be the girl Cal first fell in love with again, but I'm having trouble getting back there."

"You can't go back any more than I can. All you can do is go forward, Kathleen. And he must love the woman you are, because he's still with you, isn't he?"

His no-nonsense, no-holds-barred attitude left little room for argument. Too bad he couldn't stand back and see himself with such clarity. "It doesn't hurt to look back on what was good in the past to shape your goals. How were you and Sondra when you first met?"

He fell silent for a moment, contemplative. "A lot like you and Cal. She was the flower and I was the bee."

Kathleen laughed. "Things could still be that way with a little work. My parents can't keep their hands off each other. After nine kids and forty years of marriage."

As if on cue she heard steps in the living room. Sondra's blond hair curled under her chin becomingly, and soft pink tinted her cheeks from the outside heat, giving her pale skin some color. She was slim and athletic like Callahan. A pretty woman. "I'm sorry I was longer than I thought I'd be." The anxiety in her gaze receded when she eyed Jameson first, then moved back to Kathleen.

Kathleen gave her a smile. "We've been discussing house plans. I'll go put this away." She held up her laptop.

She put the computer in her room, checked the roast, and went into the entrance foyer to look out the window. The surrounding neighborhood appeared deserted.

Hearing Jameson and Sondra's voices in conversation, Kathleen opened the door and stepped outside. Her skin immediately blossomed with moisture from the heat. She walked down to the end of the sidewalk and paused for a moment, looking up and down the street. The smell of hot asphalt reached her. They seemed to be having a heat wave, which did nothing to soothe her. The reflective light from every concrete surface forced her to squint. Next time she'd wear her sunglasses.

Her heartbeat speeded up when she looked back toward the house. The distance between her and the front door seemed to stretch, but the anxiety it caused didn't seem quite as intense as yesterday or the day before.

She walked farther down the sidewalk to the corner of the lot, where the green scent of freshly cut grass wafted to her. She faced the house again. Her pulse beat in her throat and wrists, and her skin took on the hypersensitive feeling of eyes watching her, crawling over her body. Though the need to run back to the shelter of the house rose up so strongly she trembled, she forced herself to stand firm. No one was there to hurt her.

A man with dark hair wearing shorts and a T-shirt exited one of the houses, got into a cherry red Mustang in the driveway, and backed out into the street. As the car approached, Kathleen attempted to focus on the vehicle. She'd always wanted a Mustang. And cherry red would be the color she'd choose. The man waved when he drove by, and she threw her hand up.

She was in control. She was not going to allow anxiety to destroy her life.

One-one thousand, two-one thousand… she counted out three minutes.

The front door opened before she ever reached it, and Sondra handed Kathleen a bottle of water as she joined her inside. "You went farther today and stayed out longer."

Kathleen nodded. "And a car went by, and I actually returned the man's wave." Her hands felt numb and her face hot. She pressed the cold bottle to her cheeks, until her breathing finally eased, and with it her pulse.

She'd had no choice but to share her anxiety issues with Sondra when she'd talked Kathleen into joining her for a walk around the neighborhood. Though having Callahan's mother with her had eased some of her symptoms, she'd been hyperaware of their surroundings and distracted enough that Sondra was concerned.

In crowded spaces, she was fine. Indoors she was good. Out in the open she experienced the sensation of being watched, vulnerable, open to attack.

Most of Hillary's attacks on her had taken place in enclosed spaces. Why was she experiencing anxiety outside? It made no sense.

She still had issues visiting the building sites. What had been a slight case of vertigo had grown worse. She couldn't afford for it to take over, because it would affect her livelihood. So she was determined to face her fears.

"What did you say to Jameson?" Sondra asked, leading the way into the kitchen.

"What do you mean?"

"He was just less…"

Kathleen waited for Sondra to find the right word, though several flitted through her mind, nosy being one of them.

"He seemed less angry."

"We just talked about the business of building homes. And family." What would it hurt if she tried to do a little matchmaking between the two? They had lasted thirty years together. Maybe if she encouraged them both to think back on how things were in the past, they'd be able to reconnect now. It would never be that easy, but it was worth a try.

"He said Cal and I reminded him of the two of you when you were dating. You were the flower, and he was the bee."

Sondra's cheeks flared pink and she laughed. "We were quite young back then, and adventurous, and we couldn't get enough of each other."

Kathleen cocked her head and smiled. "When he gets back on his feet and the doctor gives him the go-ahead, there's no reason why you can't be adventurous again. He'll have some time on his hands, and he'll need to exercise."

Sondra laughed and gave her a hug. "Cal talked about you whenever I called, and I thought he was exaggerating. He wasn't a bit. I'm so glad he convinced you to come for a visit."

CHAPTER 34

ZACH OPENED THE back door of Piper's car and lifted Gracie onto the seat. He talked to the Malinois while he secured her with the seat belt through her harness. "You're now a certified therapy dog, Gracie. Your master chief is going be so happy to see you. I'm sure you're going to be tickled to see him, too." He cupped the dog's chin in his hand and rubbed up her nose and over the top of her head. Her tail thumped on the seat. He was going to miss her like hell when he had to hand her over in a few more weeks.

Piper came out of the house. "You're sure you have a ride home?"

"Yeah. Bowie's going to come by and visit with the master chief and give me a ride home. Chances are Flynn and Gracie will be worn out by then."

He closed the back door and hopped into the passenger seat of her car. Neither of them discussed whether or not he'd checked the vehicle before they put Gracie inside. As per Flash's suggestion, he checked her car every time she had to go anywhere. And they either went together or he followed her.

"I know you're getting tired of driving back and forth to my office." Piper said. She glanced into the rearview mirror before changing lanes to get on the interstate. "I thought maybe we could change back and forth between my house and your apartment.

That way no one would know where we'd be staying from one night to the next. Why stay in one spot and make it easy for him?"

"Are you getting homesick?"

"Maybe a little. It isn't that I'm not comfortable at your apartment, Zach. And I love waking up with you there. It's…"

"Your own space," he finished for her. "It's what I miss when I'm down country. I'm talking seven other guys, sometimes more, piled into a space the size of my bedroom, unbathed, unshaven, and…well, you get the picture."

Piper laughed. "And I complain when Trouble rolls in something smelly to change his scent, then jumps in my bed."

"You smell so good in the mornings. When we go wheels up and I'm trapped in some cramped barracks with my teammates, I'm going to try to remember how you smell in the mornings." Warm, sexy woman with just a hint of jasmine. He got aroused just thinking about it.

He couldn't believe he was talking about clinging to something so personal when he had assured her he didn't want to get too involved. Where was the guy who'd lectured her about keeping her distance?

"Maybe I'll take your pillow home with me," she said, with one of her secret little smiles. She checked her rearview mirror again, switched lanes, and turned on her blinker to exit the interstate. "I'll give you a handkerchief to carry with my body spray on it."

"It won't be the same, but I'll take it."

Her cell phone rang and Zach reached for it. He listened for a moment and relayed the message about an emergency. A dog having puppies in major distress. "You need to go straight to the office. Gracie and I can go onto the hospital alone while you deal with this."

Piper glanced at him. "Are you sure?"

"Yeah. We'll be fine."

Piper wove through traffic, and, bypassing the hospital by a couple of blocks, turned northwest. Her hands gripped the steering wheel, her focus on the distance between her and the distressed animal. Ten minutes later, when she turned into the office parking lot, Zach climbed out and went around to take her place behind the wheel. "Good luck," he said and brushed her cheek with a kiss. "See you at nine." He could tell her mind was already on the dog.

"Be careful," she said over her shoulder and broke into a run toward the front door.

Zach called Bowie to let him know about the change of plans. The drive to the hospital was less fraught, but he found himself looking in the rearview mirror every few seconds for Lester's black car. He did catch a glimpse of Bowie's Camaro following him to the parking lot, but he arrived at the hospital without being stopped, parked the car, and he and Gracie caught a tram from the lot to the front of the hospital.

His phone rang before he went into the building. "I've decided to keep an eye on your vehicle. I can visit Master Chief Flynn tomorrow," Bowie said.

"Okay. He'll probably be entertained better by Gracie than either of us."

"Roger that."

He approached the information desk. "Gracie has an appointment up on the fifth floor to see a patient. Master Chief Flynn. She's his therapy dog." He pulled the paperwork the hospital had sent Piper out of his jacket pocket.

The young woman behind the counter studied the paperwork, then the Malinois. She got out a badge for Zach to wear in the hospital, and he and Gracie walked down to the elevators. Gracie stood at attention, her eyes on the elevator doors and her tail waving the entire ride. The staff and visitors who got on gave the dog a wide berth, though she made no move to approach any of them.

He exited the elevator and once again produced the paperwork for a nurse at the nurse's station. She eyed the dog with a good-natured smile and offered her hand for Gracie to smell. After the introduction, she gave her a tentative stroke. "The master chief talks about her all the time. He's going to be so thrilled to see her."

Zach glanced at her name tag to put name with her face. "She's going to go wild. So I'm preparing to be dragged through the door."

"He's sitting up in a chair right now, which will be good for them both. I'll go with you just in case you need some ballast."

Zach laughed.

Gracie's three-legged progress had become familiar to him, but he didn't know how Master Chief Flynn would respond to it.

The nurse held the door open for them.

Gracie spied the master chief first. Her high-pitched whine drew his attention.

"Gracie! You look great baby."

Her whole body bowed almost in half with each wag of her tail. Zach held her back with difficulty so he could unhook the leash from her harness. She bolted to her owner, her whine almost a whistle, her body doing a serpentine wiggle as she rubbed back and forth against Master Chief's legs.

Flynn rubbed her with his one good hand and attempted to reach for her with the other, though the movement was clumsy.

"Sweet girl," Flynn patted her wherever he could reach. The dog tried to climb into his lap, and he scooted over to make room for her next to him in the chair.

Watching the two, Zach blinked against a rush of emotion. He was getting to be a real wuss where this dog was concerned. He glanced over to see Michelle unashamedly crying and smiling at the same time.

"You couldn't have done anything any better for him." She squeezed his arm and slipped out of the room, closing the door behind her.

Gracie wedged herself into Flynn's lap and rested her chin on his shoulder. The two clung together for several moments.

Zach moved forward. "Let me know when she gets to be too much for you to hold. She's a little big to be a lap dog."

"I carried one just like her in a harness, jumping out of planes, shooting during fire fights, and in much worse places than this."

Flynn's voice came out gruff, and he brushed at his eyes with the back of his wrist.

Zach filled in the moment with info to give the man time to recover his composure. "She's been great at my apartment, and Piper's house with Trouble, her Golden retriever. She's teaching him some manners and he's teaching her how to be a dog, though she still thinks she's more human than canine."

Flynn laughed. "Yeah, she does." He rubbed the back of Gracie's neck and earned a lick to the ear. "Thanks for bringing her to see me." Zach looked away and pretended not to see the tearful, glazed look in the man's eyes.

"Piper filled out the paperwork to have her designated as a therapy dog."

"She's a smart lady."

"Yeah, she is."

"I can see you're treating my girl good. How 'bout Piper?"

"I'm doing my best."

"She calls and checks on me most every day."

Zach's brows rose. He wasn't actually surprised. Piper had such empathy for injured animals and people. "Have they said when you're going to be able to go home?"

"They want me to stick around for a couple more weeks to do physical therapy and get this arm and hand working better. Well, actually, the whole right side. It's strange. I can think how I want it to move, but it's like having a limb you've slept on that won't wake up. They think with therapy I'll be able to regain some movement."

Zach limped forward to sit in the only other chair in the room. "Good. While you're busy doing physical therapy, I'm doing massage therapy with Gracie. The hip is mending well, but she still avoids putting much weight on the leg. Which is normal at this point."

Zach rose to help the dog get down. She continued to lean against Flynn's legs. Master Chief Flynn scratched her behind the ears.

"Later she'll do some water therapy at Piper's office."

"She's doing well with you, I can tell."

"She's a lot of company for me. My hip is healing, but it's slower going than I thought it would be."

"Any word about deployment?"

Zach shook his head. "I'll have to go wheels up with the team even if I have to recover after I get wherever we're going. But Piper's great with Gracie. She'll be in good hands."

"And what about Dr. Bertinelli?"

He had to go. He didn't have a choice. The thought of leaving her turned him inside out. "She understands I have a duty."

"I've had a couple of years of retirement to look back on the choices I made in the past. And I've had some time in the last two weeks to mull things over in detail. I've come to the realization I was a fool. I had a girl who was crazy about me when I was your age. But I shipped out and let everything I was going through come between us. I didn't attempt to keep in touch like I should have. Didn't tell her how I felt about her nearly as often as I should have."

Zach's thoughts leapt to Patricia. There had been no promises made there, but what about Piper? He couldn't leave and ask her to wait for him. Jesus, they'd been dating two weeks. Well, not exactly dating. What would you call what they'd been doing? Living together?

Flynn went on. "Dotty stuck with me through three deployments, wrote me letters, sent me care packages, met me for R and R on her own dime. She wanted marriage, kids, and I wasn't ready to take on that responsibility. I felt what I was doing was more important." His attention dropped to the dog lying at his feet. "It wasn't, Zach. I could have had a wife and kids coming to see me right now. Maybe some grandchildren."

"They won't send me home and let me do therapy as an outpatient because I don't have anyone to stay with me. I won't be able to drive for a long time, so I can't get to the grocery store or even the barbershop for a haircut. My parents are both gone now. My brother lives across the country in Tennessee. He has his own family to think about. Plus he has two kids in college and not enough money to come even if he wanted to."

"I'm not saying get involved or get married just to have someone to take care of you when something like this happens. I'm saying don't let the teams be the only thing in your life, because it leaves you barren."

This was the second person telling him the same thing in the past three weeks.

"Gracie's my kid, but she can't talk back when the walls get close." The dog sat up and stuck her nose beneath Flynn's semi-paralyzed hand, begging for a rub. He guided his one hand with the other to give her what she wanted. "In five or six years Gracie may be gone and I'll be alone."

The man's gray eyes focused on him. "If you think Dr. Bertinelli might stick with you for the long haul, and you have feelings for her, at least give it a shot. If it doesn't work out, you may come away with a few bruises, but you'll still have time to try again before you end up like me."

"You're not that old, Master Chief. You still have time to meet someone."

"Maybe." There was no conviction in his tone. "I may not regain full use of my arm and leg, so my mobility issues may make it difficult."

"My sister's boyfriend is missing a leg, but she didn't let it interfere with getting to know him. You're telling me not to miss out on my opportunities. You don't have them unless you make them. The nurse who showed us in here might be a start...if she's not married. You don't want to get into a one-legged ass-kicking contest with a husband."

Flynn laughed. "No, I don't. Michelle's a little young for me."

"She's, what? Mid-forties? Sounds about right to me."

Flynn's cheeks flushed. "I'll have to give it some thought."

"Look. Women in the nursing profession are nurturers. So what if you have some mobility issues? Hell, I was hobbling around on crutches and could barely move, and Piper was all about taking care of me and making sure I took care of myself. You have to show the ladies you have some qualities that outweigh all the baggage you drag around with you. And remember they have baggage, too. And you have one thing I don't have right now."

"What's that?" Flynn asked.

"You're going to be on CONUS. And you won't be shipping out. You'll be here in person if you're needed."

"Yeah, I will be." The master chief shot him a look of compassion.

One of Flynn's teammates showed perfect timing by joining them at that moment. The rest of the visit was listening to the two reminisce about past exploits.

Aware of Bowie waiting in his vehicle, Zach rose. He hooked the leash to Gracie's harness and waited while Flynn said his good-byes. "I'll bring her back in a couple of days, Master Chief."

"Thanks, Zach."

He exited the room and lifted Gracie to carry her. She appeared a little fatigued from the excitement and the walk from the front entrance.

Michelle, the nurse, was waiting at the desk. "I thought Gracie might need a ride downstairs," she said, pushing a wheel chair forward.

"What a truly excellent idea. Thanks." He set the dog on the wheelchair and smiled when she settled in.

"It's a shame she can't stay with Master Chief Flynn while he recuperates," the nurse said. "He lights up when he talks about her."

"She's the only family he has here. Is there any kind outpatient program that would transport him from home to the hospital for his therapy?"

"Not unless he could afford to pay for someone to stay with him. He's not quite mobile enough yet to be alone."

Zach's cell phone vibrated and he reached in his pocket to retrieve it. Seeing it was Bowie he said, "Sorry, I have to take this." He touched the screen and stepped away. "Yeah."

"You'd better meet me at my car. Some fucker just showed up and fucked with Piper's car. He opened the driver's door with a lockout tool and put something inside. Looked like he shoved something under the seat. I got video with my cell phone."

Zach's face flushed with heat as his anger raged. "Did you get his face?"

"Yeah. It wasn't your guy, but how much you want to bet me it was somebody he paid?"

"I'll be there in a few minutes. I'll call when I'm at the lot so you can bring me in."

"Roger that."

He ended the call, his mind racing while he thought of and discarded a number of ideas for how to handle the situation.

Though the nurse offered to accompany Gracie downstairs, Zach said he thought he could handle it and wheeled the dog onto the elevator alone. He turned in his badge at reception and carried Gracie onto the tram.

His hip was aching and he was winded by the time he'd carried the seventy-pound dog off the tram and across the parking lot. He eased her to the ground and called Bowie.

"I'm to your right two rows back."

Zach got Gracie secured in Bowie's back seat, then climbed into the passenger seat.

Bowie's features were grave with anger. "This fucker sure has it in for you and your girl. He's bound to know Piper's at the office. And he has to have some kind of tracker on her vehicle to know where it is. He's probably waiting for the car to move to call it in so you'll be stopped on your way home."

"I'm calling Sherman. I don't have any other options. I have the video of Lester in the parking lot at the marina watching us leave the dock, then pulling out just before the two cops showed up to search the boat. And you have this. The moment I leave the parking lot, they're going to stop me and search the car. If Sherman's following and watches it go down, he'll know what Piper's told him is true."

"If he'll show," Bowie said.

"If he doesn't, we'll search the car and remove whatever the guy planted. We'll document everything and I'll send the videos to Tess and go public with it."

Bowie nodded. "Sounds like a plan."

Zach scrolled for Sherman's number and put the call through.

CHAPTER 35

CAL SLID KATHLEEN'S hand through the bend of his arm while they walked along the river. The smell of greenery and the water bathed his senses while they walked across one of the arched footbridges over the river to their hotel.

They paused to watch one of the boats float down the channel. It darted under the next footbridge and disappeared with its passengers around a curve in the water's route. Hotels, restaurants, bars, and shops lined the sidewalks running parallel to the water's course. Large trees set at equal distances shaded areas of the walkways, a welcome respite from the afternoon heat. They had done a tour of the Alamo earlier, a boat tour of the river walk, and eaten ice cream at one of the shops.

"Your mom and dad won't mind us spending the night away?"

"No." He cupped his hand over hers where it rested over his arm. "They know I want to spend some time alone with you before you go back to San Diego." He brushed his lips against her temple. "You've spent more time with Mom and Dad this week than you've been able to spend with me."

"Have you given any thought to how your family is going to continue with the business if you don't stay?"

"I've thought about it. They can hire a project foreman in my place when I go back to San Diego. Or take on a partner."

Her green eyes settled on his face. "Your father wants that partner to be you, Cal."

"I'm not going anywhere without you, Kathleen."

He read relief in her expression. She rested her head against his shoulder.

"Did you really think I'd leave you behind?"

"My heart was telling me no, but a girl likes to hear the words, Callahan."

"The first week I was here, Doug took me out for a beer. We ran into two ladies he knew, and they bought us a beer. I couldn't wait to finish mine and get out of there. It felt wrong to even have a drink with another woman."

Kathleen ran her hand down his arm and laced her fingers with his. "I can't say I'm not glad you felt that way. I'd have felt the same."

A large group walked by behind them, then they were once again alone. Would Kathleen think this place romantic enough for a proposal? The water glistened below them, its sound like a soft sigh as it rushed past, and the light softened as evening approached. Kathleen's skin looked satin-smooth against her dark hair.

Mother Nature had brushed her cheeks with a natural color and given her lips a coral tint. He knew she looked just as beautiful climbing out of bed mussed and well-loved as she did spruced up to go out. She'd be beautiful when she was eighty. He hoped he was still around to tell her so when he was old.

"What time is our reservation for dinner?" Kathleen asked.

"Seven."

"We have a little more than an hour to get cleaned up."

He'd bring her back to this spot after dinner and pop the question. Their hands linked, they walked south to their hotel, the Valencia. They passed through the lobby of the hotel, past a sitting area where a large sectional couch was arranged before a wall of lighted sconces. On their way to the elevators, the vaulted ceiling's architectural design drew Kathleen's interest, just as Cal had known it would.

Their sixth floor room had a streamlined, masculine feel due to the geometric shapes of things used to decorate the space. Square lamps with cream-colored shades cast a soft glow on either side of the king-sized bed. The leather headboard and a roomy leather armchair added a west Texas flavor, and a wide floating shelf created a desk space. Everything was spotlessly clean and neat.

"I'm so sticky from the heat, think I'll take a quick shower," Kathleen said. "Unless you want to join me and we could make it a bath?"

"Think we can both fit in there?" he asked.

"I think we could give it a try."

If he slipped and fell and injured his stump, he'd never get to pop the question. "I think if we start out in the tub, we'll never make it to the restaurant."

Kathleen laughed. "You're probably right. I'll only be about ten minutes."

"Take your time, hon. I'm not going anywhere."

A little antsy, he wandered onto the balcony outside their room and leaned on the railing to watch the river traffic while he waited. The heat of the day had passed, and a nice breeze brushed against him to dry the tacky sweat from his skin.

She loved him. She was going to say yes. Then why was he so nervous?

Because he was trying to create a special memory for her, for them both, and it was damn hard. He should have planned more. He should have popped the question on the footbridge. He should have popped the question before they ever came to San Antonio.

Hearing the bathroom door open, he turned to lean back against the balcony railing and smiled when Kathleen, clad only in a towel, came out of the bathroom. Unable to resist, he sauntered back into the room and closed the balcony door.

He shed his shirt, T-shirt and belt along the way. At the sound of the belt hitting the carpet, Kathleen looked up. Cal scooped her up and headed for the bed. "I have to have you right now,

Kathleen," he murmured and knelt on the bed to place her in the center of it. He peeled away the damp towel and bent his head to press his open lips against the sensitive area between shoulder and breast. "You smell so good." He loved her scent, like citrus body wash and her. Her skin was cooled from the air conditioning and still dewy with moisture from her shower, and her hands were warm as she stroked his shoulders and back.

He slid down to press open-mouthed kisses to her breasts. Her stomach. Her thighs. Her legs trembled when he slipped between them, parting her nether lips with his thumbs, revealing her, flushed and wet, open to him. He feathered her clit with his tongue. Kathleen caught her breath and wiggled, getting closer to the caress. When he plunged his tongue inside her, she murmured, "Oh, God." The sweet-salty taste of her drove his own need higher. He deepened the intimate kiss and at the same time put pressure the sensitive nub, and Kathleen cried out and climaxed.

He unzipped his pants and slid upward, guiding himself inside her and groaning as her wet heat gripped him. He couldn't get close enough, deep enough. Her breathing was ragged in his ear, her hands caressing him while she rose to meet his thrusts and counter them with her own, creating a drag against his flesh that tossed him up and over into a climax so strong his lungs seized and his hips jerked again and again. He collapsed atop her murmuring her name.

She stroked his back, her caresses moving from passionate to soothing.

Several moments passed before he could lift his head, and when he withdrew from her, his muscles shook.

He'd gotten carried away and missed another opportunity to pop the question.

Kathleen brushed a hand over his close-cropped hair, her eyes searching his face. "You love me so well, Callahan. I'm such a lucky lady." She drew his lips to hers for a kiss. "But I think I need some food. Good sex burns a lot of calories, and I'm starving."

He laughed. "Me too."

He rolled off the bed and hiked his jeans back up. It was becoming a habit to make love partly clothed because it took too long to remove his prosthetic leg and then his pants. He needed to take more time next time. "Want to come back into the shower and clean up again?" he asked, offering his hand. His mind was already on the logistics of removing his prosthetic and balancing in the shower. But they'd done just fine before. Kathleen thought nothing of seeing his stump.

She slipped off the bed. "I'll wash your back."

CHAPTER 36

IN THE TINY security office of the parking structure, Zach paced back and forth impatiently. How long did it take for Sherman and his forensic team to go over the car? They'd been at it nearly thirty-five minutes.

"Sit down and chill, bro." Bowie said. He seemed to be dividing his time between toying with his phone and petting Gracie. The two of them stretched out on the small couch in the office. "Time's not going to pass any faster just because you wear a ditch in the floor."

"You always piss me off the way you can sit for hours screwing with your phone or just staring off into space. Especially when I'm about to crawl out of my skin."

Bowie chuckled. "I'll tell you my secret if you'll sit your ass down and relax."

Zach sank into the one of the chairs positioned in front of the desk in the room, straight-backed and uncomfortable. "All right, tell me."

"I think about the wildest, kinkiest sex I've ever had, and time just gets away from me."

Zach had to control the urge to roll his eyes. "You, my friend, are full of shit."

Bowie laughed. "Got you to sit down though, didn't I?"

Five minutes later Sherman joined them. "There are definite

scratches where he used the lock bar to unlock the car and put the drugs in the car, and there's a GPS tracker installed under the dash." Detective Sherman did not look happy. "And there's a small bag of cocaine under the front seat. Enough to suggest dealing. And someone's broken the back right taillight."

"Jesus!" Zach couldn't help but voice his rage. He'd searched the vehicle but hadn't thought to look for a GPS. "How much do you want to bet that as soon as the car moves there'll be a patrol unit, waiting to pull me over and search the vehicle?"

"You're probably right," Sherman sounded tired. "I probably shouldn't tell you this, but…I traced the call from the marina, and it came from a burner cell located in the parking lot, so it was untraceable. But there's a security video of Lester making a call from the parking lot while he watches you come back into the marina. If we recover the phone and get the serial number, we'll be able to trace it back to the store where it was sold. They may have cameras there which recorded the purchase. Or then again it might have been borrowed from a CI. But I got a copy of the tip that came into dispatch. It sounds like Detective Lester's voice. We can have it analyzed and compared to make certain while we build a case."

"And the convenient description of the subjects sent to the K-9 guys?"

"It was dictated to dispatch by the tipster, Lester, and put out on the call."

He drew a deep breath. "I also viewed the footage of his behavior during the grocery store episode Dr. Bertinelli reported to me. She was right. He was pursuing her. He followed her into the store, and when she slipped away, continued to search for her. What he would have said or done had he caught up to her, we'll never know."

"And now this," Bowie said. Gracie raised her head from his thigh for a moment, then lay it back down.

"We'll need to pull the recording directly off your phone, Ensign Rivera, so we'll have a direct chain of evidence. And we'll be pulling security footage here at the parking lot as well. I've already forwarded what you sent me to one of our forensic guys, and he's created a still and is searching the facial recognition database. And we've already sent out a BOLO on the guy as well. We'll identify him, and when we find him, and put some pressure on him, he'll crack and tell us who paid him to do this. He'll be up on distribution charges if he doesn't."

"In the meantime?" Zach asked.

"I have a big favor to ask of you, Ensign O'Connor."

Immediately wary, Zach eyed him for long moment. "What?"

"Let this play out."

"No. I can't be arrested for drugs or anything else. The brass will kick me out of the teams." Zach shot Bowie a look, and Bowie immediately raised his cell phone and held it into position to tape Sherman.

"There won't be any record of your arrest once we've reeled Lester in. Nothing will be recorded on paper."

"Once a computer record is made of anything, we both know it's impossible to delete. It's always there. We have a friend who worked on an FBI investigation and got burned, Detective. His career will never advance. He damn near single-handedly brought down a dirty agent and a drug kingpin, and he's still stuck at the starting line and will be for as long as he's a SEAL."

"I'll have my CO put it in writing. I'll call your top brass. Once you're brought in, Lester won't be able to resist coming down to the station to rub it in and say I told you so. I'll make certain he gets word you're there and sits in on the interview. It will be up to you to bait him into admitting something."

"Why do you need that?" Bowie asked. "Find the fucking guy who planted the drugs and get him to talk."

"A confession would be better. Whatever we do, we need to do it fast. You've already been here two hours. We stall much longer, and Lester will be wondering what the hell you're doing. Or we could call Dr. Bertinelli and have her come down and be the one to go through the process."

Zach's temper flared. "God damn you, Sherman. You know I'm not going to let anyone arrest Piper."

Bowie cut into the conversation, his hand never stopping as he stroked Gracie's ear. "There has to be at least a couple of thousand dollars' worth of cocaine there. I saw the size of the bag. Would Lester have access to that kind of money? Or would he borrow something from the evidence room?"

"I've already got a call into IA about it," Sherman replied. "They're going down to evidence right now to see if he's signed out anything."

Zach raked his fingers through his hair. "He'll try to get me to roll on Piper."

"Yeah, and he'll try to get to her by using you."

"They'll bring her in, too, because the car belongs to her. And Lester can say it was an arranged drop, unless you can get the guy to talk."

"We'll get him to talk."

He wished to Christ he believed the man. "There's something else. If I get Lester to talk, this is going to throw into question every arrest he's been involved with. How's the District Attorney going to feel about that?"

"Not my problem. I'm just interested in getting a dirty cop out of my division. Whatever goes down afterward is the DA's problem."

Bowie eased out from under Gracie's head to stand. "You need to know I've already sent a copy of the video to a trusted friend on the San Diego paper, Detective. Zach's already shared everything with her."

Zach raised a brow. The only person he'd sent copies of the marina videos to was Detective Sherman. "You try to fuck Doc like the FBI did our other buddy, she'll release stills and a story that will rain down shit on your department and Lester."

Sherman's Joe Friday act almost deflated. Color stormed his face, but he held it together.

Bowie continued, "And I've been recording this conversation and sent that to her as well."

Sherman's eyes narrowed. "For the record, Ensign. It's against the law to record a private conversation without all parties' knowledge."

Zach smiled at Bowie's smug, don't-give-a-shit expression as he glared back at Sherman. "You were just notified. I'm going to be covering my buddy's six during this takedown. When they stop him, there better not be any provocation. I'll be videoing the entire thing."

Sherman's phone rang and he stepped out of room. When he returned his demeanor had lightened. "We've picked up the guy. One of the other detectives in the office recognized him. He's one of the CIs Lester cultivated when he was in the drug unit. The guy's already singing."

Zach breathed a sigh of relief.

"I still want to see what you can get from Lester, O'Connor."

Fuck! When had he agreed to this? "You need to take Gracie with you, Bowie. The officers will call animal control, and she'd end up at the animal shelter."

Bowie nodded. "I've got her covered."

"You'll need to pick up Piper for me, too. Keep her calm. Let her know what's going down." She'd be upset and he wouldn't be there to reassure her.

"I will."

He messaged an ache across his forehead and his heart rate rocketed. "You fucking better come through on your end, Sherman. If brass gets even a whiff of this, I can kiss my promotion good-bye and be stuck here twiddling my thumbs while the rest of my team goes wheels up. This isn't just about Lester, this is about men's lives at stake if I'm not where I'm supposed to be."

Sherman's enthusiasm dropped to his regular Joe Friday seriousness. "I'll stand by my part of the deal. I'm calling my CO now, and he'll get in touch with yours."

"Hawk will have to take it up the chain of command. I'd better call him and give him a heads-up."

"Okay."

It was a difficult phone call. Hawk was no more pleased with the situation than Zach was. Hawk was even more pissed because Zach hadn't bothered to share everything that had gone down in the past week.

"What would you have told me to do, Hawk?" Zach asked.

"Step the fuck away from this, from her."

"And leave her completely vulnerable to this asshole cop. Would you have done it if it were Zoe?"

"You're going to end up in jail in her place."

"Maybe not. He wants her, not me, and it's not my vehicle. I just have to play dumb while he tries to get me to turn on her."

"Fuck, Doc!" Hawk's voice was rough with frustration. "I'm coming down there."

"Wait until after I'm interviewed. If it looks like things are going south, Bowie will call you."

"I don't like this."

"I'm not real crazy about the situation either. But if there's a chance I can get Lester to say something incriminating...well, there's no telling how many innocent people he's done this to, Hawk."

"Do you care enough to risk your career for her Doc?"

Why was no one but he outraged about this travesty of justice? "She's *innocent*."

"That isn't what I asked."

He'd been avoiding acknowledging the emotional aspect of being with Piper. Ignoring it. But with Hawk waiting on the other end of the line, he couldn't dodge it any longer. "Yeah, it is. I care about her. She's beautiful, and brave, and she might be the one."

There—he'd left himself some wiggle room. Who the fuck was he kidding? There wasn't enough wiggle room on the whole planet. He was crazy about her. But he didn't have time to deal with his feelings right now. "I can't turn away and leave her facing this alone."

"I'm not going to call the brass unless this thing goes south. What they don't know never happened. Damn it, you have a promotion coming down the pike, and this could fuck it up. Have this Detective Sherman call me as soon as you get to the station."

"Will do. His CO should be calling you any minute."

"Fuck!" Hawk breathed into the phone for a couple of seconds, his frustration palpable. "Okay. Watch yourself. If they take you in, don't resist in any way. Don't give them a reason to fuck you up. We need you on the plane when we go wheels up. And besides that, I don't want you stuck stateside in a jail cell."

"I know, Hawk."

He hung up the phone and beckoned to Bowie. "You need to bring Piper to the station when you pick her up. I don't want police coming to her place of business, or her house, and taking her away in handcuffs. You know that will be the first thing Lester does to fuck with her."

"I'll take care of it."

"Thanks."

Bowie extended a hand and they fist-bumped.

"There's one more thing I need you to do, Bowie." He took out his cell phone and shot Bowie the number he'd need to dial. "If they take Piper in for questioning, I want you to call Piper's mom. Someone in her family has the money, or had it. Maybe the threat of having her arrested for something they've done will make them come forward. They've probably already spent it, but they may own up to taking it."

Sherman ended his call and wandered over to join them. "We're good to go."

"I'll be following you and taping everything," Bowie said again.

"They may not stop me. Lester may bide his time."

"Then we'll put someone on you and Dr. Bertinelli until he makes his move." After a pause, Sherman added, "My bet is that he's waiting right now for you to move the car."

The sooner Zach got this over with, the better. But in a way he was looking forward to sitting across the table from this guy and seeing what kind of game he planned to play.

CHAPTER 37

THE CITRUS RESTAURANT was beautiful, the service excellent, the salmon delicious, and the banana nut cheesecake they shared for desert melted in her mouth and was almost as good as Sondra's chess pie. Almost.

"I think your mother could sell her pie recipe to the chef here and make a fortune," Kathleen commented while they strolled down the winding sidewalk toward a tributary of the river walk.

"You couldn't get her to part with that recipe from for a million bucks," Cal commented.

"Wonder if she'd share it with me?"

"Only under very special circumstances."

"Like what for instance?" Kathleen asked.

"If she were passing it down to the next generations of Crowes."

Surprised by the comment Kathleen remained silent. Cal directed her to a bench set beneath one of the big trees next to the river. The light shone from one of the hotels in a dappled pattern across the concrete sidewalk and over them.

"I've been trying to find the perfect moment, the perfect place, all day, because I have something I want to say to you, Kathleen. Ask you."

Her heart leapt against her breastbone as it took off like a flock of birds beating to get out.

"I think about you all the time when you're not with me, and I can't get enough of you when you are." He kissed her gently. "I'm off the market to any other woman, and I know you feel the same about me. I love you. I want to be your partner, your lover, your husband. Will you marry me?"

Kathleen had sensed he was working up to something, but had expected a proposal to live together, not a proposal of marriage. Shock stole her ability to speak for several seconds.

All she could think of how much she loved and wanted him. But there were things he needed to be aware of. "I'm still having PTSD issues, Callahan."

"I know, darlin'. I still have some issues too. I don't mind being your support while you work through things. You were mine and still are. That's what being a couple is all about, isn't it?"

She struggled not to tear up, but it was a hopeless cause. "I want to be better before we get married."

He kissed her again with the same soft, tender emotion behind it. "You will be. You're stronger than you know, Kathleen."

She felt strong sitting here with him, being held in his arms. But if he were to walk away ten feet, twenty, what then?

With his gaze so expectant and filled with love, she had to say what was in her heart. "I can't imagine spending my life with anyone but you. I'm so grateful we found each other. So, yes, I'll marry you."

The emotion in his face undid her. He pulled out his keys. "I've been carrying this around with me for a month. He worked something loose from his key ring.

"Oh, my God! Tell me you haven't had that on your key ring for a month."

Cal laughed. "No. I just put it on there before we left the room. I was afraid I'd lose it." He slid the ring on her finger.

In the dull glow of the streetlight, Kathleen studied the princess cut diamond flanked by alternating smaller diamonds and rubies. It was a gorgeous ring, perfect for her. He knew her so well. "It's beautiful." Tears blurred her vision, and she rested her forehead against his shoulder. "Thank you, Callahan. I thought you were going to ask me to live with you. Possibly move here. You surprised me."

His lips brushed her forehead. "You're so good for me, Kathleen. No way would I leave you."

"Want to go back to the room and celebrate?" she asked.

"You don't have to twist my arm, sweetheart." He rose and offered her a hand up. "I kind of jumped the gun earlier."

"Is that what you call it?" Kathleen said with a laugh. They wound their way back the way they had just come.

He leaned forward to nuzzle her ear. "I almost popped the question while I was still inside you."

"I'm so glad you didn't. I'd have thought it was the sex talking."

Cal laughed. "I don't remember having enough breath left to talk."

A figure stepped out of the shadows into their path. Kathleen caught her breath. The man's face remained in shadow. Not so the thirty-eight revolver he held pointed at Cal. Cal eased in front of Kathleen, putting himself between her and the gun. Her breathing hitched and she gripped his arm hard.

Oh, God! Please don't pull the trigger. Please.

"Both of you give me your wallets and jewelry."

The word jewelry seemed to ping like the vibration of a bell. Her beautiful engagement ring. She'd only had it on her finger for a matter of minutes.

"Take it easy," Cal's tone remained even, quiet. He reached behind him to retrieve his billfold. He tugged his watch off over his hand.

The tiny purse she carried only held a few dollars, one credit card, and her cell phone. He was welcome to that...but her beautiful engagement ring. But every time the gun swung in Cal's direction her legs wanted to crumple and her stomach hollowed out. She handed the man the small bag and the sterling silver bracelet her mother gave her when she was sixteen.

He jerked the purse from her. "Where's the ring he just gave you?"

So he'd been watching them. "Please don't."

"Give me the fucking ring, bitch!" He lunged at her and grabbed her arm. The light struck his face. His very young, childish, white face. He couldn't be any more than fifteen or sixteen. But his sneer of aggression was older, at least double the age.

Cal moved so quickly Kathleen only saw the boy stumble back while Cal added his weight and momentum until they crashed through the landscaping and against the building behind it. Cal gripped the gun, and twisted it. A dull pop was followed by a high-pitched scream. Cal jerked the weapon free. He flipped the kid forward onto his face and had him pinned to the ground in a matter of seconds. With his knee in the center of the kid's back and his hand gripping his wrists, Cal growled, "Kathleen come get the gun."

"You fucking broke my finger, motherfucker," the kid whined while he twisted and heaved, trying to break free, and when he couldn't, groaned in pain.

Her feet seemed to have taken root, her knees as though turned to stone. After the first step, she shuffled forward.

"You're going to have to pull back the hammer and release my hand first, honey."

Kathleen's stomach threatened to revolt. The thin strip of skin between the base of his thumb and forefinger was caught between the hammer and the frame of the revolver.

The kid had pulled the trigger.

Cal could have been killed. She could have been. Someone close by in the dark could have been hit had he not grabbed the gun just right. Her whole body began to shake as she edged back the hammer and released the fold of skin.

"You okay, Kathleen?"

"I should have given him the ring."

"I wasn't going to let him so much as touch that ring. And he damn sure shouldn't have touched you." The controlled rage in his voice did more to calm her than anything. "Dial nine-one-one, honey."

Her phone was in her purse, but at the moment she didn't know where her purse was. She pulled Cal's cell phone from his back pocket and backed away from the two of them. Placing the gun on the ground close to the sidewalk, she dialed the number.

While she spoke to the dispatcher, she caught the reflection of light on the broken crystal and scattered pieces of Cal's watch, trampled during the struggle. They'd been so lucky.

THE ONLY FURNITURE in the room was a table and two chairs. The chairs were about as comfortable as a prostate exam. There was no padding in the seat, and after nearly an hour of waiting, Zach's backside was numb.

Officially he was there for an interview, not under arrest, and at least he wasn't handcuffed. Which meant he could move around the room. And they hadn't taken his phone. So Bowie could text him updates.

There was no window and nothing to look at. The florescent light beamed down and reflected off the eggshell white of the walls and the tile on the floor. It seemed overly bright in so small a space.

He hooked a toe around the leg of the other chair, dragged it close, and propped his feet in the seat. He folded his arms, made himself as comfortable as possible, and closed his eyes. He could take a power nap anywhere. If asshole Lester was watching, his disinterest might aggravate the man enough to speed up the process.

Pretending to be the concerned guy caught with a bag of cocaine weighing almost ten ounces tucked under his driver's seat would never play for him. Lester would never buy it. Poking holes in his logic would be the only way he'd gain ground on the guy. That and straight-up painting a picture of what he believed had happened.

Lester was a linear thinker. He couldn't see the big picture. As his dad had mentioned, the guy had tunnel vision. Maybe Zach could open his eyes to other possibilities.

He tilted his head back against the wall, and breathed in deeply to relax the tension from his body so he'd become drowsy.

Had Bowie brought Piper in yet? Had he called Piper's mother? Would it do any good?

He hoped so.

When the door opened ten minutes later, he actually was on the edge of sleep, but hadn't tumbled into it yet.

"They say when a man takes a nap in an interview room, he's exhausted from guilt. An innocent man is so nervous he can't close his eyes."

Zach parted his lids and pinned Lester with his gaze. He raised one brow. "Or he's used to catching twenty winks with bombs and bullets whizzing overhead."

Lester's mouth tightened while he gripped the back of the chair Zach rested his feet on and waited until he dropped them to the floor before pulling it out and sitting down.

He laid a folder down on the table. "The cocaine in the car is good quality. Where do you suppose it came from?"

"I don't know, Detective Lester. Why don't you tell me?"

"I warned you that day at your apartment to distance yourself from her. It isn't your car, but you were driving it. If you can offer me a plausible explanation as to how it might have gotten there, I might be able to do something for you."

Zach paused to think his reply through. "I have no history of drug use. No arrest record in any state. And I was driving a borrowed car. You won't find my fingerprints on the packaging the drugs are in. I don't think you have much chance of building a case against me. So just what do you think I might need you to do for me?"

"Your CO probably wouldn't be too thrilled about having one of his team members brought in for driving a car where drugs were discovered. They hold you to a higher standard than that, surely?"

"Yeah. They're sticklers about staying drug-free and keeping our noses clean, on post and off."

"No one needs to tell your commanding officer you've been brought in for questioning, Ensign. All you have to do is stand back and let the person responsible take the blame."

With an effort Zach controlled the rage that worked its way up from his gut and threatened to explode out of the top of his head. His face felt hot. He leaned forward to rest his forearms on the table in an attempt to ease the desire to grab the man's head and ram it into the table. Several times.

Zach delved into the other man's dull blue gaze. "I don't think the guilty party is going to own up to it." Because he was sitting right here in front of him.

"You'd think Dr. Bertinelli would consider the repercussions of her actions before doing something stupid like this. I believe she cares about you, and she might take the hit if she thinks you may be charged."

"I don't need to hide behind an innocent woman, Lester. We both know it wasn't Piper who put drugs in the car."

"Are you admitting to doing it then?"

"They weren't there before we left my apartment. I drove her car earlier, and I had to adjust the seat for her when she took the driver's seat. I'd have felt or seen the bag. That means someone else put the cocaine in the car while I was at the hospital visiting Master Chief Flynn." He raised a brow. "Who do you suppose might have done it?"

"Perhaps she contacted someone to drop it off while you were in the hospital."

"As much as you wish it were true, we both know it isn't. This was a sloppy and ill-conceived way to get her back into an interrogation room so you can have another go at her."

"It isn't a smart move for you to maintain her innocence, En-sign."

"It isn't a smart move for you to continue to persecute an innocent woman in some twisted power play, either. She got the better of you. Embarrassed you in front of your colleagues. Cost you some money. So now she's got to pay no matter what you have to do to make it happen."

Lester's bulldog scowl was not a pretty sight. "She has to pay because she's guilty."

"Guilty of what, Detective? Dating the wrong guy? Trusting an asshole with a badge to protect her from the bad guys instead of becoming one of them? What would it take for you to finally recognize her innocence?"

"The money."

"How can she produce something she never had?"

Lester's eyes narrowed. "How can you be so certain she didn't?"

"Because when a woman's being stalked and harassed, she'll do anything to get the *monster* off her back. If Piper had had the money she'd have given it to you to end the harassment years ago."

Lester's scowl deepened at his use of the word monster. "She spent it at vet school. Twenty bucks here, forty there, and it would be gone in next to no time."

How the hell did the guy expect her to produce something that was gone? "If all she wanted was money, she'd have taken you and the department to the cleaners when she had the opportunity. Instead she worked her ass off to earn scholarships and took out loans. If she'd gone after you in that lawsuit, her student loans would have been paid already. I'm sure you've looked into her financials."

Zach leaned closer to Lester. "Think with your brain instead of your ego. None of this adds up."

Then he leaned back and crossed his arms. "Especially having a broken taillight that wasn't broken three hours before, to give the cops—who just happened to be Johnny-on-the-spot—a reason to stop me. Then there's their insistence on searching the car *when they had no grounds for it* and finding cocaine that wasn't there two hours before. Something stinks, and I won't be the only one who thinks so."

Lester's phone dinged at the same time Zach's phone buzzed. They both checked their screens. Piper was here, and Detective Sherman had put her in an interview room. Bowie had called her mom and laid it on thick. Mom and company were on their way. They'd dropped Gracie at Piper's house with Trouble.

Lester rose and picked up the file folder. Zach hadn't even attempted to reach for it or read it.

"I'm sure you were a good cop at one time," Zach continued. "Your determination to put the bad guys away is still admirable. But you're a linear thinker, and to be a good detective you have to be able to see the bigger picture. You have a blind spot when it comes to Piper."

Lester snorted. "She's got you snowed. That doe-eyed innocence she projects has blinded *you* to who she really is."

Zach shook his head. "I'm not so easily manipulated. I've spent a lot of time with Piper in the last two weeks. She's driven to be exact about everything she does. She worries if she's doing the right thing with every decision. She has trust issues because of her experience with Henderlight and you. She's desperate to feel safe. And she's constantly looking over her shoulder, expecting some kind of attack."

He clenched and unclenched his hands in an attempt to redirect the emotions threatening to choke him. As a man and as a SEAL, he did not show his emotions. He hadn't cried since he was a teenager, but he grieved for Piper. What kind of person had she been before Henderlight, Acosta, and Lester? What kind of person could she have been without them?

He'd never have the opportunity to know the person from the past. But he loved the person she was now. Quirks and all.

His throat felt clogged when he continued. "How does it make you feel, knowing you've made her cower behind a checkout counter like she's being hunted—which she is? That just the sight of you makes her go white with dread?"

Lester looked away. His throat worked as he swallowed. "Sometimes you have to intimidate people to break them. To make them own up to what they've done."

He didn't deny he'd followed her into the grocery store. "I'd say you've gone way beyond that, Detective."

That got the detective to turn and face him. Silence stretched between them.

Zach leaned back in his chair. "Why did Henderlight leave the money in her car?"

"She was holding it for him."

"Bullshit. They'd just had a contentious break-up. You don't give the woman you just broke up with money to hold for you."

When Lester remained silent, Zach continued. "Why would he leave the twenty-five thousand dollars he owed to a drug distributor and gunrunner in the car of a woman who'd just broken up with him? A man who could easily kill him for stiffing him. A man Henderlight called as soon as he made bail and directed to where he claimed he'd left the money." He leaned forward again. "I believe he arranged everything that went down. He used Acosta like a loaded weapon to get rid of a problem. But Acosta killed the wrong person."

Lester's gaze shifted and he remained silent for a moment. "That would be soliciting a murder."

"He never paid Acosta. He manipulated him. Piper was threatening to go to the cops if he didn't stay away from her. Hiding from him so he couldn't get access to her himself. Her roommates and family were protecting her from him. What's the worst crime you can be convicted of and do prison time for, besides child molestation? And what if he believed she had proof that would guarantee a conviction? What if she had witnesses? Roommates who maybe picked up the pieces afterward?"

Lester placed his hands on the table palm down and leaned forward. "How long are you going to continue to buy into her lies?"

God, he was a hardheaded asshole. "I've spent time with Piper, Detective. And one thing we're taught as a SEAL is that details matter." In his job they could mean life or death. "What was it that Henderlight said to you that cinched her guilt for you?"

"She was holding the money for him for a cut. She needed it for college. She was working two jobs, living on a shoestring. Her parents helping as much as she'd let them. Drugs are easy money."

Zach shook his head. "He played you, Detective. And he

played Acosta, too. Everyone who knew him said he was a con artist. A chameleon. He'd become what each person wanted him to be to get what he wanted. He's a sociopath. And possibly more dangerous than just a small-time drug dealer. Take a look at the psychological evaluations that have been done on him while he's been in prison and see if I'm right.

"Piper's survived despite you. And despite Henderlight and Acosta. You're the one who purposely drove the wedge between her and her family, isolating her so you could do a more thorough job of *breaking* her. You have no concept of even half the damage you've done."

Zach's anger nearly got away from him, and he had to look away from the man. "Are you going to attempt to send an innocent woman to prison to salve your ego? Because we both know she had nothing to do with the cocaine in her car."

Zach got to his feet. He'd had enough quality time with this guy. "If you're not going to charge me, I'd like to leave now. If you're charging me, I'm asking for a lawyer."

Lester stared off into space, his obstinate features cushioned in thoughtfulness. "I don't have a strong enough case to hold you, Ensign. Not yet. So, you're free to go."

Zach strode out of the room and shut the door behind him. Detective Sherman approached him and beckoned for him to follow. He led him into an observation room down the hall. "You didn't get him to admit to any wrongdoing, but damned if you didn't make a convincing case."

"I thought it was more important to give him a reality check so maybe he'll do the right thing."

"He'll lose his job if he does. So the odds that he'll own up to what he's done without a hard nudge are slim."

"We'll see. Where's Piper?" The need to go to her was overwhelming.

"She's in one of the interview rooms. And no, you can't go in with her. She has to face off with Lester. If you're right about how things went down, then Henderlight is guilty of more than selling drugs. He's culpable for inciting a murder."

"But he didn't pay Acosta to kill Piper, he just withheld his money and told him to go get it. He'll never be convicted, because you can't prove his intent." Fuck! "How much longer does he have in jail?"

Sherman hesitated long enough to have every muscle in his body contracting with dread.

"He got out two weeks ago." Sherman said with obvious reluctance.

"Jesus Christ! We've been so tangled up with covering our backs with Lester, what if he's been coming around, too?"

"It's unlikely. He just got out and is staying with his parents."

"Yeah like they kept such a close eye on him before. That's how Piper ended up..." he cut himself off. "Is there any way you can put some people on him?" He knew the answer before he asked the question.

"No."

"She can't live under siege her entire life. Hasn't she been through enough already? You and this department owe her."

He wouldn't be here to protect her, and the fucker was out of jail. "I'm going to ship out in a few weeks. She'll be alone. He's dangerous, Detective. More than everyone thinks."

Sherman lost his deadpan expression when a flicker of frustration creased his brow. "I've read his file extensively, Ensign. Something Lester should have done and probably hasn't, since it's a closed case and he was just interested in the drug angle at the time, and has been fixated only on Dr. Bertinelli since. And I think you have Henderlight pegged. He could be the next Ted Bundy, and I still can't touch him until he does something. My hands are tied."

Sherman and he stared at each other. He read the regret in the man's face.

Fuck!

CHAPTER 38

PIPER CLUNG TO the strap of her purse while she sat at the small table in the interview room. Running her hand back and forth over the denim fabric soothed her. She wished Trouble were here, or Gracie. Their presence was comforting, calming.

Bowie had reassured her Detective Sherman was on top of everything that happened in the hospital parking lot. They knew she hadn't bought drugs or hired anyone to deliver them to her car. But why would Detective Lester do something so stupid? It would have been more realistic had he placed Acepromazine or Xylazine in her car. She had more contact with those medications than those used by humans.

The door opened and Lester sauntered in. She couldn't control the immediate rush of fear and loathing that threw her heart and breathing into panic mode. She couldn't run from him here. She was trapped behind the table, and even if she attempted to leave, he could force her to stay.

She twisted the purse handle tight around her hand.

"Dr. Bertinelli," he greeted her. He pulled the chair opposite her out and sat down. "I just want to ask you a few questions, then we'll be done here."

Piper nodded.

For a long moment he seemed to think through what he wanted to say. When he finally looked up, she tensed. "Did David

Henderlight rape you?"

The unanticipated question hit her with the force of an open-palmed slap. Quick tears filled her eyes and spilled down her cheeks. She lunged to her feet and staggered, her vision narrowing to a dark tunnel and she nearly fell. She grabbed at the edge of the table to steady herself until her vision cleared.

How had he found out? He'd use this against her. He'd find a way to hurt her with it. "I'm not talking to you." If he told Zach... If he told her family... She had to keep him from telling anyone.

"I'm not letting you hurt me anymore. If you tell anyone...anyone... I'll-I'll sue you and this department." Her voice shook. "I have the right to my privacy." She choked back a sob. "I have rights."

"Jesus!" He shoved free of his seat and took two long paces away from her. He gripped his head between his hands and twisted about to pace the narrow space. When he dropped his hands, he seemed to have trouble swallowing.

"Did you receive any medical attention?"

She sidled around the table, her throat burning. "I'm not giving you this. You've taken all you're going to take from me." She shrank away from him when he came close. "Get away from me. Don't you touch me!" She hated the tearful sound of panicked pain in her voice, but was helpless to prevent it.

"Okay. Okay." Lester held his hands out in a placating gesture he'd never used with her before. "Take it easy."

He moved back, giving her some breathing room. She leaned her shoulder against the wall to steady herself and turned her face away from him. She would not let him do this to her. She would not give him the satisfaction of seeing her fall to pieces. Tremors shook her and she drew several breaths.

If she looked at him again, she'd lose it. She wanted to scratch his eyes out. She wanted to hit him and hit him and hit him, until she hadn't the strength left to raise her hands. But she couldn't. He'd have just cause to arrest her and she'd go to jail. She stared at the floor and choked back the rage. "You've tried every way you could to destroy me. But I'm not going to let you. If you're going to charge me, do it. But I'm not talking to you anymore. I want my lawyer."

The door opened and Detective Sherman stepped into the room, his attention shifting from her to Lester and back again. "Dr. Bertinelli's mother is here, Detective Lester. She has something with her I think you need to see. I think you need to come too, Dr. Bertinelli."

Piper charged toward the open door and freedom.

She forced herself to maintain a moderate pace when the urge to run from the two of policemen was so strong her leg muscles twitched.

The main office seemed too bright, too open after the claustrophobic closeness of the interview room. Several desks and chairs, arranged two to a group, were spaced in random order. Four detectives sat behind their desks, one doing paperwork, another talking on the phone, while two more seemed to be conversing with each other. One standing off to the side observed everything.

Zach and Bowie stood together tall, broad-shouldered, arms crossed, an island of safety in the midst of the threatening chaos. Piper squeezed in between them. Zach placed an arm around her and held her against his side. He scanned her face and his features hardened, his wide, generous mouth flattening into a grim, thin line. His focus shifted to Detective Lester when he and Sherman reached the group. His body went taut, his eyes taking on a flinty, intent look, similar to the one Gracie got when Tony came near. It was a promise of violence barely held in check.

As much as she wanted to see the man lying beaten at her feet, it wasn't right for Zach to pay the cost for such an action. She placed a hand against his broad chest to distract him. "I'm okay." She said the words to sooth him, and felt a hand squeeze her shoulder in silent support. It was Bowie's.

Her mother sat in a chair next to one of the desks. Benito, Armando, and Lorenzo stood behind her. At her feet sat a backpack, gray with grime.

Piper's attention settled on the bag. The money had to be in it.

But where had it been hidden? And who in her family had taken it? The fresh wave of betrayal built inside her. Someone in her family had purposely allowed Detective Lester to prey on her, and for what? For what?

"Go ahead, Mrs. Bertinelli," Detective Sherman laid a hand on her mother's shoulder.

Her beautiful, youthful mother looked as though she had aged ten years since the last time she saw her. Her hair, usually immaculately arranged, hung around her face.

"Seven years ago," she said, "all was right in our world. Our children were grown, leading their own lives, independent, happy. Our baby, Francesca, was in college, working toward her dream. Luca and I were settling into our empty nest, just the two of us. Though it was never truly empty. Our children came by nearly every day. When I look back on those days, I sometimes think they were too good, too idyllic."

"Then Piper came home from college for a weekend. She hid in her room upstairs, barely eating, upset, so upset. She had broken things off with David, and he was stalking her. Her roommates kept calling to check on her several times a day."

"Please don't say it. Please." Piper turned her face against Zach's shirt, gripping the knit fabric. His arm tightened around her.

"She'd turned her cell phone off, so he was calling the house phone constantly. If he saw her car in the apartment complex parking lot, he pounded on her door and harassed her, so she asked to use my car to attend classes because he wouldn't recognize it."

"The day he came to the house, I threatened to call the police on him myself if he didn't leave Piper alone. He and Mando almost came to blows, and would have if Benito and Lorenzo had not pulled Armando off of him."

She shuddered. "It was after Piper left for class that I found the backpack. I was moving the car into the garage and saw the reflection of it in the back window. I thought maybe it was Piper's and she'd forgotten it in the rush to get to class. It didn't feel like books, so I opened it."

Carlotta focused on the floor, her expression distant. "I called my husband to come home from the restaurant, and we sat in the kitchen for the longest time, talking about why David might have left the money. We knew where he'd gotten it. We knew he was stalking our child and had done something horrible to hurt her."

Pain flickered across her face and a single tear tracked down her cheek. "She had such an open heart, always wanting to heal injured creatures and people. Always eager to help us at the restaurant and at home." She raised her eyes to focus on Piper. And she hiccupped, as though catching back a sob, while a flood of tears rolled down her cheeks. "And then she was so wounded, pulling into herself, and she wouldn't speak about the breakup at all. But she was scared."

Piper gripped Zach's shirt harder. She couldn't think about that time. The hopelessness. The feeling of floating in a numb vacuum when at home, and abject terror when she was away from its security. Her mind dull and sluggish. Going to class and hearing nothing of the lecture. She'd taped them and spoon-fed the information to herself so she could keep up with the work. And later, when the grief for her father was eating her alive, she'd wanted to die.

Pain rose in her, a burning claw, and tears poured down her face.

Detective Sherman stepped forward to offer Carlotta some tissue and she blotted her eyes. Bowie did the same for Piper.

"Luca, my husband, took the bag. He said he would turn it into the police, but there was something he had to do first. We had many policemen who came by the restaurant with their families and in groups. He was friendly with some of them. I think he called one of them and told him what was happening. David was stopped for being under the influence, arrested and put in jail while a warrant was issued to search the car."

She looked up at Detective Sherman. "I don't know why Luca didn't turn the money in then. We never spoke of it. We were just holding our breath, waiting to see if David was going to get out and start harassing Piper again. Then Acosta came into our restaurant a few days later and shot Luca. And our lives just— stopped."

Two of the other detectives wandered over and stood on the periphery of the group.

"He never told me where the money was hidden. I looked everywhere for it. The police searched for it. And after a while I began to think perhaps he had donated it to the church or to a women's shelter. I knew he hadn't spent it or put it in the bank. He wouldn't have touched it because of what it represented."

She focused on Detective Lester. "Then you started coming around, hounding my daughter, accusing her of taking the money. Treating her like a criminal. Threatening to arrest her if she found the money, or even if she didn't. And she went further into herself, hiding away her hurt, and burying herself in her studies. She was like a shadow moving through her life."

Her voice rose open pain in its pitch, her eyes alight with rage. "Could you not see it? Could you not see how frail, how broken she was? Could you not have a moment of pity?"

Lester opened his mouth as though to speak, then closed it and looked away. His features looked pasty, his expression slack.

Benito's movement as he wiped his eyes with his shirt cuff, momentarily drew Piper's attention. She remembered the hug he'd given her at the restaurant. His silence at the dinner table at her mother's. His insistence that she couldn't allow Lester to harass the others. Had he found the money before then and remained silent?

Armando and Lorenzo would not meet her eyes.

"Piper took a job at an animal shelter caring for the animals after the semester ended. I went to see her there. I wanted her to come home. I was afraid for her." Her attention shifted Armando, Lorenzo and Benito. "She wasn't the Piper she had been. She'd lost so much weight she looked frail. And Lester was still harassing her. She left for San Francisco a few days later. And I thought at least that far away she would be safe from being tormented. But I was wrong."

She sent Lester another stony-eyed, accusing glare.

"Ten days ago, the freezer went out at the restaurant, and we had to call a repairman. He found the backpack, and Benito brought it to me. It was on top of the freezer unit, hidden in the ceiling panels. Acosta killed the only person who knew where it was and could give it to him." Carlotta dragged in a breath and seemed to drag her composure in around her with it.

After a few moments, she straightened, blotted her eyes again, and blew her nose. With a sigh, she rose to her feet and reached for the handle of the backpack. She walked deliberately to Lester and dropped it at his feet. Tears streamed down her face again. "The pain you've caused my daughter and our family is something we will never forget or forgive. It has forever changed us all."

She paused before Piper. "Please forgive us, Francesca. Forgive me."

Piper cleared her throat but still her voice came out a hoarse whisper. "Why didn't you tell them Daddy had the bag, mamma?"

"I kept thinking I'd find it and turn it in. By the time I accepted that I wasn't going to find it, that it was out of reach, you were already gone away from us."

"You could have told them." She nodded to her brothers. Every moment of pain she'd experienced at their hands rose up to rip at her.

"The longer you remain silent about something, the harder it is to speak of it. You just want to forget it's there. By the time you came back…I was afraid they'd blame me, like they did you."

She understood, but the weight of her mother's betrayal, the one person she had believed would protect her, threatened to crush her.

Detective Sherman touched Carlotta's arm. "I'll need you to give us a written statement and sign a chain of custody voucher documenting how the backpack came to be in your possession."

She nodded. It was she who looked frail now as she allowed him to direct her to an empty desk.

The man who'd stood back and observed everything approached Lester first. His words were just a whisper but the tone could have cut steel. Lester bent and picked up the backpack and disappeared with it into an office.

The man approached Piper, all hard edges and steel gray coloring. His suit was charcoal, his hair dull silver, and even his eyes gave the impression of metal. "Dr. Bertinelli?"

"Yes?"

"My name is Frank Terrance. I'm the Captain of this homicide unit. Would you and Ensign O'Connor mind if I had a private word with you?"

Emotionally exhausted, Piper shrugged when Zach looked down at her. How much worse could it get?

Twenty minutes later, when they walked out of the police station, it was to find Bowie waiting for them in the parking lot. Zach opened the passenger door and saw her seated before slipping into the back seat.

"So how much ass-kissing did the captain do?" Bowie asked when everyone was belted in.

Zach spoke from the back seat, but there was no satisfaction in his tone. "Major."

CHAPTER 39

"**A**RE WE GOING to tell your parents what happened last night?" Kathleen asked.

Cal wove through traffic and turned northwest to get out of town. "It will just upset them and detract from our other news. The cop said we probably wouldn't have to show up for court. His lawyer will probably plead it out."

"I'm not sure they should. I think he intended to kill us both, whether or not we gave him our money and jewelry."

"You can't guess what was in the kid's head. But he has escalated from shoplifting to armed robbery in a short time. He has a drug problem."

"How did you find that out?"

"One of the police officers was forthcoming. They suspect him a couple of other robberies in the area. If they can link him to them, he'll do time."

Kathleen focused on her engagement ring. "It's a real shame. He's so young."

"Maybe this will serve as a wake-up call for him." Callahan turned back to the road. "I thought you handled yourself fantastically last night, Kathleen. You kept it together like a pro."

She thought about it for a moment. "I didn't feel together. Every time he pointed the gun at you..." She pressed her hand to her chest. "I was just paralyzed. I couldn't think."

"But you stayed calm, Kathleen. You didn't scream or cry or make a fuss. You kept your head. You did well."

He could see when the tension drained from her body. She'd nearly gotten sick afterward, but she had still maintained her composure. He just hoped this one episode didn't trigger more episodes of anxiety. He worried about her being alone in San Diego. Zach was shipping out soon, and because of her PTSD, she hadn't made any close friends. But she was fighting back from it.

"I wish you could stay, Kathleen. I don't know how long it's going to be before we get things settled about the company."

She remained silent for a moment. "I know you're having a hard time deciding what to do. You'd be your own boss, and you could take on hand-picked projects that excite you, big and small. But on the other hand you'd be running a company, making a payroll, and paying health and liability insurance for your workers. And you'd be working with your brother. Even though I noticed things seem to be better between you, you'll need to discuss how having two bosses will impact the company.

"The most important thing is you have to make sure it can be your dream, Cal. I know what your father wants, but you're the one who will have to take up the torch and do the work. If it can't be your dream, truly isn't your dream, then walk away. If it's what you want, though, I'll look for a job here. My boss will give me a good recommendation, and I can come here to interview."

He was relieved she was so willing to relocate. Now if he could just make up his own mind. "And what about Zach?"

She fell silent for a long moment. "It will be hard to leave him. We've gotten close again since I moved out. But he's getting ready to ship out for six months, maybe longer. He wouldn't expect me to put my life on hold for him. He knows how I feel about you, and he'll want me to be happy. It helps that he likes you. And I can call him every week and check on him."

"He can fly out to see us, and we can fly out to see him whenever he's on CONUS again. Besides, he's got a new girlfriend and seems very involved with her. Maybe too involved. I'm going to check her out and find out what's going on as soon as I'm back in San Diego."

"He's a grown man, Kathleen. He may not appreciate you vetting his girlfriend."

"He didn't hesitate to vet you."

Her indignant expression amused him. Cal laughed. "That's a brother thing. And boyfriends expect that."

"His girlfriend better get ready to accept it as well."

"She probably won't mind that you're looking out for him, but you may have a problem with your brother. He's a SEAL, Kathleen."

"He can fight terrorists, blow up a building, and shoot a gun, but none of that makes him an expert when it comes to women. I just want to be sure he isn't being latched onto by someone out to take advantage of him."

Cal bit back another warning. The two of them would have to work it out. He wasn't getting in the middle. But he'd like to be a fly on the wall to find out how they worked it out. Kathleen's family's dynamic was so different from his own.

"I've noticed Dad's a little easier to get along with since you arrived."

"He's just on his best behavior right now. He's been trying to bribe me to get you to stay."

"Bribe you how?"

"I showed him the plans I've drawn for a house I really like, and he's been hinting around about how much cheaper it would be to build here than in California. How much cheaper the property values are, things like that."

Cal smiled. "Wily old bastard, isn't he? He's wooing you with promises of a house because he knew I was going to pop the question. I told him as much when I first got here. He's hoping you'll influence me. I don't get why he's so wary of talking to me man-to-man."

"He painted himself into a corner before with you, Cal, and if it's possible, I think it's twice as hard for him to say he's sorry as it is for any of my brothers. Which is saying something."

"He hasn't bitched at mom or Doug as much lately, though."

"It's only been a couple of days, and he's slept quite a bit of those." She chuckled. "Teasing aside, it may not last once he feels better."

"I'm hoping mom will bring him by once a day and just let him look things over so he'll feel he's still involved."

"Would you be satisfied with that?" she asked.

He grimaced and shook his head. "No. Actually, hell no."

Kathleen chuckled. "I think he needs a completely different outlet until he's well enough to go back."

"Such as?"

"Your mom."

Cal glanced at her.

"She's beautiful, Cal. And sweet. Neglected. She's been just another part of the machinery to get things done. And she deserves more. Your dad needs to wake up."

He could feel his mouth hanging open and shut it. "I'm their son, Kathleen. Not a marriage counselor. What do you expect me to do?"

"Just point out the obvious to them both when you see an opportunity. Make comments about how young your mom looks, and compliment her when she looks pretty. Make him see what he has right in front of him. He's built his whole life around building houses instead of doing his part to maintain his marriage."

Cal shook his head. Wow. Kathleen had walked into the house five days before and seen everything he had and then some. "If I ever fall into that hole, smack me upside the head."

"You won't. You're different from your father, Cal, but just in case, I'll remind you of this conversation." She reached for his hand and held it against her cheek. The ring he'd given her flashed in the early morning light.

He was a lucky man. But he had to make a decision. It wasn't fair to either of them to be apart and held in limbo because of this situation. It wasn't fair to Kathleen to have to relocate, either. She'd have more career opportunities in California than in San Antonio.

"You're still working on your AXP. How much more do you have to do?"

"Another two years at least. I did quite a bit during my master's, working for a firm. And during summers. Competitions and things like that, construction work, mostly during the summers. I have to have a licensed architect as a mentor during the process, and I've had to change mentors a couple of times. Then once I've completed the work and uploaded my final portfolio entries, I have to take the Architectural Registration Exam. Once that's behind me, I'll be licensed to practice in any state in the US and in Canada."

Jesus, he hadn't realized it would be such a big deal for her to move. He should have. She had to report hours every week, do paperwork, submit her work. She stayed right on top of it. Yet she was willing to risk all her hard work to be with him.

KATHLEEN WASN'T SURPRISED CAL was weighing the options before making a decision. But he thought to ask about her internship program, and even remembered the name of it, which gave her confidence that he was thinking way beyond a knee-jerk reaction.

Doug met them at the door when they came in.

"Everything okay?" Cal asked.

"Yeah. I just came by for a piece of pie before going back to the site." He looked from Cal to Kathleen, then back again. When neither one of them said anything he said, "Well?"

Cal grinned. "She said yes."

Doug's smile was genuine. "Congratulations." He hugged his brother then turned to Kathleen. "I know you probably think I'm an asshole, but I'm awfully glad you're marrying my brother."

Kathleen smiled and accepted his hug. "Thanks. I have a few assholes in my family, too, but you're young, so you still have time to grow out of it."

Doug laughed. "I'll work on it. Where's the ring?"

Kathleen thrust out her hand. He whistled. "Very nice, and it suits you, Kathleen. Cal has good taste...and better credit than I do."

"I paid cash for it, little brother. I am frugal. I know how to save money. I am a squirrel harboring nuts for the winter."

"You are full of shit, too. Mom and Dad are in the den. She laid down the law this morning over something Dad said, and he's toeing the line...for the time being. Things are a little strained. I have to go. Are we having a celebratory dinner tonight since Kathleen's leaving in the morning?"

"Yes," Cal replied. "I thought I'd get mom to fix her garlic mashed potatoes and I'll grill some steaks."

"Maybe our announcement will put them both in a better humor," Kathleen suggested.

"Let's hope," Cal said. "Later," he pointed at his bother. He laced his fingers with hers and drew her through the living room to the den. Sondra stood at the window looking out at the pool, but she glanced over her shoulder at them when they entered the room. Jameson's attention flicked from her to them, his expression sullen.

Sondra attempted to pull herself together, but her lips had an unhappy tightness. She forced a smile. "You're back early. How did you like the river walk, Kathleen?"

"It was lovely. And the Alamo was much smaller than I expected, but it's a beautiful place. Surprisingly peaceful."

"Where did you eat supper last night? I hope Cal took you somewhere nice."

Cal answered, "We ate supper at the Citrus, then took a walk and sat on a bench under one of the trees next to the water. I asked Kathleen to marry me. She said yes. We're engaged."

Sondra strode across the distance to hug Kathleen first, then Cal. "I'm so glad. He's been carrying around the ring, but wouldn't let me see it."

Kathleen interpreted it as an invitation to share and extended her hand. But the other woman's misery dimmed the moment. Sondra's eyes turned bright with tears. "Cal, this is gorgeous. I'd never have thought of rubies in an engagement ring."

"Kathleen looks good in red, and I decided she deserves something non-traditional." His hand on her shoulder squeezed gently.

"It's perfect."

"Let me see, Kathleen," Jameson said.

She walked across to where he sat in his recliner. He didn't attempt to take her hand, but studied the ring thoroughly. "It's very nice." His chest rose as he sighed. "When Sondra and I got married we had no money. Couldn't afford anything but a tiny diamond you needed a magnifying glass to see. She wore it so long the band wore through in the back." He fell silent for a moment. "I bought her a new one a couple of years ago, a little fancier, a little bigger."

"It isn't so much the ring as the meaning behind it," said Kathleen. "The love it's given with. The sacrifice it took for you to buy that tiny diamond, and the meaning behind it, probably meant more to her than anything else in the world."

"It did," Sondra spoke up, and for a moment Jameson and she connected with a glance. He looked away first.

"We need to do something to celebrate. Maybe a bottle of champagne at dinner. I'll fix something special."

"Doug and I can grill steaks outside, and you can fix your garlic mashed potatoes and rolls, Mom."

"That sounds easy and perfect," Kathleen agreed. "If you'll make the grocery list, I'll run and get whatever we need."

Sondra gave her waist a squeeze. "You're too easy to please, Kathleen."

"I suppose I'll get a boiled potato with no butter or salt," Jameson complained.

"I'll fix you one of my famous feta salads with a grilled chicken breast, and you can have a glass of red wine with us instead of champagne," Kathleen suggested. "I'll eat chicken, too. I splurged last night. Or we can have turkey burgers."

Jameson turned a scowl in her direction. "You do realize you're talking to a Texan about eating hamburger made with turkey instead of beef?"

"You realize you're talking to a woman who's fought middle age spread since before her twenty-fifth birthday? You're not getting any sympathy from me."

Jameson laughed. "Okay. I'll settle for the chicken breast. Buy one that's Texan-sized."

Kathleen gave his arm a squeeze.

"You and mom go ahead and make the list." Cal said. "I have to go by a couple of the sites and check some things, and I need to speak to Dad for a minute."

Taking his father on now might not be a good idea. But there was little she could do. She left the room with Sondra, but concern dogged her steps.

CAL PULLED ONE of the chairs closer to Jameson's and took a seat. "We need to talk, Dad."

"It's about the business, isn't it?"

"No. It's about Mom."

"Stay out of our business, Cal."

"I don't know what was said, and I don't care. You're going to keep it up until you find yourself sitting here alone. She could walk away now and take half of everything you have and start a new life with someone else. She's young enough, and pretty, and deserves better than a broken-down construction worker with a sour attitude. You said you dealt with things and moved on because that was life. Well, I have to tell you, you're not dealing, and you're not moving on. You're clinging to what used to be, and you need to look forward to what you can have now."

"What—" Jameson cut off what he started to say.

When had his father ever put his mother first? Kathleen was right. His mom was there to make the machine run smoother. Nothing more than a cog in the wheel, in his dad's mind.

"Kathleen has offered to relocate here so I can continue help-ing run things. She loves me enough to do that, even though it will disrupt some things for her. Some very important things."

He resented the hope he read in his father's face, because he didn't have a clue how little the business meant to him in comparison to Kathleen. So he added, "You do realize she has put a lot of effort into her education to do what she does."

"Yeah. I can tell she's put in some time."

"She has to finish an internship, which requires quite a bit of paperwork, documenting her hours and submission of her work, before she takes an exam to be licensed. She has two more years and she'll be finished. I don't want to screw it up for her. It's too important."

"She doesn't know you're telling me this, does she?"

"No. She's all about family. And she'd put my needs ahead of hers. This family's needs ahead of hers." Just like his mother had, and where had it gotten her? The more he thought about it the angrier he got. "Kathleen's offered to do it. Even if it screws things up for her. But I'm not going to let her."

Jameson's features blanked in disappointment, then he frowned, his lips a thin, taut line.

Cal let the silence stretch.

"We all made sacrifices to keep things running, Cal," Jameson said.

"Mom made more than anyone else. I remember her chauffeuring Doug and me to and from school, ball practices, academic stuff, working in the office, and still having dinner on the table. She'd still be working after you were sacked out here in front of the television. You've done the work of two men? Well, she's done the work of three women."

He let that sink in.

"Have you ever put her first, Dad? If I asked her, would she be able to think of a single time she could say you did? There's more to life than this *goddamn business*. You need to see that for your own sake, and for hers."

He jerked to his feet and walked away from his father, too frustrated to stay seated.

"Doug's doing okay, but he can't handle it all," Jameson said.

God, he was still fixated on the job. What did it take? "He's doing better, but he still isn't you. No one is. You've done all the work instead of delegating it to other people, and now you've paid a high price for it. You don't want Doug to pay the same price, do you? Because he'll try to be you, and he won't make it."

He ran a hand back and forth over the top of his head, then forced himself to stop. He would not allow this stress to get to him. "I have a solution I think may work."

One brow rose in interest. "What is it?"

"You hire Strom Michaels to be job foreman to take my place. He's worked for you for twenty years, knows the business up one side and down the other, and is good with the men. But he's getting some age on him. He's talking retirement in two years."

Jameson shifted in his recliner. "By then Kathleen will have finished her exams and you could step into his shoes when he retires." There was a stilted uncertainty in the way he said it. "If you move here, she can open her own architectural practice, or find a job at a big firm. She may even decide to do residential architectural design and throw in with us. She seemed excited about doing some of that."

Cal remained silent a moment. "Why do you want us to move here, Dad? For the business?"

"It was supposed to be my legacy to the two of you. It was supposed to be the three of us working shoulder to shoulder. And I ruined it." Jamison looked up and Cal gripped his shoulder in alarm when he saw tears glazing his father's eyes. Never had he seen his hard-as-nails father cry, but he was close now. Cal's own emotions ramped up in sympathy.

"I made it harder for you than it should have been." Jameson's voice was gruff with emotion. "I didn't believe in you like I should have."

He brushed his broad, work-roughened hand over his face to brush away the tears. "I want the opportunity to make it up to you, Cal."

It was as close to an apology as he was ever going to get. "Don't waste your energy making anything up to me, Dad. I'm focusing on the future, not the past."

Jameson tried for a chuckle, but it sounded more like a sob. "Getting engaged will do that to you. Has Kathleen shown you the house?" he asked.

"No." Cal narrowed his eyes at him. He decided to cut him some slack. "But I heard you've been attempting some bribery."

Jameson grinned, though his eyes were still wet. "Told you about that, did she?"

"Yeah."

"You better start putting plenty aside for that project. It's one hell of a house. It would look real sweet on three or four acres somewhere, ten would probably be better, but you don't want to be chained to the upkeep. And it has a basement, and you can't have one in California."

Cal gave up trying to control his smile. Was there anyone as stubborn as Jameson Crowes? He was thrilled to see the light of excitement in his father's eyes take over the emotion of a few minutes before. If he was so interested in the project, he needed to see Kathleen's plans. "How 'bout you keep your eyes peeled for a nice piece of property, and we'll see about the rest."

"I can do that. There's not a damn thing wrong with my eyes."

"There won't be anything wrong with the rest of you, either, if you follow doctor's orders…and you treat Mom right."

"Seems Kathleen's been filling her head with ideas." Jameson folded his arms.

"Kathleen's ideas are usually beneficial. Why don't you try doing things Mom's way for once, and see if you don't reap some of those benefits in about six or eight weeks?"

He grinned when a blush colored his father's cheeks.

Kathleen's words had been so true. "You've spent your life building houses. It's time you tried building something else now." *Why couldn't he try wooing Mom a little instead of always showing her how big an asshole he could be?*

His father's expression grew obstinate. "You've been engaged for ten minutes and it makes you an expert on marriage?"

"I don't think anyone's ever an expert on anything. It's all just trial and error. What are you so afraid of?"

As his father's silence stretched, Cal said, "I've had to start over several times since high school. Construction worker to Marine to amputee and back to construction worker. And next I'll be a husband, maybe one day a father. You've already covered most of that ground. You can be something more too, Dad."

Jameson looked like he might tear up again. "You trying to build me up? Keep me in the game?"

"Something like that. You still have time. I know something about second chances. You've been handed one. What are you going to do with it?"

His dad had clearly had enough, because his skin was a bit gray and his hands shaky. "You need to rest until dinner. I need to check out the sites and make sure the men got their work done."

Cal made it to the door before his dad said, "Will you ask your mom to come in here for a few minutes?"

"Sure."

"Maybe we'll swing over to see you and Kathleen in three or four months, when I have my legs under me again."

"You're welcome any time. I have a spare bedroom."

"You'd best start planning the wedding right away. You know how your mother is about the sleeping arrangements."

Cal laughed aloud. "I'll see what we can do."

CHAPTER 40

Z ACH PULLED THE faded quilt Piper used as a bedspread up over her shoulder. He rolled onto his back, bent his arm, and propped the back of his head in his hand.

The soft early morning sunlight crawled across the bed, touching her arm and cheek with gold, and setting off the reddish highlights in her hair. He couldn't take his eyes off of her.

In the three weeks they'd slept together, he'd never known her to sleep so soundly or be so relaxed. She literally hadn't moved all night. While he'd been on the phone with Hawk, filling him in on everything that had gone down, she'd crashed, hard.

He hadn't asked about her interview with Lester. He didn't want to know. He knew Lester would be a dick because he didn't know how to be anything else. But he hadn't expected to see that terrorized, shocky look in her eyes. Every time he thought about it, he wanted to hunt the asshole down and pound him into the ground. He tugged at the lock of hair that had begun to flop down over his forehead until it hurt.

There was justice, though. If nothing else, Lester must have somehow realized what Zach had told him was true. Otherwise he wouldn't have had that sick look on his face afterward. Everything Piper's mother said had only piled it on.

Piled it on for him, too. How had she endured it? Raped, her father killed, her family freezing her out, and Lester hounding her.

Why hadn't her mother told her what her father had done? Why hadn't she told the rest of her children? It would have saved Piper a world of heartache. That last painful betrayal might have forever severed any kind of tie she had with her family.

And why the fuck hadn't any of her brothers attempted to approach her afterward? They left before he and Piper had finished their interview with Captain Terrance. Fuck! What kind of family did that?

Trouble padded to the door and, seeing him awake, came into the room. He rested his large head on the mattress only inches from Zach's face and panted. Zach ran a hand over the top of his head and caressed his ears. "You need a ticktack, my man," Zach complained in a whisper. He slipped out of bed and bent to grab his collar and lead him out of the bedroom before he jumped up on the bed in the warm spot he left behind and wake Piper. Once in the hall, he gave Trouble a quick rubdown and urged him toward the living room.

Gracie rose to greet him at the back door and he knelt to pet her. "Need to go out?" Both dogs went into wiggling fits. He opened the back door and Trouble bounded down the steps and out into Piper's pocket-sized backyard while Gracie followed at a more dignified, three-legged pace. She was beginning to use her back leg again for balance, and even put a little pressure on it.

He stood at the door and watched the two dogs, but his mind covered the same ground it had all night. Eventually, once the shock wore off, she'd realize where Lester got his information. How could she not?

He should have never clued the man into his suspicions about Piper. He'd done what he needed to end things with Lester for her, but guilt was already eating him alive. And she was going to be pissed as hell at him.

Dressed in a sloppy sleep shirt that hit her mid-thigh and panties, Piper padded into the kitchen barefoot. Zach admired her legs while she moved zombie-like to the sink and began to make coffee. She usually wore jeans, and the only time her legs were bare was when they made love, or at times like this. For the most part she covered herself from top to toe. Was it another way of coping with what had happened?

Zach pulled out a chair from the small kitchen table and sat down. She crossed in front of him to get a coffee cup and he caught the hem of the T-shirt and reeled her in between his legs. He buried his face between her breasts and breathed her in. She smelled warm and musky, with a hint of the jasmine body wash she used. He ran his hands up the backs of her legs to her buttocks and pulled her in against him.

Piper's slipped an arm around his neck while she smoothed his thick auburn hair with the other hand. "How long have you known?"

Zach's hands stilled beneath the shirt. He had hoped to have longer. He continued to hold her but laid his head against her breasts. "Since the first weekend we spent together." He swallowed. "You hadn't been with anyone in three years. You were hesitant and unsure sometimes when you touched me. Wary of me being on top. Innocent in a way I haven't experienced in a long time."

He eased back to look up at her and recognized the weary acceptance in her expression. And the hurt.

INNOCENT. HER INNOCENCE had been stolen by a hyped-up junkie determined to take what he wanted. Her throat felt dry, and she backed away from him to lean against the cabinets and turned to glance out the window at the dogs. "You didn't ask me anything."

"I was a dumb ass. I told you we needed to keep it light, simple. I made it impossible to ask you. And I had a feeling if I came at it straight on, you'd leave and I'd never see you again. I didn't want that to happen. I hoped once we got to know each other better, you might trust me enough to tell me."

She half turned, presenting her profile, but avoided looking at him. She'd cried a lifetime of tears, and she wasn't wasting any more on any of this. This was Zach. He'd believed in her when no one else did. She believed in him, believed he had done it for a good reason. But she needed to know why. "How could you tell the one man who hated me most what I couldn't tell anyone?"

"It wasn't like that, Piper. I asked him what crime was guaranteed to cause a man grief while he was in prison if the other prisoners knew about it. And suggested he might have arranged to have you taken care of so it wouldn't happen. He planted the money *before* he was arrested, Piper.

"His arrest was a lucky thing. It guaranteed him an alibi. He was always going to send Acosta after you, because he couldn't reach you himself. If Acosta had come after you at your parents' house, or your apartment, whoever was there would have been killed. He planned the whole thing."

She felt a little light-headed and gripped the edge of the sink. She had always wondered. "I thought if the money existed he might have been trying to pay me off. I didn't want to think he was evil enough to arrange have me killed." She raked her fingers through her hair, pulling it back from her face. "I suppose I've always known it, though. I'm the only one who's seen him at the moment when he wasn't able to hide the monster."

Zach went over and leaned next to her at the counter. "Detective Sherman is working to find a way to charge Henderlight for inciting your father's death."

His parole was an event she'd been dreading since he was sentenced. "The statute of limitations has run out. There'll be no reason for him to come after me again."

"You don't know that, Piper." He ran his fingertips down the back of her arm before gripping it lightly just above her elbow. "I won't be here much longer. Do you know what it's doing to me, knowing you'll be here alone?" His green gaze delved into hers, a look in their depths that threw her stomach into a free fall.

She cupped his face in her hands. "The same thing it does to me, knowing you'll be somewhere far away, facing off against men worse than he is." She lifted up on tiptoe to slide her arms around his neck and hold him close. "The first time you kissed me, I didn't think I'd ever be able to breathe again if you didn't keep kissing me. You offered me trust. You believed in me. And you gave me back a part of myself I never thought I'd have again. The thought of being apart from you for even a moment…"

His arms tightened around her. "You've been through the ringer in the last three weeks. We both deserve some time together that isn't filled with looking over our shoulders for stalkers and having daily conversations with policemen. Just to be sure."

Now who was the wary one? But it had only been three weeks. If he wasn't sure yet…She could give him time. "Okay, Zach."

A cell phone's ring carried down the hall from the bedroom. "That's mine," he said as he eased away. "No one calls at this hour if it's not important." He strode down the hall.

His gait was easier, his movements more fluid. His hip was healing and he'd soon be out the door, training with his team. Between her hours and his, they wouldn't be able to see as much of each other.

He held the phone against his ear while he wandered back into the room. His responses gave her little clue as to who he was talking to or what they were saying. When he ended the call, he stared at the screen for a long moment. "That was my CO. I've been ordered to report to base on Monday morning." She handed him a cup of black coffee.

Piper pressed a hand to her midriff, trying to ward off the sinking feeling. "Is it because of what happened last night?"

"No. It has nothing to do with that. Officially there was nothing to report. I was just taken in and interviewed, never arrested. This order came from our Captain."

"You think everything is okay, then?" She sipped her own coffee cautiously, allowing relief to soothe her. Would she ever stop expecting a crisis around every corner?

"Everything's fine."

Another phone rang and they looked at each other. She set aside her coffee and rushed into the bedroom to retrieve her cell. It was Detective Sherman. Did the man never sleep?

"Lester has resigned."

The news was spoken so baldly it took a moment for her to take in the words and recognize their importance. "Really?"

"Yeah."

"I have no idea how to feel about that. Relieved, of course, that he can't send policemen after me whenever he gets the notion, but I don't know about the rest."

"It will take some time. And your car is being returned to you. The taillight has been repaired, free of charge, by the SDPD. Patrol officers should be at your front door any moment with your vehicle."

"Oh. Thank you, Detective."

"I just want to say…I'm sorry for everything he put you through, Dr. Bertinelli. I'm sorry for every moment you didn't get the support from us you deserved. I'm going to make it my business to monitor David Henderlight. We'll try to keep him as far away from you as possible."

Why would he have to monitor David? He was in prison. Or was he? Tears welled in her eyes and for a moment she couldn't breathe, let alone speak. She forced the words from a throat gone dry as windblown sand. "Thank you, Detective Sherman. For everything."

"Good luck to you and Ensign O'Connor. Tell him if he ever decides to leave the SEALs, I'll put in a good word for him with the brass here."

"I'll tell him."

When she ended the call, Piper sank down on her bed. It was finally over. The hand, forever clamped over her shoulder, ready to jerk her back, had been lifted. But another had taken its place. What if he came after her?

She curled in on herself and rocked. He'd have no reason to. The statute of limitations had passed. He couldn't be charged for the rape. Even if the police had saved the kit. He would not come after her. It was going to be okay.

The tap at her front door had her scurrying to slip on her robe.

Zach came to the kitchen door when she opened the door to find a uniformed officer standing there with her keys. She looked past him at her car and the patrol vehicle parked in front of it.

"Special delivery, ma'am," the young patrol officer said with a smile, offering her the keys.

"Thank you, officer."

"I don't think I've ever seen a car in the impound delivered back to its owner before." Curiosity burned behind his gaze. He looked young, but he was probably close to her age.

Piper thought how she might explain. "A SDPD officer damaged the back taillight during an undercover operation and was nice enough to have it repaired. It was probably parked at the impound because it's safe there. I don't suppose they would have handed it over to me if I'd come to pick it up without his intervention."

"Probably not. You usually have to sign away half your bank account to get them back. Thanks for satisfying my curiosity."

Zach turned from the stove where he stirred scrambled eggs in a skillet with a fork. His thick brows rose in inquiry. A wave of love and tenderness struck her. Her gaze moved downward and a clenching heat of desire rushed from breast to thigh as she took in his bare chest sprinkled with rust-colored hair and the muscular slope of his stomach, his pajama pants riding low on his hips.

"That was a smooth way of explaining the situation without lying," he commented.

"I'm a terrible liar. But he was so curious, I hated to send him away without some kind of explanation."

"You don't hold any animosity toward the other officers for what Lester did?"

"No. But if Detective Sherman hadn't called and told me they were coming, I'd have been anxious about opening the door."

She slipped in against his side when he lifted the skillet off the burner.

"I don't have to work today. It's Ryan's turn to take the half-day rotation. I want to cook."

"Sure. But I've already fixed eggs."

"No. I mean *cook*. Do you think Bowie and Flash and your commanding officer would like to come to dinner tomorrow night—with their wives and girlfriends, of course? Your sister will be back by then, too. She knows them, too, doesn't she?" She looked over her small kitchen. "Well, maybe your back patio would be better. I don't think four people would fit inside my dining area."

"Honey, there's not a SEAL alive who'll turn down free food. And Kathleen's been dying to grill you about whether your intentions are honorable."

Piper laughed. "I want to celebrate, and I don't have that many people to celebrate with. My partners, maybe, but they're more colleagues than friends."

His expression telegraphed what he was thinking before he spoke. "Maybe if you make the first overture, Piper."

She shook her head and shoved away the aching grief that threatened to swallow her mood. "I don't have the emotional energy for their drama, Zach. It was all about their loss the whole time. It will continue to be. I haven't been a real part of their family for a long time. It was too easy for them to…I just need things to be…simple right now. I just need to breathe." Would she ever get over this?

"Okay." He brushed his lips over her forehead. He divided the eggs and put two slices of toast on each plate.

She got silverware from the drawer, reached for the coffee pot to freshen their cups, and poured two glasses of orange juice. "What should I fix? What do you think they would like?" She placed the glass of juice next to his plate.

Zach chewed and swallowed. "I've been eating your cooking for three weeks now, and I can say with confidence, they'll love anything you fix, honey."

"What has been your favorite thing I've fixed—" she held up a finger "—besides steak and loaded potatoes?" The eggs were a little overcooked, but she ate them anyway because he'd fixed them, and it was her fault for distracting him.

He grinned. "Your lasagna and that chicken dish you fixed the other day."

"Chicken Caprese. Lasagna is so common. I'll fix the chicken instead." She rose to check noticed the dogs with their noses pressed against the storm door, and got up to let them in. She gave each one a treat and shooed them into the living room.

"To start with, bruschetta," she said when she sat back down. "And stuffed mushrooms. Then the chicken, baked orzo with garlic, spinach, tomatoes, and mozzarella, parmesan-crusted zucchini, and bread sticks with marinara sauce or garlic cheese sauce. And for dessert ricotta pie with chocolate chips."

Zach paused with the fork halfway to his mouth. "Jesus, Piper!"

"I can fix the pies, bread sticks, stuffed mushrooms, and the sauces today and put the chicken in the marinade. Then all I have to do is fix the orzo and slide everything into the oven to bake before dinner. While you grill the chicken, because you're so much better at it than I am, I can fry the zucchini and bake the bread sticks just before I serve them."

"Won't you need two ovens to cook so many different things?"

"No, the secret's in the timing." She sipped her juice.

"I guess we'll have to hit the market once we're done here." He finished the last of his eggs and took a swallow of orange juice to wash them down.

"There's something I'd like to do first," she slid from her seat into his lap. "Lester has resigned." She brushed his thick hair back from his forehead.

His brows shot up. "No shit?"

"No shit."

"That probably saved both him and the SDPD embarrassment, and saved them having to rehash every arrest and prosecution he's been involved in."

"Probably." She nibbled his earlobe to get his attention refocused and smiled when he shivered and his breathing hitched. "There's no horrible shadow standing between us now. No police officer stalking us. It's because of you all this happened. I don't think any other man would have stood by me. No other man ever has. Not since my father." The tears rose up, but she pushed them back down. "I want to start here…" she kissed his forehead, "and kiss every freckle on your body."

His quickly inhaled breath made her smile.

"That would take at least two weeks," he commented. "Why don't you just try to hit the spots with no freckles instead?" He pointed out his lips with an index finger.

She kissed him. He tasted of orange juice and Zach. He scooted back from the table and rose with her in his arms. She looped her arms around his neck.

"I'm so glad your hip is better. But on Monday, when you go to see your captain, limp a little more so they won't want you to go straight back to work."

Zach laughed and carried her through the hall and into the bedroom. "I can't do that, honey, but if I was tempted to do it for anyone, it would be for you, Piper."

"I know." He'd done so much. She'd never be able to show him enough gratitude, and he wouldn't want it. But when he went wheels up, as he called it, she'd wait for him. Gladly. All he had to do was ask.

When Zach lowered her into the center of the bed, she drew him down with her, but pushed him onto his back. She shook free of her robe. "I don't think it will take two weeks, but let's see how far I can get."

Using teeth, tongue and lips she began to seek out the freckles she'd noticed in the most sensitive areas. She didn't get far at all before he was pressing her back, covering himself with a condom and thrusting inside her. When they both lay breathing hard and sated with pleasure, she pressed an open-mouthed kiss on a freckled patch on his shoulder.

"I missed a spot."

Zach chuckled and shook his head. "Couldn't prove it by me, honey."

CHAPTER 41

CAL LIFTED HER SUITCASE onto the scale at the check-in desk. She handed her ticket to the man there and waited for him to compare it and her photo ID to the reservations she'd made. When he handed back her paperwork, they walked down to an area of benches to sit together for a moment.

"You called Zach and told him what time you'd be in?" he asked, clasping her hand between his.

"Yes. Piper's planned a dinner party for a few of his teammates and their wives. He's going to pick me up and take me to his apartment to eat before he runs me home."

"Call me when you get there, so I know you're okay."

"I will." She was already feeling a little weepy. She dreaded going home without him.

"I've been waiting to tell you something."

"What is it?"

"I'll be home in a little over a week. I've already got my ticket booked. Dad and I have hashed things out about the business. He's hiring a foreman I suggested to take my place, Kathleen. I'm just going to finish out a couple of projects this next week, then pass everything off to him."

She found herself tearing up in relief. "Are you sure you want to do it?"

"Positive. You've worked too hard to take a chance on a

move that might screw things up for you. Once you have your internship behind you and you've taken your licensing exam, we'll revisit everything."

She couldn't say she wasn't relieved, but at the same time she'd been a little excited about possibly designing some residential projects. But she could still do some of those outside of her work for Wiley Design. She did need to complete all the internship requirements in order to move on with her career. But in Texas they could have a home without having so much on the line financially. With Cal's family nearby, she'd have a support system for when they started a family. Her own parents and siblings were so far away.

"When the time comes, I'll be ready to do whatever you want, Cal."

"I told Dad that's what you'd say." He kissed her hand.

"Tell him I still want that deal on construction rates in two years."

Cal laughed. "I will." He was quiet for a moment, and looked serious. "I don't think either of us would have been ready to mend fences if he hadn't had this heart attack. So at least something good has come out of it."

"Maybe more will, if he and your mom can continue to work toward each other."

"They're in a better place than they were, Kathleen. You helped make it happen. You bring light and humor with you wherever you go. Mom said she hasn't laughed so much in ages. Dad even smiled and laughed a time or two. But you also stood up to him in a way he couldn't argue with, and inspired Mom to do the same. They have a way to go, but I even caught them cuddling together in his recliner this morning when they thought they were alone."

Kathleen smiled at the thought. "I thought he might have some moves left in him once he got his head out of his ass. There's no way you could ever be as stubborn as he is."

Cal laughed. "I told you so."

"I think having his son back has put him in a better place.

And what about Doug?"

"He's finding his feet. I want to give him another week, though, before I come home. He's realized it takes more than he can give to keep things afloat, so he's settled down."

Kathleen glanced at her watch and stifled a sigh. "I'd better go through the security station and find my boarding gate." She got to her feet reluctantly, leaning into him to rest her cheek against his chest, her arms tight around him. She felt secure within the answering pressure of his. "Most people refer to home as where they were born or where they grew up," she commented when she drew back.

His blue-green gaze settled on her face, and he lowered his mouth to hers and kissed her with slow, deep thoroughness that left her breathless and weak. When he raised his head, he brushed the backs of his fingers against her cheek. "Home is where you are, Kathleen."

ZACH DECIDED THE only thing more sensual than watching Piper eat food was watching her prepare it. She smelled or tasted everything before it went into the recipe she was preparing. The pots and pans, bowls, whisks, knives, and other tools she used shone like new, even though she'd been using them since starting college. It seemed he'd moved them all to his house by the time they unloaded the food and other things into his larger kitchen.

Though she'd done the lion's share of the work the day before, she still packed a box of ingredients to do some last-minute tweaks to everything before she served the dishes. She whipped cream and grated chocolate atop the ricotta pies, and added more freshly-grated Parmesan to the stuffed mushrooms. When he left her to go pick up Kathleen at the airport, she was preparing the pasta dish she meant to serve with her chicken and cutting up zucchini to fry.

Halfway to the airport, Zach pulled over into the parking lot of a parts supply store. He couldn't believe he was doing this, but the phone call from Hawk with the invite to the Captain's office had him antsy. They were probably shipping out, and the thought of leaving her unprotected with Henderlight on the loose was driving him crazy.

As soon as Piper told him Lester had resigned, the idea had popped into his head. He opened the sheet of paper he'd collected from his room and dialed the number on it.

The phone went to voicemail, and he went into his spiel, laying it on thick with Lester about how he owed Piper something for what he had done. Now he was on vacation for a while he'd have time to do something useful. By the time Zach pulled back onto the road, he felt he'd done everything he could for the time being.

Kathleen was beaming when he pulled up beside her outside the airport. When he got out of the car, his hip only twanged a bit. "Well how was it?" he asked.

"I'm engaged!"

"About time." Zach said with a laugh and gathered her close for a hug. "I thought I might have to take Cal aside and do the 'when are you going to do the right thing' speech." She was glowing.

Kathleen poked him in the stomach with a finger. "You wouldn't dare."

Like hell. He raised one brow. "Let me see the ring."

She extended her hand, a grin on her face.

He whistled. It was a beauty, and he could only wonder what Callahan had paid for it. "It's gorgeous, sis." He hugged her again.

"How was Texas?" he asked.

"Warmer than here, and beautiful. I had the usual picture in my head of deserts and cattle and all that, but it's got so much more to offer. San Antonio is one of the biggest cities in Texas. Some of the homes I saw were just gorgeous. Cal's mom's and dad's is beautiful, not a showplace, but a real home."

Zach put the suitcase in the back of the SUV and closed the door.

"How's his dad doing?" he asked after they were in the car.

"He's doing well. He sleeps a lot, like Nana Rose did. He's tough as an old boot. But under it, I think he's got some soft spots. His sons are one of them. I think he must have finally apologized to Cal, because things were better when I left."

"Good." He looked in the side mirror and the rearview mirror before pulling out into the flow of traffic.

"How have things been going with Piper?"

"I have a lot to tell you, but we'll do it when I drive you home later."

"Good stuff or bad stuff?" she asked.

"Some of each, but it's mostly good now." It felt good to share something with her after clamming up before she left for Texas. Family was hard. Piper was right. But he'd no more be able to keep everything that had happened from Kathleen than he would Bowie or Hawk.

"Has she gotten an appointment with Dr. Dowling yet?"

He glanced at her. "No. Not yet."

Kathleen sank back against the seat. "I read about her father's death. I can't imagine…"

His phone rang and he glanced at the screen. "I have to take this, Kathleen. It's important." He answered the call. "Hold on a minute. I'm pulling off the road so we can talk." He pulled into a restaurant parking lot and found a spot at the back under the shade of a catalpa tree. He motioned for Kathleen to stay silent and turned the phone onto speaker. He motioned "You still there?"

"Yeah. I've been ordered to stay a thousand feet away from both of you and no phone contact."

Lester would never be able to let things go with Henderlight. He was counting on it. "Then why did you call me back?"

"You know why." Lester's tone was sullen.

"I found out last night he's been out for two weeks and no one called her." What the fuck was up with that?

"They wouldn't have had reason to. There wouldn't be a note on any kind of list, because she never reported what happened."

"She might have later if things hadn't gone down like they

did."

"We'll never know that now, will we?"

"No." He closed his eyes while he reached for patience. A sudden wave of grief hit him. "She was nineteen, scared, traumatized."

"Have you told her he's out?" Lester asked, his voice subdued.

"She needed a day or two to recover. I'm going to tell her tonight." Zach messaged his forehead.

"What the hell do you expect me to do about it?" Lester demanded.

"Nothing you weren't willing to do when you were after her. You put a GPS on her car to monitor her. Do the same with his. Shadow him like you did us. Stay on his ass until he does something stupid."

"I'm not a cop anymore. Even if I witnessed him doing something, my word won't mean squat. Not now."

"Video doesn't lie. You can think of something. Don't you want this bastard? He was the root of it all."

"Yeah. Yeah, I do."

"He's going to dodge a solicitation to murder charge. He's smart enough to keep his mouth shut about what he planned to do. And if Acosta was going to take care of him, it would already have happened."

He waited for Lester to reply. He rested a hand on Kathleen's arm. She had lost some of her glow. He regretted letting her sit in on this conversation.

When Lester remained silent, Zach gripped the steering wheel hard in frustration. The asshole could stalk a helpless woman, but when it came to a psychopathic rapist, he wanted to back off. "He's going to go after her."

"Yeah. He probably will." The flatness of Lester's tone carried a surety Zach was had hoped only in his mind.

What was it Piper had said the day before? She was the only one who'd seen him lose control of the monster. She didn't deserve to spend her life looking over her shoulder again, not after she'd had a taste of freedom. He dragged his fingers through his hair and tugged. "You owe her something for everything you did, Lester. She's alone because of you."

"She has you."

"Uncle Sam has my number. When he calls I'll have to go."

Another pause followed. He ground his teeth as he waited. "Come on, man, it will give you the opportunity to refill your karma account."

"I'll see what I can do. Hell, I don't have anything better to do."

"Catching a psychopath will look good on your resume. If he so much as sneezes in her direction I want to know about it."

"Okay."

He drew a deep breath. If Lester put in half as much time and effort stalking David Henderlight as he had Piper... "Thanks."

Kathleen barely waited until he ended the call before exploding. "Jesus, Zach! What the hell is going on?"

"I'll tell you on the way."

It was a relief to share everything. By telling her, he thought to clear his head of the accumulated emotional baggage he realized he was carrying around. To tone those feelings down, he explained it as though he were giving a report.

"How did she endure it?"

He shook his head. "She's developed coping mechanisms." OCD, her animals, obsessively checking her environment for threats. Jesus! "She's the strongest person I've ever met. She doesn't think she is, but she is."

"And this man you just talked to is the detective who stalked her?"

"Yeah."

"You're offering him a way to redeem himself?"

"Yeah. He's a single-minded son of a bitch. Once he gets on the scent, he will not give up. The very last person you'd want on your tail. He'll land on his feet as long as they don't bring charges. The DA won't be eager to do that since it might throw some of the convictions based on Lester's work into question. He'll do fine in the private sector doing investigations for insurance companies or lawyers."

He needed to focus on Piper and her big night. "She's never hosted a dinner party before. Hasn't had any kind of get-together with friends since college. She's a little nervous, wanting everything to be perfect."

"Everything will be fine. Good food, good friends. What could go wrong?" She rested her hand on his arm. The hand with her engagement ring.

"I'm sorry I spoiled your big moment. You know I'm thrilled for you and Cal."

"I know. I've been bitching about you never sharing anything with me. I know it's because of your work, and because that's just how you are." Her eyes were glassy with tears. "I knew Cal was the one five days into our dating. Time isn't relevant when it comes to feelings. You care about Piper."

He pulled into the driveway and shut off the engine. "Of course I do. If we could just catch a break and have two minutes without some asshole coming out of the woodwork, waiting to fuck things up for us…"

Kathleen started to tear back up again.

"You have to hold it together, Kathleen. If Piper thinks I told you this, she'll get self-conscious and stiff."

"Okay." She fanned her face as though that might dry her tears. "I promise I'll keep it together. And if I don't, I'll blame it on the emotions attached to Cal's and my engagement. Which wouldn't be too wrong. I'm sure the guy who sat next to me on the plane thought I was a basket case."

"I want you to be able to see her when she's relaxed and happy. The real Piper." The Piper he fell in love with that first weekend.

CHAPTER 42

THE HOUSE SMELLED wonderful. Like home. Spices and yeast, marinara sauce, and the dish of pasta baking in the oven all scented the air. She refused to think about her family today. She was moving on without them.

Piper twisted her hair back into a bun to fit at the crown of her head and stuck in some pins to hold it in place. She touched her lips with gloss and gave her eyelashes a quick brush with mascara, then slipped the apron back on over her summer sweater and long skirt. She'd take it off once she got everything out of the oven.

She looked up from stirring the cheese sauce and smiled when Zach and Kathleen arrived.

"How was Texas?" Piper asked.

"A little warmer than here and beautiful." Kathleen raised her nose in the air as though scenting. "It smells wonderful in here. Italian is one of Zach's favorites. Mine too."

"Hopefully it will taste as good as it smells. Let me pour you a glass of wine, and we'll visit while we wait for everyone to arrive."

They wandered outside while Zach went to change. They'd set two long tables side by side to make one wide table. Piper had spread a long white tablecloth over both and smoothed a square of brightly colored fabric over the center, creating a diamond of color. Two quart-sized canning jars were spaced equal distances apart, the long tapers inside anchored by clear glass marbles. They looked both homey and elegant. The plates, glasses and silverware gleamed.

"The table looks beautiful, Piper," Kathleen said. "I don't have a knack for decoration. Maybe you can help me brainstorm some ideas for the wedding. We're not talking about a large, formal thing, but just family and a few friends."

"Oh, you're engaged?"

"Yes, Callahan popped the question day before yesterday."

"Congratulations!"

While Piper studied her beautiful ring, Kathleen said, "Callahan and I decided to forgo the large, formal thing for a large family thing."

"Won't that be the same?" The two of them laughed.

Would she still be in Zach's life when Kathleen married? If he stuck to his adamant stance of no contact… Surely he wouldn't. Not after everything they'd been through. But until he said otherwise….

Zach joined them wearing in khakis and a light green knit shirt, Flash and Samantha in tow, leaving her little time to dwell on it. They greeted her with an easy friendliness. With her strawberry blond hair and creamy skin, Samantha had a fresh, country girl prettiness that complimented Flash's blond good looks and more worldly intensity.

"I'm so glad you both could come. I can't begin to thank you," she said to Flash. "The advice you gave us made a huge difference."

"I'm glad it worked out, and that it's over for you."

"I am, too. There are soft drinks and beer in the cooler. And I have wine and tea in the kitchen."

"I'd like a soft drink," Samantha said.

"I'll get it, hon," Flash volunteered.

"Is there anything I can do to help?" Kathleen asked.

"It's all done. I'm just going to take the pasta out of the oven and put the mushrooms in for a few minutes. I'll get you a glass and some ice for your drink."

The light had softened some while the sun was setting. Kathleen and Samantha were settled at the table, the men congregated at the grill. The deep murmur of their voices was somehow soothing to her.

Hawk, Zach's commanding officer, and his wife Zoe wandered around the side of the house just when Piper stepped out onto the patio. They paused to introduce themselves. Hawk was imposing, large, and had an intense disposition, but his smile as he shook her hand eased her anxiety. Zoe was beautiful, with hazelnut brown hair streaked with blond and blue eyes. She wore a long skirt much like Piper's, and a silk blouse with a wide belt around her narrow waist. Piper poured Zoe a glass of wine while Hawk helped himself to a beer.

Piper watched Zach's Lieutenant with interest. He talked about him more than the others. He admired and trusted him and Bowie above everyone else. "I need to ask your husband something."

Zoe smiled. "He doesn't bite. I promise."

Piper laughed. "Did I look that anxious?"

"Only a little."

"It's just that Zach's been helping me solve some personal issues, and I was worried it had caused him a problem at work."

"I can't guarantee Adam will tell you if it has. They're so closemouthed. But if it hasn't, he'll tell you that. It will at least ease your concern."

"Okay."

Piper rose and approached the large man hesitantly and touched his arm. "Lieutenant—Hawk?"

He turned with the same animal grace Zach exhibited now his hip wasn't causing him such pain. "Yes?"

She moistened her lips. "I never intended for Zach to get involved."

Hawk offered her a wry smile. "An infinite force met an immovable object. Sometimes it's better to save the energy."

A short burst of laughter bubbled from her. "That's a very good description of how it went."

He shrugged. "It's what makes him a good SEAL."

"I can see that. He's been an unstoppable force and an immovable object all rolled into one. It's the first time I had someone who believed in me without question. He was in my corner from the start. I can't tell you how much it's meant to me."

"His faith was justified, based on what I heard from Detective Sherman and his boss."

Piper drew a deep breath. "I know how much what he does means to him. Being a SEAL is everything. He has a meeting with his Captain on Monday. I don't want what's happened recently to interfere with his career. So if I need to speak with anyone and explain everything…on his behalf…"

"No. It won't be necessary. Everything's fine." Hawk gave her arm a brief squeeze.

She searched his face for several seconds. Her shoulders dropped with relief. "Okay. I thought he might be trying to downplay the fallout."

"There's nothing to worry about."

She drew a deep breath. "Thank you."

He nodded. "Well there is one thing. How good are you about keeping secrets?"

Piper thought a moment. "My safety deposit box can't even come close."

He grinned. "On Monday you need to be sure he gets out the door on time. I'll have Seaman Sizemore send you a Skype invitation this evening. Zach will be receiving a commendation, but we wanted to keep it on the down low. I can't get you or Kathleen on the base in time to be there for it, but I know he'll want the two of you to see him get his Lieutenant bars."

"Oh, yes, I'd love it. I'll slip you my email address in a few minutes. And I'll tell Kathleen."

When she returned to the table to sit with the women, Zoe smiled. "I could tell from his expression and yours everything's okay. I've been dying to meet you. Hawk told me Doc had met someone. The way he tried to play it cool, I could tell you were important."

Sometimes when Zach looked at her she felt he was on the verge of saying everything she wanted to hear, but he didn't. "Is that how they all are—holding everything close, I mean?"

Kathleen leaned forward. "It's like pulling teeth to get Zach to share anything."

"Maybe he doesn't want to let anyone see the heart on his sleeve," Zoe said.

Bowie swung around the side of the house alone, and Piper hurried over to greet him. He presented her with a bottle of white wine. "How you doin' today, little lady?" His golden brown eyes searched her face.

She smiled at the concern she read there. "I'm good. Wonderful, actually. Thank you for everything you did."

He shrugged. "I was just in the right place at the right time."

"You must have the best luck of anyone I know."

"Actually, I was hung over from lack of sleep. We'd been doing night maneuvers, and I wanted to take a nap."

Piper laughed. "Your nap saved me from a jail cell. You know that, don't you?" Tears rushed to surface before she swallowed them back.

"There was never any chance of that. Zach and Detective Sherman had you covered. I heard Kathleen had some good news. I'll pretend I don't already know it and let her break it to me."

"How do you know?"

"Osmosis. Once one of us knows something, we all do."

Piper narrowed her eyes. "I think it's called texting."

He grinned. "Or that could be it."

He sauntered over to the table and slid in next to Kathleen. "Who needs a date when I can sit with one of my favorite ladies for dinner?"

Kathleen smiled, her lovely face radiant. "You're sitting next to an engaged woman, Bowie." Kathleen presented her hand with the ring.

"Damn, I missed my chance!" He studied the ring with open admiration. "I'm really happy for you, Thorn. And envious as hell of Cal."

He placed an arm around Kathleen with easy affection and kissed her forehead.

Piper slipped away to open the wine and take the stuffed

mushrooms out of the oven. Zach was busy grilling the chicken breasts and hanging with the men close to the grill. Piper got Samantha another soft drink and took the bottle of wine she'd opened earlier to fill Zoe's glass and top off Kathleen's and her own, though she'd only had a sip or two.

She listened to the easy way the other women conversed. Sam had just gotten a new job with an insurance agency. Zoe had been offered a promotion to take over a managerial position in the physical therapy department at the hospital. It would be less physically demanding and the pay was better. She was debating whether or not to take it, because she loved working with patients.

Piper went back inside and plated the bruschetta and stuffed mushrooms on two large, oval serving platters and slipped the bread into the oven. She placed a plate in the center of the table in front of the ladies, then wandered over to the men with the other and placed it on the small table next to the grill, within reaching distance.

Zach slipped an arm around her waist. "Chicken will be ready in just a minute. Those aren't going to last long." He nodded at the plate that was already emptying.

Piper smiled. "Thanks. Everything but the bread is done. I think the Orzo is still hot enough without going back in the oven."

Zach brushed a kiss against her temple. "This crowd is used to grilled burgers and hot dogs or fish. They're eating this four-star treatment up." He grinned. "Literally."

The chicken was done to a turn, the bread golden brown. Everyone served themselves from casserole dishes on the table next to the grill. Piper set a basket of bread on each table with bowls of marinara sauce and garlic cheese sauce.

She felt she could finally relax with everyone eating. Conversation flowed about the fishing trip the guys wanted to take before they went wheels up, and they wanted her to fix the same Parmesan-crusted zucchini to go with the fish they'd fry.

Everyone had a suggestion for Kathleen's wedding. The four women wanted to organize a cooking class for her to teach them how to make bread sticks and marinara sauce. They made her feel like a member of the group. She was no longer standing on the periphery as she had always done in the past. Would it last after Zach left?

After the last piece of pie was eaten, the women rose as one to help her clean up, and the men bundled up the trash and brought things in. From the easy way they all pitched in, she surmised it was a normal part of their get-togethers.

"Joy loves the kitten. It sleeps with her every night. It's so funny. It bounces sideways at toy mice and flips them in the air. Maybe it will help fill the void a little when Flash ships out."

"I hope so. They're constant sources of entertainment, and good lessons in responsibility. I'm glad you could give her a home." She loaded the plates and flatware into the dishwasher and flipped it on.

Zoe nudged her away from the sink. "You did all the hard work, Piper. Kathleen and I will take care of this." She started water for the pots. Kathleen stood ready with a towel. There was little left for Piper to do but stand back and watch.

"Animals can be excellent therapy. I don't know what I'd have done without Trouble, my golden retriever. He gave me a warm, loving, uncritical being to cling to when I needed someone."

"Don't you have family close by?"

"We're estranged, and I don't see them anymore." The sooner she accepted it, the better. "It's just me and Trouble."

"That's a real shame. After my Gran died, it was just Joy and me for a while, then Flash came into our lives. He just filled every empty space, including our hearts."

Piper's gaze strayed to Zach out on the patio with the other men. "I understand what you mean. I was hoping for more time."

Zoe folded the dishcloth over the divider on the double sink. "There's never enough, Piper," Zoe said. "Never. But the time they're with us is more precious because of it."

Piper nodded. "I've been lucky to spend these few weeks with Zach. My work hours are split, so we've had afternoons together, and nights. I can't imagine what it will be like not to see him every day or talk to him."

"It's lonely. But they call, Skype, and email when they can,"

Samantha said.

Zach insisted he wouldn't call because he couldn't be distracted by the emotions it would trigger. With no contact between them for at least six months, would he forget her, forget what it felt like to be with her?

"I live for those Skypes, because I don't entirely trust Flash to tell me the truth about how he is when he calls. If I can see him, I feel better."

"I know what you mean," Kathleen said with a nod. "Zach could have a broken leg and he'd swear it was a sprain."

Piper nodded. "He could barely walk and he was throwing a ball on the beach with Trouble."

Kathleen arched a brow. "Typical."

"If they're injured they have to work through their pain. So they don't want to give into it even when they can," Zoe explained.

Piper could understand the drive. She'd worked toward a goal because it was the only thing she had left to hold on to. If she were in physical danger and in pain she'd do the same. "Sometimes it's easier to keep putting one foot in front of the other and focusing on a goal, because it shoves the real issue that's eating at you to the back of your mind for a while so you can...survive it."

"I know how that is," Sam said.

"I think we all do," Kathleen said.

Piper looked around at their faces. Zach had told her about each of them. Kathleen had suffered her best friend's betrayal and the ending of her first engagement to a womanizing prick, Zoe with her limp and scars caused by a drunk driver, Sam with her abusive ex-husband who'd stalked and tried to kill her. She had a lot in common with these women. She had been isolated for so long. If anyone could understand what she'd been through, it would be them. When she was ready to talk about everything, and when they knew her well enough to want to listen.

She suddenly felt like she was taking her second step toward normal when she said, "Okay, when would you like to do your cooking class?"

CHAPTER 43

Z ACH CHECKED HIS APPEARANCE in the bathroom mirror. He hadn't been in uniform for more than three weeks, but he certainly looked more professional than he had before his injury. The trim Kathleen gave him after dinner last night had spruced up the new haircut. Maybe a plus, since he'd be in Captain Jackson's office in about an hour.

His physical assessment to return to duty wasn't scheduled until Wednesday, but if they needed him right away, he could reschedule. He felt the first stirrings of excitement. He'd be back to work, doing what he was meant to do. The only down side was it would cut into the time he and Piper spent together.

He was already feeling the pull between work and her, and he hadn't even left the house yet. And then there was Gracie and Trouble. He'd grown attached to them. They'd filled an empty place inside him. Which was both great and scary as hell.

Piper, already dressed for work, came to the open bathroom door and leaned against the frame. "You look very handsome in your uniform."

The khaki-colored summer uniform was not his favorite, but he had been instructed to wear it by the Captain's aide. "Thanks."

"Will you call me and let me know how it goes with your Captain?"

"Yeah. I'll call."

"Thanks. I'm going to take the dogs with me." She turned to scoop up the bag of dog toys at the foot of the bed.

"I'll help you load Gracie."

"You might get dog hair on your uniform, and you need to get going. I'll do it. They've gotten very good about staying in their seats while I buckle them in."

He didn't need a sign to tell him she was a little anxious about his returning to duty. He caught her arm and drew her in close.

"Piper, she weighs more than seventy pounds."

She shot him a wry smile. "I have a clothes brush in the car."

"It may look a little fancier than the regular Battle Dress Uniform, Piper, but it's made to withstand a lot more than dog hair."

She touched the gold bar on the corner of his collar.

He smiled. "I'm going to work, just like any other guy, honey. This is probably just a meeting to let me know something about my current assignment, or to ask me to conduct some kind of course on the medical techniques I've learned in the field. It could be about anything. His aide didn't tell me what to expect. I'll probably be home at five, just like any other guy. If I'm not going to be, I'll call and let you know."

"Okay. I've gotten used to having you here or at my house when I come home for lunch. I've gotten used to having you whenever I want."

He grinned when she squeezed his ass.

"It's going to be an adjustment."

"For me too, Piper." He kissed her gently, with care, then with more, because now she'd pointed out the obvious, he was feeling the pinch, too. A swift rush of desire followed her response and he hardened in an instant. When he lifted his mouth from hers, her mahogany eyes were nearly swallowed by her pupils and her cheeks were flushed. "We'll finish this tonight, okay?"

She nodded.

"You say break a leg to theater people when you want to encourage them to give a good performance. What do you say to a SEAL to offer encouragement?"

Zach grinned. "Saddle up, big boy?"

Piper laughed, giving him another charge of desire that left him throbbing. If they had time...

He dragged his mind back to her question. "Hooyah. Which can mean anything from 'yes, sir' to 'fuckin' A.'"

Piper laughed again, then grew serious. "Hooyah, Ensign O'Connor."

"Perfect." God, she made it sound so sexy, he was tempted to kiss her again. But once he did, he'd want more, and he'd be late for sure. Not a good way to start back to work.

He forced himself to be satisfied with a quick brush of the lips, then stepped back.

Outside, he laid his hat atop her car, lifted Gracie into Piper's back seat, and secured her, leaving the leash attached to her harness. Piper did the same with Trouble.

"Are you taking them to work with you or the house?" he asked, tucking his cover under his arm as he stood in the open car door. "If I get off early I can go by and hang out with them."

Piper jumped up into the driver's seat. "To my house. The office can't handle but one at a time. They want to lie right under everyone's feet."

Zach laughed. "We've created two monsters. I'll call and let you know one way or the other."

"Okay. You're going to be late if you don't get a move on."

He shut the door and stood back when she started the car and backed out of the driveway.

He checked his watch, then double-timed it to his car. Traffic was light, and he made it across the bridge into Coronado, then hit a bottleneck entering the base. By the time he made it to Captain Jackson's office it was crunch time, and he jogged down the sidewalk, past ruthlessly sculpted bushes, to the main entrance, ignoring the twinge from his hip. How fucking long was it going to take to heal? He arrived with only a minute to spare.

"Good to see you Ensign O'Connor. How's the hip?" Seaman Sparks, the Captain's aide of only a few months, asked.

Zach wondered how the guy knew about the injury. "Much better, thanks."

"Go down this hall to a set of double doors. It's a conference room. Captain Jackson is in there. You don't have to knock, just go straight in."

He nodded. "Thanks."

Zach paused outside the doors to smooth back his hair and tuck his cover under his arm. He reached for the doorknob, and twisted it.

He saw Hawk first, then Bowie and the rest of the guys standing at ease, shooting the shit. Captain Jackson stood with Admiral Cooper. They shook hands, then Cooper peeled off from the group and started toward the door.

Zach reached for the knob, and, holding door open, went to attention with a salute. Cooper returned it with a nod and moved on past and out. Zach strode to Captain Jackson and saluted.

Jackson never changed. His prematurely gray hair looked a little grayer, but the man never aged. He had been known to be a real hard-ass at times, but after being held hostage by a group of terrorists for three days, he seemed to have found his center. There was a more decisive bent to his decisions. He seemed to weigh in more often on behalf of the men under his command.

"At ease, Ensign. How's the hip?"

"I'll be ready to return to duty as soon as the doc releases me, sir."

"When will that be?"

"I have an appointment at ten on Wednesday, but I can call and try to get them to push me through today if you need me, sir."

"Not necessary. Wednesday will be soon enough."

"Aye, sir."

"You can join the others until I call this meeting together. We're waiting on a couple of guests."

"Aye, sir."

He'd almost made it to a seat beside Bowie when Zoe entered the room with A. J. in tow. Captain Jackson crossed to her and shook her hand, then bent to shake A. J.'s.

Hawk joined them, and they spoke for a few minutes. He bent and picked up A. J. and placed a hand against Zoe's waist to usher

her to a seat. Once they were settled, Hawk stretched an arm out along the back of Zoe's chair.

Zach caught a seat next to Bowie and hunched forward to brace his elbows on his knees.

He was getting a clue as to what he was here for, and it wasn't special duty. His heart raced and he was sweating a little. If his promotion hadn't gone through, he would be disappointed. If Hawk was being promoted, he was glad to be here. He'd have been majorly disappointed to miss it.

Seaman Jeff Sizemore, aka Bullet to his teammates, the sniper of their team, slid into the seat next to him. Sizemore's smile stretched across his face and he slapped Doc on the back.

"How you doing, Doc?" Bullet asked.

"I'm good. I'll be back on Wednesday."

"I heard you've been wooing a real babe, while you've been *laid* up." Sizemore emphasized the word laid.

Zach eyed Bowie who threw up his hands and shook his head.

"Watch yourself, Bullet," Zach warned. "Piper's a lady.

"What does she do for a living?"

"She's a veterinarian."

Bullet nodded. "See, when you say vet, I immediately get this picture of the vet back home, Dr. Chalmers, horsy face, long nose, big teeth."

"She's a vet and a babe," Zach cut in.

"A beautiful babe," Bowie added.

"A beautiful, classy babe." Zach felt like he was being set up somehow, and narrowed his eyes at Bowie in warning.

Whatever they were doing was cut short when Captain Jackson said, "Everyone please take a seat." His voice carried well in the small room.

The noise died instantly and everyone moved to the nearest chair.

Captain Jackson cleared his throat. "I seldom get the opportunity to do presentations like this. I'm proud and pleased to do so today.

"There are two men among you who have fulfilled their duty

as SEALs in ways all of us hope to emulate. Both of them have shown great courage, dedication, professionalism, and leadership. They have gone above and beyond without being asked or ordered to do so. That in itself is saying something in the company they are among today. Each and every one of you has put your life on the line for your men, family, and country, numerous times. You stand between the innocent who cannot protect themselves and those who would bring them harm. And you do it at great risk to yourselves. What these two men have accomplished is what each and every one of you can aspire to.

"I wish to ask Ensign Zachary Tobias O'Connor and Lieutenant Adam Yazzie to come forward."

Zach waited for Hawk to rise before doing so himself. He followed him to the front of the room.

"Lieutenant Yazzie. You may not know this, but every SEAL who has been under your command, past and present, has said the same thing. You are the ultimate example of what a SEAL should be. You remain calm and professional during times of extreme stress. You fight with the fierceness of your warrior ancestors. And you lead your men by example, yet you are always looking out for them. You are always searching for ways to improve their performance, and you do it with the idea of making sure every one of them returns home safe."

Zach found his throat tightening with emotion while he listened to Captain Jackson. Every word was true. They all admired Hawk and attempted to follow his lead.

"Today I am honored to present you with a promotion to Lieutenant Commander."

Captain Jackson reached for a box on the table and removed two insignia and a ribbon. He removed the insignia from each point of Hawk's collar and replaced the bars with the gold oak leaves of a Lieutenant Commander. He saluted Hawk, and Hawk returned the gesture. The two men shook hands. He handed Hawk the ribbon.

Hawk stepped aside and took a place to Captain Jackson's right.

"Ensign O'Connor. I know you have put yourself at great risk to treat the injured during battle, even dragged or carried them out of the line of fire. A team medic has possibly one of the most dangerous jobs, because the instinct to protect your wounded comrade is strong. I also know you've volunteered to act as a corpsman at the field hospitals where you've been deployed.

"But that's only one area where you've excelled. Lieutenant Commander Yazzie has told me how you've taken over many of the leadership roles during missions, taken over the shooting drills and instruction, and mentored some of the newer members of your team to sharpen their skills. All the qualities of a leader."

"It gives me great pleasure to present you with your promotion to Lieutenant Junior Grade."

Captain Jackson reached for a box on the table and removed the silver bars and a ribbon. The transfer from the gold bar insignias on his collar to the silver of a Lieutenant went quickly. As he returned Captain Jackson's salute, shook his hand, and accepted the ribbon to go over his uniform pocket, all he could think was how much he wished Piper could have been here to see it.

The men in the room erupted into applause. Hawk shook his hand, then jerked him into a hug and pounded him on the back. A crowd gathered to congratulate them.

Bullet grabbed his arm. "Smile for the ladies, Lieutenant O'Connor," Bullet said and pointed toward a camera on a tripod hooked to a computer. "We couldn't arrange passes for your sister or Dr. Bertinelli to attend, so we Skyped the whole thing so they could watch you get your bars."

He strode to the computer to see Kathleen and Piper at Piper's house. "Hey."

"We're very proud of you, Zach," Kathleen said, while she sniffled and wiped her eyes with a tissue.

"Thanks, sis."

"I hope they've taped the ceremony, because Mom and Dad and the rest of the clan would love to see it."

He glanced at Bullet, and he nodded. "I'll see what we can

do."

"Congratulations, Zach," Piper said her composure only a little better than Kathleen's. "Hooyah, Lieutenant."

Naturally he got hard, and he had the feeling that every time she said it in the future, it would happen again. "When I get home, I want you to say it again, just that way."

Piper laughed. "I will."

Captain Jackson waved to him. "I have to go, the captain's calling."

"Okay. We'll see you later."

PIPER CLOSED THE LAPTOP and reached for another tissue to dry her eyes.

"Does he always refer to your house as home?" Kathleen asked.

Piper hesitated to think about it. "My house and his. Wherever we've decided to stay."

Kathleen smiled. "Callahan said something to me before I got on the plane. I think I cried all the way home because it was probably the most beautiful thing he's ever said to me. And he's said plenty."

"What was it?"

"He said home is where I am. Don't you think it's telling that Zach's doing the same thing?"

Piper attempted a smile. "I hope so, because I love him so much it hurts. He thinks it's because of everything we've been through. But it isn't. I fell in love with him our first weekend together. When he goes, I'll wait for him if he wants me to. Probably even if he never says a word."

Kathleen put her arms around her and gave her a hug. "He'll figure it out, Piper."

If she loved him enough, maybe he would.

CHAPTER 44

PIPER RUBBED HER burning eyes, then returned her attention to the chart she was updating. She'd sleep better once Zach was home from the team's weekend training. Just one more day.

At least she knew Zach was okay. He was just out in the desert somewhere, training with his team, instead of in some dangerous place out of the country. He'd been reassigned, and was now leader of his own team. He loved it. And though it meant more responsibility, he was finding his feet.

And he'd be home on the weekend. Excitement like a bubble expanded inside her. It was like that every time. She could hardly wait to see him.

She missed being held, missed him reaching for her in his sleep, missed making love with him. The dogs were restless, particularly Gracie. They were grieving his absence, and were clingy when she was home, following her every move.

Like last night, when they thought they heard something outside and barked for nearly half an hour.

She propped her head on her hand and continued to write the notations in the chart. Almost done. She blinked to clear her vision, then closed her eyes tight. Maybe if she just rested for a moment.

ZACH'S PHONE WAS ringing when they hit the locker room. A successful day of maneuvers left the men loud and keyed up, hot and sweaty. They all smelled like Gracie and Trouble after a day at the beach. Whoo! He didn't smell like any bed of roses himself.

He glanced at the number and frowned. He hadn't heard from Lester in a couple of days. He walked out into the hall and closed the door behind him. He swiped the face of his phone. "Hello."

"Our boy's making a move finally. He's been parked in the lot adjoining your girl's office for over an hour, but he hasn't made a move yet. I have eyes on him."

"Where's Piper?"

"According to the GPS, she's still at her office."

Zach glanced at his dive watch. Ten-oh-five. "That's late for her. She's usually out of the lot by nine fifteen. Are you sure he hasn't slipped by you?"

"I'm watching him right now. He's got binoculars trained on her office."

"I'm on my way. I'll call you back."

He stepped into the locker room and gave a whistle to get everyone's attention. Most of the men had peeled out of their tactical vests and were in the process of stripping and cleaning their weapons.

Crossing the room with a speed that gained everyone's attention, he reached for his personal Sig Sauer 226 and holstered it, then secured the lock on his locker. "I have an emergency at home. I have to bug out." His attention snagged on Petty Officer Rankin. "Rankin?"

"Yes, sir."

"Weapons cleaned and secured. Everything else stowed and shipshape before anyone steps foot off base. As long as everything is as it should be before they leave, everyone can report Monday morning, zero seven hundred."

"Aye-aye, L.T."

"Do you need backup, L.T.?" Seaman Clarence asked, his gaze drifting to the weapon on Zach's hip.

It wouldn't do for anyone but him to take the hit if something bad went down. "No. But thanks."

Zach broke into a jog as he hit the outside door. His heart was beating fast and hard when he hit the key fob and unlocked his SUV, where he started the engine and dragged the seat belt over his shoulder at the same time.

Once he was on the way out of the base he reached for his phone, hit Lester's number, and speaker. "I'm going to call Piper and check on her. Don't take your eyes off that SOB. If he so much as steps foot outside his vehicle take him down."

"We won't be able to get him for anything if I make a move too soon, Ensign."

"I'm not risking Piper."

"Understood."

An annoying ringing pierced Piper's sleep-addled brain. She was reaching for the bedside clock and knocked over a small cup of pencils instead. Her cheek rested on the chart she'd been updating. The pen was still in her hand, but had made a long streak up the page. She jerked up, blinking against the harsh overhead light. She reached for the phone in her lab coat pocket, and swiped the face to answer the call.

"Hey, babe. You home yet?"

Zach's voice brought her to complete wakefulness. "I'm at the office. I fell asleep at my desk."

"Piper, it's ten-fifteen, and I'm on my way home."

"You're coming home early?"

"Yeah."

"I'm on my way right now." She scooped up the spilled pens, put them back in the container, and set it on the corner of her desk. "I just need to turn off the lights and set the alarm."

"Stay on the phone while you do it. I don't like the idea of you being there alone this late."

She smiled at his concern. "Okay." She stood, shook free of her lab coat, and draped it over the back of her desk chair. She set the phone to speaker and placed it on the desk while she retrieved her purse from the bottom desk drawer. She paused a moment to rub her eyes and stifle a yawn. "Is the training going well?"

"Yeah. We're beginning to come together. What have you been up to?"

She gathered her things, unlocked her office door, and scanned the hall each way before stepping out. She brushed the light switch off in her office. "I had two surgeries this morning. The rest of the day's been pretty routine. A cat came in with bladder stones. I'll have to do surgery on him on Monday." She went into the front office and turned out all but the security lights. "He actually got up in the sink and urinated right in front of his owner like he was showing her what was going on. He had blood in his urine, so she brought him in."

She turned and wandered back down the hall toward the surgery, turning off lights as she went.

"Any word from your mom?" he asked.

"No." A twinge of pain caught her unaware, and she dragged in a breath. "Dante called to check on me, and we spoke for a few minutes. He's going to come by tomorrow and have lunch with me—us, now that you'll be home."

She stopped to check the animals in the recovery kennels. Then turned out the overhead lights. A single security light shone overhead.

"I'm going into the boarding kennel area. It will be loud." She opened the door and the dogs immediately started barking. She checked their water as she went through…all good for the night, keyed in the code, and set the alarm, then opened the back door and scanned the yard before stepping out. The exterior motion lights they'd installed to go along with the cameras came on, but it still made her nervous walking around the back side of the building.

"I was just so tired tonight I couldn't keep my eyes open. The dogs have been restless the last few nights, barking at shadows, so I haven't slept well. Now you're coming home, I'll get a better night's sleep."

"What do you think they were barking at?"

"I don't know. I looked out, but I didn't see anything."

She reached inside her bag and withdrew the pepper spray Zach had given her, and her car keys. "I'm almost at the car."

"Don't do this again, Piper. It's dangerous for you to be there alone this late. In fact, you need to leave with the others. There's safety in numbers."

"I was going to leave as soon as I finished that last chart. I just fell asleep." She hit the button on her key fob to unlock the car, making the headlights flash and the interior lights came on. She checked the back seat, then the trunk area, before climbing in behind the wheel and locking the doors. She placed the phone on the passenger seat along with the pepper spray. "I'm locked in the car." She fastened her seat belt and started the vehicle. "I'll probably be home before you are."

"Be careful. I have another call coming in. I'll call you back as soon as I've answered it."

"Okay."

LESTER'S BREATHING WAS loud in his ear. "He's following her, and I'm following him. This might be it."

The note of excitement in the man's voice made Zach's stomach pitch.

"I hope the fuck he's going to try something. I've been watching this son-of-a-bitch for three weeks. He's dealing again. And he's not the skinny twenty-something he was back in the day. He's buffed up, so be prepared for a dude as big as you."

"I know, I saw the pictures you sent. What kind of car is he driving?"

"A brand new Cadillac Escalade. Black on black. Nothing too good for mama's boy. They traded in the car he drove before and bought him this one."

"I'm going to try to get there ahead of her."

Lester's voice held an edge. "For God's sake, don't get pulled over."

"I won't."

Crossing the bridge from Coronado to San Diego seemed to take forever. He punched Piper's number again. "You doing okay?"

"Yes. It's slow going with the traffic."

"From my end, too." He whipped around a truck turning into a grocery store parking lot and turned right at the next corner to take a short cut. "Take your time, Piper. We have the whole weekend free."

"Good. Maybe we can go out on the boat."

"Sounds good. Let's do it on Sunday." Zach swore under his breath when he hit a red light. His heart rate doubled and he had trouble getting a deep breath. "I think you're going to make it home before I do, Piper. I need you to do something for me."

"Sure."

"When you get there, I need you to lock yourself in the guest room with the dogs. Act like you're getting ready for bed. Make sure you turn the kitchen and living room lights off and just lock yourself in."

She fell silent.

PIPER FELT HER HEART beat in her throat and wrists, and a tremor struck her. "What's going on, Zach?"

"I wanted to be there so I could explain in person."

"Maybe you'd better do it now."

"Lester's been tracking David Henderlight for the last three weeks. Keeping an eye on him. Henderlight's in a new, black Cadillac Escalade following you. And Lester's behind him."

"You sicced Lester on him?"

"Yeah. He needed to atone for what he did to you, Piper, so I came up with a way for him to do it that would benefit you. I've been trying to keep you safe."

Piper's arms shook and her knee bounced as she put pressure

on the brake to stop behind the car in front of her. Her muscles had turned to water.

"Why don't we just call the police now?"

"And tell them what, honey? That it appears he was following you in bumper-to-bumper traffic? We need to catch him doing something so he'll break his parole and be sent back to prison."

What he said made sense until she thought of being in the same room with the man who'd raped her. "Detective Sherman told me they'd monitor him."

"When did he say that?"

"The morning they brought my car back." She attempted to control the shaking of her limbs. "He was telling me he was out and I...just erased it from my mind—didn't want to hear it."

"I should have told you. I just wanted you to have a little time, Piper. Lester says he hasn't been close."

"The dogs have been barking at night lately. What if he's been there and Lester didn't know? He couldn't watch him twenty-four hours a day." Her skin crawled at the thought. She checked the door locks and glanced at her side mirror to try to see if a large black SUV followed her. She turned onto her street and followed the winding curves in the road.

"If he was, he didn't come inside the house, Piper. Don't focus on what might have been, just on what is."

How could he be so calm?

"I'm almost to the house," he soothed.

"I'm here." She pulled into the driveway and shut off the car. She slung her purse over her shoulder, grabbed her phone in one hand, and the pepper spray in the other. She'd left a light on over the front door. Cut the bushes back, away from the windows, so there'd be nowhere for a prowler to hide. She had locks on the windows and a stop on each one to make them hard to raise. She'd gotten a dog.

But she hadn't bought a gun. Why hadn't she asked Zach to teach her how to shoot? Why had she given in to her fear, and let it keep her from learning to protect herself?

How was she supposed to unlock the door and hold her

phone and the pepper spray?

"I'm going to come in from the back so he won't know I'm here." Zach's voice remained calm.

"I have to put the phone in my purse."

"Leave it on, Piper."

She scanned the yard for moving shadows, and, seeing none, shoved open the car door. Every shaking nerve in her body seemed to rise to the surface of her skin. The soft, moisture-laden breeze carried the smell of freshly cut grass and the fragrant white clematis that grew up a trellis in the neighbor's yard. She rushed to the front door, key in one hand, pepper spray in the other.

She heard one of the dogs barking, but not just inside the door as they normally would. Maybe Zach had already gotten inside from the back door. Her hands shook so she could barely get the key in the lock and turn it. She stumbled inside the entrance and twisted the deadbolt to lock it behind her.

She fished for her phone. "I'm in the house with the door locked." Where were the dogs? The muffled sound of a whine came from down the hall. "Trouble?" If someone was hurting him or Gracie...

She dropped her purse by the door and flipped on the over-head light. A large, masculine form stepped out from the hall. She staggered back against the door.

CHAPTER 45

THE INSISTENT CALL waiting tone sounded on Zach's phone again and again. He was a block away from the house. "Hold on, Piper, I think Lester's trying to call me again."

"It isn't him driving. It's his vehicle but it isn't him driving." Lester's panicked tone came over the line so loud Zach jerked the phone away from his ear. "Jesus, is she okay?"

Such a surge of fear raced through Zach that for several seconds he couldn't breathe. "She's locked inside the house."

"He might be inside waiting for her."

"Call nine-one-one. I'm going in."

Zach twisted the wheel, sending his SUV to the curb two doors down. He tore his seat belt free and leapt out, leaving the door standing open. Adrenaline surged through his system. He pushed himself into a full-out run. His hands shook as he stabbed the key into the back door deadbolt and turned it. He drew his weapon, chambered a round.

He paused for a second, reaching for control. Piper's life might depend on it. He touched his fingertips to the face of the door and pushed gently, easing it open an inch at a time. He slid through the gap into the kitchen. Gracie's frantic barking came from somewhere deep in the tiny house. But closer voices were distinguishable. A man's voice and Piper's. Placing each foot as though walking on eggshells, he eased toward the door leading into the living room.

DAVID HAD CHANGED. His face was fuller, his body, bigger, broader, more muscular. His red hair glinted with copper, instead of the rich, dark reds in Zach's. His hazel eyes held a gleam as he ran his gaze over her body then back up.

Piper shuddered.

"Hello, Piper. You look good." He'd wrapped Trouble's leash around his hand. He had threaded the clip end of the inch-wide strip through the loop handle and pulled it tight around Trouble's throat. The dog was cowed, his tail down, his entire posture one of fear and pain.

The bastard had abused her dog. Her loving, gentle, friendly dog, who had never harmed anyone, ever. Rage burned away her fear, and a tear of outrage ran down her cheek. Where was Gracie? She could hear her frantic barking from somewhere in the house. He hadn't dealt with her as easily. There was a bandage wrapped around his left arm with spots of blood darkening it.

"You always liked animals more than people, didn't you?"

"No. Not always." Not until you. Her hand tightened around the palm-sized pepper spray canister, and she had to remind herself not to press the trigger, not yet. She turned her body, hiding any hint of the weapon. "Why are you here, David?"

"We have some unfinished business." His bicep bulged as he pulled up on the leash, forcing Trouble's bent head up and nearly raising him off the ground. The dog coughed and twisted against the pressure.

How many times had he done to him? She spoke quickly, hoping to appeal to him. "He's just a harmless dog. Please don't hurt him."

David lowered the leash, placing Trouble's feet on the floor. The dog gasped and wheezed as he tried to catch his breath, then gagged. His throat might be swelling from the abuse, and he could choke to death. Fear, cloying and clammy, crept up her spine at

David's dispassionate expression while he watched the retriever suffer.

"The statute of limitations has already passed. I can't bring charges against you."

"It's never so easy Piper. Prison has taught me that."

Piper motioned toward Trouble. "Is that what you did to your mother's poodle?"

He smiled as though the question evoked pleasant memories. "You remember Clara? Mom thought she'd been hit by a car. It was actually a hammer."

God, he truly was a psychopath. "I didn't call the police and report you." While Trouble continued to struggle, Piper edged closer, wary, yet determined. If she could get within five feet of him she'd spray the bastard.

"Your father did, though. I read the newspaper article in yesterday's paper." His features tightened. "It brought back some not-so-good memories."

"Had you left me alone, he wouldn't have had any reason to report you, David. I didn't tell them."

"Had your roommates not interfered, I'd have had my fill of you, and it would be over."

Her stomach rolled and nausea hit her. "And I would be as dead as Clara."

David cocked his head. "I didn't want to kill you, Piper. I wanted to… *possess* you." He said the word as though savoring it.

"Like your car."

"Much more than that." Her skin crawled at the intensity lighting his eyes. "I'm here to see if reality can match the memory. I've never been as hard as I was while I had you. Never come as hard." He reached toward his waistband behind him and drew out a large knife. It had come from her kitchen. A gift from one of the chefs who worked in the restaurant. It was sharp as her scalpels, and would be deadly.

ZACH CLOSED HIS EYES against the images of Piper helpless, trapped beneath that monster. Anger fired his skin and nearly choked him. He could not allow his emotions to distract him. It could get her killed. He had to hold it together. Wait for an opportunity.

Listening to their voices, he could tell Piper was to the left, just inside the room from the direction of the door. Henderlight was in the hall, or just in front of it.

Trouble's choking and gasping was growing more disturbing by the moment. He had to distance himself from his concern for her and the dog. He couldn't think about how much he loved them. But he trembled with it.

DAVID KNELT AND gripped Trouble's jaw, forcing his head up.

"No. Please don't hurt him." The need to protect the dog overruled everything else. He was her companion, her child, and he loved and trusted her to protect him.

"Come to me and I won't have to." He flicked the knife and golden brown hair floated down onto the hardwood flooring.

Piper took two large steps toward him. He started to rise, the knife held out to the side. Piper threw up her hand and pressed the pepper spray trigger. A cloud of spray hit him in the face and he roared and threw up an arm rubbing at his eyes. Piper grabbed Trouble's leash and pulled with all her strength, but it was looped tight around David's hand. He swung the knife at her and she dodged.

Zach pivoted into the room from the kitchen, a gun raised in a two-handed grip. "Get down, Piper."

A sharp, piercing pain struck her shoulder and trailed like fire down her back. She cried out in shock and pain, twisting away from it, and tumbled on top of Trouble.

Two loud, ear-jarring pops sounded in quick succession. David fell to the floor next to her and lay still.

ZACH HOLSTERED HIS WEAPON. He'd fired too late. She was hurt. Blood spread across the back of her shirt even as she scrambled to her knees and struggled one-handed to remove the leash from around Trouble's neck. He reached around her and got the leash off, but it took both hands and some strength. The dog lay still, panting weakly. He tried to examine her injury and she jerked away.

Lester ran into the room from the kitchen, a gun in his hand. The distant scream of sirens came closer. "Go outside and tell them what the situation is so they don't come in here with guns blazing. We need EMTs and emergency transport for an injured dog to the vet's office. Hurry."

Lester rushed to the front door, unlocked it, and ran out.

"I'm okay. We have to take care of him first. He's going into shock, Zach. Get a blanket from the bedroom." She ignored her own injuries to stroke Trouble and murmur reassurances to him while she examined his neck. His tongue looked swollen and protruded from his mouth, and his poor face was swollen, too. How long had Henderlight been in the house and tortured her precious dog?

"Call Ryan." Piper said. "He may be an asshole, but he'll go to the office and meet the transport. I trust him to take care of Trouble."

Zach tugged his cell phone free of his pocket and keyed in the number she dictated. While he spoke to the vet and filled him in on what had gone down, he rushed into the bedroom and jerked the quilt off of Piper's bed, then went into the bathroom for towels. Gracie's barking in the guest room grew more frantic. He paused to speak to her through the door. She quieted, listening, then began to whine. "I'll come back for you, baby."

How had Henderlight gotten past her? He hurried to the living room and dropped the quilt over Trouble. With a quick tug he lengthened the rip in her shirt to expose the knife wound.

He took a relieved breath. It was long and thin, and ran from the top of her shoulder down her shoulder blade, but it wasn't deep. It wasn't from lack of the asshole's trying. Partially blinded by pepper spray and enraged, he'd meant to kill her. Her tug on the leash had allowed him to home right in on her. It was a miracle he hadn't killed her.

Zach folded a hand towel and placed it over Piper's wound. He slipped an arm around her to hold her and put pressure on the bandage. "I'm sorry, Piper. I couldn't find an opening until you sprayed him." Tears blurred his vision and streamed down his face. He could no longer fight back the rush of emotion.

She gripped the arm around her waist. She half turned to look up into his face. Seeing his tears, her composure broke and tears coursed down her cheeks. "We're okay." She leaned into him. "He was going to kill Trouble and me, probably Gracie, too. You stopped him."

Police sirens wound to a crescendo outside.

He glanced at the dead man. Yeah, he'd stopped him.

CHAPTER 46

ZACH TILTED HIS HEAD back and closed his eyes, breathing in the late evening breeze with its briny scent, allowing the sound of the waves to wash over him. He had forgotten how noisy these family deals were. It had been a good distraction for the two of them, since they were both wound up about the deployment. He raised the beer to his lips and took a deep swig.

He scanned the back patio and beach. Piper's sister Teresa sat under the protection of a beach umbrella watching her children play in the surf. She was the toughest nut to crack. The rest of the Bertinelli family had been ready to meet Piper and attempt reconciliation. Teresa still clung stubbornly to her resentment.

Tom, Teresa's husband came up beside him. "I understand you're leaving tomorrow?"

"Yeah."

"You okay with that?"

Zach studied the beer in his hand, his throat tight. "You're never okay leaving the people you love. But there are innocents we need to protect. And I'm needed there. My men need me, and this is who I am, what I'm called to do."

He straightened and looked Tom in the eye. "She needs her family around her. She needs backup…just in case." In case she needed a shoulder to cry on, or an emergency arose. In case something happened to him while he was gone. He didn't want her to be alone.

Tom nodded. "We'll look after her while you're gone. I'll make sure of it."

"Thanks." Zach offered his hand. The two men shook.

"I think Teresa's had enough for the day. Even though she's finished her chemo, her energy level still isn't back to normal."

"I hope she continues to do well."

Tom remained silent a moment. "Thanks. It's always a sacrifice and a blessing, loving someone in peril."

He thought about seeing the knife come down at Piper, hearing her cry of pain. "I know."

"I guess you do. Everything okay with the police? No repercussions from the shooting?"

"No. He broke in to the house, stabbed her, and I took him down. It was justified." A fresh wave of rage and pain swamped him every time he thought about David Henderlight. "Piper doesn't know, and I don't want her to, but he'd brought a rape kit with him. Duct tape, rope, devices. He'd fine-tuned his skills and his appetites while he was in prison, preying on some of the other prisoners."

"Jesus!" Tom's expression hardened. "I'm glad to know my hatred for the bastard is well-deserved."

He'd learned it was a waste of time to hate a dead man. It was easier to love and protect the living. He looked around for Piper. She'd gone inside with her mother and little Armando and hadn't come back out. Maybe the two women were hashing things out. Things were still strained, but they were trying.

"I'm going to gather my crew and clear out so you and Piper can have some time alone."

Zach smiled. "I appreciate it."

Tom laughed. "If you need anything…"

He nodded. "Thanks."

Tom walked down the beach to his wife.

Zach wandered over to where Master Chief Flynn sat in the shade, Gracie lying alongside his chair. Piper's family had embraced the older man. Her brothers had sat around talking to him for some time, listening to his war stories and stories about the dogs. Benito, Lorenzo, Dante, and their dates had already left.

Armando sat in a lounge chair, his very pregnant wife between his thighs, leaning back against him.

Zach remembered how he had done that very thing with Piper on their first weekend together. He took a hasty swig of beer to wash the knot out of his throat.

He lowered himself into a lawn chair next to the master chief. "How you doing, M.C.?"

"I'm good."

"Want another beer?"

"Naw. I think I better stick with just the one. They may not like it if I'm weaving on my feet any more than usual when I get back."

Zach chuckled at his attempt at humor. But he knew the master chief was enjoying the rehab much more than the hospital. "When you're ready to go, Piper's mom is going to give you a ride back to the rehab facility."

"Whenever she's ready." He was silent for a moment. "My girl got a piece of that bastard, didn't she?" He brushed his fingertips along Gracie's back.

"Yeah. The police said she'd bitten his arm and done a pretty fair job of ripping it up. He must have beaten her off with something, stunned her maybe, shoved her into the bedroom and closed her up. Piper's checked her over twice to make sure she's okay."

"I'm surprised he didn't kill her."

Zach had wondered about it, too. "He needed one of them to bark so Piper would think everything was okay when she came in. Trouble couldn't."

Master Chief's clenched a fist. "Bastard! Goddamn bastard!"

Tom and Teresa came up from the beach with their two children to say their good-byes, saving him from dwelling on Henderlight. He'd done it enough already. Alana struggled to rise from the lounge, and Zach went to offer her a hand. She smiled shyly and thanked him. "I'll go in and get little Armando," she said. "Thank you for having us."

"You're welcome."

"Thanks, sweetheart." Armando focused on Zach. "You've done more for my sister and our family than any of the rest of us were man enough to do." His features crumpled in pain and he dropped his head. He struggled to maintain his composure. "Thank you for saving my sister. For ending this for us."

"I was just in the right place at the right time."

Armando shook his head. "Piper loves and needs you. Please take care of yourself."

"I will."

Armando offered his hand and Zach shook it.

He tried to turn loose of his anger with Armando. It did no one any good to hold on to any enmity for past deeds. He'd said it to Piper when he talked her into this get-together. Armando and Teresa had been the most viciously vocal about Piper's supposed culpability in her father's death, and it was good to know Armando was obviously regretting it.

Zach wandered back to the Master Chief. "You know you have a forty-minute drive with a beautiful woman back to the facility. Guys like us have to seize our opportunities when they present themselves."

Flynn's wide grin was answer enough.

Zach leaned forward in his seat. "I need you to do me a favor."

"Name it."

"Call Piper now and then, just to check in on her." He didn't want her to mope or be lonely once he was gone.

"Gladly."

Twenty minutes later Carlotta came out to collect Master Chief Flynn. Zach walked next to Flynn with his walker through the house to the car. Piper came out to say good-bye and give the master chief a hug. Zach helped him get into Carlotta's Altima, shook his hand, and closed the door.

When Carlotta hugged him, he automatically put his arms around her. "Please be careful." Her eyes were bright with tears when she released him, ducked her head, and got into the car.

He turned to go back into the apartment. Piper stood at the door, thinking again that the red sundress she wore wasn't her normal style. It left her shoulders, arms and legs bare. He wondered when she bought it.

Trouble wandered up to the door, Gracie at his side. He was still unable to lift his head or bark, but in the week since the attack, the swelling had greatly reduced, and he actually wagged his tail to greet Zach when he went back in.

Zach knelt before the retriever so he could see his face while he carefully stroked his head, back, and shoulders, avoiding the tender areas. "You're a good boy, Trouble." The dog wagged his tail in answer, licked his cheek, and laid his large head on his shoulder. He continued to pet him until he pulled back.

It was useless to be angry at a dead man, he reminded himself. But it would be a long time before the feelings of rage passed about the dog's treatment at Henderlight's hands.

"He's doing much better. He actually ate a little of his dry food. It's just going to take some time."

Zach rose to his feet. "If it's less traumatic from him to stay here during the day, you have a key, and the bills are automatically paid out of my account."

"I think I'm going to continue to take him and Gracie to work with me for awhile. He's a little anxious about being alone."

"Understandable."

"Did you see Kathleen today?"

He nodded. "She came over for a few minutes while you were gone to the market. Callahan's back home, and he came with her." His sister hadn't held it together too well, and he hadn't wanted her to get Piper worked up. Hell, she'd almost gotten him going. Callahan finally managed to maneuver her out the door after half an hour. He was going to buy him a case of beer the next time he saw him. "She said she'd call in a couple of days, and the two of you would go out and do something together."

"Okay." She brushed at a strand of hair that lay against her cheek and he tucked it back behind her ear.

"I still can't believe Tony was involved in the Master Chief Flynn's attack and the break-ins. He's worked for us for almost a year. He's great with the dogs."

The call from Sherman stunned her, and she'd been dwelling on it for the last three days.

He ran his hands up and down her arms. "I know you're disappointed and upset about it. But don't take responsibility for what he did, Piper. You weren't the only one who trusted him. No one else at the office had a single suspicion about him either."

"Only Gracie." Vindictive anger lit her eyes. "I wish she'd bitten a hunk out of him."

He laughed. "No you don't. Then she might be in trouble." He drew her close. "He'll pay for what he did. Him and the others involved. And the dogs they found will be returned to their owners."

She nodded.

He grasped her hand and tugged her toward the kitchen, then out the back door. Trouble and Gracie followed, and he left the door cracked open wide enough for them to go back in if they wanted to. He sat down on the lounge and drew her down between his legs. Piper guided his arms around her and placed her own arms atop his.

Trouble took a place next to the lounge and lay on his side. Gracie snuggled close against him and rested her head atop her paws.

"Do you think she senses he needs her support? She's very attentive to him these days."

"She probably does. I know she's missed him while he's been at the vet's office. She hunted the apartment and your house for him the whole time he was gone."

"I'll have to arrange play dates for them when Master Chief Flynn gets well enough to take her."

Zach gave her a squeeze. "Honey, I think you're going to have to arrange play dates for us."

Piper laughed. "You're right."

He pressed his lips to her temple and breathed in her jasmine fragrance. "I love you, Piper."

Her hands tightened on his arms. "I do you, too." She turned on her side to press as tightly to him as possible. "Since that first weekend."

"Me, too."

If she cried… "Let's go to bed. I need to be as close to you as I can get."

She nodded and slid down to the foot of the lounge to get up, but kept her face turned away.

Gracie scrambled to her feet and Trouble followed a little more slowly. The dogs trotted into the apartment ahead of them.

He remembered wanting to put his hand against the small of her back the first day they met. He did it now as they walked down the hall to his bedroom.

Piper's hands shook while she unbuttoned his shirt and peeled it off his shoulders, just as they had the first time. He had said it, but he wanted her to know he meant it. He cupped her face in his hands and looked into her eyes. "I love you, Piper."

"Zach." Her mouth took his and her tears wet his face.

He kissed her over and over until she calmed. "It's going to be okay, honey. You have to trust me."

"I do. With my heart, my body, my love."

He wanted to touch every inch of her, feel every inch of her skin against his own. He took his time undressing her. "You looked beautiful tonight. This red is perfect with your coloring." He released the buttons at the base of her neck to the lower curve of her back, then eased it forward and down, brushing his fingertips against the peaks of her breasts, teasing the already-budded nipples.

Piper pulled her arms free and let the dress slide to her feet. She wore no bra, and the white lace panties she wore were barely a scrap of fabric.

"If I'd known this was all you had on under the dress I wouldn't have been able to think about anything else."

"The dress and the panties were a gift from Kathleen."

"I'm going to text my sister later thanking her."

Piper laughed, and the sound eased the ache inside him until he smiled. He took great care while he slid the panties down and let them drop to her feet. He urged her to sit on the edge of the bed and knelt to slide her feet free of her sandals and place them on the floor.

He ran his hands up the backs of her calves and brushed a kiss on her knee.

Piper smoothed his hair back from his forehead. "You're still dressed," she reminded him.

He stood, and she reached for his belt and unfastened it. He loved the way she always took her time sliding down his zipper and baring him. It was as though she was savoring the moment. He shed his T-shirt in record time.

When Piper leaned forward and pressed a kiss to his stomach, right below his navel, an electric current of need raced downward, making him harden almost painfully. He rushed to kick free of his deck shoes, shorts and briefs.

Piper slid back on the bed, and he followed her. He touched the fragile peaks of her collarbones, the weight of her breasts, the shallow hollow of her stomach, memorizing the texture of her skin, the slender grace of her shape. Piper's hands were a brush of arousing sensation as she did the same to him. She traced the defined muscles of his stomach and they tightened.

He bent his head and kissed her, just where she had kissed him, and he felt her sharp, indrawn breath and knew she felt the same electric need.

"Come inside me, Zach," she murmured, her voice breathy and soft.

He did. No condom. Nothing between them.

The ripe, moist heat of her caressed him, and he held his breath while he fought for control. He wanted to stay like this for as long as he could. Feeling her hands caress his back, her lips against his throat, his shoulder. The tender way she held him. Her whispered, "I love you," with the throb of pain and joy in her tone. The way her lips clung to his with both tenderness and passion. When his control threatened to break and he had to move, only then did he withdraw, slide a condom on, and began a tender dance to drive them both to completion.

Afterward they lay for hours, clinging to each other until he could no longer stay awake.

PIPER LAID HER HEAD against his chest and listened to the strong, steady rhythm of his heart, willing the sound to soothe her to sleep. But sleep wouldn't come. All the sweet, loving things he had done played through her mind. All the protective courage he had shown in every instance. It had all been done with love. To know it gave every act a greater dimension for her.

At four, Zach woke and reached for her. They made love again, this time with a desperate intensity that left them both sweaty and spent. She finally drifted off until five, when the alarm went off.

She rose with him, and while he took a shower, she slid into the shirt he'd worn the day before. Instead of the two large dog beds they'd purposely bought for them to sleep in, the dogs both slipped guiltily off the leather sofa and greeted her. She hadn't the heart to scold them this morning, and instead gave each one a generous rub, then urged them into the kitchen. She opened the door and let them out, watching them until they returned to the door.

She fed them, and while they crunched at their breakfast, she turned her attention to Zach's. It would be the last thing she could do for him before he flew away from her. She wanted to care for him in some way.

She made coffee, poured juice, and whipped eggs for a three-egg omelet of shredded ham and cheddar cheese. She slipped three slices of bread in the toaster.

When he entered the kitchen dressed in his BDU's, he brought the energy of purpose with him. It was what had clung to him the first time they'd met. What she'd admired about him then. What she loved about him now.

"It smells wonderful, Piper," he said. He sat down at the table and she placed the food before him. He gave her waist a squeeze.

Those few words triggered a memory.

While he ate, she got a small zip-lock storage bag and slipped back into the bedroom. She collected the panties he had taken off her the night before and went into the bathroom. She found the spritzer she used, sprayed the panties with her scent, and sealed them in the bag.

She slipped her robe on and stuffed the bag in the pocket.

When she returned she poured a cup of coffee for them both and sat at the table.

"The guys will be here to pick me up any time now. I've put the key to the storage unit in the top dresser drawer in the bedroom, in case you need my SUV."

"I'll be okay, Zach." She felt calmer than the day before. Knowing he loved her helped her hold her emotions in check. She prayed it would last.

"I know."

The sound of a car pulling into the driveway was followed by the toot of a horn. He stared at her and she at him. He reached for his juice to wash down the last bite of food and shoved to his feet.

"I have something for you." She withdrew the plastic bag with the panties in it from her pocket and offered it to him. He studied the contents for a moment then a smile lit his face. "They have my scent on them. When it fades, email or call, and I'll send you another pair."

He unbuttoned his shirt and stuck the bag inside it, then buttoned it back up. "I love you."

Her heart rose to into her throat, and tears burned against the backs of her eyes. "I love you too."

He reached for her and kissed her hard. She clung to him with an answering fierceness. Lifting the heavy sea bag he'd packed the day before, he settled it over his shoulder and opened the door.

He stepped out onto the front stoop, then paused to look back at her. The early morning sun touched his hair, still damp from his shower, with deep red highlights, and his eyes gleamed a bright, clear green. "Wait for me, Piper."

Her heart swelled with both joy and love. "I will, Zach. Always."

BOOKS BY
TERESA J. REASOR

MILITARY ROMANTIC SUSPENSE:
Breaking Free (Book 1 of the SEAL TEAM Heartbreakers)
Breaking Through (Book 2 of the SEAL TEAM Heartbreakers)
Breaking Away (Book 3 of the SEAL TEAM Heartbreakers)
Breaking Ties: A Seal Team Heartbreakers Novella
Building Ties (Book 4 of the SEAL TEAM Heartbreakers)
Breaking Boundaries (Book 5 of the SEAL TEAM Heartbreakers)
Breaking Out (Book 6 of the SEAL TEAM Heartbreakers)

PARANORMAL ROMANCE/Urban Fantasy:
Timeless
Whisper In My Ear
Deep Within The Shadows

HISTORICAL ROMANCE:
Highland Moonlight
Captive Hearts
To Capture A Highlander's Heart: The Wedding Night
(A Highland Moonlight Spinoff Novel)
To Capture A Highlander's Heart: The Trilogy
(all three parts of the Highland Moonlight spinoff series in one book)
Print and ebook

SHORT STORIES:
To Capture A Highlander's Heart: The Beginning
(A Highland Moonlight Spinoff)
An Automated Death (A Steampunk Short Story) Paranormal
Caught In The Act (A Humorous Short Story) Contemporary Romance

NOVELLAS:
To Capture A Highlander's Heart: The Courtship
(A Highland Moonlight Spinoff)

CHILDREN'S BOOK:
Willy C. Sparks: The Dragon Who Lost His Fire

**ANTHOLOGIES HER WORK
HAS BEEN INCLUDED IN:**
Malice, Mischief, and Men (Breaking Free)
SEALed With A Kiss: Heroes With A Heart (Breaking Free)
Dangerous Dames (Building Ties)

www.ingramcontent.com/pod-product-compliance
Lightning Source LLC
Chambersburg PA
CBHW051433260626
47162CB00001B/76